3/12

THE
SAVAGE
GRACE

THE SAVAGE GRACE

A DARK DIVINE NOVEL

BREE DESPAIN

EGMONT
USA

New York

EGMONT

We bring stories to life

First published by Egmont USA, 2012
443 Park Avenue South, Suite 806
New York, NY 10016

1 3 5 7 9 8 6 4 2

www.egmontusa.com
www.breedespain.com

Library of Congress Cataloging-in-Publication Data

Despain, Bree, 1979-
The savage Grace : a Dark Divine novel / Bree Despain.
p. cm.
Sequel to: Lost saint.
Summary: After a brush with death, Grace Divine must find a way to prevent her
one true love, Daniel, from being stuck in wolf form, while also seeking to save her
family from destruction.
ISBN 978-1-60684-221-8 (hardcover) — ISBN 978-1-60684-222-5 (e-book)
[1. Supernatural—Fiction. 2. Interpersonal relations—Fiction.
3. Werewolves—Fiction. 4. Christian life—Fiction.] I. Title.
PZ7.D4518Sav 2012
[Fic]--dc23
2011038116

Printed in the United States of America

CPSIA tracking label information:
Printed in January 2012 at Berryville Graphics, Berryville, Virginia

For Brick—

Because we both know that you practically deserve a byline in this book. Thank you for always inspiring me.

Always,
Bree

FULL CIRCLE

He knew me too well.

Read the writing on my heart.

He knew exactly what it would take—

For me to embrace this savagery.

"However will you choose?" he asks. "You let me go, and I will kill him."

I lift the gun. Train it at his heart. "I've made my decision."

He does not falter. Doesn't even blink. "All you have to do is want to kill me, and you'll lose yourself."

"I know," I say.

I squeeze back on the trigger. A silver bullet explodes from the chamber.

I have no regrets. . . .

Chapter One

HOWL

You need to do something, Gracie.

My eyes squinted involuntarily at my phone's screen, illuminated too bright in the dark of my bedroom. I'd been staring at the black void between my bed and my ceiling for so long it was hard to focus my vision—and my mind—on the incoming text.

I blinked several times and read the message again: *You need to do something, Gracie. He's going to get himself in real trouble if he doesn't stop.*

I wish I could say that I'd been asleep when the howling started. I knew it was the white wolf without being able to see him. The high, mournful wolf's cry that filled my bedroom now sounded like he was just outside my window—but I knew it came from deep in the forest. He was venturing farther away.

Away from me.

Away from who he used to be.

I'd rolled over and sat up in my bed when the howls started only a few minutes before. I knew it was just after two a.m. without even needing to glance at the dim red numbers of my alarm clock. I'd been willing myself not to check the time every few minutes, not to count down how many hours of rest I could still get before morning—if I could just fall asleep in the first place.

The problem is, it's hard to fall asleep when deep down there's a part of you that desperately doesn't want to ever again.

Because sleep brought on dreams of Daniel. The Daniel I remembered. Dreams so wonderful and tangible that the second I woke up and realized they were just that—dreams—the terribleness of reality came crashing in on me all over again. I didn't know if my sanity could handle it one more time.

Dad and Gabriel had sent me home around eleven o'clock, claiming I needed to get a handle on my sleep debt during the weekend before I was expected to go back to school on Monday. But I think they really sent me away because neither of them could bear to look me in the eye as the hours—days—of searching through book after book on werewolf folklore, shape-shifters mythology, and even scripture, went by and we'd still found nothing.

Nothing at all that could help us change Daniel back.

It had been six nights since the terrible one Daniel

and I had spent imprisoned in the Shadow Kings' warehouse, knowing our deaths would most likely play out in the morning. It had been five days since Daniel had somehow miraculously turned into the great white wolf in order to save me from Caleb's rabid wolf pack. I'd escaped a horrific fate that day—but Daniel hadn't. He'd been trapped in a prison of bone and fur and claws ever since. Stuck in the body of the white wolf.

I could tell with each unuseful page that was turned that Dad and Gabriel believed more and more that Daniel was going to be stuck forever. And it didn't bode well that he seemed to be more the white wolf than he was *Daniel* with each passing moment.

The first few days after Daniel transformed, he'd followed me everywhere—which meant I pretty much couldn't go *anywhere*, but at least he'd been with me, and I could see him in the white wolf's deep brown eyes.

But two days ago, he'd gotten skittish, and then he'd started to wander away. Into the woods mostly. For a few hours at a time, returning to my backyard when I called for him. But then today my calls had gone unbidden, and he hadn't come back at all.

The forest is claiming him, a harsh voice whispered in my head.

I shook it off, not letting the demon wolf inside of me feed off my doubt. I didn't have the patience for mind games tonight.

Daniel's howling grew louder from the woods, and

my heart ached for him. For us. I'd wondered if his howls were as loud to anyone else, or if my superhearing was just acting up again—that was until the cell phone on my nightstand buzzed with the text from Dad.

Huh. Dad. Texting. I'll never get used to that.

I rubbed my eyes. My sight shifted from my super-human night vision back to normal a couple of times before I was able to focus on the screen of my phone again. I pecked out a response to Dad's text about my needing to do something.

Me: *I know. Are you still at the parish? How loud is it there?*

Dad had taken to staying at the parish most nights this past week. Besides doing research, he and Gabriel alternated watching over my brother Jude in his small cell-like den in the parish's basement.

The question as to what to do with Jude had been our first item of business when we'd brought him back from the warehouse with us. I think everyone was surprised when I suggested that we lock him up in the storage cage in the parish basement for observation until we could figure out what exactly was going on inside his head. My brother had been on the run for the last ten months, and he'd eventually joined Caleb's gang of paranormal teens—the same pack that had tried to kill Daniel and me. Jude had been the one who had led the Shadow Kings right to us.

In the end, he'd surrendered. Begged to come back

with us. But relieved as I was to know finally that Jude was safe—I wasn't ready to let him come home. Not until we were sure of his motivations. Not until I knew whether my *brother* was the one who had returned with us, and not just one of Caleb's death dogs.

As surprised as the others had been when I suggested keeping Jude under lock and key for the time being, I was shocked that Dad and Gabriel actually agreed. Only April had protested, but her vote hadn't counted for much.

She hadn't seen the way Jude had stood by and let Caleb try to destroy me. . . .

A new text from Dad interrupted my thoughts: *Yes, still at the parish. The howling is quite loud here.*

That wasn't the answer I was hoping for. The parish was several blocks away. If Daniel's howling was still loud there, that meant the whole town could hear it, too.

Dad: *He's going to get himself killed.*

I know, I typed, my fingers shaking a bit. Rose Crest had a history of "wild dog" attacks—and unearthly howling from the woods surrounding the town would be enough to get people talking. And what they'd talk about were all those rumors about the Markham Street Monster. Rumors that weren't really rumors at all. And then talking would lead to action. . . .

Dad: *You MUST do something to stop him.*

Me: *I'm on it.*

Except, I didn't know if there was anything I *could* do—not if Daniel wasn't responding to me anymore—but I had to at least try. I couldn't let something bad happen to him. Especially after all he'd sacrificed to save me.

I pulled on my jacket over my red flannel pajamas and tucked my phone into my pocket. My tender ankle throbbed as I sank my feet into my tall faux-fur-lined boots. I hoped they were sturdy enough to keep the newly healed fracture from shifting out of place. I slinked quietly down the stairs, even though I was the only one home. Dad had sent Charity and James to spend the week at Aunt Carol's because Mom was . . . somewhere I didn't want to think about now.

I went out the door off the kitchen into our backyard. A light blazed in the house next door—the house that Daniel used to live in all those years ago—and I saw the silhouette of Mr. Dutton standing in the window. He looked in the direction of the forest—no doubt wondering about the source of the wolf's cry that had probably awoken him—but I doubted he could see much with his own light on.

I stood on our back deck until Mr. Dutton moved away from the window. Before he had a chance to turn off the light for a better look outside, I mustered up a few extra ounces of power and took off in a sprint toward the back fence that separated our yard from the encroaching woods. Just before the rosebushes could snag at my pajama pants, I leaped over the fence. I winced at the shock of pain that ricocheted up from my ankle when my feet hit the ground on the opposite side. But other than that, I'd managed a perfect, almost soundless, landing.

For half a second I thought about how proud Nathan Talbot, my former mentor, would be if I told him about my quiet landing—something that we'd worked on in training. "For such a tiny girl, you land like a pile of rocks," he'd teased me once, his cheeks dimpling with that warm smile of his.

And then, as if he knew I'd allowed myself even to think about him, my phone buzzed with a new text.

Talbot: *Do you need any help?*

I dropped my phone back in my pocket without responding. If I could manage it, I was never going to talk—or even text—with him again.

Talbot was the last person I'd ask for help now. The last person I'd trust. *And all that crap that he'd said about loving me . . .*

I took in a deep breath and told myself not to give Talbot another thought. Daniel needed me, and I had to find him before anyone else in town—like Deputy Marsh with his rifle—decided to go looking for the source of those terrible howls.

A patch of bushes rustled off to my right. I whirled at the sound—realizing I wouldn't have noticed it without my superhearing—and crouched defensively. Panic pounded in my ears.

A large brown wolf stepped out from between the bushes onto the path in front of me, followed closely by a slightly smaller gray wolf. Their eyes glinted as they looked up at me. I nodded to them, trying to hide my disappointment that neither of them was the wolf I was looking for—but at least they weren't a couple of local hunters.

The two wolves separated and sat at attention on either side of the rocky path. Like sentinels, awaiting my passage. Only five days ago, these two wolves had been part of the pack that had been intent on killing me at Caleb's beckoning; now they bowed their furry heads in reverence as I passed between them.

While I questioned my brother's intentions, these wolves were another quandary altogether. I mean, I still didn't quite understand why they treated me this way—like I was practically their queen.

I'd asked Gabriel about it a couple of days ago. "As I told you in the warehouse, Daniel is their alpha now," he'd explained as we stood in Dad's office together, watching as the white wolf lay next to an untouched bowl of canned stew I'd set out for him by my dad's desk. "And apparently, Daniel has done something to choose you as his . . . mate. The wolves recognize this somehow and have accepted you as their alpha female."

And of course it turned out that my dad, the pastor, was standing behind us, and even though he was usually a pretty even-keeled guy, he went totally nuts over the word *mate*.

Until that moment, I'd completely pushed aside the worry of explaining to my father what had happened during that dark night Daniel and I had spent together in the dungeon of the warehouse. But the look on his slightly purplish face made it clear that an explanation was needed before his imagination got the better of him. "Daniel . . . kind of proposed to me," I'd explained. "Before Caleb threw me in the wolf pit. And I said yes."

"Ah, that would explain it," Gabriel had said, as if getting engaged at nearly eighteen was a perfectly normal thing to do.

But Dad's face went an even darker shade of violet, and he started going on and on about how young we were and how even though he and my mom had gotten married when they were twenty, it was no excuse for such irresponsible behavior on my part. And because I hadn't been able to get a word in explanation-wise, I'd finally shouted, "I only said yes because I thought we were going to die! I wanted him to be happy."

My dad had closed his mouth with a snap, and his eyes got all shiny with tears. He reached out and grabbed me in a death-grip hug at the reminder that he'd almost lost me only a few days before. With a pang of guilt, I glanced back at the white wolf that lay next to the desk with his eyes shut, seemingly asleep.

I could only hope now that it had been purely a

coincidence that Daniel had started his wanderings into the forest only a few hours later.

I used my guilt, and the adrenaline created by the sudden appearance of the two wolves, to muster up enough power to start running despite the pain in my leg. I'd been able to use my abilities to speed up the healing process of the injuries I'd suffered because of Caleb's cruelty, but Gabriel had cautioned me to take it easy. I ignored the echo of his warnings and jogged along the rocky path in the direction of the howls. The two wolves loped behind me, so close I could feel their warm breath against my back. I dug down deeper inside of me for more strength and picked up my speed, sprinting faster and faster until the two wolves dropped behind me—but I knew they still followed.

I ignored the ache in my lungs from the crisp, autumn air and the searing sensation in my ankle, and veered off the dirt path into the thick of the forest's trees, with only Daniel's mournful howls to guide me. I melted into the run, let it take me over for fear that I'd lose all steam if I slowed even a little. I was nothing but a pounding heart, sharp breaths in and out, and feet that slammed against the forest floor.

I didn't want to be anything else anymore.

Not without Daniel.

If it hadn't been for a sharp bark from one of the wolves behind me, I probably wouldn't have snapped back into reality in time to stop myself from sprinting right over the edge of the ravine. With the warning, I grabbed onto the crooked branch of an old tree just as my boots slipped on the muddy cliff's ledge. I steadied myself against the trunk and looked out over the twenty-foot drop that lay right in front of me. The ravine was about another twenty feet wide. I realized as I scanned the terrain that this was the same spot where Baby James had taken his near-fatal fall last Thanksgiving.

The warm, tingling memory of Daniel miraculously saving my little brother in this very place filled my mind—only to be tarnished by the sight of the great white wolf standing on a rocky outcropping on the other side of the ravine. His head arched back as he howled up at the three-quarter moon like he was desperate for it to answer his cries. The shrillness of his howling screams pierced my oversensitive eardrums, and I fought the urge to cover my ears.

"Daniel!" I shouted, not sure the sound of my shaky voice could penetrate his cries. I pushed myself up taller against the bowed tree trunk, clinging to it for support. My legs burned with lactic acid, and my ankle kept trying to bend in the wrong direction—threatening to buckle. If I thought it had hurt when it was first broken, that was nothing compared to the extreme stabbing that shot through my ankle, up into my body, now that the adrenaline from my run had washed out of me. "Daniel, stop!"

The white wolf's head arched farther back, and

another desperate howl ripped through the night, louder and more deranged sounding than ever. The two wolves behind me picked up Daniel's cry and joined in with their own howls. *Great, just, great.* Surely, the whole town would be at their windows now. I imagined bullets being locked into the chambers of more than one shotgun.

"Get!" I snapped at the two wolves that had followed me here, and stomped my good foot in their direction. "Get out of here, now!" I said, harsher than I'd meant to. The two whined and backed away with their tails low to the ground. When they were gone, I turned back to the sight of the howling white wolf.

"Daniel!" I screamed louder, my voice echoing his desperation. "Daniel, please. Dan—" A sinking feeling pulled at my stomach, and I realized that if by chance I wasn't the only one in the woods searching for the howling wolf, I shouldn't go shouting Daniel's name. "Stop, please . . ." I left off his name, even though I hated to. Like doing so was acknowledging that he wasn't "Daniel" anymore.

"Please stop! You have to stop this, now." My voice caught in the back of my throat, and I clutched my hand over my mouth. I couldn't let myself cry. "Please. Stop before you get hurt," I whispered against my fingers.

The white wolf's howl trailed off suddenly, and when I looked out across the ravine, I saw him staring at me. His furry head cocked with curiosity. I met his glinting eyes for a moment, and then he backed up slowly on his four paws.

"No," I said. "Don't leave." I held my hand up as if to signal "stop"—the same motion I learned when training my old three-legged dog, Daisy. "Don't run away again, please."

The wolf took two steps forward to the edge of his side of the ravine and looked at me again with that curious tilt of his head. *Did he still recognize me?* Hope burned in my chest, and I stayed as still as I could so as not to frighten him away. And I swear, in the silence that engulfed the dark woods now that his howling had stopped, I thought I could hear his heart beating.

His solitary heartbeat. Not two heartbeats like every other werewolf I knew. I still didn't know what that meant. I still didn't know *what* he had become.

For a moment it looked like the Daniel wolf contemplated making the jump over the ravine to get to my side as he crouched back slightly on his hind legs.

"Come," I motioned to him. "Please, Daniel," I said softly. "I need you. We need each other."

The Daniel wolf seemed to startle at the sound of his name. He dropped my gaze, and my heart felt like it fell right into the depths of the ravine as I watched him turn away from me.

"No!" I shouted, both of my hands extended as if I could reach out and grab him, stop him, as he bounded away into the trees, deeper than we'd ever ventured together in these woods before.

For half a second I contemplated trying to go after him—trying to jump the ravine, even if I didn't have the strength to make it in one piece. Anything to be near him again. But without the support of my hands against the tree trunk to hold me up, my ankle finally gave out, and I collapsed at the base of the tree.

I pulled my knees into my chest and listened for the howls to start up again from some unreachable part of the forest, counting my own lonely heartbeats as the minutes passed and no sound followed. A sigh of over-whelming exhaustion shuddered through me—mixed with relief that the howling had stopped and remorse that I wasn't able to get Daniel to come back to me—and for the first time since we escaped Caleb's warehouse, I allowed myself to cry.

I let out a string of long sobs against the forest floor until a terrible voice whispered inside my head, *You're losing him. And there's nothing you can do.*

Another wail tried to escape my throat, but I swal-lowed it back down. "No," I told the monster in my head. I pushed myself up and wiped the muddy tears from my face, hating myself for giving in to that weak-ness. "Daniel and I have been through too much, we've come too far, and I am *not* going to lose him. I won't let that happen."

No matter the cost.

Chapter Two

LOST BOYS

"Are you cold?" Daniel asked from behind me as I sat on a stone bench, working on a charcoal drawing for art class. His arms wrapped around my shoulders, and he pressed his chest against my back. Warmth radiated through his shirt, and my skin tingled in response under my thin sweater. I shivered, but not because I was cold. Not anymore.

"Mmm," I said, and set my notebook on the bench.

Daniel moved his hands down and up my arms to warm them, and nuzzled his nose against my neck.

"I'll give you an hour to quit that," I said with a quiet laugh, even though we were pretty much the only ones who ever came to the Garden of Angels.

"How about two?" he asked, and pressed his lips softly against my skin. I wanted to melt. He brushed my hair back and kissed behind my ear.

I sighed, and my charcoal pencil slipped from my fingers. It hit the edge of the stone bench and then rolled to the base of the statue I'd been sketching. It was the sculpture of Gabriel the Angel that Daniel had shown me the first time he'd brought me here.

Daniel's firm lips trailed down my neck until they reached the delicate chain of the necklace I almost always wore now. Something stirred inside of me, and my hand clutched at the moonstone pendant instinctively. Daniel pulled back a bit.

"Does it help?" he asked. His breath was so warm and wonderful against my hair. I shivered again as a tingling sensation ran up my neck into my scalp. My hand closed tighter over my pendant, and I let the almost hot, pulsing sensation that emanated from the stone send its calming strength through my body.

"Yes," I said, but I didn't mention that I seemed to need it more often now than I had in the first couple of months since my infection. I didn't want him to worry.

"Good," he said. "I wish I'd had a moonstone from the very beginning like you." Daniel's hands slipped away from my shoulders, and he stepped back, taking his warmth with him. "I wonder if I would have been able to stop myself from ever giving in to the wolf the first time. . . ." His voice trailed off, and I didn't have to wonder why. So much pain had come into his life— our lives—because of what happened that night.

I shifted on the bench so I was looking at him now.

His shaggy blond hair blew softly above his deep brown eyes in the chilly March wind. "Will you ever forgive yourself for that night?"

Daniel shoved his hands in his jacket pockets. "When your brother does."

I bit my lip. That required *finding* Jude in the first place. A prospect that seemed more unlikely with each passing week that he remained missing. "He has to. Eventually. Don't you think?" My dad once said that someone who refused to forgive would eventually become a monster if he held on to his anger and let it burn inside of him for too long. But I guess that had already happened to Jude. He'd turned into a monster—in a much more literal sense than my father had meant—a werewolf who had infected me and then tried to kill Daniel. All because he couldn't forgive Daniel for infecting him the night he first succumbed to the werewolf curse himself.

"Do you think he can come back from what he's done?" I asked. "I mean, even if we find him—do you think he'll ever be the same person he was before . . . ?" My arm twinged with a sharp pain in the spot where Jude had bitten me. I rubbed my hand over the scar that hid under my sleeve.

"I don't know," Daniel said. "I did—with your help. But that doesn't mean everyone can. Jude won't change unless he wants to. And once you've gone wolf, its influence is so overwhelming that it's almost impossible to remember who you used be."

I nodded, wondering if that fate awaited me someday.

Daniel stepped toward me. He reached out and
brushed the moonstone pendant that rested against my
chest. His finger traced along the stone's rough edge
where it had broken in half when Jude had pitched it
from the roof of the parish three months before.

"I just thank God every day that I was able to find
this for you. Even if it's only half the original stone, it's
still enough to help keep you safe. Help stop you from
losing yourself like I did. Like Jude. It'll help keep
you human." Daniel's fingers left the pendant, and
he cupped my face in both of his hands. His thumbs
brushed my cheeks, and he stared deep into my eyes.

"Thank you," I whispered.

"For what?"

"For the moonstone. For believing in me." I half
smiled. "For not dying. I would have killed you if you'd
died on me like that." I jabbed him in the chest with my
finger.

Daniel laughed. I loved the sound of it. Then he
leaned in and pressed his mouth against my upturned
lips. I pressed back, and our mouths melted together
into a kiss that told me that everything I felt for Daniel,
he felt for me.

I shuddered in his arms. "You *are* cold," he said
when our lips parted, and he held me tight in his warm
embrace.

"Is she dead?" a voice asked somewhere nearby, waking me from a deep sleep.

"No," a second, slightly younger-sounding voice responded.

"I think she's dead."

An "unnnmmmm" sound escaped my lips. *Why did my ankle ache so badly? And why did my mattress feel more like wood slats?*

"Yep, she's dead. He's going to be so mad."

"She just made a noise, and her . . . um . . . chest . . . is moving up and down. Obviously, she's not dead."

"Dead, dead, dead. Do you think he'll kill us? That's what Caleb would have done. Do you think we can request how we want to go out? I don't want to drown. That just looks so unpleasant on TV."

"He's a wolf. How would he drown you? Most likely he'd rip out your throat. And anyways, she's *not* dead."

"It's 'anyway' not 'anyways.'"

"What?"

"Guys," I tried to say, but it came out more like, "Gaaaahh." I cleared my throat. *How early was it?*

"You said it wrong. It's 'anyway.' Putting an 's' on the end makes you sound like an idiot. And *anyway*, she's dead. How fast do you think we need to run to get to Canada before he finds out?"

"You're the idiot!"

I heard a scuffle and a shout. One of my eyelids cracked open just enough to see Ryan grab Brent in a headlock right next to me. Everything else in my vision was still blurry.

"Guys!" I shouted. "Cut it out!"

Ryan dropped his hold on Brent, and the two snapped to attention. They stood straight as rails with their hands at their sides, like soldiers responding to the bark of their drill sergeant. I'd never get used to their response to my commands. Brent leaned slightly toward Ryan and whispered—loudly—"I told you she was dead."

Ryan's nostrils flared. "Why you effing—"

I burst out laughing at the look on Brent's face. He could pull off that innocent, yet sarcastic "Whaaat?" look like nobody else. I'd known him for only a few days, but the kid knew how to crack me up—and I was thankful for anything that could make me smile lately. My laugh turned into a coughing fit. The two boys leaned over me like they were afraid I actually *was* going to die.

I waved them off and regained my breath. "Now, would you like to tell me what the hell you're doing in my bedroom?"

"Oh great, now she's lost her mind," Brent said.

Ryan shoved him away. "You're not in your bedroom, Miss Grace. We helped you home last night, and you fell asleep on your porch swing. We stayed to protect you. Don't you remember?"

I opened both my eyes now and gave them a few

seconds to focus on my surroundings. Brent. Ryan. The top branches of the walnut tree. Purple early-morning sky. Porch swing. And apparently, that thing jabbing me in the back was my cell phone, which I must have fallen asleep on top of. A vague recollection trickled into my brain, and I remembered following Daniel's howls into the forest, then attempting to limp home on a newly rebroken ankle. I'd given up about halfway through the forest and allowed one of the two wolves who followed anxiously at my side to carry me home—only to discover that I'd locked myself out of the house. I remembered sitting on the porch swing with the intention to call my dad for help, but I must have fallen asleep before dialing the number.

Asleep.

Truth hit me like a smack in the face as I realized—once again—that the time I'd spent with Daniel in the Garden of Angels last night had been just a dream. It was the same vibrant memory that played in a loop in my head every time I'd allowed myself to sleep since we'd escaped from the warehouse: Daniel and me in the Garden of Angels about six months ago. Before Jude came back. Before Caleb and Talbot. Before Daniel became trapped as the white wolf. It felt like heaven.

Last night, the dream had kept me warm as I slept in the frosty November air. But now I felt colder than even before, realizing all over again that Daniel hadn't really been there to wrap me in his arms.

And he may never be able to again.

"Did you two stay out here with me all night?" I asked.

Ryan and Brent were the youngest of the five of Caleb's boys who had chosen Daniel as their new alpha. Ryan couldn't be more than fourteen. Brent was probably almost sixteen, but he had a boyish roundness to his face, and he pressed his fingers against the bridge of his nose often enough to make me wonder if he'd worn glasses before he'd been turned into an Urbat. And there was something just plain ironic about "Brent the Werewolf."

In fact, it was hard for me to imagine either of these two as part of the vicious werewolf pack that had tried to attack me at Caleb's command. I couldn't help thinking of them as a group of lost boys. Like in the *Peter Pan* play my mom made us put on at the parish when I was ten. The way they'd never really grow up. And how they lived in that warehouse next to the Depot club. I'm sure it was all fun and games—until the killing-people part started.

Ryan nodded. "Your safety is our first priority. It's what he wants."

I sat up and scanned the yard. If Brent and Ryan were here, I wouldn't be surprised if the other three boys weren't far off. They were a pack, after all.

Zach and Marcos sat at the base of the walnut tree, but Slade stood so far down the street that I wouldn't have noticed him without my sharper-than-average eyesight. While it was hard to imagine Brent and Ryan as bloodthirsty werewolves, I had the opposite reaction to Slade. His ripped arms were painted with tattoos of flames that extended from his wrists to shoulders. He had a steel bar in one eyebrow and ten other piercings in his ears. And he almost always had a lighter in his hand, which he'd flick to life just to watch the flame dance for a while before singeing off the hair on his arms—seemingly just for fun. But it wasn't Slade's appearance that made me shiver in his presence. It was the way he looked at me. I was almost certain he had been the large gray wolf that had sunk his venomous teeth into my leg when I was attacked by Caleb's pack in the warehouse, because every once in a while I'd catch this look in Slade's eyes, like he'd tasted my blood—and he just might want more.

I glanced away from Slade. Unlike the other boys, I couldn't help questioning just how devoted he was to Daniel as his alpha. Or whether he might be a danger to us all.

"Who wants you to keep me safe?" I asked Ryan.

"Alpha."

"You mean Daniel?"

"The great white wolf. Your safety is to come first and foremost."

I smiled slightly at the idea that Daniel still cared, in some way, about me.

"We only left you for a while—to change back." I knew Ryan not only meant to transform back into human form, but to also change back into their clothes. That was one of the difficulties of the werewolf transformation—clothing usually wasn't optional.

"Thanks," I mumbled, glad not to wake up in a yard full of naked guys. That definitely wouldn't go over well with the neighbors if anyone were to look out their window this early in the morning. And I was glad they weren't hanging out in their wolf forms anymore, either. With all that howling last night, it wouldn't be safe.

"I'm just glad you didn't die while we were gone," Brent said. "He'd be so pissed. And you know, you'd be dead. So that would suck."

"Thanks for the concern. I'm pretty sure I'm safe on my front porch, though."

"With all due respect, Miss Grace, our father—I mean, Caleb—and the rest of the Shadow Kings are still out there somewhere. You should be more careful."

I nodded. "You're right." It really had been stupid of me to drop my guard like that. That was "rule number one," as both Daniel and Talbot used to tell me. Caleb was still out there, and it was impossible to predict what a madman like him was capable of doing next. Considering the state of my stupid ankle, I wouldn't have stood a chance if I'd encountered him or any of his still-loyal boys last night.

I stretched forward and concentrated my healing

powers into my throbbing ankle until the pain subsided into an uncomfortable ache. Then a thought hit me. "How do you know what Daniel wants? Can you . . . can you talk to him when you're in wolf form?"

A trill of hope ran up my spine, and I no longer cared about the soreness of my ankle. Maybe I could get one of the boys to talk to Daniel for me. Tell him . . .

"No," Brent said. "It's just like we *know* what he wants. And we do it. That's how it works with an alpha."

"Like telepathy?" My brain was running much too slow this morning. But it couldn't be any later than six a.m., so I didn't blame myself for being so sluggish running on less than three hours of sleep. But there was a much quicker thought—too quick to be my own—that flitted through my mind. *If you were a wolf, you could communicate with Daniel, too. You could be together.*

"No," Ryan said. "We can't read each other's thoughts."

"Thank God," I heard Zach mumble. He and Marcos had edged closer to the porch.

"All animals have their ways of communicating," Brent said. "Facial expressions, vocalizations, and such, but with the alpha, it's more like a *feeling*. Sometimes it manifests as images or impressions. But mostly, it's like we feel what he feels."

I mulled that over quietly in my head for a moment.

"What does he feel?" I finally asked, even though I was afraid I already knew the answer.

Ryan and Brent exchanged a look, but I couldn't read the meaning of it.

Marcos stepped forward. "He loves you very much," he said in his Brazilian accent. "He wants us to keep you safe . . . but at the same time, it feels like part of him is . . . I don't know quite how to say it. Like part of him is *leaving*."

I nodded and bit my lip. That is exactly what I'd been afraid to hear. I didn't need to be one of his wolves to be able to feel that a part of him—the part that was *Daniel*—was going away.

You can't stop ƒ*im. Not as a weak* ƒ*uman,* the monster in my head growled. I hated how often I heard its voice now. My hand went to my neck, hoping to clasp my moonstone to help sooth the beast away. But of course the stone wasn't there anymore. Caleb had smashed it against a wall in his warehouse, along with most of my hope that we were ever going to escape his evil plan.

I'd worn that pendant every day for almost a year, and I kept forgetting it wasn't there anymore until I'd reach for it. And then my neck would just feel empty and bare without it. In my dreams, Daniel kept telling me that he'd given me the moonstone to help me stay in control—to help me stay human. And sometimes now I wondered if I had the strength to stay myself without it. . . .

"That's it!" I jumped out of the swing and practically

knocked Brent over. "Oh my goodness, I think I know the answer."

I ran down the porch steps, my hands to my head like I was trying to hold in my racing thoughts so they couldn't escape. Brent, Ryan, Marcos, and Zach bounded up to me. Even Slade came closer, standing at the edge of the yard now.

"I keep seeing Daniel in my dreams—the same dream over and over again. What if he's trying to tell me something? What if *I'm* feeling what he feels? What he wants me to feel? He and I could be connected somehow, too. So what if he's trying to tell me how to help him?"

"It's plausible," Brent said.

"What is he trying to tell you?" Marcos asked.

"My moonstone!" I jogged down the driveway, once again ignoring Gabriel's warning about running on my fragile ankle. I had to get to the parish. I had to tell Gabriel and my father what I'd realized. The boys followed after me. "In my dreams, I keep reliving a memory where Daniel keeps telling me that my moonstone will help me stay human. But what if he's really trying to tell me that a moonstone is what *he* needs to turn him back into a human?"

Could it really be that easy? Why hadn't Gabriel thought of it before me?

My hand went instinctively to my neck again to clasp my moonstone pendant—the thing that could save

Daniel—and once again I was caught by surprise that it wasn't there.

"No!" I practically howled and stopped in my tracks. I should have known there was no easy answer.

Every moonstone I'd ever known to exist had now been destroyed.

Unless . . .

I closed my eyes and thought through every moment of that dream about Daniel and me in the Garden of Angels: the sketchbook. Daniel's tender kiss on my skin. His warm fingers lingering on my moonstone pendant. The pendant that was half the stone Daniel used to wear before it had been broken by . . .

The beautiful image of Daniel in my head suddenly shifted to one of my most horrible memories—the night Jude fell to the werewolf curse. The night he infected me and almost succeeded in killing Daniel. Jude had pursued us on to the roof of the parish. He'd confronted Daniel, but Daniel had refused to fight. Anxiety ached in my muscles as I remembered the way Daniel had removed his moonstone necklace—the only thing keeping him from going wolf in the light of the full moon—and offered it to Jude. Begged him to take the stone.

I remembered how for a second it looked like Jude was going to take the moonstone, like all was going to be well. As I watched the memory replay in my head, I knew what was going to happen. I remembered the way

I'd screamed when Jude took the stone and pitched it from the roof of the parish, and it disappeared into the dark void beyond the roof. . . .

And then it all clicked. My eyes popped open. I *knew* exactly what my dreams had been trying to tell me.

Half a moonstone!

"Daniel was only able to find *half* the moonstone that Jude threw from that roof . . . and I might just know where to find the other half."

Chapter Three

Hope Stone

I stood in the cold, dead grass in the churchyard near the willow tree where Daniel and I used to share occasional picnics after Sunday service. Dad and Gabriel sat on the parish steps. The five boys stood behind me—they'd insisted on coming along, which was good since I was going to need all the help I could get. No doubt they were all wondering why I'd been staring up at the roof of the parish for the last few minutes like a total loon. Only one member of our little group was still missing, and I was taking advantage of what time I had left to gather my thoughts before I shared my revelation with the others.

I heard the screech of brakes in the parking lot. I could smell April's pear-scented perfume as soon as she got out of the car—along with another mixture of scents, like maple, donuts, and . . . bacon?

"What's the big emergency?" she asked as she came up to me. Her voice sounded oddly chipper for six thirty a.m. on a Saturday.

I took my eyes off the parish's roof for a second to glance at her. I'd given the others only a ten-minute warning to meet me. Dad had creases on his face like he'd fallen asleep at his desk in the parish's office with only a book for a pillow. Gabriel was just as bleary-eyed, but April looked like she was headed out to the Megaplex in Apple Valley on a Friday night with perfectly placed curls, jewelry, makeup, and an outfit that looked like it was straight off a mannequin at the Gap. I, on the other hand, was still clad in my red pajama pants and shirt under my jacket.

I gave her one more quick glance and noticed the paper bag from the Day's Market Bakery sticking out of her large pink purse. The mixture of smells suddenly made sense, and if I had only one guess, I'd bet ten bucks that bag contained a couple of bacon-maple donuts—Jude's favorite.

I frowned. *No wonder she looked so good.* April had spent almost every waking moment in the past week outside Jude's makeshift cage.

I ignored April's question. She must have been headed over here already before she got my text because she'd gotten here a lot faster than I'd expected, and I still wasn't quite ready to share my idea.

I'd spent almost a year repressing my memories of

what happened that fateful night on the parish's roof, and now it took most of my concentration to force myself to recall every last detail.

"Grace has proposed the hypothesis that we need a moonstone in order to help change Daniel back into his human form," Brent said, as if he could sense my reluctance to speak.

"What makes you think this?" Gabriel asked me. "I've been exploring that possibility myself."

"She thinks he's been trying to psychically communicate it to her," Brent answered for me, "in her dreams."

Gabriel stood. "Interesting. Perhaps it has something to do with your being his alpha mate." He stared into my eyes for a moment. "Or something else . . ."

Dad started grumbling about the word *mate*. I held my hand up to silence him before he could launch into another lecture and break my concentration.

"Of course, the issue would be *where* to procure another moonstone," Dad said, instead of getting all preachy.

"Can't we just buy a moon rock off the Internet?" April said. "I've been doing some looking around for Jude, and I found a dude on eBay who says he's got a moon rock from the actual moon mission back in the sixties. We can buy it now for only three thousand dollars. I've got some college savings—"

"Whoa. Hold on to your wallet," Gabriel said.

"First of all, most of the moon rocks you see being sold out there are fakes. Secondly, there are only a relative handful of moonstones in existence that work to counteract the Urbat curse. They were a gift to me from a Babylonian moon priestess who had been taken as a slave. She blessed a few moon meteor rocks and gave them to me in exchange for freeing her from her master. No other moonstone I have ever encountered has the same effect as these."

"Oh." It was almost possible to hear April counting all the money she'd almost lost on eBay in her head—although I did find it heartening that Jude might have been the one who *asked* her to find him a new stone. "Then let's call this priestess lady," she said, "and get some more magic rocks."

Gabriel gave her an overly patient look. "That was over seven hundred years ago, my child."

"Oh." April gave a sheepish grin. "I forget you're so *old*."

"Grace thinks she may know where to find a moonstone," Brent said. "She just hasn't shared it yet."

"Any time now would be fantastic," Slade grumbled. "It's cold out here."

"Then get a jacket," I snapped. He obviously wasn't a native Minnesotan if he thought *this* was cold. "Because we're all going to be out here for a while." I kept my eyes on the roof and backed up farther so I could get a better view of the steeple—what Daniel had clung to that night to keep himself from falling. I pictured where Jude had stood in relation to Daniel, and then tried to map out the trajectory of his throw in my mind's eye.

"My moonstone, the one I wore for almost the last year, was a piece of the moonstone pendant Daniel used to wear. Jude threw it from the roof of the parish. Daniel searched for it in the snow a few days later, but he was able to find only *half* of the moonstone for me. The rock must have split when it hit the ground. Which means the other half is possibly *still* in the churchyard somewhere."

April gasped. I could always rely on her for a good reaction.

I backed up a few more paces, sending the boys scattering to get out of my way. Then I turned and walked slowly, trying to figure just how far the moonstone must have traveled when Jude threw it. The others trailed behind me as I walked with calculated, yet limping steps around the church building. I stopped when I came to what I guesstimated was the approximate area—the gravely overflow parking pad behind the parish for busy church days like Christmas and Easter.

"It's here. It has to be here somewhere." I dropped to my knees and started picking through the rocks. There were thousands of them—*hundreds of thousands*—but I started by picking up a rock that had a blackish-gray tint, and tested it for that pulsing heat that emanated only from a moonstone.

Nothing.

I set it aside and tested another and then another.

"You've got to be kidding me," Slade said. "It could take an eternity to pick through all those rocks."

"Then get started," I said.

Brent and Ryan followed my order immediately and bent down beside me to start searching. Then Gabriel, my father, April, Marcos, and Zach joined in. Even Slade sat in the gravel and halfheartedly poked at a few rocks.

"Set aside any rock that is gray or black: that way I can test them for the pulsing. The stone we're looking for might still have a crescent moon carved into it, but it might not. Who knows how it could have broken. There might even be more than one piece."

It had been almost a year. Three seasons had come and gone. Snow and rain and plenty of cars had passed through the churchyard. But there was still a *possibility* that the other half of Daniel's moonstone was here, which meant I wasn't going to stop searching until I'd actually turned over every stone in this place.

Chapter Four

INTERVENTION

SUNDAY EVENING—

ALMOST THIRTY-NINE HOURS LATER

"If you think I'm going to give up now, then you don't know me at all," I said.

"We're not telling you to give up." Dad reached across the desk and gently scooped up the pile of rocks that sat in front of me.

We'd moved most of "Operation: Find the Moonstone" into Dad's office at the parish because eight people picking through rocks in a church parking lot was bound to bring on questions from townsfolk passing by. Plus, Dad wouldn't let us keep working out there once it was time for church services earlier today. The others took shifts discreetly bringing in buckets of rocks from the churchyard and dumping them on Dad's desk for Gabriel and me to sift through. The others had stopped for dinner an hour ago—and had apparently decided to turn against me while they were out.

"We're telling you to take a break," Dad continued. "You haven't eaten, you've barely slept, and you've got so much caffeine in your system your hands are shaking."

I glanced at the empty cups from the Java Pot and the several energy drink cans that littered the desk as evidence, and then folded my trembling hands into my lap. "I'm fine."

"You need to go home and get some sleep," Gabriel said. He, my dad, and April all stood on the opposite side of my dad's desk.

I shook my head. I didn't want to sleep because I knew I'd have that dream of Daniel and me again—the one that told me to find the moonstone. The dream had grown more and more urgent the few times I'd tried to rest my eyes while sifting through the stones, making me wake up a few minutes later, all the more frantic to keep up the search.

Without thinking, I grabbed the coffee cup closest to me and gulped down the dregs.

April snatched the cup out of my hand. "Geez, Grace. You've got circles the size of hockey pucks under your eyes. I'm totally going to have to get you some heavy-duty concealer before we go back to school tomorrow. People are gonna think—"

I shot an accusatory glare at April. As my best friend,

she was supposed to take my side in this. "I don't care what I look like, and I don't care what people think." At least I wasn't still in my pajamas. At some point in the last twenty-four hours or so, April had brought me fresh clothes along with the supply of caffeinated beverages. "And I'm not going to school tomorrow. How can I without . . . ?"

My voice caught in the back of my throat, but I pushed down the rush of emotion that rose up from deep inside my chest when I tried to say Daniel's name out loud. "How can I sit there next to his empty seat in class and pretend he's just at home sick?"

That was the story Dad had come up with to explain Daniel's absence from school so he wouldn't lose his scholarship now that the midterm break was over and we were supposed to head back to class tomorrow. Dad had filed a "home and hospital" release for Daniel, and as far as everyone else in town was concerned, Daniel had a nasty case of walking pneumonia. I still wondered how Dad had actually gotten a doctor to sign the release without examining Daniel . . . or if *Pastor Divine* had forged the report himself.

He never did answer the question when I'd asked.

"You're not missing school, Gracie." Dad pulled the rock away that I'd tried to snatch from a pile on the desk. "College applications are due soon, and you can't afford any more difficulties with your grades. Your future is too important."

"My future? What future? If we can't turn Daniel back into a human, I don't *have* a future." *Why didn't they understand?* "The cure could be in this very room right now. I am not giving up."

"We told you, Grace, we're not telling you to give up. We're telling you to take a break. It could take weeks, maybe even months, to go through all these rocks." He swallowed hard, no doubt trying to hide the hopelessness that echoed in his voice. He didn't believe we were ever going to find it. "You won't be any good to anyone if you get sick or lose it. . . ." He paused again, and I knew he was thinking about Mom. Mental instability *did* run in the family. "April is going to take you home so you can get some sleep. Gabriel and I will pick up here where you left off with these rocks tomorrow."

I stared at the three of them as they stared at me, and I realized what exactly this was: an intervention.

How dare they try to stop you from helping Daniel? a soft but harsh voice whispered inside my head. *They've given up already, and they want you to also. They don't understand how important this is for you. Nobody knows you like I do.* I shook my head hard, trying to get rid of the demon wolf's voice. My hand flew to the nape of my neck, searching for the moonstone necklace that wasn't there. I tried to disguise the move by scratching at the collar of my shirt.

But I couldn't fool Gabriel. He nodded with recognition. "The more tired or stressed or emotional you are,

Grace, the more the wolf will be able to invade your thoughts. You're making yourself vulnerable by wearing yourself out. How would Daniel feel if your fears for him are what led you to losing your own self to the wolf?"

I clenched my hands at my side. The voice inside my head wanted me to lash out at Gabriel and tell him that he was wrong—he and I had never really gotten along—but deep down I knew he was right. Losing my moonstone at the warehouse meant I needed to be more careful and guarded than ever against the wolf . . . *oh!*

"I need to go back to the warehouse," I blurted out before I'd even finished processing the thought.

"Why the heck would you want to do that?" April fidgeted with the beaded bracelet on her wrist—no doubt one of her new creations. I'd think it was an odd digging-through-rocks accessory if she hadn't spent an extra-long lunch break downstairs with Jude. "I'd never want to go back there if I were you." April shivered dramatically. "I get the willies just thinking about that place."

I shivered, too. *So do I.* "We need a moonstone. And Dad's right, it could take months to go through every rock in that gravel-strewn parking lot." I indicated the buckets and bowls full of rocks, trying not to feel defeated admitting that it was a near-impossible task. "But Caleb smashed both my and Jude's moonstones at the warehouse, and since a pack of teenage boys aren't exactly the best housekeepers, I'm guessing there're going to be moonstone fragments scattered all over the place there. What if I can find enough pieces—maybe April can weld them onto some sort of necklace or dog tag?" Finding enough fragments to make a difference seemed like a long shot—but not a shot as long as going through all these rocks. "I'll go now."

"Absolutely not," Dad said.

"But Dad, I have to—"

"You're tired, Grace, and you're not thinking rationally if you believe I'm going to let you go waltzing back into the place where you were almost killed. Your mother would never recover if—"

"If what?" I asked. "You tell her the truth again?"

Dad and I still didn't see eye to eye on that one. When I'd disappeared from the Halloween festival with Talbot (i.e., gotten myself kidnapped), Dad had taken it upon himself to tell Mom the truth about what all was going on. And let me tell you, that hadn't gone over so well.

Especially considering where Mom was now. She'd earned herself a one-way ticket to mandatory lockdown in the psych ward at City Hospital, courtesy of Dr. Connors.

"Um, not to make you madder at me, but your dad has a point," April said. "I mean, what if Mr. Caleb 'I'm a scary nut job' Kalbi is watching the place, just waiting for you to come back?"

"I doubt he'd go back there. Besides—"

"No," Dad said. He locked eyes with me. "And don't you forget that you promised me you wouldn't go running off without my blessing again. I am not letting you go back there, and that's final."

"But part of that promise was that you'd hear me out. That we'd work together—as a family. Daniel needs a moonstone. I know it. I can *feel* it. And now you're telling me to give up before I can—"

"What we're telling you to do is be safe." Dad reached across his desk and tried to take my hand. I pulled it away. "I've seen the way you've been limping around here all weekend. Not to mention the internal injuries you suffered because of Caleb. You're in no shape to be heading into potential danger again."

He had a point about the ankle. Crouching in the gravel for so long had done little to help it reheal. I stood up and pretended not to feel the sharp twinge that shot through my leg when I put weight on it. I stood as tall as I could. "I'm fine."

"I suggest you go home and rest." Gabriel scrubbed his hands down his weary face. "We'll talk about this later. Come up with a more sensible plan."

"Think of the big picture, Gracie," Dad said. "Your life is a lot bigger than this moment. You need to remember that you can't let the trials you face right now derail your course forever."

"I *am* thinking about the big picture. Not only has

the boy I love been turned into a wolf and he's *stuck* that way, but we also have a psychotic werewolf with a gang of bloodthirsty demons after us, not to mention Sirhan and his pack, and whatever the hell they want with me. . . . Daniel may be the only one who can stop Caleb from killing us and then taking over the strongest werewolf pack in the country and doing who knows what horrendous things with his newfound power. Because when Sirhan dies, Daniel will be the only *true alpha* left on this side of the planet, if not the whole world. That sounds pretty 'big picture' to me!"

My voice had risen louder than I'd meant it to. From the expressions on their faces I could tell I must look all wild-eyed and insane. *How could I make them understand?*

"And I miss him," I said, my voice much softer now. "I miss him so bad, it makes my heart ache like there's something inside of it, pushing out, and the whole thing is just going to burst open at any moment if the pressure gets any greater. I miss being held in his arms." I turned to April because I felt more comfortable telling her these things than my dad or Gabriel. "I miss that look he gets in his eyes when he's really in the groove with a new painting. I miss the look in his eyes when he looks at me. I miss how everything I said to him was important. Like I was the most important person in the world to him. And now, I don't even know if he understands me when I speak."

"Gracie . . ."

I shook my head to stop Dad from interrupting. "It feels like he's dead. Only it's worse because he's still here. Only it isn't him. Not completely. He's physically here, stuck inside that white wolf, and at the same time he's never felt so far away. He's not *Daniel*. We don't even know *what* he is." I looked back at Gabriel and Dad. "I swore I wouldn't give up on him. And I'd move a whole damn mountain if I thought it would change him back. So how can you ask me to give up and go to school when all I have to do is search some abandoned warehouse for a few priceless stones that might change him back?"

"Letting *you* go to the warehouse in this condition is not an option—"

"Then I'll go to Sirhan," I said, even though that idea scared me more than the warehouse. "He's the keeper of the rest of the moonstones, isn't he?"

Gabriel nodded solemnly, and I knew he'd been thinking the same thing.

"Over my dead body," Dad said. "The warehouse is foolhardy, but going to Sirhan is akin to suicide. I barely survived my encounter with him, and I'm not allowing any of you to go. He hates Daniel for being Caleb's son, so what makes you think he'd want to help him?"

This time I *could* see my dad's point. I knew Gabriel was in hot water with Sirhan for not returning weeks ago—with me as his unwilling guest. If we sent Gabriel to get a moonstone for Daniel, I had serious doubts we'd ever see him again. And I didn't know what Sirhan wanted with me, but the pure fact that he had ordered Gabriel to bring me to him made me fear him even more than Caleb sometimes. If I went to Sirhan, I probably wouldn't be allowed to come back. And then there was the fact that Daniel had been banished from Sirhan's pack, not only for being Caleb's son but also because Sirhan recognized Daniel as a true alpha. I had no idea what they might do to him now that he'd embraced his own true alpha–ness. Sirhan might see Daniel as the ultimate threat.

"I won't go to Sirhan if you let me go to the warehouse. But I need to go soon. I'm afraid if Daniel keeps wandering farther into the forest . . . that he won't come back again at all." We'd heard him howling again last night, and it had sounded much farther away. I'd sent Marcos and Ryan to quiet him down, and they'd told me they'd had to run for almost a half hour at full speed to get to him in the depths of the woods.

Dad sighed. "Then let me go for you."

"That's a terrible idea, Paul," Gabriel said. "If anyone should go, it should be me."

"You and the girls have school. I'll go tomorrow while it's daylight. I can at least have a look around to see what I can find."

"No way. *You* don't have any powers at all. That's

even more dangerous than me going." I couldn't believe how quickly this conversation had turned surreal. I was used to Dad trying to convince me not to wander into dangerous places—but the vice-versa situation suddenly made me understand why he worried so much. "What if someone *is* waiting there—?"

"So you acknowledge the danger now?" Dad folded his arms in front of his chest.

I opened my mouth, but I didn't have a response.

"I'll go with him," came a familiar voice from the doorway of the office.

I spun around to find Talbot standing there. He wore his favorite blue baseball cap and held a bowl from the parish kitchen filled with parking lot gravel in one hand. The thumb of his other hand was jammed into one of his belt loops next to his Texas Ranger star-shaped belt buckle. He gave me a look like someone who was crashing a party he knew he wasn't invited to.

I scowled. "What the heck is he doing here?"

"Good evening to you, too, kid," he said, and tipped his baseball cap to me and then winked at April.

My hands balled into fists. I'm pretty sure I'd warned him what I'd do the next time he called me "kid."

"I come bearing gifts, at least," he said, and indicated the bowl of rocks. "Those boys out there looked like they were about to fall over. I sent most of them home. Marcos and I are sharing rock duty for a while."

By *home* I assumed he meant Maryanne Duke's old

house, where the boys had been crashing for the time being—until Dad and I can figure out what the heck to do with five homeless teenage werewolves.

"But that still doesn't explain *why* you came here in the first place," I said. "I told you to stay away from me."

"I asked Talbot to take the night shift with Jude," Gabriel said. "I need to get some rest since I'll have to deal with a couple hundred high school students tomorrow." He stifled a yawn that must have been brought on by the very prospect of it. I still found it hard to believe that Dad had hired an eight-hundred-some-year-old werewolf to teach religion at the Christian private school I attended. But I found it even harder to understand why Dad and Gabriel would trust Talbot—like he'd had *nothing* to do with Caleb.

"You've got him babysitting Jude now?"

Not that I didn't agree that Jude needed someone to keep an eye on him while he . . . adjusted to being back in Rose Crest. I just didn't think that person should be Talbot. I know it'd been revealed that Talbot was Gabriel's great-great-add-in-a-few-dozen-more-greats nephew, but I hoped the sudden familial obligation Gabriel felt toward Talbot didn't come back to bite him.

"Thank you, Talbot," Dad said, ignoring my comment. "I'll take you up on the offer to accompany me to the warehouse." He picked up a couple of books and stuffed them in his briefcase. "So it's settled. Grace, have April take you home so you can get some sleep before school tomorrow. I have to do some visits at the nursing home in the morning, and then Talbot and I will head over to the warehouse around lunch. I want to make sure we get out of there before nightfall."

"Sounds good," Talbot said.

"But—" I tried to protest.

"I said it was settled." Dad snapped his briefcase shut and gave me a look that said that if I pushed one more time, *nobody* would be going to the warehouse. Then his eyes softened. "Let me do this for you, Grace. Let me be your father and protect you when I still can. Let's make sure Daniel has a future to come back to."

"Okay," I said softly. "Marcos is still outside, isn't he?"

Talbot nodded.

"Ask him if he'll go with you, too." I didn't want to say it out loud, but I didn't want my dad going anywhere alone with Talbot.

"Okay," Dad said.

I grabbed my jacket.

"Maybe you should go visit your brother on the way out," Dad said. "I think he'd appreciate seeing you."

"Not tonight," I said softly; then I sidestepped around Talbot and went out the office door.

April gathered up her things and followed me out

into the foyer. She stopped when I passed the stairwell that led to the basement of the parish where Jude was holed up—locked up—for observation.

"I'm going to drop off some dinner for Jude." April held up the paper sack from the Rose Crest Café. "Do you want to come down with me? Your dad is right. I think Jude would like to see you."

I shook my head and leaned against the wall. "I'll wait."

"You've been practically living at the parish for the last few days, and you haven't been down there to see him once. After everything you went through to get him back . . . it just doesn't seem like you to ignore him like this."

"I know." It wasn't very *Grace-like* at all. It's just that there had been something in my brother's eyes the last time I looked him in the face—back in the warehouse when I found out he'd asked to come home— that'd scared me. They didn't look like *his* eyes at all. Like my brother wasn't *my brother* anymore. I didn't know if it was just a flash of emotion I'd seen—guilt, anger, remorse—or if his eyes were telling me we'd brought a monster back with us instead of Jude.

I wasn't ready to go see him yet because I was afraid of what I might find if I looked him in the eyes again.

What if I didn't see my brother there at all?

April gave me a sad smile and then headed for the stairs.

"Be careful," I said. "We still don't know why Jude asked to come back home. I don't want you to get hurt." *Emotionally or physically.*

April nodded, and I felt a pang of guilt as I let her go down the stairs without me.

"Grace?"

I sighed heavily and turned away from Talbot. He'd followed us out into the hall—I should have known that I wouldn't get by him so easily. I pursed my lips, determined not to talk to him.

"What you said in there, about Daniel not being able to—"

"Stop," I said. I'd never been very good at holding my tongue. "You don't have the right to ask me anything about *him*."

"Then can I ask when you're going to give me another chance? When are you going to trust me?"

"I trusted you before, Talbot. I trusted you when I thought you were the only person on my side. You were supposed to be my mentor. I thought you were my *friend*. But you were working for Caleb all along. You were the enemy." *You're one of the people responsible for what happened to Daniel.*

"You seem to be forgetting the part where I turned on Caleb and tried to help you escape. And then I used my powers to help heal you. Do you know how difficult that all was? But I did it because I care about you. Because we *are* friends. I'm on your side now." He sighed. "So what more do I have to do to prove to you that I'm a changed man?"

I was quiet until I heard April's footsteps coming back up the stairs from the basement. "Keep my father safe tomorrow," I said, and stepped outside through the exit doors without looking back.

Chapter Five

SILVER BULLETS

If Dad had thought a day at school would be good for my sanity, he couldn't have been more wrong.

Part of the "home and hospital" arrangement for Daniel was that I was supposed to gather his missed assignments from his teachers through the day. Which meant I was hit over and over again in the gut each time I was asked how he was doing, and had to lie through my teeth about how his doctor thought it should only be a few more days, and how appreciative he was that they were willing to let him make up his assignments. I swear my neck must have looked like it was on fire considering how many fibs I had to tell.

To add insult to injury, Daniel's homework pile was so heavy I had to use some of my superstrength just to heft my backpack around. He'd missed almost a whole week of school before the midterm break, and since the policy for sick leave was that he still needed to turn in his assignments by the end of this month—it meant that *I* was going to have a lot to do in the next few weeks if I wanted to keep Daniel from flunking out of high school.

As if I didn't already have enough on my plate.

But things only got worse in fourth period when Mr. Barlow handed me two thin manila envelopes in addition to a stack of drawing exercises for Daniel. "I think you'll be needing these," he said. "I'm sure Daniel has been asking about it. Thought I'd put his mind at ease so he can rest and get better."

My expression must have said something like, *Huh?* because Barlow tapped the envelopes on top the pile and said, "They're your and Daniel's letters for Trenton."

"Letters for Trenton?"

"Don't tell me Daniel's forgotten about the application due date? If so, we'd better get a whole team of doctors in there to look him over. Might have fever-induced amnesia or something."

Oh no! I almost dropped the whole stack of papers. *How could I have forgotten about our Trenton applications?* If there was one thing Daniel wanted (other than to regain his human form, I suppose), it was admission into the Amelia Trenton Art Institute. It had one of the best industrial design departments in the country—and was pretty much everything Daniel had staked his future on.

"No," I said. "Of course not. He's just been a little slow at getting things together. Being . . . sick and all." I bit my lip. "Is there any chance they'd accept a late application?"

"I'm afraid not." Barlow stroked his jowls. "It's a competitive school. All their slots and the waiting list will fill up just from the applications that are turned in on time. Both you and Daniel will need to get your applications, essays, letters of recommendation, and your portfolios turned in by Friday of this week, or neither of you stands a chance—no matter how good your work is." Barlow put his hand on my shoulder. "I wish there was something more I could do."

"No." I indicated the letters. "These are enough." I left Barlow's office and headed for my desk. My hands were shaking, and I wanted to put all those papers down before I lost them all over the floor.

"You okay?" Katie Summers asked as she slipped into the empty seat that should have been occupied by Daniel. I wanted to tell her to move, but instead I gave a slight smile and said, "Yeah. I'm just worried about Daniel, you know."

"I bought him a little present to help him feel better." She smiled sweetly, but I couldn't help noticing that the regulation khakis and polo shirt required by HTA's conservative dress code looked down right salacious the way she wore them. Katie was one of those girls who could make anything seem sexy. "I was thinking I'd stop by his place this afternoon to drop it off."

"No!" I practically shouted. "I mean, he's like super-freaking-contagious. You don't want to go over there." The last thing I needed was for Katie to show up at Daniel's place to find not only that he was missing, but also that a pack of teenage were-boys lived there—especially looking like she did.

"Oh, okay," she said, scrunching her nose. "Will you give it to him for me then?"

She pulled a small package from her knapsack. It was wrapped in paper decorated with an exquisite, intricately hand-drawn design I didn't doubt she'd done herself. A lot of work on her part for a present to *my* boyfriend.

"Yeah, sure." I know Daniel had sworn that nothing had ever happened between him and Katie—but I couldn't help getting the feeling that she *wanted* something to.

I glanced from the present to Daniel's Trenton letter sitting on my table. An old sneaking thought trickled into my mind—in between everything else I had to worry about—what if Daniel and Katie were the ones who got acceptances to Trenton, and not me?

The two of them headed off to college together. . . .

Gah. None of this was good for my sanity. I took the present from Katie and shoved it into my backpack with all of Daniel's and my assignments.

What else could this day possibly throw at me?

The ring of the lunch bell couldn't have come soon enough.

"I'm gonna go to Day's to get Jude some lunch," April said, with the keys to her car in her hand. It's a good thing she was around, or my brother would probably starve, considering everything else I had on my mind.

"I'll hitch a ride with you," I said. I needed to get away from the school for a while.

She gave me a hopeful smile. I'm sure she was thinking I'd changed my mind about visiting Jude. I hoped she wouldn't be too disappointed that I was only planning on going with her to the grocery store.

I know I shouldn't have been surprised by the fact that Ryan, Slade, Brent, and Zach were waiting outside the school when April and I headed out to the parking lot. You'd think they'd be able to figure out what to do with themselves other than wait around for me all day.

Then again, I was glad they weren't left to their own devices. . . .

I let them ride over to Day's with us, but Brent was in one of his more sarcastic moods—driving both Ryan and Slade to the brink of punching him in the nose—so I insisted they wait outside while April and I went into the store.

April headed over to the deli to order a couple of sandwiches. I wandered down one of the aisles until I found a stash of PowerBars. Just what I needed to get through this day. I picked up three that sounded the least disgusting and grabbed a bottled iced tea from the refrigerated section.

Brunch of champions, I thought as I got in line at the cash registers with the realization that I'd forgotten to eat this morning. The emptiness in my stomach was so distracting I didn't pay much attention to anything, until I heard Mr. Day ask the customer in front of me what he planned on doing about all that howling last night.

My head snapped up, and I realized that I was standing behind none other than Deputy Marsh. Pretty much my least-favorite person in town—and the last person I wanted *doing* something about Daniel's howling.

"Few of the guys from the lodge are itching to get a hunting party together," Marsh said as he handed a pastrami sandwich and a prepackaged protein shake over to Mr. Day to ring up. "That howling can't mean anything good coming our way, not with this town's history. And it looks like we already have a victim on our hands."

"Who?" Mr. Day asked, with no incredulity evident in his voice. I could tell by the look on his face that he was thinking about his granddaughter Jessica, who had supposedly been a victim of one of this town's infamous wild-dog attacks almost a year ago.

"Just got word that the doctors over at City Hospital are saying that Pete Bradshaw kid was attacked by an animal rather than a person, like we first thought. There are bite marks to prove it. The kid's still unconscious, but he's stable. I'm eager to find out what he knows."

Part of me had wanted to sigh audibly after hearing that Daniel would no longer be a suspect in the Pete Bradshaw case—Deputy Marsh had jumped to the assumption that Daniel was gunning to take down Pete for what he did to me last December—but I almost dropped my grocery basket because of what Mr. Day did next.

"If you get a hunting party together, I'll supply the ammunition," Mr. Day said, and pulled a small box out from under the counter and set it in front of Marsh. I squinted at the writing on the box. Most of it looked like words written in a foreign language, but there was one line in English that said: HANDCRAFTED SILVER BULLETS. "Special ordered these from a guy in Romania."

Deputy Marsh chuckled uneasily as he picked up the package. "Silver bullets? What kind of wolf do you think we'd be hunting?"

"You can never be too careful," Mr. Day said, his tone dead serious. He'd been a believer in the Markham Street Monster ever since his granddaughter's body had been discovered, mauled and mutilated, in the Dumpster behind his store. I should have known it wouldn't take long for someone like him to put two and two together and realize that the monster had to be a werewolf.

"You're a crazy old coot, Day, but I won't go passing up an offer for free amo."

I was about to protest when Michelle Evans, who was buying a five-pound bag of dog food from Stacey Canova at the next register, spoke up before me. "You can't just go shooting wolves." She gave Deputy Marsh the evil eye. "They may have been removed from the endangered species list, but you still need to apply for a permit."

"We did, ma'am." Deputy Marsh tipped his hat to her. "One more attack and Fish and Wildlife Services will expedite a permit—and then I'm going hunting."

I watched with horror as Deputy Marsh tucked the box of silver bullets into his jacket pocket and sauntered away. It took Mr. Day asking three times before I realized I was next in line. "How's Daniel feeling?" he asked as I stepped up to the counter.

"Still the same," I mumbled. If only Mr. Day knew his favorite employee was the one he was endangering with those silver bullets. But Deputy Marsh had always hated Daniel, so the truth would probably put Daniel even more at risk.

"We sure do miss him around here."

"Me, too," I said.

April was still waiting at the deli counter, so I paid for my stuff and went out in front of the store before anyone could notice just how badly my hands shook.

Silver bullets. Hunters after Daniel was bad enough, but ones equipped with weapons that could actually kill him . . .

The boys were gathered near a tree at the far end of the parking lot. Ryan and Brent were engaged in some sort of wrestling match, with Zach egging them on. Slade held a cigarette to his lips and took a deep drag. I watched as Deputy Marsh veered from heading to his patrol truck and started to make a beeline toward them. No doubt thinking he was going to bust a gang of truant kids from the public school in Oak Park. "No loitering," he shouted.

"They're my cousins," I said as I passed him. "Visiting from . . . Michigan. They're on fall break. I'll tell them to go somewhere else."

Marsh looked at me with narrowed eyes. "Whatever. I'm on my lunch break," he said, and headed back toward his car.

"Put it out," I said to Slade as I came up to the guys. Brent dropped his sleeper hold on Ryan when he saw me.

Slade gave me a snide look.

"I said put it out!"

I grabbed the cigarette from his lips and flung it to

the ground, then stomped it out with my foot. Slade growled as if he wanted to lunge at me, but the other three boys stepped in between us.

"We've got more important things to do than for you guys to be hanging around getting hassled by the police. That very deputy is looking to get a wolf-hunting party together—with silver bullets! That means all of you are in danger, and Daniel, too. Which means I need all of you to head over to the warehouse to help my dad look for a moonstone. Now!" I should have told Dad to take all of them in the first place, not just Marcos. But if they went quickly, they'd get there in time to help out. Dad said he and Talbot wouldn't be able to go out there until lunchtime.

Slade gave me an indignant sneer, but Zach and Ryan bowed their heads to acknowledge the order. Brent grabbed my arm.

"The Shadow Kings' warehouse? We can't go back there!" he said, his voice sounding more urgent than I'd ever heard it. Not a hint of humor.

"Why?"

"Caleb's backup plan. He always has a backup. There's a fail-safe in case he had to abandon the building."

"What do you mean? Is the place being watched? Are the SKs back there?"

"No. They wouldn't go back there. Nobody should.

That building is wired to explode!"

"What?" I dropped my grocery bag. The bottle of iced tea shattered when it hit the concrete. "How do you know?"

Brent's face went absolutely white. "Because I built the explosives myself."

Chapter Six

FIRESTORM

My cell phone was out, and I'd dialed Dad's number faster than I thought possible. The call went straight to voice mail.

"Ahhhh! Why do you never charge your phone?!" I shouted at the recording. *But what if that wasn't the reason his phone wasn't working? What if . . .*

"What's wrong?" April asked as she bounded up to me in the parking lot with her deli purchase.

"April, I need your car! Give me your keys. This is matter of life and death."

"Yeah, right. My mom forbids me from letting anyone else drive it because of insurance."

"No, like, *literally* a matter of life and death! My dad is in danger."

"Now see, there's someone who knows how to use 'literally' the correct way," Brent said, smacking Ryan on the back.

"Not the right time for that," I snapped at him. I turned back to April. "The warehouse is rigged to explode. I can't get my dad on his phone, so I've got to try to get there before they go inside."

"Oh!" April grabbed her keys from her purse and threw them to me.

"Which one of you can drive the fastest?"

"Slade," Zach said. "He used to be a street racer."

Of course it would be Slade.

"Zach and Ryan, can you two make the run to the city?"

They nodded.

"Go as fast as you can. You might beat us there. Brent, you come with Slade and me. Tell me everything you know about that bomb."

"What do you want me to do?" April asked.

"Go back to school," I practically ordered. I didn't want April coming along.

Who knows what we'd find when we got there.

IN THE CAR

The next thing I knew, we were flying down the freeway in April's jelly bean of a hatchback. I'd dialed Dad five more times for good measure, and then thought to try the phone in his office at the parish—just in case he hadn't left yet. Someone picked up on the seventh ring.

"Thank goodness, Dad—" I started to say, but was cut off by a voice that wasn't his.

"Grace," Gabriel said. "Listen. Whatever you do, do not come back to the parish or the school this afternoon."

"Why—?"

"Your dad left his phone charging here," Gabriel said. "If you see him, tell him not to come back here, either." And then he hung up.

I held my phone for a second, stunned. What on earth was that all about? Should I call him back? No, I didn't have time to waste trying to figure out why Gabriel was being so cryptic. Dad was in trouble, and that's all that mattered. At least I knew why his phone wasn't working, and not because it had already been blown up.

Tension mounted in my muscles, and the anxiety only increased with each moment that passed and we weren't in the city yet—despite Slade's insane driving.

I shifted in the passenger seat so I could look at Brent in the backseat. "Tell me about that bomb."

Brent leaned forward. "The bomb was Caleb's backup plan in case he had to abandon the warehouse. He wanted a way to destroy any evidence he might have had to leave behind—or take down anyone who might have overthrown him. He's really into getting the last laugh."

"So why didn't he just blow up the building after

he escaped with rest of the Shadow Kings? We were in there for hours after he was gone. He could have gotten rid of all of us in one fell swoop."

"It doesn't work that way—at least not yet. I wasn't finished working on a remote trigger before we left. The way it works now is that there's a keypad in Caleb's bedroom. Every night, he has to punch a code into it. If he misses a night—like if he had to abandon the building—the trip sensor will be activated. The bomb is rigged to blow ninety seconds after someone unlocks one of the entrances into the warehouse. That way the victim will be well inside the building when the explosives go off"—he swallowed hard—"making escape almost impossible."

"You made that system?" Slade asked, swerving into the left lane at what felt like a hundred miles per hour. "Dude, I had no idea you were so hard-core. I shouldn't have given you such a bad time. I knew you made those flash bombs we used when we robbed places—but man, you've got some real skills."

"Tell that to my long string of foster parents. Nobody is too keen on a foster kid who enjoys making explosives in their garage. That's how I ended up on the streets when Talbot found me and brought me to Caleb. I think they wanted me for my 'skills,' as you say."

"Why didn't you tell us about the trap?" I asked, trying to get us back to the topic at hand.

"I didn't think you'd be crazy enough to go back there."

"But wouldn't Talbot know about the explosives?" Was he intentionally leading my dad into the trap? *I knew he couldn't be trusted.*

"No," Brent said. "I'm the only one who knew. Caleb is super-freaking-paranoid. That was his backup plan to get revenge on anyone who might turn on him. I'm probably still alive only because I stalled on making the remote trigger. No way Talbot knows about it."

"Talbot!" I grabbed my phone and dialed Talbot's number. It rang six times and then went to voice mail. I left a message of warning and then dialed the number over and over again. "Why aren't you picking up?!"

Slade swerved the car between two semis and then jutted in front of one of them, cutting it off. Perhaps Caleb had chosen him for his special *skills*, too. I clutched at my stomach as the car took a hard right turn onto the exit. But we were still a good five minutes from the warehouse. I opened my phone with the intention of sending a couple dozen texts to Talbot—anything to get his attention—when my phone suddenly rang in my hand.

It was Talbot's number. Relief gripped me so hard I almost missed answering it in time.

"Talbot!" I said into my phone. "Thank heaven—"

"Wow. Twenty missed calls? And you *claim* not to like me—"

"Shut up," I said. "I need to tell you, *don't* go to the warehouse. You can't go—"

"We're already here. I'm keeping watch while the others head inside."

"No! There's a bomb. Whatever you do, *don't* let them go inside."

"There's a what? Sorry, you cut out. I'm in the underground corridor between . . . Depot and . . . warehouse. Just a sec."

I could tell from the distance in his voice that he'd lowered the phone from his ear before he'd finished talking. I shouted as loud as I could so he might still hear me, "No! Listen to me—"

"Go ahead. It's just Grace," I heard Talbot's voice call to someone on his end of the line.

"There's a—" But I didn't get a chance to finish my sentence. I didn't need to. Because I heard what had happened: a horrible explosive crescendo mixed with a sound so terrible it could only be a human scream before the line went completely silent.

TWO HORRIFYING MINUTES LATER

I saw the smoke almost immediately, billowing from a few blocks away. Slade hit the gas, and the car practically flew through the few remaining streets. To me, it felt like we couldn't possibly move any slower.

I don't know how I did what I did next. I don't know

how I had the presence of mind to call 911, but I did. I wasn't sure if they understood anything that I'd said—that there had been an explosion at the warehouse next to the old train station on Murphy Street, and there were people inside—but I shouted it out before the phone fell from my shaking fingers.

I was out of the car before Slade had swerved to a stop half a block from the flaming warehouse. Onlookers stood in the street, all staring at what I could barely stand to witness. The building that had once been the warehouse was now mostly a crumbled mass of burning rubble. Debris from the explosion littered the street, and tongues of flame lapped up at the sky from what remained of the building. Even from this far away, the black smoke and ash made me cough.

How could anyone have survived this?

"Dad!" I screamed, scanning every face in the small crowd of spectators. "Talbot!"

Where were they?

"Come on," I cried to Brent and Slade. "Let's go, we have to find them." I started toward the warehouse, expecting the boys to follow, but when I turned back to say something, I realized that neither of them had moved from the car.

I pulled open Slade's door. "I said come on, and that's an order."

"I can't," Slade said. He gripped the steering wheel like he was afraid I was going to try to physically pull him out of the car—and he was holding on for dear life. He stared at the flames, as if entranced by their deadly dance.

"What do you mean you can't? I need your help."

Slade just shook his head, not taking his eyes off the fire. I looked at Brent. His face was paler than morning frost. And then I realized what was going on. Something I'd read somewhere in all that research but I'd thought it was just another myth—werewolves were supposedly petrified by fire. Not a small flame like from Slade's lighter, or the burn of a cigarette—but real, raging fire. Like the one that engulfed the warehouse.

"I know you're freaked out. I'm scared, too, but we need to find them."

Brent reached for the handle of his door, then he pulled his hand back. "I don't think I can . . . I'm sorry . . ."

Slade didn't say a word. I slammed his door. Ignoring the twinges of pain in my ankle, I bolted down the street toward the decimated warehouse, knowing I was on my own. I broke through the crowd—someone tried to hold me back from the building, but whoever it was wasn't strong enough to stop me—and got as close to the fire as I could.

"Dad! Talbot!" I shouted toward the building. Of course, there was no response.

I stood absolutely still, the heat of the fire baking my face, and used all my concentration to let my senses guide me to where they might be. The ground underneath my feet shifted like it would during an earthquake. Talbot had said he was in the corridor between the Depot and the warehouse. That meant they had gone in through the secret underground club in the basement of the abandoned train station next door.

I ran down what remained of the alley between the two buildings and came to the thick metal door that led to the Depot. Normally, I'd need a key card to open it, but the explosion must have fried the sensors because the door was unlocked. I pulled it open. Heavy, black smoke mixed with concrete dust smacked me in the face. I choked and sputtered, then pulled off my jacket and used it to cover my nose and mouth as I ran through the doorway and navigated my way down through the blackness of the stairwell. I passed the entrance to the empty club, and opted for the second door that I had never walked through before—which I realized now must have been the secret entrance to Caleb's lair all this time. It looked like it was normally guarded by a similar powerful electronic lock system as the one outside—but the door stood almost wide open now.

I hoped it had only been left open by Talbot, and not blown open by the force of the blast. Could anyone survive an explosion that strong?

I stood silently again, willing my pounding heart to quiet, until a faint sound reverberated in my sensitive ears. A low, airy noise accompanied by a high-pitched wheeze. Almost like a cough.

Someone was alive in the corridor!

I entered the pitch black of the hallway. Even with night vision, I could barely see anything in the thick smoke. I held my jacket over my mouth and nose with one hand, crouching low to stay out of the worst of the smoke, as I made my way through the dark of the corridor toward the source of the noise. I coughed into my jacket, grateful for the noise of it to help block out the howls of the wolf inside my head. It feared the fire even more than I did. It screamed at me, *Turn back, turn back!* I pushed forward instead.

It felt like it took an hour to traverse the corridor, but I knew it had been only a few minutes. I finally came to the end, only to find my way blocked by a flaming wooded beam that had fallen from the ceiling, cutting off the end of the corridor. Rolls of flames curled and lapped at what remained of the corridor above me. My lungs burned and ached, and my inner wolf grew more frantic. *It's not worth risking your own life. They're all dead anyway. Turn back!* Just when I thought the need for fresh air was going to force me to retreat, I saw something move behind the fiery barricade.

I willed my power into my eyes, and through the smoke and flickering flames I saw him. He was collapsed against the wall at the end of the corridor, just on the other side of the barrier—with what looked like my unconscious father in his arms!

I lowered my jacket just long enough to scream his name, "Talbot!"

"Grace," he choked out. "Help me."

My muscles surged with adrenaline. I forced power into my good leg. *Don't!* the wolf shrieked as I sent a kick into the burning wood beam, flames licking at my pant leg. It cracked, splintering from the impact of my foot. One more kick broke it completely, sending cinders swirling around me. *Run away! Get out of here!* I used my jacket as a shield as I passed through the opening in the barrier in order to get to Talbot. I pulled my father from his arms.

"The smoke . . . too much." Talbot coughed. His head lolled back.

"Stay with me! I can't carry both of you."

I pulled Talbot against my side. He clutched at my arm for support, and I tried to concentrate all my supernatural strength into my muscles as I hitched my large father up in my arms. But the lack of oxygen must have been getting to me, because he felt like a giant, limp rag doll—his dead weight almost crushing me.

Dead weight . . . No. I didn't know that. *He's just unconscious,* I tried to tell myself.

I took three lumbering steps, carrying my father and practically dragging Talbot at my side. I could barely see anything with the smoke stinging my eyes, but I could hear Talbot gagging and wheezing next to me.

"Marcos?" I asked, with the realization that he was missing. "Where's Marcos?"

Talbot shook his head.

At first I was confused, but then I knew what he meant without his saying it out loud.

Marcos was dead.

I didn't have time to react to this revelation. A loud cracking noise above my head warned me that another portion of the corridor ceiling was about to fall—and it would come down right on top of us. I pushed all my emotions into my powers and made a run for the exit with my father in my arms and Talbot trailing behind me. My left ankle throbbed, threatening to break for a third time in a week, and just when I didn't think I could go any farther, Brent, Ryan, and Zach appeared at the end of the corridor. I blinked at them through my smoke-stung eyes, wondering if this was a miracle or a mirage.

"Help," I gasped.

The boys approached slowly at first, like their own inner wolves were physically trying to hold them back from the fire. Then, with what looked like a burst of unified courage, Ryan and Brent grabbed Talbot, and Zach took Dad from my arms. Together we pulled them from the corridor, just as the ceiling caved in behind us.

LATER

Four cop cars and three large fire trucks cordoned off the street outside the burning building. Their red-and-white flashing lights mixed with the yellow-and-orange flames, creating a garish portrait in front of me as I watched through the open doors from the back of an ambulance. My breath fogged inside an oxygen mask that sent clean air down my burning throat and into my aching lungs.

Dad was in the next ambulance over. I couldn't stand not being able to see what they were doing to him. *Why hadn't they left for the ER already?* I suddenly remembered seeing in a TV show once that paramedics can't move the ambulance if they're using a defibrillator. *Oh, no!* I clawed at the mask and pulled it from my face. I'd started to climb out of the vehicle when the paramedic who had looked me over grabbed my arm.

"You can't go yet, miss."

Without thinking, I pushed him away—harder than I'd meant to—and he stumbled into the gurney I'd just left. "I need to be with my father," I said, and staggered out of the truck.

"No, miss"—a fireman tried to stop me—"go back."

"He's my father!" I pushed past him toward the other ambulance.

"Let her through," a female paramedic shouted. "She's needed."

The woman waved me over. I followed her around the big open doors of the ambulance and almost lost my footing when I saw the scene unfolding inside the back of the truck. Two paramedics worked over my unconscious father, who lay so still on a gurney, strapped to a backboard. One held an oxygen mask over my father's face while the other prepared an IV. Dad had absolutely no reaction to the needle the woman stuck in his arm. I tried to imagine that he was just sleeping. Tried not to think about how he looked barely alive.

"Daddy?" I hadn't called him that since I was eight.

The paramedic looked up from kneading a bag of liquid into the IV.

"This is his daughter," the woman who had called me over told her before she could protest my presence.

The paramedic in the ambulance nodded. "My name is Jen, honey. What's yours?" Her voice was soothing but urgent at the same time.

"Grace," I said, my voice barely audible. "Why haven't you left yet?"

"We've assessed his needs, and we're doing what we can for him before we leave. He's lucky, I'm certified to give him pain meds before we reach the ER."

My breaths started to come much too quickly.

"Is your father allergic to any medications?"

"Um, I . . ." My head felt light, and suddenly my brain didn't want to work. I knew he *was* allergic to something, but I couldn't think of what it was. I couldn't think of anything other than watching the way my father's chest barely moved in response to the oxygen pump. My own breaths came so fast now I feared I was going to hyperventilate. Just then, I felt someone else's presence next to me. I looked up and found Talbot standing there, wrapped in a thick blanket that was supposed to help prevent shock. Soot smudged his face, and his hair looked gray from the ashy dust that clung to his disheveled mane.

He put his hand on my back. "Deep breaths, kid. You won't be able to help if you pass out."

I nodded and took in several deep breaths and concentrated some of my healing power down my ragged throat. "Um, penicillin." I finally remembered that's why my mom never let any doctors prescribe it to us kids—just in case we were allergic like my dad.

"What's his blood type?"

"O negative."

"Are you a match? They may need to do a blood transfusion at the hospital."

"Transfusion?"

I looked back at Talbot—only one question playing on my mind. If Dad were given a blood transfusion with *my* blood, would he be infected by the werewolf curse? Talbot gave me a look like he understood my unspoken question. His eyes seemed to say, *I really don't know.*

"No," I lied. It was too risky.

"Anyone else in your family? His is a hard blood type to match."

Jude, I thought. As a nurse, my mom insisted we all know one another's blood type. She kept them written on a laminated card in her wallet.

"No," I lied again. Jude's blood would be even more dangerous, considering he was a full-blown werewolf.

"Damn," Jen mumbled under her breath. "Hopefully, the hospital will have enough."

How much blood does he need? Why is he still not moving? "How bad is he?"

"Critical," she said, and grabbed a long needle. I didn't even want to know what that was for. "Your father must have been thrown several feet by the blast. He's showing signs of internal bleeding. Still don't know how the rest of you got out of there with barely a scratch." She nodded to Talbot and me. "You're damn lucky."

Talbot ducked his head. "Yes, the *rest* of us were lucky."

I looked at him, wondering about the inflection in his voice. Then I remembered . . . Marcos had entered that building with the others. Now he was gone. And Talbot didn't want me to mention him. Marcos was dead, and it would be better if no one knew he'd ever existed.

And you're the one who sent him to his death, the wolf told me inside my head.

I wasn't sure how much longer I could keep standing. My legs felt far too soft, and the ground underneath my feet seemed suddenly off-kilter. Talbot's hand on my back felt like the only thing holding me upright.

I'd known Marcos for only a week, and now he was just gone.

"We need to get your father to the hospital," the male paramedic said. "I think it's best if you ride along." He held his hand out to help me climb into the back of the ambulance. I clung to it for support.

"I'll meet you there," Talbot said as they shut the doors between us.

I suddenly felt very alone in the crowded ambulance.

Dad's eyes flickered open for a second and then closed.

"I'm here, Daddy." I leaned forward and reached for his hand, but I could barely loop one of my fingers around one of his for all the wires and tubes that protruded from his hand and arm. I could see him straining to open his eyes again, but he couldn't.

How could I have let this happen?

Chapter Seven

BACKFIRE

SEVERAL HOURS LATER

"I need to be able to do something," I said to myself as I paced in the corner of Dad's small ICU room.

Dad hadn't opened his eyes again since that one time in the ambulance. Doctors and nurses had worked over him in the ER for what felt like an eternity, and then they shuffled us off into this room with grave looks on their faces. At one point someone examined me, and then I was told to wash up in the shower of an empty patient room. One of the nurses gave me a pair of pale green scrubs to change into. She wrapped my tattered and bloody clothes in a plastic bag and then threw them away in a canister marked BIOHAZARD.

When had I bled? It must have been my father's. . . .

I guess they thought being clean would help me cope better with bad news, because as soon as I was dressed, someone with a clipboard took me aside. She'd said words relating to my father, like *trauma* and *invasive surgery*, along with a long string of other phrases that I couldn't comprehend over the loud pounding of my heartbeat in my ears.

How can I have all these powers, yet there's nothing I can do?

A muffled stream of what sounded like French curse words came from the sliding glass doorway. I turned to find Gabriel standing there, his hands clasped over his mouth as he looked at my father lying there, helpless and slipping further away.

I was about to mutter something horrible like, "Took you long enough," because I'd left a string of urgent messages for him, but when Gabriel lowered his hands from his face, I saw a long, pink, newly healed scar marring one of his cheekbones. His reddish beard almost hid the faintest hints of purple bruises along his jaw. He hadn't had those injuries this morning when I saw him last.

"Are you okay? What happened?" I knew immediately this had something to do with why he hadn't wanted me to return to the parish. "Did Jude do this to you?" I hated to ask, but I had to. Jude acted placid, but I'd feared he was volatile, like a ticking time bomb . . . *Oh hell.* Tears stung my eyes from the reminder of the explosion that had harmed my father.

It's all your fault, the evil wolf inside me growled.

"No," Gabriel said. "Something else entirely, but it's

not important now. We'll discuss it later. How is your father?" Gabriel stepped farther into the room, and the glass door slid closed behind him. "I had to convince the nurse I was his brother so she'd allow me in."

"Critical. That's all I know."

The ICU was a busy, noisy place, with nurses and doctors bustling about, but I still felt like I'd been completely alone for the last couple of hours. Talbot had never showed up like he said he would. I hadn't wanted to call April—because if April knew, then Jude would, too, and I didn't know how the news would affect him—and after I couldn't get ahold of Gabriel, there was no one else left to call who could come be with me. Not Daniel. Not Charity. Not even my mom. "They wanted to use my blood for a transfusion, but at the time I thought that would be too risky. It might infect him, you know? But maybe I was wrong. Maybe letting him get infected would help his body heal. Or my blood might do nothing at all."

"Could you live with yourself knowing you had passed this curse on to him?"

I'd heard Daniel, who had suffered with the effects of the curse most of his life before he was supposedly cured, say that he'd rather die than live with the potential of becoming a monster again. Giving Dad healing powers might help him live, but he might never be the same person again. And I didn't know what he'd choose if he could.

"But there has to be something I can do. I mean, I'm a freaking superpowered, demon-slaying, pseudo-werewolf, but all the power I have inside of me isn't worth crap if I can't use it to help my dad."

"Perhaps there is a way . . ." Gabriel said hesitantly. "It is risky, though. And I cannot guarantee it will work. I have only tried it three times, with varying degrees of success. Yet it helped you some." He seemed to be debating it out more with himself than explaining it me.

"What do you mean?" Then my mind flitted back to something Talbot had said to me last night, and I realized what he was referring to. "You and Talbot used your powers to help heal me—after I was attacked by those wolves in the warehouse. You did some sort of power transfer to help my body heal itself when I was unconscious and wasn't able to do it myself?"

"Yes," Gabriel said.

My memories surrounding the aftermath of what had happened in the warehouse were still fuzzy, so I'd never quite gotten the implications of that before now. Gabriel and Talbot had helped *heal* me. But I hadn't known that was even possible—that healing other people was one of the many powers of the Urbat. Yes, they could heal themselves, but other people? I'd been the recipient of a power transfer before that day—when Daniel and I ran through the ravine in the woods after saving Baby James. I hadn't had the ability to keep up with him until I felt a burst of energy travel through

Daniel's body into mine, tethering us together, making his power mine for a few moments. He'd shown me later that same night how he could heal himself, but he'd never mentioned that he could heal other people.

"Why didn't Daniel tell me about this power?"

"He probably has no idea. It is a closely guarded secret. I did not know myself for hundreds of years. Not until Sirhan asked me to help him try it on his wife, Rachel. It did not work as well for her as it did for you. I believe that was the first and only time Sirhan had attempted it." Gabriel scrubbed his hand over his bearded chin. "It is a remnant from the original Hounds of Heaven, the ones who were called by God and imbued with powers to help and protect the people of their clan. Legend has it that, in addition to being strong warriors, they were also great healers and teachers. They were like angels here on Earth, gifted with every power to help mankind. That is, until their power corrupted them, and they coveted their abilities for themselves. They succumbed to the same fate as the fallen angels of heaven, forsaking their duty and blessings to become as lowly as the devil's demons. The power to heal others has been forgotten by most Urbat. They deal death now instead of life, and I am not sure the gift has been used on a normal human since those primitive times."

"But you think it can be still?"

"I have never attempted it on a human before. It is

extremely taxing, and dangerous if done wrong." He studied Dad's monitors like he understood what all the lines and numbers meant. "In your father's condition, I think it is worth trying. If you will allow it."

"Yes," I said. "Please help him."

"It takes two. I will need your help." He gave me a soft, reassuring smile. He looked just like a priest consoling one of his parishioners. "You must have complete focus and clear your mind of negativity in order to be a conduit for your positive energy to pass into him. No negative thoughts or feelings. This must be a gift of love."

I glanced over at Dad. A large brace supported his neck, and most of his swollen face was obscured by the oxygen mask. All I could really recognize of him were the creases of his closed eyes. He looked so utterly helpless. *Why did he insist on going to the warehouse? Why did I let him go? What if I couldn't do this? What if I wasn't ready? What if I couldn't open my mind?*

Deep breaths.

Deep breaths.

I had to clear all those doubtful thoughts away.

"Show me what to do, then. I have to do something for him." I held my hands out like the healing power was something tangible he could actually hand to me.

Gabriel pulled the hospital curtain partially closed over the glass observation window and door—I imagined to obscure an outsider's view, but not draw too much attention by closing it completely. The nurses were letting me visit my dad's room for only twenty minutes at a time, which meant we had less than ten minutes of privacy before someone returned to shoo us back into the waiting room. Gabriel took my hands in his and walked me over to my father's bed. He placed my hands on my father's shallow chest. The rise and fall of his breathing felt completely unnatural. Strained and thin.

"Your hands go here, over his heart. And mine go here." He placed his hands softly over mine. "Clear your mind. Open a pathway for your positive energy to flow from your heart, through your hands, and into him. Negative emotions feed the wolf inside of you, but you must be able to push them completely away in order to do this. Deep breaths. Meditate. Clear your mind. Open your heart."

I almost pulled my hands out from under Gabriel's. "But what if I can't do this?"

"I believe in you, Grace." Gabriel had never said anything like that to me before. I'd started thinking of him as the world's oldest skeptic. "You're the girl who withstood the wolves. The Divine One, they say."

"I don't feel very divine."

"You must try, for you father."

I nodded. Gabriel pulled in a long breath and then let it out between his lips. I did the same. He closed his eyes. I did also.

"Concentrate on your love for him. Clear your mind of doubt, and imagine him becoming whole."

Gabriel was still for a moment, but then his hands clasped tightly over mine. Heat swelled from his fingers and pulsed into my hands. I tried to picture my father well again, tried to call up memories of him from my life. The way he smiled. His patient voice. But as the heat swelled in my hands, growing with intensity, my memories flashed to the scene in the fiery corridor. The way my father looked, limp and lifeless in Talbot's arms, when I found them. I couldn't stop him from getting hurt, so what made me think I could actually help him now?

You're too weak, my inner wolf snarled. *You can't help him. You can't help anybody.*

I winced. The heat radiating off of Gabriel's hands was almost too much to bear. I gritted my teeth, trying to hold on. Dad needed my help. He went to that warehouse because of me. . . .

Images of the fire ripped through my mind. The sound of the explosion I heard over the phone. Words the nurses said. My father lying so still.

It's your fault. It's your fault. It's your fault. It's your fault.

No, I tried to tell the wolf's voice. *I didn't tell him to go there. He insisted on going. It should have been me in the corridor. He shouldn't have gone.*

It's his fault!

Gabriel cried out like he'd been stabbed with a sharp pain. His hands lifted off mine and the intense power dissipated with a sudden surge that made my eyes pop open from the shock. Gabriel stumbled away from the bedside, his hand clasped over his cheek.

"Are you okay?" I asked between panting breaths.

Gabriel moved his hand away from his face. The scar on his cheek looked like a fresh cut now, oozing blood. The once faded bruises on his jaw now looked fresh and painful, like someone had slammed a mallet into his face several times. Gabriel looked at his blood-stained fingers. "I need to take care of this," he said, and staggered toward the door. "I am sorry. I thought you were ready."

He left through the sliding door before I could ask him if he needed my help.

You did that, the wolf said in my head. I looked down at my father. *What if I'd hurt him more, too?* My fear was confirmed a few seconds later when one of his monitors started making a frantic beeping noise.

Two nurses rushed into the room. I felt numb, completely unable to react, as they pushed me away in order to get to his bedside.

ANOTHER HOUR LATER

I stayed outside the room, watching through the small opening of the curtained glass window, until the doctor was able to do something to Dad to make that horrible beeping monitor noise stop. One of the nurses told me I could go in for one more short visit, but then I *must* go home. I knew the drill from last year when Daniel had been trapped in one of those hospital beds. Even though the ICU had open visiting hours, I was still a minor, and I wasn't allowed to stay here at night. I'd nodded and told her I would go, but it still took me another few minutes before I could tear myself away from Dad's bedside.

I wanted to squeeze his hand to let him know I was leaving, but I hesitated, afraid my very touch might hurt him again. Instead, I left a note on the table by his bed just in case he woke up and I wasn't here. I didn't want him to feel as abandoned as I did at the moment.

I left the ICU and went out into the lobby. I started toward an elevator that would take me down to the main floor so I could leave the hospital. But I stopped in front of the closed elevator doors and stared at the triangular up and down arrow buttons—not knowing which one to push. Down would take me to the exit. Up would take me to the psych ward.

To my mom.

When Dad and I came into the ER from the ambulance, someone had asked me where they could find my mother. When I told him where she was, the man said they'd have to call Dr. Connors first and let him decide if my mother should be informed about what had happened.

The fact that she hadn't come down here to see Dad yet didn't bode well to me.

I knew if Dad had been awake, he would have told me to go visit her, just like he'd wanted me to visit Jude. I hadn't seen either of them since I'd come home from the warehouse, and I knew Dad would have said something about how, by not visiting them, I wasn't acting like myself. Just like April had.

The thing is, Dad had been my go-to parent for the last few years, but there had been a time in my life when Mom had been my rock. Back when I still wore pigtails and lived off of peanut-butter-and-honey sandwiches with the crusts cut off. Back when I thought a mother's kiss could heal any hurt, whether it was a wound of the flesh or of the heart. I longed for the days when I could bury my head against her side and she'd stroke my hair, telling me everything would be all right.

I'd spent the last year shutting her out. Keeping her away from my secrets. Maybe it was out of some noble idea of protecting her. Maybe I thought she was too fragile to handle it. Or maybe the real reason I'd kept her in the dark was because I worried that she'd be afraid of what I'd become.

But as much as I'd grown and changed recently, no matter how strong my powers made me—I knew now that I still needed her.

But would she still want me?

It took what little strength was left inside of me after the failed power transfer to muster up the courage to do what I did next: I stretched my fingers out to push the Up button, then waited for the *ding* of the elevator doors. As much as I dreaded what was about to happen, I knew what needed to be done. It was time to tell my mother . . . well, everything.

Chapter Eight

Inside Out

UP THE ELEVATOR

An old beige phone hung on the wall outside the locked psych-ward door. A sign instructed me to pick it up and dial a number for assistance. "I'm here to see Meredith Divine," I told the nurse who answered. I hung up the receiver as the door buzzed and swung open on a mechanical arm. I took a few steps into the ward and was greeted by a wide hallway with pale green walls, the smells of stale vending machine candy and ammonia, and another sign that read, HIGH FLIGHT RISK AREA. ENSURE DOOR CLOSES COMPLETELY.

I did as I was told and watched as the large door closed behind me. I felt a sudden impulse to pull it open again—and make a run for the parking lot.

I can't do this.

The handleless door locked with a heavy click. It was too late to turn back now. I'd have to visit the nurses' desk to get the door opened again. I might as well ask about my mother.

I made my way down the hallway, passing a young woman perched on a bench that looked like it should have been replaced sometime in the 1980s. She braided a long lock of her hair in front of her face, rocking back and forth. I entered the main area of the ward and signed in at the desk. I could see a glassed-in room where a group of people sat in a circle of chairs. A man dressed in khakis and a button-up shirt seemed to be leading some sort of discussion. Everyone else was dressed in plain gray sweats, like the woman I'd passed in the hallway. Patients, I assumed.

"You said you're here for Meredith Divine?" asked the woman behind the desk. Her name tag said LATISHA. Her eyes held a look of recognition in them when she said my mother's name.

Before Mom started to lose it, she'd been a nurse at an outpatient psych clinic in Apple Valley, but sometimes she'd filled in here at the main treatment center, whenever Dr. Connors needed substitute staff. I'm sure there had been a lot of talk among the ward nurses about one of their own being a patient now. That kind of gossip would have killed my mother if she were fully with it. Reputation had meant everything to her.

I nodded. "I don't have to see her, though . . . if this is a bad time. It looks like there's a group meeting going on."

"Nonsense, girl," Latisha said. "Meredith isn't in group, and a visitor is just what the doctor ordered."

"Indeed it is," Dr. Connors said as he came up to me. He held a clipboard in his hands and wore a long white coat over a sweater and slacks—the same sweater he'd worn to our family's ill-fated Thanksgiving dinner last year. He smiled warmly down at me, but his eyes told a much graver story. "How's your father doing? I called down to check on him earlier, but I've been unable to make it down there personally."

"Same as earlier."

"I see." He cleared his throat.

"Has she asked to go down to see him?"

"No. I was hoping that . . ." He cleared his throat again and tucked a pen into the top of his clipboard. "Walk with me, Grace."

I took a few strides in the direction he led me, until I realized we were headed toward the patient rooms rather than the visiting area. I still wasn't sure I was ready for this. Dr. Connors glanced back at me expectantly. I swallowed my apprehension and fell into step with him.

"Normally, we'd have you meet with her in one of our visiting rooms, but I think in this case . . . it would be best if I were to take you to her."

"What . . ." I bit my lip. "What exactly is wrong with her?"

Mom had always had OCD-like tendencies that

amplified whenever things got stressful at home. Like, the worse things were, the more she had to make everything seem perfect. Then after Jude ran away, she really started to lose it. Like she'd developed her own designer brand of bipolar disorder—going from a manic overprotective mother bear when it came to me and my siblings to slipping into a zombie-esque state in which she was obsessed with doing nothing but watching news reports in hopes of spotting my missing brother in the background. She'd refuse to do anything else for days, and she'd totally lose all consideration for her children who were still home. Who still needed her. Dr. Connors had advised my father more than once that she might need more than counseling and medication—might need to be admitted—but she must have really snapped when I disappeared for my dad finally to have brought her to the main clinic. He'd known that she'd probably never forgive him for it.

Dr. Connors stopped in front of a patient room. A little card under the door number had my mother's name on it. "I've known your mother for a long time. She was a godsend during my residency. However, as you're probably aware, she's always had a tendency to create a facade of perfection around her—a false reality, so to speak. It's a coping mechanism. Yet as I gathered from our counseling sessions over the last year, that facade has been crumbling—and now, something, whatever it is, has torn apart her fake reality so completely, she can no longer cope at all."

He pushed open her door and I saw her for the first time in over a week—yet I barely recognized her. She sat up in her bed, staring at what seemed like a black smudge on the wall, wearing gray sweats like all the other patients—but without a drawstring in the pants waist, I realized now—and slippers on her feet. Both items she wouldn't have been caught dead wearing outside of the house in the past. Her normally beautiful hair hung stringy and unwashed around her face, which was so hollow looking, I wondered just how long it had been since she'd eaten anything at all.

"She hasn't voluntarily left that spot since she got here," he said. "She won't go to group or eat with the others. She won't even say a word to me."

I swallowed hard. I'd lived through many of my mother's bad days in the last year, but now she just seemed . . . vacant. "Will she ever get better?"

"Not until her mind can come to terms with her new reality—the true one—whatever that may be. What is it your father is always saying, 'The truth shall set you free'? That's what your mother needs to process: the truth. Whatever happened that caused this—it's rocked her off her foundation. Until she can find her footing again, both mentally and emotionally, this is the only way her mind knows how to function." He indicated her catatonic stare.

I nodded, as if I actually understood. So what Mom needed to do was tell her doctors she's accepted the fact that her oldest son is a werewolf and her daughter is a superpowered demon hunter? *Yeah, I don't see that earning her a ticket out of the psych ward anytime soon.*

"I'll give you ten minutes alone with her. Short visits are best."

I checked my watch, pretending I didn't have much time anyway. A short visit was all I had the energy for. *Maybe I don't have the strength at all. . . .*

"It's good you came," Dr. Connors said, and gave me a nudge into the room. He closed the door behind me. I felt trapped all over again.

Three eternal minutes ticked by on my watch as I stood there, not knowing what to do. Or what to say. Mom didn't move. She didn't even try to glance at me.

"Mom?" My voice sounded so awkward. I felt like I was talking to that smudge on the wall. I took two small steps closer to her. "Mom?"

No acknowledgment.

But maybe I didn't want her to look at me. Dad had told her what had happened to me . . . about the curse . . . and maybe now she'd see me only as a monster. Maybe that was what she couldn't accept.

"Mommy?" Tears pricked my eyes. "I don't know what all Daddy told you, but it's true. I know it's hard to believe—what happened to Jude . . . and me. But

I'm still your daughter. And Jude's still your son. And he's back now. And he needs you. We all need you."

Nothing.

"James and Charity are staying with Aunt Carol—but they can't stay there forever. And Dad's been hurt. Really hurt. He needs someone to take care of him. But I have so much on my plate. I'm trying to find a way to turn Daniel back into a human. And Jude needs someone to help him, too. There's a madman with a pack of demons that wants me dead, and another werewolf pack that wants me for heaven knows what reason. And then I've got my own pack of five—four—werewolf boys, who keep looking to me to be their leader . . . or mother . . . or something. But I don't know how to do it all. And I can't do it by myself. We all need you." I stepped even closer. What I wanted to do was throw my arms around her and bury my head against her like I did when I was a child. Instead, I placed my hand on her thin fingers. "I need a *mother*. We all need one."

She didn't move. Not even a twitch of her fingers.

"Please, Mom. That's who you are. That's who we need you to be. That's your reality, no matter how crazy any of this is. Be my *mother*. Please."

Tears stung my face as they slid down my cheeks. Mom hated public crying just as much as I did, but I let them flow. She didn't notice. She didn't react. Just kept staring at that damn smudge. I don't know how I'd thought this was going to play out, but in my imagination I thought she would at least care.

My muscles ached as I felt a deep rumbling surge up from a dark place inside my heart. The wolf in my head whispered for me to lash out at my mom—or at the shell of the woman who sat in front of me now. The impulse made me sick. I clutched at my stomach and took deep breaths, focusing on purging those emotions from my mind. I hadn't come here to get angry. I'd come here to get my mother back.

I let go of her hand and left her room. Covering my tear-streaked face with my arm, I passed the nurses' station and asked Latisha to buzz me out the door.

What I needed now was to get away.

I almost ran into an older couple waiting outside the elevator when I exited the psych ward. The woman leaned her weight into her husband, and he clasped his arm around her for support. I noticed she bore a striking resemblance to the young woman I'd seen when I'd first entered the ward. I wondered if these were that patient's parents, and I couldn't bear the thought of sharing the confined space of the elevator with them. Like I might absorb their pain on top of mine.

Instead, I pushed open the heavy stairwell door and let it slam closed behind me. I darted down a couple of flights of stairs, my echoing footsteps chasing behind me. I made it all the way to the landing that would take me back out to the ICU floor before I fell against the wall.

Sobs quaked inside my chest and sounded even louder in the isolated stairwell. I hated myself for thinking I could make my mother understand how much I needed her. Like I could snap her out of her catatonic state just like that. I hated the horrible thoughts that had raced through my head when I'd failed. Deep down, I knew I couldn't blame her for being mentally incapacitated, just like I couldn't blame my father for being unconscious in his hospital bed.

But all the same, it still meant I was completely alone.

I let myself cry until the ache inside of me was replaced by a deep fatigue that pulled at my body, filling my muscles with the strain of everything that had happened in this harrowing day. It felt like I'd completed an Ironman triathlon—without my powers.

I closed my eyes with a heavy sigh. It took only a few moments before one of my dreams of Daniel trickled into my brain.

This one was different from the usual dream. I was standing rather than sitting on a bench, and Daniel stood in front of me. His almost devious, playful grin edged on his lips for a moment, then his face shifted into a look of deep concern. It all felt so real, it was hard to remember the image of him was purely an invention of my sorrow.

"Are you okay?" Daniel asked.

I tried to take a step closer to him, but my body swayed dangerously. Even in my dream I was exhausted. Daniel reached out and steadied me with his strong hands. I knew I shouldn't indulge the dream—I'd only regret it when I fully realized it was fake—but I could feel his warmth so close to me, I couldn't help grabbing him around the middle and nuzzling my face into his chest.

Daniel's arms wrapped around me, engulfing me in his warmth. He rested his head against the top of mine, his breath tickling against my hair and scalp. The sensation was so wonderful and needed that I sighed out loud.

"I love you," I whispered against the fabric of his shirt.

He took in a sharp breath. "I love you, too," came a whisper so quiet I could *feel* the words spoken against my hair more than I could actually hear them.

I slid my hand up his chest and let my fingers linger on the warm skin exposed at his collar. "Why are you trying to leave me, Daniel?"

The arms holding me stiffened. I heard a throat clear, and even though the sound was familiar, it didn't belong to Daniel.

And the fabric nestled against my face felt very much like flannel.

Oh no! My eyes shot open, and I stared up at the face that belonged with the arms that held me—in the real world, not in my dream. He looked back at me with bright green eyes almost hidden under the brim of a red baseball cap.

"Talbot?" I pushed myself out from his grasp. "What on earth do you think you're doing?"

"Hey." He held up his large hands defensively. "I just came into the stairwell and saw you standing here, looking like you were about to fall over. I asked if you were okay, and *you're* the one who hugged me."

"I did not!" My neck burned with the red splotches that formed there whenever I was lying. Which I wasn't! "I was asleep. I thought you were someone else. You took advantage of me."

"Took advantage? How about saved you from collapsing?"

"I'm fine! No thanks to you."

"No thanks to me?"

"You said you were going to meet me here, like, five hours ago. Do you have any idea how alone and afraid I've been? Where were you?"

"I had to pull a disappearing act with those paramedics, who tried to force me into the ER. You should see how freaked out medical people get when they hear two hearts beating in my chest. I had to lay low for a while, and then the ICU nurses wouldn't let me in there to see you guys because I'm not related. So I went home to clean up and change my clothes. I lost my lucky blue hat today, by the way. And then I had to take care of something before I could—"

"Your hat? You're worried about losing your freaking hat? I almost lost my father today!" A sudden rush of power surged through my muscles. I pushed against his chest, hard enough so that he had to step backward to regain his footing. "Why didn't you protect him?" I shouted. "Why didn't you stop him from getting hurt? I asked you to do one thing for me, and that was keep him safe. And look where he ended up!"

I went to push him again, but Talbot grabbed my wrists to stop me.

"I tried, Grace. I went into that burning building and tried to carry him out because I knew that's what you'd want me to do."

"Well, you didn't try hard enough!"

I attempted to wrestle my hands from his grasp. I wanted to hit him. Hurt him. Make him feel the pain I had inside. *He should have been the one who got hurt!* But Talbot pulled my arms around him and hugged me in a tight embrace, holding me against his chest, like he had before I realized he wasn't Daniel. And for a few short seconds I contemplated melting into his arms, letting him hold me, letting everything go for just a few moments.

But I couldn't.

"Let go," I said. "What are you doing?"

"This is what you need, isn't it?" Talbot said. "I heard what you said in the parish, that you miss having someone to hold you in his arms. I can do that for you."

I struggled out of his embrace. "No, you can't. I said that I missed *Daniel* holding me. And you're not him.

You never will be. So this can't happen." I pushed his arms down and stepped away.

He stared at me from under the brim of his baseball cap. "How do you mourn someone who isn't dead?" he asked.

"What?"

"At the parish, you said that it feels like Daniel is dead, even though he isn't. When someone dies, you mourn him for a time and then you can move on. But how will you ever stop mourning Daniel if you haven't accepted that he's gone? At some point you're going to have to realize that the part of Daniel that was Daniel *is* dead. That he isn't coming back. That he'll *never* hold you in his arms again—"

"Shut up."

"Once you accept that, you'll be able to move on."

"I said shut up."

Talbot put his hand on my arm like he wanted to pull me against him again. "He can't hold you in his arms, but I can."

I yanked myself out of his grasp. "You don't *get* to do that. Leave me alone."

"I'll wait for you until you're ready to move on."

"That's never going to happen!" My hands balled into fists.

Talbot stepped back. He dropped his arms to his sides, as if showing me that he'd submit himself to an attack. "I'm sorry." He lowered his head. "I shouldn't have said all that. I just . . . I just don't like seeing you do this to yourself. I look at you, and I don't see my *Grace* anymore. And I miss her."

"I haven't gone anywhere . . . and I was never yours to miss in the first place."

"You might be standing right here, but you're not the *you* I met a few weeks ago. That girl had fire. That girl wanted to be a superhero. The you I see now is someone who is wasting away, forgetting everything she wanted for herself. When was the last time you trained? Or even ate?"

"You make it sound like I've done nothing but curl up in a corner and cry for the last week." Okay, so I had just been crying in a corner of a stairwell—but still. "I'm not some weak little do-nothing. I'm doing everything I possibly can to bring Daniel back."

"And that's the problem. The only thing you have passion for anymore is trying to find something that can't be found." He lowered his voice, looking down at his large hands. "And I'm afraid you're going to lose whatever is left of your old self in the process. You need to give up this search. The warehouse is gone, and you're not going to find that moonstone in the parish yard."

My fists loosened, and I found my own arms dropping to my sides. Talbot was right. I wasn't going to find a moonstone by searching for it. I'd just said I was doing everything I could to try to bring Daniel back, but I wasn't. There was still the thing I'd promised my father would only be my last resort. . . .

"Please don't hate me, Grace, for saying all of this. But someone had to. I just want to be your friend. I've been on my own since I was thirteen, so I kind of suck at interpersonal relationships."

"Yeah, you do," I said, my mind still preoccupied with the revelation that was unfolding inside my head.

"I'm trying my hardest." He shoved his thumbs through his belt loops. "Are you ever going to trust me again?"

I thought about how Talbot was trying to make things up to me. I remembered how terrified even hardened Slade had been by the fire at the warehouse, and I realized just how much guts it must have taken for Talbot to go into the burning corridor by himself in order to pull my father out. He was right. He'd tried his best. He might say idiotic things, but he deserved more from me than my perpetual disdain.

"Thank you," I finally said.

Talbot looked down at me.

"You did what I asked you to do. You tried to keep my dad safe." I put my hand on his arm. "We can be friends again. It's what I need right now."

"You have no idea how much that means to me." He smiled. "All I want is for you to realize how much I care about you."

"Don't get too excited," I said softly. "It doesn't really mean much now . . . because I'm leaving."

"You're what?"

"I'm leaving," I said with sudden conviction, even though I hadn't known that was my decision until I said it. "You're right. I'm never going to find that moonstone piece at the parish. It's hopeless. And with the warehouse destroyed now . . . I have only one chance left to get a moonstone before it's too late and Daniel leaves me forever. And that's to go to Sirhan."

"Sirhan? That's crazy, Grace. You can't go there." His eyes were stern, and he gripped my arm like he could physically hold me back. "You go to Sirhan, and there's a good chance you'll never—"

"Return? I know. But if that's the price I need to pay to get Daniel back, then that's what I'm going to do. I'll trade myself for a moonstone."

"And then do what? How will that even help Daniel?"

"I'll send it back to April. I don't know." I hadn't thought that much of it through. "I'll figure it out if . . . *when* . . . I get to that point. But I'm going, and there's nothing that can stop me."

"What about your dad? The rest of your family?"

"There's nothing I can do to help my dad by staying here. I tried to do that healing thing on him with Gabriel, but it backfired and I ended up hurting him more."

Talbot's eyes widened when I said this.

"And my mom . . ." I bit my lip. "There's no way to get through to her." I didn't even mention Jude, because I had no idea how to start helping him. I couldn't even bring myself to look him in the eyes again.

Talbot brushed his hand through his wavy milk-chocolate-brown hair. "What about me? I can try to stop you."

"No, Tal," I said, using the close-friends nickname he asked me not to use once because it sounded too good coming from my lips. "There's nothing you could do, short of miraculously making a moonstone appear out of thin air, that could make me change my mind. I'm going to go home to pack, and then I'm leaving in the morning."

He opened his mouth as if to speak, but then closed it again as if reconsidering whatever it was that he'd wanted to stay. For a second, I thought I saw a deep pain flash behind his eyes.

I rocked up onto my tiptoes and brushed a light kiss on his cheek. His whole body shuddered with a sigh at the touch of my lips on his skin. He cared *too* much about me. "Just let me leave. Don't make this harder than it already is."

I brushed my hand down his arm, and he tried to snatch at my fingers as I turned away from him.

"No. Grace?"

My back was to him now, but I could hear the pleading urgency that filled his voice.

"Let me go." I reached for the stairwell door.

"I can't," he said. "I can't let you trade yourself to Sirhan."

"I have to."

"No you don't." He grabbed my hand and pulled me around to face him. "Because I have this." He pressed something hard, flat, and warm into my palm, then pulled his hand away so I could see what he'd given me.

I almost didn't recognize what it was at first. It was shaped like a rounded-off triangle, and the color was almost silver instead of the usual blackish hue. A large chink in it exposed an almost crystal-like center under its smooth surface—but the heat that pulsed off of it was unmistakable.

It felt just like hope.

"A moonstone?" I gasped.

Chapter Nine

FLAT-LINE

SIX MOONSTONE PULSES LATER

"How did you . . . ? Did you find this in the warehouse? Why didn't you tell me right away?"

Talbot cleared his throat and turned his head so he wasn't looking me in the eyes.

My gaze flitted back to the stone. It looked so weathered and tattered. Was that from the exposure to the fire in the warehouse? *No*, I realized. This stone was too large to have been one of the shattered fragments he could have found at the warehouse. I ran my finger over the surface of the stone, noticing the small hole drilled into one of the points of the triangle, probably where it had been strung onto a chain or leather string. My inspection of the stone lingered on the raw chink in the surface. It almost resembled the shape of a crescent moon that had been worn away by almost a year of being exposed to the elements. . . .

"This is the stone we were looking for in the church-yard, isn't it? The other half of Daniel's moonstone?"

I could see the tension in Talbot's clenched jaw. He gave the slightest nod. He was hiding something, and I was pretty sure I knew what it was. The thought of it made my stomach churn.

"*When* did you find this?"

"Before."

"Before when?"

"Before today."

"You mean you found this yesterday? Before you told me to accept that it was hopeless that I was going to find it. Because *you* had it already. You had it all that time . . . before we decided to search the warehouse? Before you volunteered to go with my dad?" Raw power surged through my body, and my muscles clenched with a fire that burned just as strong as the betrayal I felt. "Before my dad got hurt!"

"Yes," he breathed out.

"So you were just playing along? You had this stone all that time, and you didn't tell me. You took my dad to that warehouse even though you knew he didn't need to go. Were you only going there so you could hide anything he would have found there, too? My dad wouldn't have gotten hurt if it weren't for you! Why the hell would you keep this from me?"

He opened his mouth, but I didn't let him speak.

"I know already," I said. "You didn't want me to

have this moonstone because you don't want Daniel to come back. Because you know you can't compete with him. You think if he never comes back, I'll eventually choose you. Well, you're wrong."

"I did it because I love you, Grace."

"You don't love me. You don't even know what love is. You're a selfish bastard. Anyone who would do *this* is a monster. You only tried to save my dad because you thought it would endear you to me, make me love you. Not because it was the right thing to do." This realization made my insides lurch. "I could never love someone like that. I could never love someone who would hide *this* from me." I held up the moonstone in my fist. But what I really wanted to do was let that fist fly. I wanted to punch Talbot in the face more than anything. No, I wanted to rip his face off. *He deserves it.*

My muscles rumbled with adrenaline.

How could he have done this to you?

"I will never love you!"

"Grace, please. I'm sorry. It was stupid and selfish, and I shouldn't have . . ." He reached out to grab my arm.

"Don't you touch me!" My hand went sailing and slammed into his chest in a wing chun–style punch. A move *he'd* taught me. The hit landed hard. I felt bone crack on impact. Talbot flew backward and hit the stair railing with the satisfying crunch of body impacting with metal. He cried out, clutching at his rib cage. I had no doubt I'd broken at least one of his ribs.

The wolf in my head whispered promises of all the things it would do to Talbot if I'd just let it free, and I wanted to do more damage. . . .

No. I couldn't. I clutched that moonstone to my chest and willed its calming power into my body. I couldn't let *Talbot* cause me to lose control. I had to get away from him. Away from his deceit. Away from his lies.

"I never want to see you again." I pulled open the stairwell door and burst through the doorway into the lobby outside the ICU.

I hit the Call button next to the ICU door. I told the nurse I'd left my car keys in the waiting area, and she let me into the unit. I stormed down the hall, past my dad's room, and kept going deeper into the ICU until I was certain Talbot hadn't followed me. I stopped and leaned against a window, clasping the moonstone against my chest, trying to get ahold of my senses. That is, until I noticed a shrill beeping noise, like the one from my father's monitor that had gone nuts after I'd tried to heal him.

I was about to bolt back to his room when I realized the noise actually came from the room behind the window I leaned against. I peered through the glass and watched as a doctor used two large defibrillator paddles to shock the chest of a guy lying in the hospital bed. The guy's body arched and shuddered with the jolt of electricity, but then it collapsed, limp and lifeless on the bed. Something about the guy looked familiar. . . .

He was young. Maybe my age or a little older . . .

I concentrated my superhearing beyond the high-pitched alarm so I could hear what was being said by the small army of medical personnel in the room. "I don't understand it. He was fine last time I checked on him," one of the nurses said frantically. "His cousin was just here to visit."

"Clear!" someone else shouted.

I stood and watched in shock—no one noticing me at the window—as the guy in the bed was jolted twice more. His face looked like a bloated mask, but beyond the bruises and bandages, recognition finally clicked in my head.

"It's been too long. It's time to call it," one of the nurses said.

The doctor pulled off his latex gloves and placed them on a metal tray. He looked up at the clock above the bed. "Time of death: eight twenty-three p.m."

I stumbled away from the window and ran down the hall, down the empty stairwell, and out of the hospital—knowing I'd just watched Pete Bradshaw die.

Chapter Ten

TENDER MERCIES

By some small miracle, he was outside the hospital. The white wolf lingered in the grove of trees beyond the parking lot. He watched me as I watched him, my eyes locked with his glinting ones in the evening moonlight. Did he know what had happened? Was he here because I needed him? Did he know I had the moonstone now?

I took a step in his direction. He turned and disappeared into the grove. I wanted to shout to him to stay, but I couldn't draw attention to him in such a public place. I was about to take another step to go after him when April's red hatchback pulled up in front of me. Slade and Brent waited for me inside. I hadn't seen Slade since he'd refused to follow me into the fire. I wondered how many hours he and Brent had been sitting out here in the parking lot.

"He wants us to take you home," Brent said solemnly through the open window.

I tucked the moonstone into the small pocket of my scrub shirt, just over my chest, before approaching the car. After Talbot's betrayal, I was hesitant to let anyone know I had the stone now.

I slipped into the backseat and could almost taste the dark mood that radiated off the two boys in the front. I gathered that they knew what had happened to Marcos. They'd known him so much better than I had, and I didn't know what to say. So nobody said anything, and Slade started the car and headed back toward Rose Crest, driving much slower this time.

Their pack mate had died because of me.

Two people I knew had died today, and my dad was in *critical* condition.

And it's all your fault, growled the wolf inside my head.

We drove in awkward silence until we pulled into my neighborhood and I noticed something strange. Even though it was after dark, almost all my neighbors were outside of their houses. Some sitting on their porch steps. A few standing in the street. They looked like they were waiting for something. Almost like they didn't know what to do with themselves until it happened.

I rolled down my tinted window to get a better look, and peered out at the Headrick family, sitting on their porch, just staring out into the night. When Jack

Headrick saw me pass by in the backseat of April's car, he stood and motioned to his wife and kids. Much to my surprise, they started following the car as we drove down the street. Other neighbors followed in a quiet procession.

"What's going on?" I asked.

Slade seemed to flinch at the sound of my voice breaking the silence.

"They know," Brent said, speaking for the first time since I'd gotten into the car. "Reports about the explosion have been on the radio all afternoon. I imagine the television, too. Someone must have leaked your dad's name to the press. They all know what happened to him."

Slade pulled into the driveway of my house. The long line of people following us suddenly felt like a funeral march. I sat there, unable to get out of the car yet. I wanted to shout at them through the rolled-down window to go away. I didn't want them here. I didn't want to see the concern on their faces. Didn't want to answer their questions. They'd all want news. They'd want to know why my dad had been at that warehouse in the first place. They'd want someone to tell them what they could do for us. They'd want someone to care that *they* cared.

*He's **your** father. What right do they have to invade your space, acting like they'd almost lost him, too?*

I opened the car door and bolted toward the house,

careful not to run unnaturally fast, though. Not with so many people watching. I just wanted to get inside, away from all these people. But as I approached the porch, the front door opened and April stepped through the doorway. She shook like a nervous cocker spaniel, and her puffy face was splotched with red tearstains. *So much for keeping this from April.* Before I could react, she padded down the porch steps and threw her arms around me in a bear hug so tight it reminded me of my old friend Don Mooney.

"Oh, honey, are *you* okay?" she asked.

"Yes," I said, tearing up over the fact that her first question had been about *me.* "But I just want to go inside. I need to get away from *them.*"

The moonstone pulsed in my pocket between us as April rubbed her hand up and down my back. It felt so reassuring—the first *real* hug tonight—that for the first time this evening I didn't feel quite so alone.

"They're here because they need to be," April said.

I turned my head and looked out at the yard. By now, most of the neighborhood had converged on my lawn, although a few people hung back in the street. It reminded me of when Baby James had gone missing, the way practically the whole parish had shown up to help search for one of their own.

I realized then that the wolf in my head had been wrong. My dad belonged to these people, too. He was their pastor—their father, too. They had every right to feel like he belonged to them. They had every right to be concerned. If this were a werewolf pack, Dad would be their alpha.

No, they were more like a flock without their shepherd.

I mustered up my strength and let go of April. I turned and faced my neighbors. I could see the same question forming on all their lips. "Thank you for your show of support," I said in my best impersonation of Dad's authoritative-yet-reassuring voice. "I am truly moved by your love for my father. His condition is still critical, but he has improved some in the last hour. I will make sure someone spreads the word whenever I hear something more."

I was immediately bombarded by a string of questions about how it happened, and I told them the same lie I'd told the police who had questioned me in the ER: that Dad had been scouting out a new location for a rescue shelter in the city, but I had no idea what had caused the explosion.

More questions followed, and then at least three of my neighbors offered to bring over dinner.

"Thank you for your offers," I said. "However, someone else in the parish needs your help more than I do. I was at the hospital just now when Pete Bradshaw unfortunately passed away."

April gasped next to me, along with several others in the crowd.

"I am sure his mother could use your love and good-will more than I can at this moment. Please, put your energy to use for her." I knew that was what my father would want them to do. Pete had his problems, but his mother didn't deserve to lose her only son.

I thanked everyone again and then turned to go inside. April followed me up the rest of the porch steps. We ducked into the house, and as I closed the door behind us, I watched a few of my neighbors slowly head down our street toward Rose Drive, where Ann Bradshaw lived.

"You almost sounded like a pastor," April said. "Maybe you have a future in public leadership."

"I doubt that," I mumbled.

"I do not," came Gabriel's voice from the kitchen. I peered down the hallway and saw him rise from his seat at the table. "And that future may be sooner than you think." He set what looked like a sketchbook on the table and looked at me. "We need to talk, Grace."

FIVE MINUTES LATER

April made her excuses to leave, as if by a pre-arranged cue from Gabriel. I knew exactly where she was headed.

"Is someone with Jude now?" I asked.

"I sent Ryan and Zach."

"Does he know?"

"He knows there was some sort of accident, but I told the others not to say anything yet."

I sighed with relief, but then I knew what needed to be done next. "You should tell him. But keep Ryan and Zach there with you, in case. . . . I don't know how he'll react."

I knew I should be the one to break the news to my brother, but I just couldn't do it. What if he didn't react at all? What if he didn't care? I just couldn't bear to see that happen.

And I have something more important to do now, I thought as I patted the moonstone in my pocket, just to reassure myself that it was still there.

As April went out the front door, Gabriel beckoned me to the table. The sketchbook I didn't recognize sat in front of him, and he clenched a charcoal pencil in a white-knuckled grasp. I wanted to tell him that I didn't have time to talk—that I needed to focus all my energy on figuring out how to use the moonstone to bring Daniel back now that I had it—but the grave look in Gabriel's eyes, and the way April had bugged out of here, told me that whatever he had to say was serious. And honestly, I still didn't know if I was ready to trust anyone else with the truth that I had the moonstone.

I pulled up a kitchen chair and sat next to Gabriel.

"First of all, I'm sorry," he said. "As your father's junior pastor, it should have been my responsibility to address his parishioners outside. However, considering the circumstances, I did not think it was wise with all of this." He indicated the bandage on his face that covered the cut that had reopened during our failed healing session, and the bruises that painted his jaw. It had been a couple of hours since I saw him last, but they looked just as dark and painful. I wondered how long they would take to heal.

"I am the one who is sorry. I was just so desperate to help my dad. I should have known I wasn't ready."

"It is my fault. I should have been aware of how much anger you're holding inside of you."

I stared at him.

"Are you familiar with the story of the unmerciful servant?"

I really wasn't in the mood for a Bible story, but I could tell Gabriel's mind was set, so I nodded my head.

"Then you know that a merciful king forgave his servant's great debt when he could not pay. But when that same servant went to collect a lesser debt from a fellow countryman, and found that he could not pay, the servant was angry and threw him into prison. When the king heard of this, he was wrothful with the servant for not showing the same compassion he had been shown, and the king threw the servant into debtors' prison as well."

"I'm not sure what that has to do with anything right now," I said, with more frustration than I had intended.

"You are so full of anger, Grace. I could feel it when we were connected. All that anger swirling inside of you—it will eat you alive if you do not deal with it. It is a power just as strong as love. You channeled it instead of your positive energy. It is like letting your inner wolf attack somebody else—but from the inside. That is what caused this." He indicated his damaged face. "You reopened my wounds. I just hope I took the brunt of the attack, and not your father."

I dropped my head. So I *was* the reason those monitors went off in Dad's hospital room. "You mean, I can hurt people—literally—with my anger?" I clasped my hands together. They felt like dangerous weapons.

"Not as much as you can hurt yourself. We have discussed this before, but the wolf inside of you feeds on your negative emotions. You must recognize your anger and get rid of it before you give your wolf more power. I know you are strong enough to withstand an attack from the outside—you proved that in the warehouse. Yet letting the wolf attack you from the *inside* is much more insidious." He picked at the bandage on his face. "Tell me, Grace, who are you angry with?"

"I don't know. No one." *That wasn't true.* "Everyone." *They've all let you down, and now he's giving you a lecture?* I concentrated on the stone in my pocket to help regain some control. "I'm angry at my father for not letting me go to the warehouse and insisting that he go instead. I'm angry at Talbot for letting Dad get hurt, and for being a lying son of a . . ." I let the sentence drop off.

"But your anger runs deeper than that. The anger I felt in you stemmed from before today." Gabriel took a deep breath and looked me right in the eyes. "Are you angry with Daniel?"

"No."

"Are you sure about that? It would be easy to resent him."

"Resent him? How could I be angry with someone who sacrificed everything for me? He was the one who was supposed to get away. I made him promise to escape the warehouse if he got the chance, but instead he tried to save me. How can I resent him for not being here?"

And there it was, just under the surface. All Gabriel had to do was scratch at it, and it came oozing up, like blood from a scab. I *was* angry with Daniel. Part of me resented him for not being here. He was the one who had left me alone. He should have been with me in the hospital today, wrapping his arms around me, reassuring me that my father was going to be okay. It was irrational, I know. He couldn't control the fact that he wasn't there.

Your father wouldn't have gone to the warehouse if Daniel were here. It's his fault your father got hurt.

Hell.

I knew it was the wolf who had said it, but only because it had uncovered the idea buried deep inside my subconscious. How could I have thought something so terrible? Tears pricked at the backs of my eyes.

"Why am I so angry at him? It isn't right. He sacrificed everything for me."

"Because he was not *supposed* to sacrifice himself for you. He was not *supposed* to try to save you."

"I made him promise to escape if he had the chance. He was supposed to let me die so he could save himself and my family. But he broke that promise. He threw himself over that balcony to save *me*, and he was turned into the white wolf."

"And now he is stuck that way."

And that's why I'm so angry with him. "Does that make me a horrible person?"

"It makes you human." He reached out and placed his hand on my shoulder. "But you must consider this, Grace. You and Daniel are connected—deeper so than we were at the hospital. You feel what he feels. You know that he needs a moonstone, and that part of him is leaving. But have you considered that he may feel what you feel? Perhaps your anger is what is driving him away."

Gabriel might as well have stabbed a silver knife into my heart for how much his words pained me. "Do you really believe that?"

"It is just a speculation. Yet I think you need to find a way to forgive him—before it is too late. Find a way to forgive everyone before you find yourself alone with only the wolf inside your head for company. Daniel. Your father. Your mother. Your brother . . ."

I looked away.

"God."

"God?" I glanced back at Gabriel. "I never said anything about being angry with God."

"You did not have to. I could feel what was in your heart at the hospital, and just now, you said that Daniel '*was* turned into the white wolf.' Not 'he turned into the white wolf.' As if you blame someone else, some outside force, for turning him. You blame God."

I didn't know what to say. *Had he really seen that in my heart?*

"Tell me, my child," he said, sounding very much like a priest questioning a sinner at confessional, "with all of these challenges you have been facing this week, have you prayed for guidance?"

I blinked at him. It was an intrusive question that made the wolf inside me snarl evil insults. I shook my head again to get rid of it. "No," I admitted softly.

"Do not forget who you are, Grace Divine. Your father is a pastor, and you are talking to an eight-hundred-year-old monk, but *He*"—Gabriel pointed up to the heavens—"is the one you need to turn to now."

"But what if I can't? What if I'm . . . afraid?"

Gabriel tilted his head with curiosity. "Afraid you will not get an answer? Have you lost your faith . . . ?"

"No. I know God is there. I just don't understand

him anymore. I don't get why he created the Urbat in the first place. I don't get why he let them be corrupted like they were. Why would he create this curse? Why would he do this to us? To me? Why would he turn Daniel into the white wolf and trap him that way? That's not what I wanted. It's not what I asked for."

"Asked for?"

"The last time I prayed—in the warehouse—I asked God to find a way to spare Daniel. A way to save him and my family. I told God he could let me die, but I begged Him to spare the others. I was ready to die, but then Daniel jumped from the balcony and was transformed into the white wolf, and then everything turned out the way it did. Everyone was spared, in a way. My plea was answered, but not in the way I expected. The price was not what I was ready to pay. I don't want that to happen again." I bit my lip, and we both sat in silence as my thoughts finally started to come together. "I guess deep down I really am angry at God."

"There are times I have doubted. Times I have lost my way—without my anchor I would probably be lost still. Yet I know there is a purpose in all of this—even if after almost a millennium, I still do not know exactly how God works. But I do know that you need to work out this anger, find your own anchor, and—unlike the unmerciful servant in the story—learn to forgive in order to be forgiven. Even if God is the one you need to forgive. Even if it is *yourself*."

I dropped my gaze. Perhaps *I* was the one I was the most angry with in all of this. I laughed uneasily to break the tension that was thick inside of me. "Remind me to never do a mind-meldy thing with you again. You're far too perceptive."

"Mind-meldy?" Gabriel asked. It sounded extra ridiculous with his weird mixture of a European and American accent.

"Oh yeah. I forgot you don't watch movies."

"You would think in all these centuries I would find the time."

"So what's your anchor?" I asked. I'd never thought of Gabriel as necessarily my friend—but he knew so much about me now, I figured I deserved to ask him a few personal questions. "Eight hundred years is a long time to go without losing your grip."

"I never said I do not lose my grip sometimes. Quite the opposite." A dark look passed over his eyes, and I knew asking about those times *would* be too personal. Then again, I already knew what had happened to his sister, Katharine. She'd died by his hands—teeth—shortly after he'd fallen to the werewolf curse. "But I always find my way back because of her." Gabriel opened the sketch-book that sat in front of him. A drawing of a woman's face decorated the page. She was beautiful, with light-colored hair and delicate features, drawn with so much care that they could only have been done by a true artistic master—a master who obviously loved his subject.

"Did you draw this?"

"Yes." Gabriel tapped the pencil next to the book. "Drawing is one of the things I do when I am agitated. Not quite as effective as tai chi, but people stare at you less for doing it in public."

"This is beautiful." I'd thought of Gabriel so much as a monk and a werewolf, and even a high school religion teacher, that I had all but forgotten that he was an artist. He had been one of the sculptors who'd created the gorgeous statues in the Garden of Angels. "May I?" I reached for the sketchbook, eager to see more of his work.

Gabriel nodded and pushed the book toward me. He didn't make a sound as I flipped through the pages. Every sketch was of the face of this same woman. There was something beyond her beauty, something in her eyes. Like she was in great pain but trying not show it. A weak smile curved her lips, like she was trying to be brave, despite her fears.

"Who is she? Your sister?"

"My wife."

I glanced up at him. The bruises on his face still looked tender, but they didn't seem as painful as the look in his eyes—like a reflection of what the woman in the drawings felt.

"You never mentioned that you have a wife."

"Her name was Marie." He pronounced it Mah-ree with his strange accent. "She died in childbirth hundreds of years ago. Before I became a monk. Before the Crusades. Before I was cursed."

"I'm sorry," I said, even though it couldn't make any difference.

"She made me promise before she died that I would someday come find her in heaven. That is why I became a monk. I thought if I lived a life devoted to God, I would be pure enough to keep my promise to her. Obviously, my plan did not work out that way. I feared all was lost when I fell to the werewolf curse. I forsook my promise to Marie for quite some time. You know some of the things I did. . . ."

I nodded, thinking once again of his sister, Katharine.

"Yet it was Marie who brought me back, by showing that she has not given up on me."

"How?"

"The Babylonian priestess—the woman who gave me the moonstones—did not find me by coincidence. She told me that Marie's spirit had spoken to her and told her what I needed. She said that Marie was still waiting for me to join her in heaven. That she would never stop waiting for me."

I gasped.

"Those moonstones changed my life. I devoted myself to a path of strict nonviolence, and I have been trying to atone for all of my terrible misdeeds ever since."

I felt a pang of guilt for not sharing the moonstone I had with him yet. It wouldn't have even existed if it weren't for him. "But you fought at the warehouse even though you said you never would again?"

"As I told you before, you inspired me." He pulled the sketchbook back in front of him. His fingers lightly brushed over the drawing of his Marie. "You know, it was not until Daniel told me about what you did for him that I truly *believed* that it is possible for someone like me to be cured. The *idea* of you gave me hope that I might be able to fulfill my promise to Marie. Yet after so many centuries of doubting I could truly make it back to her, I was afraid to let that hope take root inside of me. That is why I came here, to see you for myself. Alas, I was so afraid to lose you before I figured you out, that I thought you needed to be coddled and protected. Which in the end turned out to be the wrong thing to keep you safe. I am just grateful that you were able to show me that there are some things worth fighting for."

"Or I'm just really stupid for running into danger all the time."

Gabriel chuckled a bit. "Yes, that, too. However, you are right about many things. A long time ago, I thought I could help the Urbat reclaim their blessings. I had lost hope that was truly possible, until you came along. Do you want to know something interesting that you and the priestess have in common?"

I cocked my head. "What?"

"Violet eyes. I remember that now. She had eyes just like yours."

"Really?" Violet eyes are extremely uncommon. My mom once told me that when my baby blue eyes had developed into violet, Grandpa Kramer had tried to convince her to change my name to Liz—after his favorite actress, Elizabeth Taylor, who was famous for her supposedly violet eyes. But Jude was the only other person I really knew of with eyes like mine.

"There's an old Egyptian legend about people with violet eyes. They call them 'spirit people.' The priestess I knew could commune with the dead. Fulfill their requests. Maybe that is why your connection to Daniel is so strong—how you know what he needs."

My mouth went dry. "Are you saying Daniel is dead?"

"No, no." Gabriel patted my hand. "I am saying you have a close spiritual connection to the world. I think you are special in many ways you are just now beginning to understand. If you can tap into that, you have the potential to become a great leader and healer—the Divine One we all want you to be. However, you will never get there unless you can let go of your anger. Otherwise, it will corrupt you just like the rest of us."

Gabriel's words rang true, even though I didn't know what to do with them. Letting go sounded much easier than it really was to do. I looked over at the sketchbook, wondering how he'd held on to an anchor that had been gone from him for so long.

"I tell you all of this, Grace, not to lecture or make you feel discouraged. That is the opposite of my intention. I do believe you have the potential to become a great leader—alas, as I said earlier, that time may come sooner than you would like."

"What do you mean?"

"I'm leaving, Grace."

Chapter Eleven

TETHER

AFTER HOLDING MY BREATH FOR A MOMENT

"Whoa. What? You can't leave. *Not now.*" Panic rumbled behind my voice.

Gabriel scratched at his bandage. "Sirhan's guards found me today. They came here to deliver a message." He massaged his bruised jaw. He must have taken quite the beating. "I have forty-eight hours to return to Sirhan or else he and the entire pack will come here to collect me."

Only a couple of hours ago, I'd been determined to go to Sirhan myself—but the prospect of his coming to Rose Crest made my stomach clench with dread. "Sirhan would really come here?"

Gabriel nodded. His eyes held that grave look. "Believe me, that is not something you want to happen."

"But you're his beta. Can't you reason with him? Ask for more time?" Two weeks ago I would have been happy to get rid of Gabriel, but at the moment he was one of the few people I had left in the world to rely on. The idea of his leaving made me want to scream at the heavens.

"Sirhan has never been quite the same since his mate, Rachel, died as a result of Caleb's treachery. And now Sirhan is dying of old age. Can you imagine how that would be for someone who has stayed young and felt immortal for almost a thousand years? The rapid aging he has gone through in the last few months has taken a toll, not only on his body but also on his mind. He is not someone who can be reasoned with easily. He is facing death in what appears to be only a few days' time, and that has made him a desperate man. And desperate men can be very dangerous."

"Then you really are in danger if you go back there?"

"If I reassure Sirhan of my loyalty by returning quickly, then I should be okay. As his beta, it is my duty to be with him in these last few days. I was going to go straightaway this afternoon, but I could not leave yet, after I heard what happened to your father."

"But you are still leaving?"

"I must go first thing in the morning. There is an additional danger to Sirhan coming here. According to pack laws that are even older than I am, the place in which the alpha dies is where we must hold the Challenging Ceremony to determine the new alpha. If Sirhan were to pass away while he was here, not only would that bring

Caleb and his pack here, it would also bring other Urbat challengers from all over the world to Rose Crest. You do not want your little town to become a battleground for every werewolf seeking to overthrow me."

No, I certainly do not.

I had so many more questions for Gabriel, but before I could ask them, we were both startled by the sound of a mournful, and terribly loud, howl that emanated from the forest behind the neighborhood.

Daniel.

"Oh no!" I shot up from my seat and accidentally knocked Gabriel's sketchbook from the table. His hand shot out and caught it before I could react. "I heard Deputy Marsh threatening to get a wolf-hunting party together. With everything that happened today, I totally forgot. They think Pete Bradshaw was attacked by a wolf, and now that he's dead . . . They even have silver bullets."

"That is a disturbing development." Gabriel stood up and gathered his drawing pencils and sketchbook into a knapsack.

"I need to do something." My hand went to the moonstone in my shirt pocket.

Gabriel put his hand on my arm. "Let me go after him. I could use a good run to think some things through, and you need rest. I will find Daniel, take him somewhere safe, and stay with him through the night to make sure he is out of danger."

He slung his knapsack over his shoulder.

"Wait." I pulled the moonstone from my pocket and placed it on the table.

Gabriel gasped when he saw it. He extended his hand toward it, and I could see his fingers itching to touch the stone. I nodded my approval, and he pressed his fingers against its surface. I could see some of the tension in his body physically drain out of him. It must have been quite the sacrifice for Gabriel to give up his moonstone ring for my brother. This was probably the longest he'd been without one for centuries.

For half a second, I wanted to snatch the stone back—afraid Gabriel might try to steal it from me like Talbot had. But then I shook my head, realizing it was the wolf's selfishness that would make me feel that way. I watched in silence for a few more moments while Gabriel soaked in the hopeful power of the stone.

"How did you find this?" he asked when he finally pulled his hand away from it.

"Talbot was hiding it from me. I just found out that he'd had it since yesterday. I . . . I wanted to seriously hurt him when he told me." *Maybe there was something to all this anger stuff.* "I want you to take it to Daniel," I said. "I want you to cure him with it. I don't know how."

"Neither do I. Not really. I have my speculations. I believe the process may be much like how we tried to heal your father—concentrating energy into him—but using the moonstone as a filter. Alas, I know that I am *not* the one who can bring him back." Gabriel picked up the stone and handed it back to me. "Only you can."

I bit my lip and closed my hand over the stone. *What if I tried to change Daniel back and only made things worse, like I had with my father?* "Why me?"

"The connection the two of you have—I believe you are Daniel's anchor. His tether to what makes him human. I believe only you have the ability to bring the human side of him back."

I nodded, realizing that I had already known what he'd just told me. I was the only one who could do it—just like I'd been the only one who could cure Daniel a year ago.

The first time I'd experienced the connection between Daniel and me—months ago when he brought me to the Garden of Angels—it had felt like we were tethered together and I was his lifeline. Like I was the one who could pull him to safety.

"Your anger is trying to sever that connection. It is even more imperative now that you deal with it as soon as possible. You must not try to change Daniel back until you have—or I am afraid you will lose him forever."

I swallowed hard, unable to respond. Even though I had the moonstone now, Gabriel knew I wasn't ready to use it.

I knew I wasn't ready.

Daniel's howls grew louder. Perhaps he knew it, too.

"I must bid you good-bye. I will protect Daniel tonight, but I will be gone in the morning." He stood and bowed to me, bending from the waist with one hand over his heart, as if addressing royalty. "I have faith in you, Divine One. I know you and Daniel are destined to do great things for the Urbat."

And then he was out the door before I could even muster up an argument to his beliefs. Instead, I let myself be grateful for his help.

I'd have it for only a few more hours.

Chapter Twelve

DO THE MATH

Dad being worse off now because of my botched healing attempt

+

Finally having the moonstone and not being able to use it

+

Fearing my anger was driving Daniel away, and not knowing how to get rid of it

+

Knowing Gabriel, the one person I had left to rely on, had to leave or else my town might become a paranormal war zone

=

PRETTY MUCH THE PERFECT RECIPE FOR INSOMNIA

I tried watching TV for a while in hopes of getting sleepy, but the only thing on was the local news. They kept showing live updates about the warehouse fire that had now spread to the abandoned train station and threatened other buildings on the block. They cut in with occasional reports on Dad's medical status (still critical). And the only other story they seemed to have to run with was the death of Pete Bradshaw. The phone started ringing so I hit the Off button on the remote just as a reporter shoved a microphone into poor Ann Bradshaw's face just outside her house.

I looked at the caller ID on the wireless handset.

Aunt Carol.

I'd found a long piece of string in the utility drawer in the kitchen and had used it to hang the moonstone around my neck as a pendant. I clutched at it now for strength as I answered the phone.

Aunt Carol immediately laid me flat with a lecture about how I should have called her right away and not let her find out about my father from the evening news—apparently, the story about the explosion was being reported as far away as Cincinnati. But then whatever latent motherly instinct was buried inside my aunt must have surfaced, because the next thing I knew I was insisting that she didn't need to drive all the way out here with Charity and James to be with me.

"I'm fine. And the ICU won't let James and Charity visit because they're both under thirteen, so I think it's better if they stay out there. I don't think they'd be able to handle being this close without being allowed to see him." I knew that reasoning probably wouldn't keep my sister away, and I contemplated asking Aunt Carol to keep the news from Charity all together. But I knew how pissed I'd be if I were her when I eventually did find out. It's just that the last thing I needed was the three of them coming here, with so many dangers looming and so many secrets that could be exposed. I'd promised James once that I'd keep him safe, and the best way to do that right now was to keep him away.

Aunt Carol definitely wasn't keeping mum on the subject, because it was only five minutes after I'd hung up with her that I had to field a call from Grandma Kramer in Florida. If it weren't for my grandfather's recent health problems, I knew I would have ended up with them on the doorstep pretty soon, too.

Once phone calls were finished, I was even less sleepy and I couldn't shake the need to feel somewhat productive—so I went upstairs and started in on some of my homework, and attempted to finish a stack of Daniel's missed assignments, too. All the while, I cursed the fact that Daniel and I had only three classes together. I was at a total loss when it came to his calculus homework, and the one assignment we did have in common—tracking the upcoming eclipse for our astronomy class—couldn't be done until the lunar eclipse on Saturday. I tucked that worksheet back into my backpack, where I found Mr. Barlow's letters of recommendation for Trenton.

I slid open my desk drawer and pulled out the large white envelope that contained my Trenton application. I'd looked at it only once since I'd gotten it, and I remembered feeling overwhelmed—now I had *two* to tackle by Friday. It might seem like a trivial thing to be worried about at a time like this, but Trenton was what Daniel had always wanted, and Dad was right: I needed to make sure Daniel had a future to come back to.

The actual application part would be easy, yet time-consuming, to fill out for Daniel. However, it was the essays that scared me. I mean, I barely knew the answers to the questions for myself, let alone how to answer them on someone else's behalf. I stared at the broken blue seal on the envelope for a long time and then stuck it back in my drawer.

Later, I thought and went back to homework.

I picked up Daniel's chem book and settled onto my bed, thinking that if anything were going to help me fall asleep, it would be chemistry. Besides, I figured I could successfully tackle a few of those assignments since I'd had that class last year. The only problem was that as soon as I flipped the book open to chapter ten, the memory of studying this assignment with Pete Bradshaw at the library last year overtook my thoughts.

I'd all but forgotten that Pete and I had not only

been chem lab partners, but also friends, before things changed between us. Before I realized what kind of violent person lurked under his letterman's jacket and that "triple-threat smile." Before he agreed to help Jude try to turn me against Daniel. Before the night my car broke down in the city and he tried to trick me into thinking I was being stalked by the Markham Street Monster—just so he could *pretend* to be my hero. Before he attacked me in the alley between the school and parish the night of the Christmas dance.

But it wasn't my fault he'd lost control. I wasn't the one who made him an entitled jerk who thought he could have whatever—or whoever—he wanted. I wasn't the one who made him get drunk and attack me the night of the Christmas dance. . . . And he obviously hadn't learned his lesson very well. He and his friends had jumped Daniel a couple of weeks ago. And who knows what he would have tried to do to me that night I ran into him at the Depot.

The night he was later brutally beaten into a coma.

But he deserved it.

"No," I told the wolf's voice. There had been a moment when the wolf had succeeded in convincing me that what had happened to Pete was perfectly deserved. But it was the same afternoon that I had almost lost complete control myself—when the wolf in my head propelled me to Daniel's doorstep and I practically attacked him in my frenzy.

You're no better than Pete. Daniel should hate you for what you almost did to him. No wonder he wants to leave you.

The wolf was overwhelming sometimes in how quickly it could change its tactics, glomming onto any doubt that flitted through my mind. Clawing me apart from the inside.

Pete and I are different, I tried to tell myself. I'd almost lost control because there was a beast inside my head driving me to hurt the ones I love. Pete didn't have that excuse. He was perfectly human.

Yet he was still a monster.

The image of Pete lying on that hospital bed, being jolted with electricity by the doctor, flashed in my head. His face had looked so different today. Like a distorted mask of who he used to be. So lifeless and pale. Pete did the things he did of his own accord, but he still didn't deserve to *die*. For the last year, I'd told myself that I had forgiven him for all the things he'd done to me, but had I really?

And now it was too late. . . .

What would happen if I waited too long to forgive everyone else?

NIGHTMARE

I must have fallen asleep eventually in the stack of books and papers on my bed, because one moment I was reading, and the next I found myself standing in the alley where Pete had attacked me the night of the Christmas dance. I wore my white dress with the violet sash, and I could feel the cold night air on my skin, even though I knew I was just dreaming.

It wasn't one of my pleasant dreams of Daniel. It was a nightmare, I realized, when I saw that I wasn't alone in the alley. Pete was there, just as angry and dangerous as he'd been that terrible night. The fear and desperation to get away from him felt just as real, too. The dream progressed, and I relived more of that horrific night. Don Mooney stabbing Pete, then almost suffocating me in an effort to quiet my screams. Daniel coming to my rescue, and then the two of us trying to hunt down Jude and lead him away from the school dance before he was overtaken by the werewolf curse. In my nightmare, I was forced to reexperience the moment when Jude found us on the roof of the parish, and I watched again as he pitched Daniel's moonstone off the roof. I remembered the way Daniel had arched his head back and howled a scream. . . .

EARLY TUESDAY MORNING

I shot bolt upright in my bed, my legs and arms tangled in my sheets. The sky outside my window was a purply early-morning gray. I thought it was the noise of Daniel's scream that had awoken me from my terrible dream, but then the noise sounded again, and I realized it was the ring of my cell phone next to my bed.

I had no idea who would call so early in the morning, but I was grateful for the reprieve from my nightmare. Part of me wondered if being forced to relive that horrific night was God's way of punishing me for neglecting Him for so long. I grabbed my phone and flipped it open without checking the caller ID.

"Hello," I said groggily.

"Grace," came April's voice. It sounded even shakier than usual. "Have you seen the news yet this morning?"

"No, it's"—I checked the clock—"barely six a.m."

"I got up early to make some breakfast for Jude. He was really upset last night, and I thought if I brought him something homemade, it might help him feel better. But I turned on my mom's radio in the kitchen . . . and I heard a report about something that happened at City Hospital . . ." She sounded too upset to finish her sentence.

"What?" *Something about my dad? Please don't let it be something about my dad!*

"A woman was found dead in the parking lot of the hospital. Near that grove of trees on the west side. An ICU nurse."

"What?" I felt a rush of relief that it wasn't news about my dad, and sudden panic at what this might mean. "Do they know what happened?"

"They're saying it was a wild-animal attack."

This was bad. Very. Very. Bad. I'd heard what Deputy Marsh had said about one more attack being all the justification he needed to get a hunting party together. Even if the attack had been all the way in the city, with two people dead now, I didn't see that stopping those hunters from going after Daniel.

Suddenly, I remembered seeing the white wolf watching me from that same grove of trees last night when I left the hospital. But no, it couldn't be. . . . He *wouldn't*. . . . Whatever Daniel was now, I didn't sense any malevolence in him.

"What time did they say it happened?"

"Just after midnight."

"Thank goodness." Daniel had been back in Rose Crest by then. We'd heard him howling just before ten p.m. Gabriel said he'd stay with him through the night. I could prove it wasn't him if I had to.

And then another thought hit me. What if someone was *trying* to make it look like Daniel had done it . . . like the way my brother had staged those attacks last year to frame Daniel . . .

I shook my head. Dreaming of Jude's misdeeds all night long must have made me paranoid this morning. Jude was locked up, after all. He would have been at the parish all last night, with Zach and Ryan guarding him and everything.

"I need . . . I need to tell you something, Grace."

"What is it?"

"I let Jude out last night."

"You did *what*?"

"He was so upset about your dad. He begged me to let him go see him. I just couldn't say no. I sent Zach and Ryan away, and then I let Jude out. He promised he'd come back. He said he wouldn't be gone longer than two hours. He swore to me he'd just check in on your dad and come right back."

"Did you stay there to make sure he did?"

"No. My mom called and got real mad because I was out past my ten thirty curfew. I left, and I have no idea if he . . ." She took in a gulp of air. "Gracie, do you think Jude could have done this?"

A nurse at my father's hospital had been killed, and my brother had been loose at the same time. He was probably still loose now—doing heaven only knows what. Every fear I'd had about Jude since the moment he *claimed* he wanted to come home came crashing in on me.

"Yes." I snapped my phone shut and sprinted from my house, headed toward the parish.

I had to see the evidence for myself.

Chapter Thirteen

DEBTS UNPAID

My ankle had healed considerably with almost a full night's sleep, but I still couldn't run at my top speed because too much of Rose Crest was already out and about this morning. It felt like torture slowing my pace down enough just to look like someone out for a morning jog—which I realize now probably would have been more convincing if I'd bothered to put on shoes before bolting from the house. And I was still wearing the pair of pale green scrubs I'd changed into at the hospital.

I ran past Mr. Day, who was setting up a display outside his shop, and then rounded onto Crescent Street. When I was sure no one else was around, I kicked up my speed and flew across the parish's parking lot and into the building. I pounded down the stairs into the darkened basement without stopping to turn on any lights.

What am I going to do if Jude isn't here?

What am I going to do if he is?

I ran right up to the storage cage and grabbed the iron bars of the gate with both hands. The gate was closed and bolted by a thick padlock, but the two "watchmen" chairs outside the cage sat empty.

"Jude?" I called into the dark cell. "Jude!"

I heard a moan. Something shifted deep inside the storage cage.

"Grace?"

I blinked several times and focused my powers into my eyes until I felt that familiar popping sensation behind my pupils. My night vision sharpened in the dark, and I was able to see Jude as he sat up on the narrow cot in the far corner of the cage. His long hair was disheveled, and he rubbed his eyes like he'd been in a deep sleep before I came crashing in on his slumber. "I thought you might finally come today." He blinked and scrubbed his hand down the side of his face. "What time is it?"

He was here! Asleep. Jude had come back. That had to *mean* something.

He's just covering his tracks, hissed the wolf. *Tricking you into thinking he's innocent.*

"Did you do it?" I asked. "Did you kill that nurse at the hospital?"

Jude squinted at me. "What are you talking about? What nurse? I've been here in this place," he indicated the cage bars, "since you decided I needed to be locked up."

"Don't lie to me. April told me she let you out last night. I know you went to the hospital. And now there's a dead nurse. She was killed by a *wild animal* just after midnight."

Jude shot up from the cot and stormed over to the gate. He clutched the bars, his hands just above mine.

"And that's your first thought? That *I* did it?"

He slammed his hand against the iron bars. The gate rattled in my face. I realized then that the padlock was just a formality. He could tear this gate off its hinges if he wanted.

I didn't back away, but I couldn't look him in the eyes. I was too afraid of what I might see. "Answer my question. Did. You. Do. It?"

"Would I have come back here if I did?"

"You tell me. What happened last night?"

"I went straight to the city, looked in on Dad, and then came right back here. I didn't talk to anyone— and certainly didn't *kill* anyone—while I was gone. I was back here by eleven." He jabbed his finger at the little TV Dad had set up in the cell for him. "I can reenact the *Late Show* for you if you want. That actor April is always going on about did a tap dance on the host's desk and accidentally kicked a coffee mug onto a supermodel. It was a real riot," he said with a bitter bite in his voice.

I let go of the bars. "I just needed to know."

"Nice, Grace. I've been back for over a week, and the first time you come to see me, you accuse me of murder. When Daniel was back for that same amount of time, you were trying to kiss him. I'm glad to know where I stand with you."

His words were so true they stung like a fresh slap. I stepped back from the gate. "Jude, I'm—"

"Get out," he snarled.

"Jude, please."

"Get out of here!" he screamed, and slammed both of his hands against the gate. The hinges groaned. "Don't come back here again. If you think I'm such a *wild animal*, then you'd better keep the hell away from me."

"Jude—"

"Out!" he roared, looking like he was about to tear down the gate.

I stumbled back toward the stairs and scrambled my way back up to the foyer.

JUST AFTER SUNRISE

I sat on the steps outside the parish, watching the sun silently change the sky above the hills of Rose Crest from a purple-gray into a crisp bright yellow that contrasted starkly with my black mood. I hated myself for jumping to such a terrible conclusion about Jude.

So much for trying to make peace.

Only I knew that I would be immensely stupid for *not* suspecting him right off—especially if he really did turn out to be the killer. . . .

Gah! There I went again.

It had to mean something that he'd come back after being let out last night.

Perfect alibi, whispered the wolf.

And what did it mean that all this time he could have ripped off the gate and escaped—yet he allowed himself to be locked up?

He's fooling you.

Urgh. I clasped the moonstone pendant in my fingers and pushed the wolf's voice from my mind.

If it hadn't been for that terrible dream last night—reliving the night Jude fell to the werewolf curse—making me so paranoid in the first place, I might have been able to be more rational before storming in on him with my accusations.

What was the point of that dream anyway?

Why would my subconscious—or Daniel, or whoever or whatever was trying to communicate with me through my REM cycle—want me to relive what happened that night on the roof of the parish?

Maybe God really is punishing me. . . .

Or perhaps Daniel was still desperately trying to tell me to look for the moonstone in the parish yard. He didn't know that I already had it. That it hung from my neck now.

But it was clear I wasn't ready to use it.

The anger I'd felt last night—the way I'd wanted to lash out at my own mother, and the damage I'd wanted to inflict on Talbot when I learned of his deceit— scared me. It was consuming me the way Gabriel said it would—and I'd unleashed it once again on my own brother just now.

I was driving everyone away from me.

I pressed the moonstone pendant tight in my palm. I might even still lose Daniel before I was able to change him back.

Perhaps I really would end up all alone with the just the wolf inside my head.

Chapter Fourteen

WANDERER

LATER

I didn't know what to do with myself now. It was a school day, but I couldn't bear the thought of sitting through classes or talking with friends who felt more like strangers with each passing moment. Instead, I spent the next few hours wandering from place to place like a stray pup looking for shelter. I remember going home to shower and change. Then somehow I was in the driveway of Maryanne Duke's old house. Then I was standing in the concrete stairwell that led to the basement apartment where Daniel had lived until he'd taken to the forest. I must have stood there long enough to look lost, because Zach poked his head out one of the main floor windows, almost scaring me half to death, and asked if I was okay.

"Yeah," I said. "Will a couple of you go sit with Jude? We had a run-in, and I don't think he should be alone."

"Sure thing," Zach said. He almost looked happy to have an order, reminding me that his former alpha had treated him like a soldier instead of a boy.

I slowly walked down the steps and unlocked the old yellow door to Daniel's apartment. I stood in the middle of his room for a few minutes, soaking in the fading scent of him there. I willed my hands and feet to move again, and I picked up a few of his notebooks from his desk, and found his half-filled-out Trenton application neatly stored in its envelope. I took that and his beat-up laptop, and stuffed them into the satchel bag I'd brought along. Next, I sorted through the stacks of Masonite boards and stretched canvas that leaned against his wall, choosing the best of his paintings and designs. I hoped they'd be the same ones he would have chosen for his Trenton portfolio. My chest felt so tight as I pulled the apartment door closed behind me when I left, thinking about how the things I took with me would be the only traces of Daniel's human side left in this world if I failed to change him back.

My next stop was the hospital, where I alternated between sitting next to Dad's bed, holding his too-still hand, for the twenty minutes of each hour I was allowed in his hospital room, and standing outside the elevator that would lead me up to my mother's room in the psych ward.

When I couldn't stand the beep of Dad's heart monitor or the *ding* of the elevator anymore, I went to the hospital cafeteria and found an empty table where I could set up Daniel's laptop. Between flipping through his notebooks and poking around in his computer files, I found six different drafts of his Trenton essays.

They were good but unfinished. I chose the best and filled in the gaps, channeling the things Daniel had always told me about wanting to use his talents to improve people's lives. I only hoped my words could do his passion justice.

Crowds of diners came and went, and I was about to log off the computer and head back to Dad's room again when I noticed a Word file titled: FOR GRACE.

I hovered the curser over the file, wondering what it could possibly contain. Wondering how Daniel would feel if he knew I opened it. Wondering if I could stand not to.

It said it was for me, after all.

I tapped the touch pad and opened the file, knowing I wouldn't be able to do anything until I knew what Daniel had left for me. What I found was a poem.

For Grace—

I was walking in the cool night air
Watching simple leaves gusted off
Blown by the same wind that blows through
    my window
Like thoughts filling boxes in crowded basements
Self-inflicted thoughts

Sorted cards and picture books
Jumbled thoughts of you

Walking slowly and thinking clearly
I was watching the moon rise and fall
Thinking about bare feet and candlelight walks
About soup-filled dreams
Smooth silk hands and violet eyes
Smelling the night air and waiting for my mind
*   to stop*
Waiting and watching as the stars rolled on

You came then and stopped the stars
Pulling the moon from the sky with those words—
I was dreaming then, that I never meant to walk
But I saw the stars and saw your face
And couldn't stand still knowing you
Knowing your humor, your brilliance, your beauty
Your grace

Knowing I love you.

My eyes flooded with tears and I was barely able to finish reading the last few lines. My heart ached so bad, I clutched at my chest. But it wasn't a pain from sorrow, it was the feeling of the emptiness inside of me being filled up again—with the rushing, pulsing, warmth of Daniel's love.

How had he known that this was exactly what I needed? How could I have ever doubted him? How could I stand to let my anger push him away?

I couldn't risk that happening.

I had to do something.

I hadn't been wandering like a stray all day long—I'd been running away from what I knew I needed to do even before Gabriel said I should last night. I gathered up the things on the table and walked with slow steps toward the small hospital chapel I'd passed on my way to the cafeteria. It looked different inside than my father's parish back in Rose Crest, more sterile than sacred, but I knew I could still find God here if I sought him out. I continued my slow walk through the empty chapel until I reached the altar. I fell to my knees in front of it, and found myself doing what I'd been afraid to do for far too long now.

For the first time since I lay bleeding and ready to die on the floor of the Shadow Kings' warehouse—I prayed.

For forgiveness.

For guidance.

For peace.

For the ability to bring Daniel back to me.

Chapter Fifteen

ON MY OWN

LATE AFTERNOON

When I finally left the hospital, my heart was lighter than it had felt in days, but the weather had turned dark and cloudy. The smell of rain hung the air. I had one last thing I needed to do in Rose Crest before I could go home and hunker down in an empty house for the impending storm. I pulled into the parking lot behind the Print & Ship shop on Main Street and carried my canvas bag inside. I paid a small fortune to print out a few documents from Daniel's laptop on résumé paper, and then express ship two packages to the Trenton Art Institute. One was a thick padded envelope, and the other was a large portfolio box tied with twine. Both had Daniel's apartment as the return address.

I was headed back out to the parking lot when I practically ran into Katie Summers, who was on her way into the Print & Ship with her own portfolio box.

"Hey," she said. "Looks like we had the same idea today. Didn't want to risk being rushed to get your application out on Friday, huh?"

"Yeah," I said, even though I still hadn't started my *own* application yet. With the way my life was going lately, who knew what this Friday would entail, but I felt some relief knowing at least Daniel's application had been taken care of.

It was the least I could do for him right now.

"I'm surprised you had time," Katie said. "When I heard about your dad, and when you weren't in school today, I just kind of figured . . ."

Was she admitting that she hoped my dad's accident would keep me from turning in my application? Narrow the competition a bit? I couldn't help scowling.

Katie bit her lip. "I mean . . . that came out wrong." She shifted the portfolio box in her arms. "I'm sorry about your dad."

"Thanks," I said. "I should get going." As I stepped around her, I couldn't help thinking about how both her and Daniel's applications would be sent out together in the same shipment to Trenton.

And yours will be nowhere in sight, said the wolf.

But that doesn't matter, I told the voice in my head. *Because I know how much Daniel cares about me. Even you can't convince me otherwise.*

"Hey, Grace," Katie called.

I looked back at her. She gave me an apologetic smile.

"My parents are out of town, and some of my friends from my old neighborhood in the city are coming to visit. They want to go to some party they heard about tomorrow night. You should come with us. Might be good for you to blow off some steam."

Katie might be my competition in every sense of the word, but she made it all too hard to dislike her. "Um, thanks. But I think I'll pass." My life was far too complicated for parties. "Good luck," I said, pointing at her box.

"Yeah, you, too . . ." she started to say, but a loud chorus of honking car horns drowned out her words.

I raised my eyebrows.

"Must be the hunters," Katie shouted over the noise that came from the street in front of the shop. "They announced a call for wolf hunters at school."

"Wolf hunters?" My stomach felt like the bottom of it was about to drop out. I left Katie behind and jogged around to the front of the building to find a cluster of pickup trucks, filled with men and teenage boys, practically blocking off all of Main Street. Almost every truck sported a loaded gun rack, and several people held rifles.

"What's going on?" I asked Justin Fletcher, who sat in the back of his dad's pickup.

"Going hunting." He grinned. "Didn't you hear, the mayor put a twenty-five-hundred-dollar bounty on the head of that wolf who's been howling in the woods, and the Bradshaw family has offered to double the amount for whoever brings back the body. Five thousand dollars for shooting a wolf—you can't beat that."

"Holy crap," is what I said, but what I really wanted to do was let out a long line of curse words so colorful every hunter in this parking lot would blush. "But what about the storm?" The gray clouds that had been gathering before I went into the Print & Ship looked positively black now.

"I imagine a few people are going to wait it out." The truck roared to life, and Justin grabbed onto the inside of the truck bed. "The radio says it's probably going to blow over, though, and most everyone in town is hoping to get a head start tonight. With a bounty like that, every hunter in the county will be in the woods pretty soon. The deputy was even handing out free amo to everyone." He lifted up a small box that I recognized. My heart crawled up into my throat. They were the silver bullets from Day's Market.

As the truck pulled away, I made a mad dash to the parish, grateful my ankle had finally healed. I went straight to the little caretaker's apartment behind the building and pounded on the door, hoping Gabriel would answer. I needed his help. Maybe he could use his pastoral influence to get those men to call off the hunt? *Not likely*—but he could at least tell me what to do. Help me find Daniel. He was the last one to see him, after all.

After my knocking went unanswered for a few

seconds, I remembered my conversation with Gabriel from the night before. He had said he would be leaving in the morning. I turned the knob slowly and peaked inside the apartment. Everything was gone except for the bed and the little desk in the corner of the room, against which I had once thrown Gabriel. Every trace of him was gone except for a slip of paper on the edge of the otherwise bare mattress. I picked it up and found a sketch that I would have said was of myself—except for the expression of confidence on the girl's face. She looked so sure of herself, ready to take on any challenge, that it couldn't be me.

I flipped the drawing over and found the words *The Divine One* scribbled on the back with another note that said, *We'll meet again. Gabriel.*

He was gone.

Gabriel was gone, and I was truly on my own now.

I left the little room and found my way back to my car. I drove home, taking a different route than the caravan of hunters headed toward the woods. I needed better clothes—running shoes and a jacket—before I could head out on my own hunting expedition.

I'd prayed for guidance in the hospital chapel, and I knew I needed to follow my gut.

It was up to me.

The time to save Daniel was now.

Chapter Sixteen

HUNTER AND PREY

Darkness had completely overtaken the skies by the time I'd changed into running pants, a T-shirt, and a jacket, and headed out into our backyard to get to the woods. Those storm clouds, black as night, blotted out any early-evening stars.

I could smell the downpour brewing in the air. Hopefully, it wouldn't blow over.

"Please, dear God, let it storm," I whispered. Maybe torrential rain would deter most of those hunters. Turn them back from the incentive of a five-thousand-dollar reward. Or at least slow them down.

I climbed over the fence into the woods just as a flash of lightning splattered across the sky, as if someone had thrown white paint against a blackened canvas. Thunder rolled just behind it. *The storm is coming.* A fat raindrop splashed on my arm as if to punctuate my thought. A few more heavy drops fell as I ran into the forest. The rain was sparse for now, but I knew it was only a matter of minutes before I'd be engulfed in the downpour.

Another thunderous crack echoed in my ears—but there'd been no lightning.

A gunshot?!

"No!" I shrieked. Power surged through my muscles like I'd received an injection of pure adrenaline to my heart. I rocketed between trees and over boulders. I couldn't tell where the echoing gunshot had come from, but I followed my instincts—or whatever it was that pulled me in the direction of the ravine, the last place where I'd encountered the white wolf in these woods.

If someone got to Daniel before I did . . .

The rain fell heavier now, pounding down almost as hard and as fast as my racing feet. I was almost to the ravine when a second shot was fired. I veered slightly to the right, able to pinpoint the origin of the blast this time. I moved with quick but deliberate steps, careful not to make a sound as I slinked behind an upcropping of bushes.

"You missed again," I heard a low voice grumble. "You never miss."

"It's these damn silver bullets," a second voice answered, sounding even more annoyed. "They don't fly right. Start cheating to the left, or you won't hit a thing."

I peaked through the bushes and found myself behind two hunters, dressed in camouflage rain gear, with high-tech-looking scopes attached to their large rifles.

One of them bent down, as if checking a print in the mud. He wiped rain from his face and signaled to his friend to be silent. He made a gesture, and the two separated, fanning out as they took off in a quiet jog after their prey. I followed the hunter who supposedly *never* missed, because he seemed the greater threat, as they headed toward the ravine.

I knew what they'd find there before I even saw him.

The great white wolf stood only a few yards away, at the edge of the ravine. He glared at the expert hunter as he raised his gun. The red dot of the gun's laser scope marked the hunter's aim, about six inches left of the wolf's heart.

The white wolf bared his teeth in a growl. He stepped back, and one of his hind paws slipped a bit on the cliff's edge.

I could *feel* the satisfaction radiating off the hunter's shoulders, and it made my insides roar with power. Just as his fingers went for the trigger, I ran up on a boulder and leaped onto the hunter's back. I hit him hard from behind with my forearms as I landed. He shouted, and his gun went off, sending a wild bullet flying before I slammed him to the ground. He landed in a motionless heap with me on top of him.

I gasped and rolled him onto his side, noticing a trickle of blood seeping from the gash in his forehead. My heart quickened with panic. I hadn't actually wanted to hurt him. I was about to feel for his pulse in his neck when he groaned. I pulled my hand back.

"Hey!" the second hunter shouted.

My head snapped up, and I saw him running toward me in the rain with his gun raised.

"What'd you do to him?" He stopped short when he got a better look at me—the teenage girl standing over his unconscious two-hundred-pound friend. "Who are you?"

It was then that I recognized the man. Pete Bradshaw's only uncle, Jeff Bradshaw. I'd met him once, when my family were guests at Pete's sister's wedding two summers ago. He looked a lot like Pete's dad, only blond, but he was only a few years older than we were. April had practically swooned when Jeff had asked her to dance at the wedding.

What on earth was I supposed to do now? I didn't have time to think of a proper excuse for what I had done—and he might recognize me, too, if I let him look at me any longer. . . .

The white wolf let out a sharp growl. Jeff started to swing his gun around, ready to shoot at the crouching animal. Before he could finish the movement, I lunged for him, grabbed the end of his rifle, yanked it from his hands, and then swung it at him like baseball bat. The butt of the gun made a cracking noise as it smacked against the side of his head—almost as if I'd hit a home run. He fell to the ground, unconscious but still breathing, next to his friend.

The rain thickened. My soaked clothes clung to my shivering body. Lightning and thunder crashed as the white wolf arched his head back in a great, earsplitting howl. The first hunter I'd knocked down let out an answering groan. He'd be conscious soon. I had to get Daniel out of here.

"Come," I said to the white wolf, motioning to him.

He whined, and I was afraid he'd try to run away.

"Come, please."

He stepped cautiously toward me until his snout was almost touching my chest. I threaded my fingers into the wet fur around his neck. "This isn't over yet. Not until you're safe."

He let out a grunt as if he understood.

"Let's go, then."

Chapter Seventeen

NOT OUT OF THE WOODS YET

Rain poured down on us as we ran. Like a full-on monsoon had blown into Minnesota. I carried the two rifles I'd taken off the hunters and ran through the forest with the great white wolf at my side. Our feet sank deep into the mud with each step, but I prayed the rain would wash away our trail. What if Pete's uncle Jeff had recognized me? Would he remember who I am? With that much money on the line—not to mention wanting to get even with someone who'd bashed you in the head with a rifle—I knew those two hunters would probably come looking for us as soon as they regained consciousness. How long that would be, I didn't know. It's not like I made a habit of knocking people out.

We headed in the direction of my house because I didn't know where else to go. Where was I going to hide a giant white wolf?

Daniel's footfalls started to falter. He slowed to a lumbering jog.

"Are you okay?"

He glanced at me with his glinting eyes. His fur was as soaked as my clothing, water dripping off his muzzle. He whined, then took another few limping steps, and then came to a halt. He whimpered as he sat, shaking his head in what seemed like frustration—or pain.

"Come on!" I whispered loudly. "We can't stay here. It's not safe."

He looked back in the direction from where we'd come—back to where the hunters were—and growled. But the growl broke off into another whine. He shook one of his front legs, and I noticed a patch of blood on his shoulder.

"Did you get hit by one of those bullets?"

He whine-growled in response.

No wonder he couldn't run anymore.

What on earth was I going to do? How could I hide a giant, injured, white wolf?

"I need you to press forward. We need to keep going."

Did he even really understand me?

He panted several times and then limped forward. We made it about twenty more feet before he stopped again, almost collapsing. I knew he wouldn't be able to run any longer on his injured leg. If only he were in human form—his front leg would be his arm instead, and he wouldn't have to use it to run.

If he were human, he would be much easier to hide. Those hunters would be looking for a wolf, not a boy. I could feel the heat of the moonstone resting against my chest, and I remembered what Gabriel had said about how to change Daniel back.

I pulled the moonstone from my neck and held it dangling from its long string. It seemed heavy all of a sudden, like the weight of my decision was encapsulated in it. Not only had I prayed for guidance, I'd also prayed for the ability to bring Daniel back to me. I held the means in my hand, but the strength to do it had to come from inside of me.

Was I ready? Could I do it?

I heard a shout from somewhere off in the distance—but too close for comfort. I didn't have much time before we'd be discovered.

I needed to do it now, or it would be too late.

I *had* to be ready.

"Dear God, I hope I'm doing the right thing."

I draped the moonstone necklace around the wolf's neck. I clasped one hand behind his uninjured shoulder, and then with my other hand, I pressed the stone as hard as I could against his chest. He struggled at first. I could feel him trying to break away. I was afraid I was hurting him—but I had to push that fear away. I took several deep breaths, cleared my mind, and opened myself up to channeling all of my positive energy into that stone. Every particle of love I had for Daniel in my heart—in my soul—I tried to direct into him. The warm stone grew hotter and hotter in my hand, searing like a piece of brimstone into my flesh, but I didn't let go.

"Come back to me," I said to Daniel, and a jolt of energy flowed through me. It started in my toes and then rushed up my legs into my chest, making my heart feel like it might burst, and then into my arms, hands, and then the moonstone. Suddenly, shards of light shone out from under my hand—emanating from the burning stone itself. Power exploded from the stone so forcefully that it pushed me back and I fell into the mud, losing my grip on the white wolf.

Lightning burst in the sky directly above. I looked up and was momentarily blinded by the sharp light. I blinked several times, and when I regained my vision, the white wolf was gone. The place where he'd sat was completely empty.

"No" I said, turning frantically in a circle, looking for him. Had the lightning scared him off? I couldn't make out his trail in the saturated ground. How was I going to find him again? Rain ran down my forehead from my hair into my eyes. I tried to brush it away, but it did no good. Even with my super vision, I couldn't see farther than a few feet in this storm.

"Daniel?" I cried out. "Where are you?"

I took a few steps in the direction we'd been heading.

Then I heard it from behind me. A raspy voice, barely audible in the roar of the rain. A voice I feared

I'd never hear again . . . And when I did, it made my heart almost seize up in my chest.

"Gracie?" he rasped.

I turned around, almost slipping in the mud with my haste.

Someone was there. Through the rain, I could make out the white silhouette of a person clutching the trunk of tree for support, his lower half obscured by branches.

I took a hesitant step in his direction, too shocked to believe my eyes. Then another step. And another— feeling like a whole lifetime could have passed in the time it took to make my body move.

He was so close now I could almost reach out and touch him. His blond hair, drenched from the storm, looked almost brown as it hung down on his forehead— still shaggy even when wet. I watched in awe as rainwater ran from his hair down his chiseled cheekbones, arched over his cleft chin, and down his neck. It pooled momentarily in his hollow of his collarbone, and then carved paths down his bare chest.

"Daniel," I whispered, afraid I was dreaming again.

"Gracie." He held a shaking arm out toward me.

I grabbed his hand, and he pulled me closer to him. He cupped my chin with both of his hands, and then our lips were together, melting in a fierce kiss—wet with rain and tears. He kissed me like he'd feared that he'd never be able to kiss me again.

I wrapped my arms around his naked chest,

shuddering against his hot skin. Never wanting to let go.

But then he cried out in pain and pulled away. I noticed a bright red, blistering welt against the taut muscles of his left shoulder—where the silver bullet had pierced his flesh. He shuddered, his body convulsing, and he cried so sharply, I knew he suffered from a pain much greater than just that of the bullet wound. As if his insides were under threat of being torn apart. More shouts sounded in the background. Coming closer. Was someone on our trail? I reached out to steady Daniel's shaking body, but he slipped through my grasp and collapsed to the ground.

It took every ounce of my will not to howl a scream as I stared down at Daniel, lying in the mud so still, as if he were dead.

Chapter Eighteen

FEVER

He was hot. So very, very hot. Even in the cool rain, the heat radiating off his skin against my body made me sweat as I propelled him toward home. It felt like he was burning up in a fever of nuclear proportions. His shallow breathing scared me, and his body quaked with a seizurelike shudder every few minutes. I didn't know what was wrong with him, but I knew I had to get him to safety. He'd regained himself only enough to stand. With his arms draped around my shoulders, leaning his weight into my side, I was able to walk, drag, and carry him—depending on his ability to put one foot in front of the other—through the rest of the forest. I wanted to pass out with exhaustion by the time I reached the back fence of our yard. I don't know how I mustered up any more supernatural strength to hoist him over it.

I stashed the two rifles under my back porch—I'd

been too afraid to leave them in the forest for those hunters to find—then carried Daniel into the house. His body was slick with mud and still just as burning hot. He moaned softly and slid out of my grasp onto the linoleum kitchen floor.

How could he withstand a fever this high?

Suddenly, I wished my mother, the nurse, was here. Not that she'd be too keen about my naked boyfriend lying on her kitchen floor—but she'd know better than I did what to do for someone so sick. I had to bring down his temperature as quickly as possible, but I doubted a couple of ibuprofen were going to help.

I grunted from exertion as I picked him up again and carried him to the upstairs bathroom. I sat him in the tub and draped a hand towel over his . . . um, middle . . . and then turned on the faucet. I let a rush of cold water pour down on his legs. I tested the temperature. Colder than the rain outside when it left the faucet, but it warmed up quickly as it came into contact with his hot skin. I ran downstairs and grabbed the entire bucket of ice from the freezer's ice maker and brought it back upstairs.

"Don't hate me for this," I said to Daniel as I dumped the ice on top of him. He groaned and his eyes half opened for a moment—at least he was still conscious. Steam curled up in wisps from his skin.

The blistered welt on his shoulder was caked with mud. I didn't want it to get infected, so I washed my own hands and arms and then scooped up handfuls of the now-cooler water and drizzled it over his shoulder. Then I grabbed the bar of soap and lathered it up. As gently as I could, I carefully scrubbed his shoulder. He winced with pain as my fingers brushed over the tender wound. As I washed away the grime, I found a second welt on the back side of his shoulder. An exit wound—the bullet had passed clean through his arm. Both wounds looked like they'd been cauterized by the burning reaction of silver meeting werewolf flesh. It looked painful as hell, but at least I didn't have to worry about his bleeding to death.

I worked the soap down both of his arms and then across his back and then down his chest—trying all the time not to linger on the thought of how much bigger everything about his body was now. Daniel had always been well cut, but with a slighter build. However, his muscles were larger now than I remembered, firmer. Even his jaw and cheekbones were better defined. Everything about him was perfectly shaped, like Adonis himself lay in my bathtub.

After I finished washing his body, I lathered shampoo into his hair and washed away what was left of the week he'd lived in the woods. As I leaned over him to brush his now clean, wet, hair off his forehead, he lifted his hand and touched my arm.

He opened his deep dark eyes and stared into mine for a moment. "Thank you," he said quietly through chattering teeth. He closed his eyes again, convulsing with a shiver.

I clasped my hand over his forehead and realized his skin felt positively frigid now, even though the ice in the water had long melted away.

Had I done something wrong?

I took a moment to change into clean yoga pants and a cami, and threw my dirty clothes into the washer with a heaping scoop of detergent to destroy the muddy evidence. Then I fetched a pair of pajamas from Jude's unused room for Daniel. He let me help him into the flannel pajama pants, but he refused the flannel shirt. "Don't want to overheat again," he said through his pale blue lips. I wondered if kissing them would help him warm up. Instead, I draped a dry towel over his shoulders and led him to my bed. He barely made it before his legs gave out from under him.

"I don't really know what I'm doing," I said as I tucked him under my bedspread. "Maybe I should go for help." Leaving him was the last thing I wanted to do, but if he needed more help . . .

"No," he said, grasping my hand tight. "Please stay with me."

I nodded and crawled into the bed next to him. I pressed myself against his side to help warm him with my body heat. But it wasn't long until he was burning up again, and I had to bring ice packs from the freezer to press against his forehead. At one point he shook and screamed, clutching at the sheets, as if some sort of invisible force was trying to drag him away.

"Are you sure you don't want me to go for help," I called desperately over his cries. "Maybe Dr. Connors would—"

"Don't go." Daniel shook his head. He grabbed me in his arms and held me to his bare chest—clutching on to me like a drowning swimmer to a lifesaver. "I need you here with me tonight. So I don't go away again . . ."

And then I realized what was happening—Daniel wasn't suffering from some sort of illness, and not from a reaction to silver. There was an internal battle raging inside his body.

Daniel was fighting to stay human.

I wrapped my arms around him and clung to him with all my strength—it was up to me to ensure he survived this fight.

Chapter Nineteen

ANGEL

I didn't let go of Daniel. I held him through fits of burning hot and freezing cold. Through screams of pain, and low wolflike whimpers that barely passed his bluish lips. Finally, well after three in the morning, he gave a great sigh and his grasp on me loosened. His skin felt neither hot nor cold, and his labored breaths eased into a normal rhythm. The tension in his taut muscles slipped away, and everything about him became heavy with sleep.

I watched him for a long while. Smoothed his golden blond hair off his face, and caressed my fingers lightly along his perfect cheek and jawbone. Careful not to wake him, I brushed kisses against his forehead. I couldn't help it. I wanted to drink in everything about him. It felt as if I'd been stuck in some sort of hell-like limbo, with the week he'd been gone seeming more like a century.

But he was here with me now, and that's all that mattered.

At some point I must have drifted off to sleep in his arms because I was awoken several hours later to the sensation of someone's fingers brushing my hair off my forehead, and then tender lips pressed against mine in a kiss.

I slowly opened my eyes to find Daniel gazing at me as he lay beside me in my bed. A weak smile curved on his lips, but it was a smile, nonetheless.

"Hey," I said, and pushed myself up on my elbows. "How are you feeling?"

"Better than last night." His deep, dark eyes were locked on my face, as if it had been years since he'd seen me. "Thank you for staying with me." He leaned closer and gently kissed my lips. I gripped him around his neck and pulled him in for a harder kiss.

"This isn't a dream, is it?" Daniel asked. "I had dreams so realistic they were cruel."

"Better the hell not be." I laughed softly against his skin. "But it is hard to believe you're actually here, isn't it?"

"Then maybe we need to convince ourselves a little longer."

We kissed again, longer and deeper. Quite some time passed before our mouths broke apart, short of breath.

"Remind me to wake up in your bed more often," Daniel said with a heartier, devious smile.

"Not allowed. Never. Ever. Again." I pushed him away with a playful slap to the arm.

"Ow," he said, grasping his injured shoulder just below the red, blistered wound caused by the silver bullet.

"I'm sorry," I said. "Do you think you can heal that?"

He shook his head. "Already tried. Must have been caused by pure silver," he said. "Not much I can do but hope it keeps healing on its own. Hurts like hell, but at least I can still use my arm. Do you know how this happened?" he asked about the wound.

I scrunched my eyebrows, concerned. "You don't remember?"

He shook his head.

"You were shot. A couple of hunters in the woods. There was a whole hunting party out there looking for you—equipped with silver bullets, courtesy of Mr. Day." I touched the reddened skin just under the wound on the front of his shoulder. "I'm glad it passed clean through. I don't know if I'd have had the nerve to dig out a bullet. You seriously don't remember getting shot?"

"It's all patchy. I've got images here and there . . . Did you hit someone in the head with a rifle?"

"Yes. But he was one of the hunters who was trying to shoot you, so it was totally justified."

"Totally," he said with a smirk.

"Do you remember how we got out of the warehouse?" I asked, wondering just how much of his memory was affected.

"Partially. I remember watching you trying to fight off those wolves. And I remember jumping from the balcony and going all superwolf. But before and after that are really foggy. It's like I remember feelings more than I do events. Like how I remember feeling like I'd do anything to save you . . ." He gave me a look, and I knew he was pained by the sudden memory of my almost dying. "And then when I was the wolf, it was like I could feel this undeniable force pulling me away. Pulling me *to do* something. Go somewhere. Find something. But no matter how far I went, I couldn't find it. I kept running through the forest trying to get to it, even though I knew I couldn't. And even though I didn't want to go, it still pulled me away. I still don't know what it was I was looking for."

"I'm just glad you're back now—and that you never felt the urge to kill anyone."

"No, I never did. All that time I never felt the urge to kill, like when I was the black wolf. Protecting you was definitely one of my impulses, though. But I never felt any malice toward you or anyone else—I still don't. It's like I'm not actually werewolf. Like I'm a completely different species or something."

Daniel pulled me closer, and I rested my head against his chest, listening to the thrumming of his single heartbeat. I touched his arm. Silver could still burn him like a werewolf, but I got what he meant about feeling like he was something different altogether. "Then what are you?" I wondered out loud, but as I said the words, a realization dawned on me.

Daniel had died that night in the parish when I'd plunged that knife into his chest to cure him—to kill the demon wolf who had his soul in its clutches. Daniel had died along with the demon. But Daniel had come back—cured. No, *more* than cured . . .

The way his powers had returned after several months—but without the evil side effects . . . and the transformation he'd gone through. Turning into the *white wolf* when his greatest desire was to help me—save me—rather than the black wolf he used to be before he was cured. And the way his body looked now. Like everything about him had been . . . *perfected.*

Gabriel had told me to think of the Urbat as fallen angels. So what was Daniel now that he was no longer fallen? "I think you're a perfected Urbat," I said. "You're what the original Hounds of Heaven were *intended* to be. I think you're like . . . an angel."

"An angel?" Daniel gave a slight laugh.

"I think so."

"Does that mean you think I'm . . . dead?"

"No. Just perfected."

Daniel gave a great sigh and rolled over onto his side. "I don't know about that. . . ."

I stared at his exposed pecs and the muscles that rippled over his shoulders and down his arms. "You should see yourself." I felt my cheeks blush with heat.

He looked up at me with his deep, dark eyes. A mischievous smile curled on his lips. He picked at my coral-colored sheets. "So I can *never ever* wake up in your bed again, huh?"

I laughed. The sound came out as a girlish giggle that made my cheeks flush even hotter. "Maybe someday, if the *conditions* are right."

He wrapped his hand around the back of my head and pulled me toward him. His lips brushed over mine and then melted into a delicious kiss. I could feel his other hand on my waist, his fingers lingering on the hem of my shirt. Then they were on my skin as his warm fingertips drifted up the side of my stomach. His kiss grew more urgent. I could feel his need for me. My hands caressed his bare back as I pulled him closer. I needed him just as much. His hand cupped against my rib cage under my shirt. I could feel his strumming pulse in his fingers against my skin. . . .

Daniel pulled his hands away. He sat up in my bed and scooted farther away still. He sat so his back was to me, his legs draped over the end of the bed.

The tingle of anticipation still lingered in my skin. "Are you okay?" I asked. I sat up behind him, hesitating to touch my fingers against the back of his uninjured shoulder.

"I'm sorry," he said. "I got carried away. I don't want my need for you to get in the way of what we decided." I knew what he was talking about—we'd decided months ago that we wanted to wait. Deep down, beyond the yearning I felt at the moment, where I wanted to place his hands, what I wanted to do, I knew I still wanted to keep the promise we'd made to each other, even if it was almost impossible to remember *why* at that moment.

I leaned forward and pressed my lips against one of his shoulder blades as I traced my fingers against the muscles underneath it. "Thank you," I whispered against his spine.

He sighed and stood up, stepping away from the bed as if one more touch from me would make him lose total control. I knew exactly how he felt. "I guess I should find a shirt or something. What time is it?"

I glanced at the clock. "Wow. It's almost nine. Guess we're not making it to school on time this morning." I laughed. *As if.*

Daniel laughed, too. "I guess we could do the walk of shame together into the cafeteria around lunchtime."

"There's nothing to be ashamed of." I pulled off the sheet covering my legs and scooted to the edge of my bed, closer to where Daniel stood. I bit my lip, not quite sure I was ready to address the issue that played on my mind. "The *conditions* I mentioned earlier . . . ? That night in the warehouse, when we were locked in Caleb's dungeon. What do you remember happening?"

"Only bits and pieces. My memory is so fragmented. Like I've got a puzzle in my head that needs to be put together, but I'm missing half the pieces."

"Do you remember asking me . . . ?"

To marry you? I couldn't finish the question out loud. What if he hadn't really meant to ask? What if he'd done it only out of panic, to try to keep me from losing hope for the future? What if he didn't remember asking in the first place? What if he thought I was completely crazy for claiming he had?

Daniel stepped closer. Leaning in, he pressed his hands against the sides of my legs. My skin tingled uncontrollably in response.

"Do I remember what?" he asked.

My heart sank in my chest, realizing I was engaged to someone who didn't even remember asking. Who maybe hadn't even really wanted to ask. Maybe his memory had blocked it out on purpose.

"Nothing," I said, and started to pull away.

"No, Gracie." Daniel grabbed my arms. An expression of pain crossed his face as he pulled me up so I was standing in front of him, gripping me tightly so I couldn't run away. "Whatever it is you wanted to ask me is important. I can see it on your face. Don't hide anything from me. That's not how we work. Not anymore. We're in this together. No matter what."

I could tell he meant it. So maybe the idea of our being engaged wouldn't be too crazy, even if he had no recollection of it. "It's just that . . . when we were locked up . . . you asked me . . . *What the hell?*" I jumped back and smacked my hip on the foot of my bed. My hearing had pricked at the sound of an unexpected noise, stopping me from finishing what I was about to say.

Daniel laughed and let go of my arms. "That's an odd thing for me to ask."

I held my hand up to quiet him and then concentrated my powers into my hearing. I felt a slight pop in my eardrums, and my hearing increased just in time to catch the noise again. I knew exactly what it was this time—the sound of a car door opening and closing. Out in my driveway.

Then another noise, one I never would have heard without my powers: a key being slipped into the lock of the front door downstairs.

Daniel's eyes widened. He'd heard it, too. "Who . . . ?" he whispered.

"I don't know." My muscles tensed. "My parents are both in the hospital . . ."

A creaking noise accompanied the opening of the front door. Then footsteps as someone crossed the threshold. Anxious power tingled under my skin. Who could be inside my house? How could they even get a key?

Suddenly, I pictured Caleb and a gang of his boys entering my house. Coming for us at last . . .

"James, don't drag your blanket," I heard a voice call.

A sigh of relief rippled through me. "Aunt Carol," I said to Daniel. I jogged over to the window and saw her yellow Subaru parked in the driveway with its trunk open. I watched as Charity pulled a duffel bag from the back, and Baby James dragged his blanket across the leaf-strewn grass. "And she's brought Charity and James. I told her not to come here."

"You're related. I'm not surprised that she didn't listen," Daniel said with a quiet laugh.

"Hey," I whispered loudly. "That's justified . . . but how am I going to explain the half-naked guy in my bedroom?"

"Just tell her the truth." He shrugged overdramatically, his hands turned up. "Werewolves are always naked when they turn back into human."

"Ha. Ha." I gave him a "Not appreciated" look, but I couldn't help smiling.

"Don't worry," Daniel whispered. "I'm good at disappearing."

I looked out the window again just as a white SUV pulled up behind Aunt Carol's car in the driveway. "Oh crap!"

"What?"

"Sheriff Wright," I said as I watched him get out of

the patrol SUV with Deputy Marsh. I could think of only one reason why they would come here. I'd almost let myself believe that we'd gotten away. "I think those hunters went to the police. You better pull that vanishing act now."

I turned to Daniel, but he was already gone.

Chapter Twenty

SECRETS UNEARTHED

HALF A MINUTE LATER

I jogged out of my room and headed for the stairs just in time to hear Aunt Carol greet the sheriff at the door. I slowed my pace and tried to go down the stairs as casually as possible. I even threw in a yawn with a dramatic stretch for good measure.

"Kind of early for a visit," Carol said to the sheriff. "I just got here."

"Is this about Dad?" Charity asked. I could hear the concern in her voice.

"No, miss." Sheriff Wright tipped his hat to them. "We're here to ask Grace a few questions." He glanced up and saw me descending the stairs.

"Gwacie!" Baby James said. He ran to me and practically threw himself into my arms.

I wrapped him in a bear hug but didn't take my eyes off the sheriff and Deputy Marsh. Their presence here couldn't be a coincidence, not with what happened last night. "Hey, little man, how was your trip?" I asked my little brother.

"Long," James said. "I hungwy."

"Hello, Grace." Marsh gave me a too-friendly grin. "We looked for you at the school this morning but couldn't find you."

"I wasn't feeling well," I said. "I would have had one of my parents call the school under different circumstances."

"Since when does the school send the police when someone plays hooky?" Aunt Carol asked. "The poor girl's parents are both in the hospital. I think a few truancies are understandable." Carol never did have a lot of patience, and I could tell she wanted to finish bringing in the luggage. They must have driven most of the night to get here this early in the morning.

"This isn't about school," Sheriff Wright said. "I need to ask you a few questions about last night."

"*Last night?*"

Oy, why did my voice always sound so weird when I was trying to act casual?

"We got a couple of hunters in the station this morning. They were part of yesterday's hunt for the wolf that's been howling so loud the whole town can hear it. The hunters claim they were on the verge of capturing it, but then they were accosted by someone who knocked them out and stole their guns. Happened a mile or so into the woods behind this neighborhood."

"Oh, that's too bad." I kept my face as blank as possible. "But what do you need me for?"

"Their description of the assailant fits you to a tee," Marsh said. "One of them claims to have recognized you."

Charity gave me a surprised stare.

"I have no idea what you're talking about." Red "lie marks" burned up my neck. *Why did I have to be such a bad liar?*

Carol gave a derisive chuckle. "You mean a couple of full-grown men came into your station, claiming a five-foot-two-inch stick of a teenage girl beat them up, and you didn't laugh them right out the door? This is ridiculous. Now if you don't mind, I'd like to get the car unpacked and Baby James down for a nap. We drove all night to get here." She started to close the door in their faces.

Marsh stopped it with his boot. "All the same, we'd like to take a look around, if that's okay?" He glared at me right in the eyes. "We're worried the same person who attacked those hunters might also be harboring a dangerous animal. The wolf that escaped those hunters may be responsible for two deaths already. A nurse at City Hospital, and Peter Bradshaw, who died two nights ago.

"What?" Charity asked softly. Her mouth had popped open at the mention of Pete's death. This was probably the first time she'd heard about it.

"This is a matter of public safety," Sheriff Wright said.

"My niece knows better than to bring something dangerous into this house."

I tried desperately to keep a straight face.

Charity gave me another strange look.

"Besides, I know my rights," Carol said, wagging a finger at Marsh. "You need a warrant if you want to come in here."

"No," I said. "They're welcome to look around. I have nothing to hide." I stepped aside and waved my hand, inviting them in. The only way for them to stop suspecting me was to give them access to what they wanted. I trusted Daniel's abilities enough to know he'd keep out of sight.

"We'll be out of your hair soon," Sheriff Wright said as he and Marsh came inside. I listened to their heavily booted footsteps as they trudged through the house, opening and closing doors.

Carol followed behind them, grumbling about the mud they were tracking around. Carol and my mom were alike in a few ways. Charity said something about needing to get the rest of the bags and disappeared out the front door.

"I hungwy," James said again, rocking in my arms.

"Let's get you some cereal," I said, trying to keep my superhearing trained on the sheriff and Marsh as they took their search down to the basement. I hoped all the mud had washed away from the clothes that were still sitting in the washer.

I set James in his booster chair and then opened the pantry and pulled out a box of cereal. I poured a bowl and set it in front of him.

"Nana, too?" James asked with a smile too cute to deny him.

I grabbed a banana from the counter and then pulled a knife from the butcher block. As I sliced into the thick peel I suddenly remembered that I'd stashed the hunters' rifles under the back porch. I'd been so concerned about Daniel last night, I'd completely forgotten about hiding them. My eyes darted toward the back door, wondering how quickly I could get to the rifles before the police came back downstairs. But then what would I do with them, throw them over the fence into the forest? What if one of them went off when I tossed it? What if I got caught?

"Nana, nana, nana," James crooned from the table.

"It's coming." I sliced the knife down a second time just as Deputy Marsh appeared through the kitchen entrance, making me flinch. "Shhhh," I hissed. I'd cut right into one of my fingers. Droplets of blood pricked up from the cut. I grabbed a paper towel and wrapped it around the wound as Deputy Marsh gave me a snide look. Like me flinching was a sure sign of my guilt.

"Sorry to scare you," he said. "You don't mind if I take a look outside, do you?"

I wished I could wipe that smirk right off his face. "Not at all."

I watched out of the corner of my eye as he went through the back door out onto the deck. He was standing right over the spot where I'd stashed those rifles. How was I ever going to explain myself if he found them? He jogged down the porch steps, whistling an all-too-merry tune, and moved out of my line of sight.

I squeezed the paper towel into my cut, concentrating on healing over the stinging sensation as I rocked up on my tiptoes and tried to spy out the window. I still couldn't see him. I took a step back and realized I was practically standing on Aunt Carol's feet.

"What are you doing?" she asked.

"Nothing." I held up my finger, still wrapped in the bloody paper towel. "I just cut myself."

Carol raised her eyebrows. She started to say something, but she was cut off by the sheriff's voice as he reentered the foyer.

"Do we have an all clear?" he asked. I heard the cut of static and assumed he was speaking into a walkie-talkie.

"All clear," another voice answered, with just enough edge of disappointment that I knew it belonged to Deputy Marsh. "Nothing out of the ordinary in the yard."

How had he not found anything?

"Sorry for invading your morning, ma'am," Sheriff

Wright said to Aunt Carol. "Looks like everything here is in order."

"What else did you expect?" she snapped. "Honestly!"

"Truly, I am sorry. But I'd be remiss if I didn't check out every lead in this case. We had an entire forest full of hunters last night, but that wolf still managed to escape. Wouldn't want any of the townsfolk putting themselves, or their neighbors, in danger."

"Nana. I want nana," James cried. I could hear the lack of sleep in his strained little voice.

I grabbed another banana and sliced it with a butter knife while listening as Aunt Carol escorted the sheriff out the front door. Every muscle in my body tensed until I heard them drive away. But I still couldn't duck off to the backyard yet to figure out why Marsh hadn't found those rifles, because Aunt Carol had decided to regale me with one of her long griping sessions about small-town life and the idiocy of Rose Crest's government.

After about what felt like an hour of listening to Carol, I realized James was asleep, one of his cheeks resting on his bowl of dry cereal and bananas like it was a pillow.

"Why don't you take James upstairs so the two of you can take a proper nap," I suggested to Carol. "You deserve it after all that driving."

Carol yawned and picked up James. As soon as they were up the stairs, I slipped out the kitchen door into the backyard. Curiosity was killing me. Why hadn't Marsh found those rifles?

I was about to pad down the porch steps when I heard someone call my name in a loud whisper. I looked up to find Daniel perched on the edge of the roof. So that's where he'd been hiding!

He stood up, his bare toes peaking over the edge of the roof. If he'd been normal, I would have worried about his falling. Instead, I watched in quiet adoration as he pushed off with his toes and did a twisting flip in the air before landing soundlessly in the grass in a crouched position. It reminded me of the night he first told me about his powers. He'd made an exit in a similar way.

"Show-off," I said sarcastically, but I couldn't help smiling with appreciation. I could seriously watch him do that kind of thing all day.

"Oh, come on. You loved it." His mischievous smile made me want to kiss it right off his face. How had I even breathed without him for an entire week?

"Yes, I did." I put a hand on my hip. "The sheriff might be gone, but there're still people in the house."

"Good point." He crouched low, avoiding the kitchen windows. "Are you okay?" He pointed at the bloody paper-towel bandage I'd forgotten was still wrapped around my finger.

"It's just a small cut," I said as I pulled off the paper towel and showed him how I'd healed it over. There wasn't even a pink scar as evidence that the cut had even happened.

"You're getting better at healing yourself," he said.

Healing had always been the hardest of my powers to get the hang of. "Yeah, I guess I am."

My ears pricked to the sound of voices coming from the house. I listened for a moment and realized that Aunt Carol was talking on the phone—complaining to her latest boyfriend about the visit from the police.

"Come on." I waved at Daniel to follow me. I wanted to find a new home for those rifles while Aunt Carol was distracted. I rounded the edge of the porch to the opening where I'd stashed the guns the night before. I stretched my hand in deep to reach for them, then peered into the opening.

"You didn't see Deputy Marsh carry anything out from the backyard, did you?"

Daniel shook his head. "I'm pretty sure he was empty-handed. Why?"

"Because they're gone. . . ." Confusion muddled my brain. I could have sworn this is where I'd hidden the rifles, but maybe I'd just imagined that part of last night. The entire experience had been completely unreal. Maybe I'd left them in the forest after all? I shook my head. I know I wouldn't have just left them there. "I think I might be losing my mind. I swear they were right there. I don't know how this is possible."

"What?" Daniel's eyebrows arched over his deep

brown eyes. He'd been so delirious, he wouldn't have remembered my hiding them.

"You're looking for this, aren't you?" asked a voice from behind us.

Daniel and I reeled around to find someone standing there, with a high-powered rifle in her hand.

ABOUT TEN SECONDS LATER

"Charity!" I jumped up. "What the heck are you doing?"

The sight of my almost thirteen-year-old sister holding a gun nearly gave me a heart attack. She had it half raised in her hands, like she wasn't quite strong enough for its weight.

"Whoa, there, Char. Be careful." Daniel reached out toward the gun. "Give it to me."

"No," she said, taking a step back. "Not until you answer my questions."

"Don't be a brat, Charity," I said in my bossiest older-sister voice possible. "Put that thing down. It's loaded."

Charity lowered one of her hands and shoved it into her pocket. She pulled something out and held it in her hand, nearly dropping the heavy gun at the same time. "You mean with more of these?" The bullet in her hand was shiny and silver. Not like the brassy ones a rifle would normally take. "These are silver bullets, aren't they?" She cradled the gun in both of her arms.

"Yes, and they're dangerous. Now put the gun down. It isn't a toy."

"I know," she said. "And I know how to use a gun just as well as you do, Grace. Grandpa Kramer taught me how to shoot, too, you know."

She was right. I did know. Grandpa Kramer had always fancied himself a bit of a cowboy. He used to invite us on monthlong trips to his summer cabin, where he'd teach us things like shooting and fishing. I wasn't a fan of guns, but I could shoot a tin can off a tree stump from thirty yards away. Charity had been a lot younger during those lessons, but it was obvious she'd remembered a few things—like how to load and unload bullets.

"Yeah, and Grandpa Kramer would flip out if he saw you holding that thing. You should know better. Somebody could get hurt." My nostrils flared. "Give. It. To. Me. Now."

"Or what? You'll tell Aunt Carol? Go ahead, because then you'll have to explain to her why you have them, and I want to know. I deserve it. You should be thanking me for finding them before the deputy did. You know how far back under the porch I had to hide to keep him from seeing me? I still feel like I have spiders crawling all over my back." She shivered dramatically, making me flinch. I really wished she'd put that gun down.

"Thank you," I said, dropping the bossy tone. "But

you can give it back to me now." I held out my hand, beckoning her to hand the rifle over. Why had she even gone looking for it in the first place?

Charity shook her head. Her arms tightened around the gun. If she wasn't careful, she was going to end up blowing someone's face off. "I knew you were lying," she said, answering the question I'd wanted to ask out loud. "Your neck was as red as the devil. I just couldn't figure out what you were lying about. I figured *if* you had been out in the forest, you would have gone over the fence, so I decided to take a look around in the backyard. I didn't actually expect to find out you were hiding guns." She tapped her finger against the gun barrel. "But now I want to know *why*. I want the truth. And I'm not giving this gun back until you answer."

Whoa. My little sister was using a high-powered rifle as leverage? Well, if there was any doubt she and I were related . . .

"You really were the one who attacked those hunters in the woods and stole their guns, weren't you?" she asked.

I started to shake my head, but Charity wouldn't have it.

"How would these guns have gotten under the porch if you didn't hide them there?"

"I don't know. Maybe someone else—"

"You're lying again." She nodded at my red-splotched neck. "But I don't get why. Why would *you* attack a couple of hunters? Why would you steal their guns and hide them? *How*, even? And why would you do all that to save some wolf? That's so not normal. Except you've been acting really strange for, like, a year now. Ever since Daniel came back."

She glanced at Daniel. He shoved his hands in his pajama pants pockets, trying to look casual—which didn't exactly make him look innocent, but did make his pecs flex in a very nice way. Charity's cheeks pinked a bit, and I assumed it was because she'd finally noticed that Daniel was shirtless. I mean, she was a *girl*, after all; even if she was wigging out, she was bound to notice the perfection of his body.

Suddenly, her eyes narrowed as she looked at Daniel. "Is that . . . a bullet hole?" She used the muzzle of the gun to point at the welt on Daniel's shoulder, making my stomach feel like I was on a rocking boat. "Or is it a burn? Or both?"

Daniel glanced at me as if asking how I thought he should answer the question. But I didn't get a chance to respond.

"Oh, my heck." The pink flush in Charity's cheeks turned a bright shade of red. I could almost see the gears turning in her head as a realization dawned on her. "Silver bullets? That wasn't a *normal* wolf those hunters were after, was it? I mean, what the sheriff said about the whole town being able to hear the wolf howling. That shouldn't be possible. A *normal* wolf can't be heard beyond a mile and a half. I studied wolves last year for my science project, so I know."

I didn't like the emphasis she kept putting on the word *normal* in her sentences. And I especially didn't like the way she was holding the gun now, pointing it at Daniel in her unsteady hands.

"Charity, I don't know what you think is going on, but—"

Charity rocked the gun in my direction, making me throw my hands up defensively on instinct.

"Don't you point that at anyone!" I cried.

"What I couldn't figure out was *why* you'd risk your life to save some wolf." She tilted the gun back toward Daniel. "But I know why now. . . ."

"What do you think know?" Daniel asked, sounding calm, like a therapist, and not like someone who had a gun pointed at his chest.

"I had to research myths about wolves as part of my project. I know what they say about wolves, or people, who can be burned by silver. And I saw you do a flip from the roof and land on two feet like it was no big deal. Normal *people* can't do that."

I gave a little gasp. "So being a show-off comes back to bite you in the butt, eh?" I said to Daniel.

He smirked. "So it does."

"This isn't funny!" Charity rocked the gun back and forth between us. "I'm not stupid, Grace. I know you think just because I'm in middle school that I should be oblivious to everything. I know something's been going on. Ever since Daniel came back . . . and people started turning up dead again from *wild-dog* attacks. And all that stuff the news has been saying about the return of the Markham Street Monster."

"I know you're not stupid. But this isn't what you think. Daniel didn't do any of that."

Charity shook her head, the gun swaying dangerously back and forth as she did it. She blinked fast, as if fighting the tears that formed in the corners of her eyes. "He's a monster, isn't he? A . . . a . . . a werewolf?"

I opened my mouth, ready to tell any lie that would convince her otherwise, but Daniel placed his hand on my shoulder.

"It's okay," he said. "She knows what I am, and it's time to tell her the rest."

"So it is true?" Tears trailed from her eyes now. The gun wavered up and down in her trembling hands. I knew how freaked out she must be—even I hadn't handled the revelation of Daniel's true origins all that well when I found out—but if she lost control of herself, that gun was surely going to fire.

Three different scenarios of how I could spring on her and wrestle the gun from her hands flashed through my mind. *Do it!* growled my inner wolf. *She's a danger to you. Take her out.*

No. I couldn't see any of those scenarios ending

without someone I loved getting hurt. "Yes, Charity. But what are you going to do about it?" I inched sideways. "Are you going to shoot Daniel?"

"I don't know." She choked on her tears. "Isn't that what I should do? Shouldn't I try to protect us all?"

"If you shoot him for being a werewolf, then you're going to have to shoot Jude. . . ." I stepped between Daniel and Charity so the gun was aimed at me now. "And then you'll have to shoot me." Because even if I wasn't a full-blown werewolf now, watching Daniel's heart get ripped open by a silver bullet would be the tipping point that would force me over the edge. "This is what we are, but we haven't done what you think we have."

"Don't do this, Grace." Daniel's hands clamped over my shoulders, ready to shove me out of harm's way if needed.

I didn't change my stance. "So what's it going to be?" I asked Charity.

Except for the bright red tearstains, her face was as white as the clouds in the sky. "You're a . . . ? I don't believe it. You can't be . . . You're just my sister. I don't understand. . . ."

"Give me the gun, and we promise to tell you everything." I held out my hand.

"Everything?"

"Yes," Daniel said.

My heart thudded against my chest at least forty times before Charity finally lowered the rifle and handed it to me. I passed it quickly over to Daniel as Charity took a lurching step forward and fell into my arms, crying like the little girl I knew she no longer was.

I held Charity for a good long while before she sank into the fallen leaves that were scattered across the dead lawn. She pulled her knees into her chest and asked us to start from the very beginning. Daniel gave her a brief overview of the history of the Urbat, but he let me tell the story of our lives over the last year—probably because his memory was still a bit spotty. I noticed he listened just as intently as Charity did when I covered the happenings of the last week.

I told Charity the truth, but I was careful to leave out personal details. Like the way I'd had to hold Daniel last night to keep him from succumbing to the pull to transform back into the white wolf. I didn't tell her the secrets Daniel and I had shared in the dungeon of Caleb's warehouse. And I figured this wasn't the time or place for Daniel to find out about our engagement if he didn't have any memory of it.

Charity flinched when I told her about Jude. About

211

the things he'd done. Where he'd been for the last several months. And where he was now. "Can I go see him?" she'd asked.

"Not yet," I said, trying to keep my shame from bubbling up in my voice. Here was my not-quite-thirteen-year-old sister, ready to take on the task I'd been dreading for days—and had botched terrifically only yesterday. "I don't think he's ready for that."

Daniel remained silent as I spoke, but he gave me a knowing glance when I said this about Jude. I wondered, when Daniel and I were psychically connected in our dreams, if he'd been able to channel the fear and the pain I felt toward my brother. When I got to the part about what had *really* happened to Dad, Daniel put a soothing hand on my shoulder, and I wished again he'd been there with me in the hospital.

Charity took it all in with a maturity I should have credited her with a long time ago. Her eyes flitted to the rifle that sat next to Daniel in the grass only a couple of times. When I'd caught her up on everything relevant, from the Shadow Kings to the hunting party looking for the wolf that supposedly killed Pete Bradshaw and, lastly, to this morning's run-in with the sheriff and Deputy Marsh, she sighed heavily and pinched her fingers above her nose like she was trying to keep all this new information from leaking out of her brain.

"Okay," she said. "But the thing I still can't figure

out is why everyone keeps saying Pete Bradshaw is dead when he's not."

"I'm sorry, Charity. But he is. I was at the hospital when he passed away two days ago."

She shook her head with such denial it surprised me. "That can't be."

"I know it's hard to hear that someone you know is dead. . . ."

"But he's *not*," she insisted. "I saw Pete Bradshaw when we stopped at a gas station in the city early this morning. He was acting kinda wacko, but he looked pretty darn alive to me."

It took me a full thirty seconds to respond. Like my brain and my mouth decided not to communicate with each other. "Are you sure it was Pete? It wasn't, like, someone who *looked* like him? He might have cousins in town for the funeral."

"Pete doesn't have any cousins. His mom said something about that when they had Thanksgiving dinner with us."

"He doesn't? I thought . . ." I recalled the fact that Pete's only uncle was barely older than we were. Even if he had any cousins, they'd be too young to be mistaken for Pete. "This doesn't make any sense." I'd been there when the doctor pronounced Pete dead in the hospital, and even the news had reported his death. There couldn't have been a mistake. There had to be another explanation. . . .

Charity bit her lip. "So if Pete died, and now he's alive again like Daniel, does that mean he's a werewolf now, too?"

"I don't know." I pushed myself up from the grass. "But I'm going to find out."

Even though it meant I was going to have to do something I never wanted to do again.

Chapter Twenty-one

TRICKS OF THE TRADE

Charity wasn't too happy that I wouldn't let her come with us. Truth is, with this new Pete development, I didn't know what Daniel and I would be heading into, and I didn't want her to get hurt. Before we left, I swore her to utter secrecy and then tasked her with the more-than-important job of covering for me with Aunt Carol.

"When Carol gets up from her nap, tell her I went to the hospital," I instructed Charity before getting into the Corolla with Daniel. "Or that I'm at April's working on a project or something. But I might not be home until late."

Daniel and I headed to his apartment first in order to find him some proper not-pajamas clothes for our mission. I waited on the sofa bed while he changed in the bathroom, and I tried not to dwell on what had *almost* happened the last time we had been alone in this room together. Because of that, I wasn't exactly *allowed* to be in here.

"Sorry I took so long," Daniel said as he came into the living area, wearing dark jeans and a white button-up shirt that was open at the collar and clung to his carved chest. "Had to try three different pairs of pants before I found one that didn't fit like floods."

"I told you I wasn't imagining things. You're *bigger* now." I rose from the bed and walked to him. My hand rested on the hard muscles under his shirtsleeve. "I can't say I'm bothered by the end result. And I'd thought you couldn't get any hotter. . . ." I rocked up on my tiptoes and kissed the curve of his jaw.

Daniel made an appreciative noise. "You looking to calm your nerves before we go?" He bent his head down so his lips could meet mine. Just as I thought he was about to kiss me, his head snapped up at the sound of the apartment door opening. "We've got company."

I let go of Daniel's arm and turned toward the door to find Brent, Ryan, and Zach crowded in the doorway. Slade stood farther behind them on the concrete stairs that led down to the apartment.

"We heard voices down here," Ryan said. "Thought we should check it out. Didn't want anyone breaking into alpha's place while he's gone."

Brent elbowed Ryan in the chest and then gestured to Daniel, who stood behind me. "Doesn't look like he's gone anymore."

"Holy crap," Ryan said. "Is that really you?"

"Last time I checked," Daniel said.

"Holy crap!" Ryan bounded into the apartment and came right up to us like an excited pup. Brent and Zach followed. Slade stood in the doorway, looking so shocked I might say he was actually a bit frightened.

"I can't believe it," Ryan said. "I guess I lost Slade's betting pool. I didn't think we'd see you in human form until Thanksgiving, at least."

"You bet a year from next March," Brent said to Ryan.

Ryan reeled on him. "No. I. Didn't."

"Yes, you did. I've got all the bets written down." Brent stuck his hand in his pocket, and Ryan made a move to pounce on him.

"Guys," I said. "Seriously?"

Ryan and Brent dropped their argument and looked at me.

"I guess it's time you officially met the lost boys," I said to Daniel.

"Lost boys? You mean like that old Kiefer Sutherland movie?"

"What? No, I mean like Peter Pan and the lost boys."

"Is she calling us fairies?" Slade asked.

"No," Brent said. "She means the lost boys who never wanted to grow up, and got into mischief with Peter Pan."

"Still sounds like fairies to me." Slade crossed his tattooed arms in front of his chest.

"Still sounds like that Kiefer Sutherland movie to me." Daniel smirked.

"We were in the play together, like, seven years ago. You were mad because my mom made you wear tights, but you wanted to be a pirate."

Daniel held his hand up. "Partial amnesia here, remember? I must have blocked out any and all recollections associated with said tights."

Brent, Zach, and Ryan laughed. Slade almost cracked a smile.

"Well, anyway," I said, "I was trying to say that it's about time you met your pack."

"In person, that is." Daniel stretched his hand out toward Zach. "I'm sorry, like I said, my memory is a little messed up. I don't remember names."

"This is Zach," I said as Daniel shook hands with him. "The youngest is Ryan. The obnoxious one is Brent."

"I respect that assessment," Brent said, and awkwardly bumped knuckles with Daniel instead of a handshake.

"And this is Slade." I gestured to him in the doorway.

Daniel stuck his fist out toward Slade, and I swear the tattooed-covered street racer flinched away from it at first. After what seemed like a second of contemplation, he smacked his fist down on top of Daniel's. A typical guy greeting.

"But there were five of you, weren't there?" Daniel turned back to Ryan and the others. "Where is he?"

"Marcos." I shoved my hands in my pockets. "He died in the explosion at the warehouse."

The boys dropped their heads, as if in a moment of silence for their friend.

Daniel nodded. "I remember feeling your loss."

"We should probably get going. I've already sent a text asking for the meet-up."

"Right," Daniel said.

"What're you up to?" Ryan asked.

"We've got a matter to take care of." I picked up the Corolla keys from the sofa bed. "Might get a little dicey."

"Bring us," Ryan said. "For backup."

"Yeah," the others agreed.

Daniel shifted uncomfortably next to me. I knew it would irritate him to have four shadows, but I was glad to see that the devotion of these reformed SKs hadn't waned one bit now that Daniel was no longer the white wolf.

"I don't mind busting some heads for you." Brent punched his fist into his palm, looking tough and yet still very sarcastic at the same time.

"I think this matter may call for a more delicate approach," I said.

"Okay," Daniel said, and propelled Brent out the door with the others. "Let's go. We'll fill you in on the way."

TWENTY MINUTES LATER

As part of the delicate approach, we decided it would

be best if I arrived at the meet-up alone—didn't want to spook Talbot before I could get answers.

The only problem was, the moment I saw him leaning against a tree at the farthest end of the churchyard, where I'd texted him to meet me, any idea of handling him *delicately* vanished from my mind.

Talbot stood up and shoved his hands into his pockets when he saw me coming. Stubble painted his face as if it had been over a day since he'd shaved, and he wore the same clothes I'd last seen him in. I must not have been able to stop my emotions from showing on my face, because a strange looked passed over his eyes—kind of like guilt—before he plastered on his warmest "aw shucks" farm-boy, dimpled smile. "I knew you wouldn't be able to stay away from me for long. You have no idea how happy I am you decided—"

"What the hell did you do?" I asked as I approached.

A confused look settled in Talbot's eyes. "Nothing . . . I was just sitting here."

"That's not what I'm talking about." My hand went flying, and I hit him in the sternum with the flat of my palm, slamming him against the tree trunk. The branches above us shuddered. A flutter of autumn leaves fell to the ground. A bright orange one landed in his brown hair. I had to stand up on my tiptoes to get in his face.

"Whoa, kid. If you wanted to get me in a compromising position, all you had to do was ask."

"Stop it!" I grabbed him by the collar of his flannel shirt. "You need to tell me *exactly* what happened to Pete Bradshaw."

Since the moment it was revealed that Talbot had been working for Caleb, that he was one of the Shadow Kings, I'd suspected that he'd had something to do with the attack on Pete Bradshaw that had put him in a coma. After all, Pete had been found in the dojo, where Talbot and I had trained, with an *SK* spray painted next to his body. Not to mention that Talbot had witnessed an altercation between Pete and me the night before at the Depot. And I'd seen how angry Talbot had gotten when he'd heard that Pete had been harassing me.

"You attacked him, didn't you? After I begged you to leave him be. What did you *do* to him?"

Talbot just stared at me. He blinked a couple of times. "What are you talking about . . . ?" He gave me a look like he was afraid I knew something I shouldn't.

"Don't pretend you didn't have anything to do with that attack on Pete. You know what happened to him. I watched him die two days ago, but my sister saw him hanging out near a gas station in the city this morning. Tell me how that's possible." I let go of his shirt. "Did you infect him? Is he an Urbat now or something?"

Talbot swore, loudly. "This is what I was afraid of," he said under his breath. "He's not an Urbat, Grace. Damn it. If what you say is true, then Pete's an Akh."

"An Akh?" Akhs were bloodthirsty and conniving,

and they could psychically control their victims by staring into their eyes.

"He must have been infected by an Akh when he was attacked." Talbot brushed the leaf out of his hair. "*I* didn't attack Pete that night . . . because you asked me not to—"

"You didn't?" My voice was more than tinged with incredulity.

He looped his thumbs behind his big brass belt buckle. "No. You were already having an effect on me. Normally, I would have torn the guy apart and not given it a second thought, but since you asked me to leave him alone, I couldn't bring myself lay a hand on him."

"Seriously?"

"Yeah." He rocked back on his heels. He took in a long breath and then said quickly as he blew it back out: "But I may have ordered a couple of Caleb's Akhs to do the job for me."

"*Nice.*" I threw my hands up. "Because that was so much better?"

"What was I supposed to do, Grace? He was harassing you. He looked at you like you were another notch on his belt. I saw the fear in your eyes after he came up to you. I couldn't let him get away with it. I did it for you."

"For me? Someone I know is dead, or undead, or whatever, and you say you did it for me. Is that supposed to make me feel better?"

"That was the old me."

"You're *still* the old you."

"If I were, then I wouldn't have tried to fix it. I tried to take care of the problem in the hospital, but those stupid monitors went off."

"Hospital?" Something that had been nagging at me since yesterday resurfaced in my head. "Oh my—*You* were the cousin." The nurse in Pete Bradshaw's room had said that he'd had a cousin come visit him right before he crashed. I thought back to when I'd accidentally hugged Talbot in the hospital's stairwell. The angle we were standing at . . . He hadn't come from *up* the stairs, he'd come from the doorway of the ICU's lobby. He'd been headed *out* of the ICU. Taking the stairs for a quick getaway, no doubt. "Pete was the *thing* you had to take care of?"

I took a step back. Then another two. "Did you go to the hospital to finish off Pete? Did you *kill* him?"

How had my life come to the point where, in less than forty-eight hours, counting my run-in with Jude, I'd have to ask two different people I knew if they'd killed someone?

I mean, *seriously*?

"No. I'd heard rumors around town that they'd found bite marks on Pete's body, which made me suspect that his coma was actually an incubation period for an Akh infestation. I went to confirm my suspicions, but his oxygen levels crashed almost as soon as I entered the room and his oxygen monitor went crazy. I got out of there as fast as I could. That's when I ran into you in the stairwell."

"And if the monitors hadn't gone crazy? What would you have done?"

"If I had been sure he'd been infected—which apparently he has been—I would have put a stake through his heart."

"You'd have killed him?"

"Only so you wouldn't have to."

My mouth popped open, but Talbot went on before I could I respond.

"Pete isn't Pete anymore. Think of it this way: he's just a demon walking around wearing a Pete suit. He might look like Pete, he might sound like Pete, he'll even have Pete's memories, but it's very important that you don't forget that he *isn't* Pete. Especially when he comes for you."

"Comes for me?"

"The Akh inside of him will not only retain his memories, he'll also take on parts of Pete's personality. The bad parts. Only amplified. Pete had it out for you before he was infected and died—which means you're probably one of the first people he's going to come looking for after he's gotten over the feeding-frenzy stage, and his memories start to come back." Talbot let out a few more swear words. "There's already been one killing— that nurse at the hospital. I should have suspected Pete as soon as I heard about it. I was so busy wallowing, I didn't even think—"

"You're saying *Pete* was the one who killed that nurse?" I felt a pang of guilt for even suspecting Jude.

"Yes. I think so. Akhs are born hungry. They need to feed off of both blood and psychic energy in insane amounts to survive the first few days. Which means he'll be killing indiscriminately at first. But after that, it's only a matter of time before he starts seeking out people from his former life. . . ."

"What?" I thought about Charity encountering Pete at that gas station, grateful she'd only seen him through the car window as they'd pulled away. But then I thought about Pete's mother, Ann. Would he go home and find her once his memories came back? And where was I on Pete's potential list of victims?

Talbot grabbed my arm and started pulling me toward his truck, which was parked behind the parish. "We're going to have to kill Pete Bradshaw . . . *again*," he said, sounding excited by the idea.

"Wait."

I put my hand on top of his. He stopped pulling me toward his truck and looked down at our two hands touching.

"Come on, Grace. You and me on the demon hunt again. Just like what we trained for. Just like it was meant to be."

I gave him a slight smile. He really was happy about

the idea of our hunting together again. "How are we even going to find Pete?"

"New Akhs are predictable because of their hunger. He'll seek out whatever place has the most psychic and sexual energy wafting off of it. He'll be able to smell it. Somewhere like a big party. Normally, new Akhs flock to the Depot. That's how we recruited so many of them to the Shadow Kings. But now that the Depot is no more, he'll have to find somewhere else." He snapped his fingers. "I know just the place."

"Where?" I stepped closer to him.

"There's a trance party tonight."

"A what party?"

"Trance party. You know how Akhs can put their victims into trances by staring into their eyes? They do it to feed off a human's psychic energy and mess with their free will."

"Yeah." I knew all to well. I'd almost been killed the last time it happened to me.

"Well, a trance party is kind of like a rave, except humans use Akhs to get high instead of Ecstasy."

"You mean people go to these parties and willingly let Akhs feed off of them?"

"Pretty much. The Akhs get to feed without a hunt. The humans get high and let someone take away their free will for a night. Some people get off on that."

"Eww." I made a gagging face. "But aren't people afraid the Akhs will feed too much off of them and they'll die?"

"It happens," Talbot said. "Especially if new Akhs are in the mix. They don't come just to get a quick fix; they feed to kill. But I guess the danger is part of the thrill for some people. And a lot of them are just stupid kids who don't really know what's going on. Most don't remember in the morning."

"And we'll be able to hunt down Pete there?" I gazed up into his green eyes. At the same time I reached into my jacket pocket and clicked a button on my phone.

"I'd bet my truck on it."

"But where is the party?"

"There's always one a week or two after Halloween in a haunted house that's just been closed down for the season. Before they strike all the creepy sets. Rumor has it, tonight's trance party is going to be at Frightmare Farms."

"That old farm outside Rose Crest? Didn't that place get shut down for being unsafe?" April and I used to frequent the corn maze at that old farm-turned-Halloween-attraction, but we didn't make it this year because it got shut down opening night after some kid fell through the rotten floorboards in the haunted barn. I'd heard the owners had left it abandoned the way it was, rather than spend the money to get it up to code.

"You can see the appeal for this kind of party then?" Talbot reached out like he wanted to caress his fingers along my cheek. "But we're going to have to cover up that pretty face of yours, find you a disguise. The party will be crawling with Gelals and Akhs. I wouldn't be surprised if a few Shadow Kings showed up for recruiting."

Shadow Kings. That's what I was afraid he was going to say.

"People wear pretty crazy stuff to these things, so you won't stand out in a costume," Talbot said. "I don't want any SKs getting wind of us being there. I imagine I'm the last person they'll feel like being friendly to."

"That's okay," I said, taking a large step back, away from him and his truck. "Because you're not coming."

"What? You think I'm going to let you go alone?"

"I won't be alone." I glanced over at the motorcycle driven by a lone rider pulling into the parking lot next to us. The green Corolla followed just behind him. Right on cue. "You're just not coming with us." I backed away quickly.

"What's going on?" Talbot started to come after me, but he stopped when the motorcyclist got off his bike and removed his helmet. Talbot's eyes widened as he recognized Daniel. The four lost boys got out of the car and stood behind their alpha.

"So he's back?" Talbot asked.

"Yep." I couldn't help smiling a bit and thinking of that song from the oldies station my Grandpa Kramer used to listen to. *My boyfriend's back, and your gonna be in trouble. . . .*

"Despite your best efforts, I hear," Daniel said, tucking his helmet under his arm.

Talbot's mouth hung open with shock, but his hands balled into fists.

"Do you need any help here?" Daniel asked me.

"Nope. I got what I came for." I looked at Talbot. "Thanks for the information. We'll be taking care of the Pete problem without you."

"This was a setup?" Talbot asked. I could see the storm brewing behind his eyes. He took a stride toward me, but the four lost boys stepped forward, creating a barrier between us. Talbot stepped back slightly. "But I thought . . . you and me, Grace. This is what we're supposed to do together. . . ."

"There is no you and me, Talbot." I got on the motorcycle with Daniel. "You're not a part of this anymore."

Tricking Talbot into thinking I was going to go hunting with him, and then leaving him in the lurch, felt cruel. But he needed to know that despite his lies and betrayal, I'd gotten Daniel back—and I didn't need Talbot anymore.

"I need you to realize, Talbot," I said to him, solemnly, "when it comes down to it, I'll *always* choose Daniel."

Chapter Twenty-two

PARTY ON

April was all over the needing-to-wear-a-disguise thing. I was starting to wonder if she had a frequent buyers' reward at the thrift shop/costume closet in Apple Valley. We'd convened at her house to get ready for the trance party, and I watched in awe as she pulled outfit after outfit from her closet.

"Wow, you're really taking your role as my Alfred seriously," I said. When April had learned about my quest to become a superhero—a quest I'd all but given up on while trying to find a way to bring Daniel back to me—she'd insisted on becoming the Alfred to my Batman. Which, unfortunately, often involved a BeDazzler.

I seriously wouldn't be surprised if she'd put "superhero stylist" as one of her qualifications on her Trenton application.

"I design when I'm anxious," April said. "And I've had a lot to be anxious about lately." She pulled a yellow Day-Glo jumpsuit with a matching cape from the pile. "I put this one together after you got kidnapped by the Shadow Kings."

Daniel smiled wryly.

It was nice to know April cared so much.

"I even collected a few things for Daniel . . . you know, just in case he ever turned back into a human." She picked up what looked like a bundle of black leather. She handed it to Daniel. "Glad you're back, by the way." She smiled at him.

"Thanks." Daniel unrolled the bundle. It turned out to be a long leather trench coat. "This I can handle," he said.

"Only twenty-five bucks at the thrift store. Can you believe it? Pair that with some black pants and black shirt, and you're good to go." She picked up another bundle of clothing and handed it to me. "Grace, on the other hand, needs a little more *oomph*."

"These are pleather shorts," I said, holding up the pair of fake black leather Daisy Dukes.

"You wear them with fishnets." She handed me the tights and a lacy black cami. "There's a jacket for you, too."

"Yeah. But. These. Are. *Pleather.* Shorts."

"And. You. Wear. Them. With. Fishnets," she responded, as if I hadn't heard her properly the first time. She pushed me toward the bathroom to get changed.

Daniel smiled so wide I thought his face was going to crack.

NEARLY MIDNIGHT

Daniel was oddly quiet as I drove the Corolla—it'd been too cold for the motorcycle, considering my short-shorts—down an old country road that led to Frightmare Farms, just outside of Rose Crest. The boys followed in April's red hatchback, borrowed as payback for my ridiculous outfit.

Shortly after the "pleather shorts incident," Daniel became more and more withdrawn as time drew closer to go hunt down Pete at the trance party. He hadn't even protested April's insistence that he wear the black mask she'd pilfered from a Zorro costume. The perfect finishing touch for his "Bad A outfit"—as she put it.

I'd figured he must have been bothered that I'd had to turn to Talbot for information, but the way he stared far out the passenger's-side window made me worry that something deeper was eating at him.

I parked in a field full of cars outside the decrepit "haunted" farmhouse. Possessed-looking scarecrows hung limp from their stands in front of the entrance gate, and part of the roof of the barn that loomed behind the house looked like it could cave in at any given moment.

I knew from experience that a corn maze stretched out for a good five acres beyond the barn. Secluded from town, I could see why Akhs would choose this place for one of their creepy trance parties—and based on the crowds of teens that headed from the parking field to the farm, they'd pulled in a pretty good turnout.

"Are you okay?" I asked as I pulled the keys out of the ignition.

Daniel shrugged.

"I'm sorry you've gotten dragged into this mess. And I'm sorry you had to see Talbot."

"It's not any of that." Daniel sighed heavily and pushed his hand through his golden hair. "I've been trying not to let it get to me all day. Move on and get the job done, you know. It's just that . . . she looked at me like I was a monster."

"Who?" I hadn't seen anything like that from April.

"Charity." He looked down at his finely muscled hands. "After I was cured, before my powers came back—when I was normal for once—there was a time when I thought I'd never have to deal with anyone looking at me like that again. Calling me that. And now, I don't even know what I am anymore. . . . Maybe 'monster' is all I'll ever be."

"Daniel." I placed my hand on his shoulder. "You are not a monster. And no, you're not *normal* anymore. You never have been, really."

He winced. Being *normal* was what Daniel had

always desired more than anything. Normal meant Trenton, and family, and having a life. But I saw in him a potential to have all of that and so much more.

"You're something greater than that. I really think you're like an—"

"Angel?" He shook his head and looked out the window instead of at me. "I don't think so."

"Daniel, I really think you can use your powers for good. I thought that before you were even cured. I know you're skeptical, and I know you've always felt that being an Urbat made you a monster. But Gabriel told me about the original Urbat, and the good things they were created to do. Like protect people. Like we're about to do now. I think, together, we can be heroes."

"Didn't the quest to become a hero almost get you killed?"

"Only because I was trying to do it alone—or not exactly alone, but with the wrong help. But now that I have you to be a hero with me, it could totally work."

A bubbling of hope trilled up my body into my heart, and I suddenly wondered, if I could convince Daniel that his powers could be blessing instead of a curse— that he could become a hero—then maybe there was a chance to convince other Urbat, like Sirhan's pack, that they could do it, too. I could help them reclaim their blessings—just like Gabriel had said I could.

"I've never seen myself as a hero," Daniel said.

"Maybe it's time you start."

I could tell Daniel was about to protest, but he then suddenly sat up in his seat. "He's here."

I looked up just in time to see Pete Bradshaw, looking all too alive, slink through the line of teens gathered outside the entrance gate. A couple of burly-looking guys stood aside to let him enter the farmhouse.

"Bouncers," I said. "I didn't think an Akh party would have bouncers."

"I'm sure they'd want to keep people like us from crashing their fun."

"Right." I took in a deep breath and let it out in a puff. "So this is it? The end of our story with Pete Bradshaw? As much trouble as he's given us, I never thought I'd be the one to kill him."

Daniel put his hand on my arm. "Are you sure you're ready for this?"

"I've killed a demon before. He was a Gelal, but according to Talbot, Akhs die the same way. They just explode into dust instead of burning acid. It should be cleaner, I guess."

"That's not what I meant." Daniel looked me right in the eyes. "I know Pete isn't really Pete anymore. But we still *knew* him. You guys were friends once. Killing a demon wearing the face of your old friend, that's got to affect you differently than just killing some random Gelal. And we both know what happened last time. . . ."

I bowed my head. "I know." The first, and last, time I'd killed a demon, I'd experienced such a power rush that I'd almost lost control and given in to the wolf. "But I think I'm ready. I need to clean up the messes I've made."

Because deep down, I knew Pete's undeath had happened, ultimately, because of me. Even if I wasn't the one who killed him the first time, it was my responsibility to do it now.

"Either way, I want you to wear this. Maybe it will help you avoid any side effects." Daniel removed his moonstone necklace and handed it to me.

"Thanks," I said, remembering what it had been like to go into battle against a demon without one.

Daniel opened the weapons pack that April had sent us with. He handed me a stake bedazzled with bright pink and orange gemstones, and he selected for himself a stake that had a gold wolf's head attached to the end.

"Sure you don't want the sparkly one?" I dangled my stake in front of him.

"I don't do sparkles," Daniel said. He cracked a smile for the first time since we left April's. "But the whole ensemble looks pretty darn hot on you."

"Wait." I pulled down the black mask, adorned with three matching pink gemstones at the temples, over the upper half of my face. "What do you think now?"

"Cute, but I prefer seeing your face." Daniel tied his own black mask over his eyes. Luckily, his was free of any sparkles. "Are you sure you're ready for this?"

I nodded. "What about you? How's your shoulder?"

The way he'd been carrying himself all day, I'd almost forgotten about the bullet wound. I realized that it might not be the best idea for us to head into battle with one of us injured.

Daniel rolled his shoulders. "It stings like crazy, but I'll be okay. I think it's even started to heal a bit."

"That's good."

"Let's go." He reached for the door handle.

I put my hand on his arm. "Thank you."

His dark eyes blinked behind the mask. "What for?"

"For not suggesting that I stay in the car while you go in and take care of things for me."

"We're partners in this."

"Good," I said.

We got out of the car. The lost boys, wearing various Halloween masks, fell in behind us and we made our way toward the farmhouse through the crowd of teens who were clamoring to get past the bouncers. Some of the partygoers were dressed in costumes, others just in assortments of black, camo, lace, and leather. I wondered if they were eager to get inside the trance party because they knew what was going on in there—or because they didn't have a clue. Part of me wanted to shout at them to run away.

"Just act like you belong here, and no one will stop us," Daniel said, bypassing all the wannabes standing in line. I called on my superpowered balance in order not to wobble in the high-heeled black boots that went with my ensemble as we strode right up to the large bouncers. Daniel gave one of them a slight nod. He let us pass.

Daniel pushed open the door, and techno music burst into my eardrums. Inside reminded me of the Depot, with strobe lights, dancers, and plenty of foggy smoke wafting in the air. The biggest difference here was the decrepit farmhouse furniture interspersed with garish haunted-house decor, looking all the more frightening in the flashing lights and smoke.

"Fan out," Daniel said to the boys. "I want you to act as lookouts only. No engaging with any of the Shadow Kings."

I knew he hadn't wanted them coming along into a potential fight—didn't want to feel responsible for them if anything went wrong. But I'd convinced him that they should be here. They were his pack after all.

"This place reeks," I said, gagging on the mixture of smells in the air: alcohol, perfume, cigarettes, decaying wood from the house itself, the must from yellowed drapes that hung from the blacked-out windows, and an underlying scent probably only someone like Daniel or me could pick out—like garbage that's been baking out in the sun. The stench of sour milk and rotting meat.

"Akhs and Gelals." I covered my nose. "This place is crawling with them."

"Feeding grounds," Daniel said. He looked at me. "You okay? I know this isn't your scene."

The first time I'd been to a party like this, at Daniel's

apartment last year, I'd run away scared. The second time was when April and I went to the Depot looking for Jude, and we'd had to be rescued and dragged out of there by Talbot. The third time, I'd had to leave before I lost control and hurt someone.

But this time, I wasn't leaving the party until I'd kicked some major butt.

"Yeah," I said, and led him toward a crowd of dancing teens in the family room of the house. "There he is," I whispered, and nodded my head toward Pete Bradshaw. He lurked in the shadows behind a group of girls dressed in matching red-devil costumes. The girls danced in a circle, close to each other in a fashion that would have been provocative if their arms and legs weren't moving in a such a weird, jerking sort of way. Almost like someone else was directing their motions. Like puppets on strings.

"Why are they moving like that?" I scanned the room, noticing more people dancing and moving in that odd way. A girl standing on a tabletop, dressed as a fairy, looked particularly horrible the way her arms moved—like she was trying desperately to get them to stop but couldn't.

"They're in trances," Daniel said. "If an Akh stares into your eyes long enough, it can keep you in a hypnotic state for quite some time, even without the continued eye-to-eye connection. These people are being controlled by someone else."

"And they do this on purpose?"

"It's quite the high," he said in a way that made me wonder if he'd tried it before in his former life. "They feel stoned. But their brains are starting to fight it. Hence the jerking movements."

I tore my sight off the gruesome dancers and looked back at Pete. He'd narrowed his sights on a girl in a curly blonde wig, dressed as a sexy vampire. Velvet cape and all. Her back was to me, and I couldn't see her face, but I watched as she tapped the shoulder of one of the dancing devil girls. "Kristy, I want to go," I heard her say. The other girl didn't respond. "Kristy, please? Answer me." Something about her voice made me cringe. It was laced with so much fear. Her friends had probably dragged her here, and she hadn't known what she was getting herself into.

Pete must have heard the fear also. He licked his lips as he stared at her. I knew what he was thinking: easy prey. And I doubted it was just her psychic energy he wanted to feed off of.

I leaned in close to Daniel and pecked a kiss against his throat, making it look like we were merely on the dance floor to make out. "Pete's on the prowl," I whispered into Daniel's ear.

"Then he'll be easily baited." Daniel kissed me. "What do you think?"

Our plan had been to find away to lure Pete to a secluded area of the haunted house—in order to kill him without attracting any attention.

Daniel caressed his finger along my face. He pecked a few kisses behind my ear and then whispered, "There," turning my head slightly toward an arched doorway, guarded by two more freaky scarecrows. A sign, painted in garish letters the color of blood, read, LIBRARY OF HORRORS: ENTER AT YOUR OWN RISK. A yellow X of caution tape blocked it off from the rest of the party.

"See if you can get him to follow you in there," Daniel said. "I'll be waiting."

"You think he'll go for it?"

"He's a horny, hungry, teenage boy. Believe me, he'll go for you. Undead or not." Daniel gave me one last kiss, and then we broke apart. "Just don't let him get close enough to realize who you are before you're alone. I don't want anyone else getting hurt."

I watched him quietly maneuver through the party and then slip into the library. I turned my attention back to Pete just in time to see him make a move for the vampire-costumed girl. He put his hand on her shoulder, making her jump. He leaned in close to her face.

"Don't look into his eyes," I whispered.

But she must have, because only a matter of seconds later, she was holding his hand as he pulled her through the crowd of dancers. She didn't seem to notice his talonlike fingernails—a classic sign of an Akh.

I started to go after them, but before I made it more than two quick steps, someone else stepped out in front of me, blocking my path. He wore a long brown trench coat over what looked a Lone Ranger costume: blue shirt, leather pants, cowboy hat, and a black eye mask that was supposed to obscure his identity. But I'd recognize his bright green eyes—and belt buckle—anywhere.

"Talbot, what the hell are you doing here?"

"I want to help you." By the smell of his breath and the whiskey bottle in his hand, I could tell he'd been drinking.

"I told you I didn't need it. Daniel and I are taking care of things." I tried to step around him, but he countered my movements.

"But there's more going on here than you think. There're other—"

"Yeah, I know. This place is crawling with Gelal and Akhs. You taught me how to recognize their scent, remember?" I looked over his shoulder so I wouldn't lose sight of Pete and the girl. They were still making their way through the crowd, presumably toward the exit door on the other side of the room that led to the grounds behind the farmhouse. So much for getting a chance to lure Pete to the library.

"Yeah, I do remember," Talbot said. "And that's why I should be the one here with you. This is what we do, you and me. We're the demon hunters." He opened his trench coat and showed me his long steel sword taped inside. "Daniel is completely untrained."

"Something tells me Daniel doesn't need training."

I pushed Talbot away from me. "Go home." I marched past him, looking at Pete and his prey as they went out the exit door. The girl was angled so I could see her face for the first time—and despite the curly blonde wig, I recognized her.

Katie Summers.

This must have been the party she'd invited me to. The party her friends from the city—who were presumably the tranced-out dancing devil girls—had heard about.

I swore and tried to go after them, but Talbot caught me by the hand, trying to stop me from getting away.

"Grace, you need me."

I did not have time for this. "I said go home!" I shouted, and punched him across the jaw with all my might. He let go of my hand and stumbled backward into a dancing girl. The two fell to the ground, tangled with each other. His bottle of whiskey sloshed all over them.

I pushed my way through the gyrating crowd as fast as I could, which didn't feel fast enough. When I made it to the door, I flung it open and dashed out into the dark farmyard. Even adjusting my eyes to night vision, I couldn't see Pete or Katie among the hay bales, scarecrows, and other freakish Halloween decorations. The heels of my boots sank into the moist ground as I headed toward the dilapidated barn, and I realized I should be looking for footprints. I scanned the ground and found two sets of prints headed for the wall of cornstalks just beyond the barnyard.

Great, I thought. *They've gone into the corn maze.*

I pulled out my cell phone and typed out a text to Daniel: *Corn maze. Pete's got Katie.* I hit the Send button, but the text didn't go through. Crap! Cell-phone reception had always been spotty in the farmland that stretched between Rose Crest and Apple Valley.

A noise that sounded like either a girl's laugher or a whimper echoed from somewhere in the maze. I hit Send one more time, then stuck my phone into the pocket of my leather jacket, hoping it would eventually go through. I jogged into the maze. The hay-strewn ground made it impossible to make out footprints, so I had to follow Pete's smell and the whimper-laugh, which sounded every few seconds, the best I could. I took two rights, two lefts, three more rights, and then rounded another left and almost ran smack into someone wearing tattered, black robes. I jumped back and almost let out a yelp, but then I realized it was just a dummy dressed like the Grim Reaper. A very real spider was busy spinning a web in the curve of the Reaper's scythe, and some sort of sticky bloodlike substance smeared the dull metal blade.

I was about to turn back, thinking I'd hit a dead end, when I heard that pitiful laugh again, coming from just beyond the Reaper. That's when I noticed the dummy was blocking the entrance to a square-shaped clearing in the maze. I ducked under the spider and the scythe into the opening to find more ghoulish dummies lurking in the square. One figurine looked like he was supposed to be both Dr. Jekyll and Mr. Hyde, and an orange-painted knockoff of Frankenstein's monster loomed in the corner. Just beyond a dummy of a totally inaccurate werewolf, I saw Pete Bradshaw holding Katie in his arms.

At first it looked like a lover's embrace, but I knew better. Katie's eyes were locked with his, and his talonlike fingernails scratched at her neck, leaving row after row of bloody cuts. With each tear of his talons, Katie would start to whimper, only for the sound to shift into a strained giggle. Like Pete was using his psychic powers to convince her that she liked it.

My stomach already felt ill from the sight in front of me, but as Pete raised his blood-smeared fingers to his lips and licked them—the way I'd relish a spatula covered in brownie batter—I almost lost the stale taquitos from April's freezer that I'd eaten for dinner.

I took three deep breaths to keep from hurling, then walked right up to Pete with my hands on my hips. "No fair!" I said in my whiniest voice. "I want a turn."

Pete's head snapped in my direction, his pointy teeth bared and his lips smeared with blood. Katie's head lolled back over his arms. "Go away," he snarled.

"Whatever." I grabbed Katie's limp body and yanked her out of the way. "Why should she have all the fun?" I made sure Katie could stand on her own two feet and then pushed her aside. "Get lost, girl."

Katie stumbled forward and then started walking in a lazy circle, like she was in a trance—which I guess is normal since she was. Hopefully, she'd stay dazed through what I had to do next.

"This one's mine," I said, stepping closer to Pete.

"I am?" Pete asked. He looked me up and down, taking in the tall boots, fishnet tights, little pleather shorts, lacy cami, mysterious eye mask, and my tough-girl leather jacket. He cocked his head in appreciation. "I am," he said.

"You better be." I grabbed him by the collar of his shirt and pulled him close like I was about to kiss him. "I was promised a trance when I came to this party. Now give me what I want."

"My pleasure," he said, and clasped his taloned hands on either side of my face. "I always loved the feisty girls." But just as he was about to look me in the eyes, I clamped my eyelids shut and kneed him as hard as I could in the groin.

Pete's hands fell away from my face, and he wailed as he doubled over, coughing—proving that even the undead feel it where it counts.

I didn't get much time for satisfaction before Pete roared and came charging at me with his fangs and talons bared. "I'm gonna kill you for that!"

I swung out of his way, and he tackled the werewolf

dummy instead of me. He tore off one of its limbs and threw it to the ground.

"Really? Are you sure?" I asked. "'Cause I'm pretty certain this is actually the part where I kill you."

"What?" Pete asked. His lips dropped over his Akh fangs.

I pulled out my stake from my jacket's inside pocket. "Yep. That's pretty much what's going to happen."

Pete screamed and lunged at me. I twisted out of his path and sent a kick into his back. He stumbled toward the Frankenstein statue. I was feeling pretty good about having him cornered, and my ability to be done with him soon, when a dazed Katie Summers stumbled and swayed right into him.

"No!" I shouted as he grabbed her by the neck, his sharp fingers wrapping around her throat. She didn't even try to scream, but I could see the panic behind her glazed-over eyes, as she tried to fight her way out of her trance.

Pete propelled her forward by his grasp on her neck. "Let me pass or I'll rip her throat out."

I scrambled out of his way—what else could I have done—and let him drag Katie by the neck to the clearing's exit. He was going to escape into the depths of the maze. I lifted my stake to throw at his back as he crouched to climb under the Grim Reaper's scythe, but then he stopped and turned halfway toward me, making it impossible for me to aim at his heart.

"Don't worry," he said. "I've got your scent. We'll find you when I'm done with her."

We?

Pete let out a cackle that sounded more like the screeching of a bird . . . but then the metal blade of the Reaper's scythe came crashing down on his head. He screamed and let go of Katie. She sank to the ground, seemingly unconscious, just as Daniel burst out from behind the Reaper's tattered robes and into the clearing.

I practically cheered when I saw him.

Pete screeched with anger.

Daniel smacked him in the head again with the scythe. It looked painful, but the blade was too dull to do any real damage. Daniel cast the weapon aside and grabbed Pete with his bare hands. Pete clawed at his grip and then went for Daniel's neck, but Daniel pushed him away just in time. Pete whirled around and made a lunge at me instead. He sent a clawed hand at my face, ripping my mask off.

It fell to the ground, and my first instinct was to try to hide my face, to keep Pete from recognizing me, but really, what was the point now? Part of me *wanted* him to know it was me who was taking him down.

A shrill laugh escaped Pete's lips. "As if I didn't know it was you."

"What?" I asked. As far as I knew, Pete should have thought I was your average mild-mannered pastor's daughter. Not a demon hunter.

I jumped out of the way as Pete sent another clawed swipe at my face.

Daniel grabbed him from behind.

Pete struggled in his grasp. "They said you'd come for me!" he snarled. "They were waiting for me outside the hospital when I was reborn. They told me that all I had to do was kill that nurse and you'd eventually come looking for me. And they'd be waiting."

"Who?" Daniel asked.

"My new family." Pete broke free from Daniel's grasp and tried to flip Daniel over his shoulder. Daniel was too quick and sent several punches into Pete's side.

Pete grunted in pain. He stumbled away to the corner near the Frankenstein monster, holding his rib cage. At that moment he looked just like the old Pete Bradshaw. Not like some monster we'd come here to kill. For a second I wondered if I could still do it.

"Who are you talking about?" I asked, afraid I might already know.

Pete took in a deep, ragged breath through his nose. "Can't you smell them coming? The people who want you dead." Pete let out a sharp scream and ran at me. He looked like a rabid bat, claws extended, fangs bared. He was going for the kill.

As much as I hated to do it before getting a real answer, I thrust my stake deep into Pete's chest. I let go, and he fell into the wall of brittle cornstalks. He clawed at the stake with his talonlike nails, scratching sparkly jewels from the hilt. He got purchase on the handle and pulled it out of his chest. It made a sound like something ripping through a paper bag. He looked at it with disdain and then threw it at my feet. A wicked smile curled on Pete's lips, and he laughed.

"They're gonna kill you," he said, as his body burst into dust.

I clamped my hands over my face, not only so I wouldn't inhale little Pete particles, but also because I couldn't believe I'd actually killed Pete Bradshaw.

"What did he mean by . . . ?" Daniel started to ask, but a loud growling noise cut him off. Both our heads snapped toward the origin of the sound. It came from somewhere behind the Grim Reaper.

Another growl followed—from the opposite side of the clearing, beyond the tall cornstalks. Then more growling from outside all four walls of the square-shaped clearing.

"What the . . . ?"

The brittle cornstalks rustled and swayed and the growling grew closer.

"They're coming through the corn," I said.

And we were literally boxed in.

Pete had said that I should have smelled them coming, and now I did. Rotten meat and sour milk. *Ahks and Gelals*, I thought, as dark figures burst through the cornstalks into the clearing. I recognized a few of them right away from my time imprisoned at the warehouse.

Shadow Kings. At least ten of them. Surrounding us from every direction.

"Guess what?" I said to Daniel. "This was a trap."

"I see that," Daniel said.

The circle of monsters slowly closed in on us, their growls melting together into a collective noise that made my eardrums rattle. I snatched up my dusty stake, and Daniel and I stood back to back, our weapons raised.

Chapter Twenty-three

Ambush

The beasts closed in on us, slowly, as if savoring the drama of it all.

"Now would be a good time to pull out some of your true alpha mojo," I said to Daniel. "Maybe convert some of these guys to our team?"

"Good idea. Except none of these guys are Urbat. My mojo doesn't work on Akhs and Gelals. Caleb is certifiable, but he isn't stupid. He's not going to risk losing any more of his followers to our side."

"Dang. So what do we do now?"

"Fight like hell," Daniel said, and lunged out with his stake at a Gelal who'd broken from the circle and come barreling at us. I was amazed at how fast Daniel moved. The Gelal went flying, clutching at the gaping wound in his chest.

"Watch out for the acid!" I yelled, just as the dead Gelal exploded into acrid green ooze that could melt through just about anything. Daniel moved quickly again, shielding both of us from the rain of burning acid with his long black jacket.

"Oh man, I really liked this coat," he said as the green slime ate holes through the leather.

"Me, too. But better that than your face," I said.

"Good point."

The growl of the demons shifted into a loud screeching, like a chorus of vultures. They chomped their teeth and clacked their claws in our direction. Daniel and I stood, ready for the next one who'd dare break away from the circle.

"I'm just glad you got my text," I said. "Or else I'd be facing these guys alone."

"Yeah. Nine against two isn't the worst odds ever," Daniel said. "Wait, what text? I didn't get a text from you."

"But then how did you know to come to the maze?"

Daniel shrugged. "I just *knew*."

"Huh. Gabriel says you and I are connected . . . Oh crap. How do you feel about the odds of nineteen against two?" I asked, as I noticed a second wave of ten more demons waiting in the stalks of corn. Ready to join the fray when needed.

Daniel swore. "Caleb's been busy."

The high-pitched screech of the monsters reached a

deafening crescendo, and I had to clamp my hands over my ears to keep my eardrums from bursting.

And then, as if someone sucked all the sound out of the clearing with a vacuum, it fell completely silent—every beast cutting off its cry at the exact same moment.

One of the beasts pointed a long claw at us, a Gelal from the smell of him. "First we kill you two, and then we kill every last human at this party," it said. "And then this city will know that the Shadow Kings rule."

"Can you say 'overdramatic'?" I asked.

Daniel snorted. "Yeah, but I don't think he's kidding."

"Kind of wishing we hadn't told the boys to stay inside. A little backup would be nice." Even if we shouted at the top of our lungs, they'd never hear us over the noise of the party. "Well, ready or not," I said as the first wave of nine beasts came rushing at us in a flurry of claws and teeth.

Daniel sprang into action immediately, pulling his coat off and using it to entrap two of the monsters at once, and then flung them into the wall of cornstalks in a move he must have picked up from a Jackie Chan movie or something. He staked both of them before they even knew what had happened. I realized he'd been holding back with Pete.

Daniel went after another one, and I had two demons of my own to deal with. I kicked one away and staked the other.

"Wait," I shouted to Daniel. "Can't you call the boys, like psychically? They always knew what you wanted when you were the white wolf. And you knew I needed you here."

Daniel kicked a demon, sending him flying into the dummy of Dr. Jekyll. "I don't really remember how I did it."

"I don't know. Maybe just think real hard about what you need them to do."

"I'll try." Daniel pointed behind me. "Watch out—"

I felt a sharp stab as a Gelal raked its claws into my back. Screaming in pain, I used my own weight to flip the beast over my shoulder. It scrambled away from me, and my stake sank into the soft ground instead of flesh as I tried to stab it. "Ahh!" I yelled, trying to regain my balance.

Daniel went after the Gelal and wrestled it to the ground.

The sound of rustling cornstalks made me look up just in time to see the ten more beasts come through the corn barrier into the clearing.

"Now would be a great time for that backup," I yelled, as an Akh came at me with vicious swings of his taloned hands.

"I'm working on it," Daniel answered. I heard him grunt, but I wasn't sure if it was in response to the force of taking out another demon, or a cry of pain.

I staked the Akh, and then tried to turn toward

Daniel to check on him, but another Gelal must have noticed my distraction. I caught the sight of it out of the corner of my eye, launching in my direction. I flinched, knowing I wouldn't have time to block its blow, but its body suddenly lurched backward like a dog caught at the end of its lead.

I saw the glint of metal protruding from his chest, and I realized it'd been skewered on the end of a sword. Talbot's sword, I saw, as he came bursting through the wall of cornstalks. He swung his arm with a forceful movement, flinging the dead Gelal off the end of his sword and onto the ground.

I jumped back to avoid the acid spray. "I told you to go home."

"Good thing I didn't listen," he said, seeming far more sober than just a few minutes ago. "I thought I heard someone asking for backup." He stepped out of the way, and Brent, Ryan, Zach, and Slade pushed their way through the cornstalks, all with weapons ready. They rushed right into the clearing and joined Daniel in the fight against the fourteen beasts that remained. Talbot followed, taking off the head of an Akh with the swing of his sword.

Not to be left out, I charged into the mix, sending another Akh I recognized from Caleb's warehouse into Ryan's outstretched stake with a roundhouse kick.

"Now that was awesome," Ryan said, as the Akh burst into dust in front of him. "I always hated that guy." He spun around and went charging after a Gelal that had Brent backed into a corner. I felt like a proud mama for a moment, watching my boys sticking up for each other.

I heard a female shriek from the other side of the clearing, near the exit.

"Look what I found," screeched an Akh.

He stood over Katie Summers, clacking his taloned nails together. Katie screamed again, throwing her arms in front of her face as she lay on the ground.

"Looks like a tasty treat," said the Akh.

"Stop him!" I shouted at Slade, who was closest to them.

Slade jumped into action, knocking the Akh away from Katie with the swing of one of his tattooed arms. He reached out to help Katie up, but then a Gelal jumped on his back and knocked him to the ground. Slade tried to roll away. Before he could, the Gelal pinned Slade down by sitting on his chest, and the Akh who'd tried to attack Katie grabbed him by the face with his long talons.

"Don't look him in the eyes!" I shouted.

But it was too late, the beast had locked eyes with Slade, trapping him in a motionless trance. The Gelal, teeth bared, went for Slade's neck. Before the beast could bite, I threw my stake like a javelin across the clearing, and it skewered the Gelal in the back. It burst to acid on top of the Akh.

The Akh scrambled off of Slade. It screeched like an injured bat as it scurried away into the cornstalks and disappeared into the maze.

I ran to Slade and pulled off my jacket. I used it to wipe the Gelal acid from his arms. He blinked at me, moaning as he came out of the trance. I was about to ask him if he was okay when I heard another shout from Daniel. This time I *knew* it was from pain.

I spun in Daniel's direction and watched as his stake fell from his hand. He clutched at his right shoulder, where his silver-bullet wound was exposed by a gash in his shirt. A Gelal stood in front of Daniel with blood dripping from its claws. The demon had raked its claws over Daniel's already-tender wound.

Daniel tried to crouch to snatch up his stake, but he was too slow, and the Gelal kicked it away. The stake went flying into the depths of the cornstalks. The beast lunged at Daniel, and Daniel dropped his hand from his bleeding shoulder to grab the Gelal by its shoulders. I could see the pain on Daniel's face as the two grappled in hand-to-claw combat. For the first time in this fight, Daniel, weaponless and injured, actually seemed vulnerable.

I reached for my own stake with the intention of throwing it to Daniel, but found that it had almost completely disintegrated, lying in a pool of Gelal acid.

"Heads up!" Talbot shouted. He elbowed an Akh in the face and then flung his sword at Daniel with all his might. It sailed through the air, spinning point over hilt, toward Daniel's face.

I was about to shriek, but Daniel whipped out his left hand and caught the sword in midair by its handle. In a move just as quick, he brought the blade down on the neck of the Gelal and lopped off its head. He spun away from the spray of green acid, and I felt my jaw drop as I watched Daniel, with moves fluid yet forceful, slice through three more demons before they even had time to react.

"Wow," I said, my heart beating quickly in my chest.

"That was killer," said Ryan, watching with just as much awe as Daniel finished off a forth demon.

The other monsters in the clearing hadn't failed to notice Daniel's prowess with the sword, and I watched as the four remaining Akhs and two Gelals backed away. They clawed their way into the wall of cornstalks and disappeared. I could hear their foot-falls as they ran at top speed through the stretches of the maze.

"Should we go after them?" Zach asked. Ryan and Brent looked just as eager to pursue their old gang mates. Slade, looking a bit dizzy himself, sat on the ground next to Katie, his hand on her back as she held her head between her knees like she was trying not to pass out again.

"No," I said. "I don't want you getting separated in that maze with them."

"Aw, come on," Ryan said, practicing swinging his stake the way Daniel had handled the sword.

"My guess is that they're already gone by now." Talbot lifted his cowboy hat and wiped his forehead.

"All the same," Ryan said. "If we chase them, they'll be less likely to regroup and come back."

"Fine then," I said. "Zach and Ryan, you two can go. Stick together and be safe, all right?"

Ryan and Zach went after the probably-already-long-gone demons, whooping and hollering like a couple of lost boys chasing pirates. Brent groaned about being left behind.

"I should go with them." Slade stood, but he didn't seem the most stable on his feet. But maybe that's because Katie was clinging to his legs for support.

"You can stay," I told Slade. "Looks like Katie isn't letting go any time soon."

She looked at me then with eyes that still made her seem a bit dazed and confused. Her mascara smeared in long streaks down her face. "Grace? Is that you? I thought you weren't coming to the party."

I sighed, relieved that she obviously still wasn't quite with it if that was her biggest question. Maybe she wouldn't actually process anything that had just happened. "I changed my mind. Can't pass up a good party." I shrugged.

"This was some party," she said slowly, bobbing her head up and down. She seemed positively high. "Wait, why did you follow me out here? Did you . . . *kill* . . . that guy who was trying to make out with me?"

Uh-oh.

Daniel stepped forward. He tucked the sword behind his back, but he couldn't cover up the bloody tear in his shoulder. "I think someone may have slipped something in your drink, Katie. We followed you to make sure no one took advantage of you."

"Daniel?" She leaned forward, squinting at his eyes behind his mask. "You came, too? I thought you had pneumonia?" She tapped her fingers against her forehead like she was trying to think really hard. "Did you just chop off some guy's head?"

Brent busted up laughing. I gave him a quick glare.

"Okay," I said. "I think Katie's had enough partying for one night." I motioned for Slade to pick her up. "Take care of her, will you?" I asked him.

Slade looked down at Katie, still clinging to his legs, and then back at me. A stricken look crossed his face. He leaned toward me and whispered, "Um. To be clear, are you asking me to kill her and dump her body?"

"What? *No!* Why on earth would you think that?"

Brent cleared his throat. "To a Shadow King, 'taking care of someone' has a very different connotation."

"Oh . . . *Oh!*" I was going to have to be more careful with my vocabulary choices in the future. "No, I mean, make sure she gets back home okay. Keep trying to convince her that everything she saw was the result of special party Kool-Aid so she doesn't go spilling all of our secrets. You know, that kind of taking care of someone. Take Brent with you."

Slade nodded. He and Brent pulled Katie up and hitched their arms around her back to help her walk.

"You saved me, didn't you?" Katie asked, patting her hand limply against Slade's cheek. She giggled and waved her hands like someone who'd enjoyed a good joint. "Did you see all the pretty green ooze?"

"Yeah, it was pretty," Slade said. Brent snorted. Slade glanced back at me with the look of someone being punished.

I watched them walk away, leaving me with Daniel and Talbot. Not the three best people to be left alone together.

Especially with weapons.

We were all quiet for a moment, tension building thick between us. Finally, Daniel approached Talbot with the sword in his hand. Daniel stood in front of him, their eyes locked, like they were trying to read each other's thoughts. I was reminded as to how much bigger Daniel's stature was now than before. Talbot, who had never seemed small to me, suddenly did, compared to Daniel. Or maybe it was just the way Daniel carried himself now—like an alpha. One whose pack had just defeated a rival's attack.

Daniel extended the blade of the sword toward Talbot, and then he flipped it upside down and offered him the handle. "Thanks," Daniel said. "You really saved us back there. We might not have gotten out of that without you."

Talbot blinked. "You're welcome," he said slowly, cautiously. "So . . . truce?"

Daniel glanced at me, as if looking for my verdict. I didn't know what to say. Talbot had helped us, but he'd also done so much to destroy my trust, I didn't know how I could just forgive him and call it good.

"I just want to help," Talbot said. "What happened here tonight was just a test. Caleb is eventually going to come at you with everything he's got. You need all the help you can get."

"He has a point," Daniel said. "Talbot knows Caleb's operations better than anyone. And he's a good fighter."

I was surprised Daniel was the one arguing on Talbot's behalf. He knew what Talbot had tried to do to keep him from coming back. Talbot owed Daniel big-time for what he did. How could Daniel be so forgiving?

I thought about what Gabriel had said to me about forgiving people their debts. Could I really move on and let Talbot back into my inner circle again?

"I don't know."

Talbot pulled off his eye mask and stared at me. "Please, Gracie? Forgive me."

I'd always been too trusting. Always tried to see the

good in people. Was that a fault or a blessing? *A weakness,* answered the wolf. I didn't know if I could trust myself to make the right choice at this moment. . . .

"It's up to you," I said to Daniel. "You're the one he really crossed."

"Are you sure?" he asked.

I nodded.

"Truce, then." Daniel offered the sword to Talbot again. "I gotta get me one of these."

"Take it," Talbot said, still staring at me. Why was he looking at me like that? Was he angry that I hadn't been the one to forgive him? "I've got more than one."

Daniel nodded in acceptance. He grabbed his now hole-ridden black coat and used it to wipe traces of Gelal acid from the blade, with a loving look on his face.

Talbot finally broke his gaze with me, but I could still feel the tension between us.

"Well, hey, how come you never gave me a sword?" I asked, trying to lighten things up. "I get stuck with a lousy stick with sparkles, and the boys get the fancy swords?" I held up the gooey nubbin, all that was left of my BeDazzled wooden stake. "Not. Fair."

"I can get you one, too, kid." Talbot smirked. "I just always thought you preferred the feel of wood in your hand."

Daniel slammed his fist into Talbot's stomach. Talbot doubled over, coughing.

"Just 'cause we have a truce doesn't mean you can

talk to my girlfriend that way," Daniel said, but he had one of his devious smiles on his face.

I dropped my stake and took Daniel's free hand in mine. I walked him to the exit before the two of them could get into a pissing contest or something—because I wouldn't put it past either of them at the moment.

Daniel turned back to Talbot, who still rubbed at his abs. "Come by the house tomorrow. I want to know everything you know about Caleb and the Shadow Kings."

Talbot nodded. That strange look passed over his eyes again. Perhaps it was just gratitude at the idea of being included in my life again?

OUTSIDE THE MAZE

Daniel and I made our way back to the farmhouse. To my surprise, the party had all but emptied out. Just a few dazed and confused teens milling about, experiencing the effects of coming out of a trance.

"Are the rest of the Akhs gone?" I asked.

"They must have smelled the dust in the air. That's as good as yelling 'police' at a normal rave."

"Good," I said. I wouldn't have felt like I could leave, knowing people like Katie were still being fed off of by demons. "I'm worried about Zach and Ryan. Do you think we should have gone after them?"

"No, I doubt they're doing much more than running

around that maze, swinging their stakes. Let them have some fun."

I gave Daniel a wry smile.

"What?" he asked.

"I feel like we're their parents or something." I laughed. "I guess in a way we are. Us being their alphas and all. Just our boys are headed off to kill demons instead of their first day of school."

"Hmm. That's kind of the problem, isn't it?" Daniel said under his breath, and looked down at the sword he'd tucked into his belt. A solemn quiet I didn't expect after all that excitement seemed to fill the air around him. We walked in silence until we reached the Corolla. "I was impressed by the way you handled yourself out there," Daniel said as he opened the passenger door for me. "You seemed so balanced. I didn't have to worry once about you losing control."

"Huh," I said, brushing the moonstone pendant with my fingers as I took it off and handed it back to Daniel. "You know, I didn't hear the wolf's voice once during the fight." The only time I had heard it was when I couldn't decide what to do about Talbot's truce. Keeping the wolf's voice away seemed to be getting easier since I'd prayed for help at the hospital. I'd been hearing it less and less.

Daniel shut my door and got in on his side.

"What about you? Are you okay?" I asked.

"I don't know," he said.

"You were amazing in there. Like seriously, freaking amazing." I poked him in the side. "Even with a bad arm! And you're always going on about not being a hero? Whatever, that was awesome."

"I don't feel like a hero." He gripped the steering wheel hard as he pulled out of the parking lot. "No matter what, I still feel like a monster."

"You. Are. Not. A. Monster. We saved a lot of lives tonight. *You* saved them. That seems like the definition of a hero to me."

"But how did I save them?" The muscles in Daniel's throat tensed. I could see the pulse of his veins. "By killing. I hate that. Even though I've changed, transformed into whatever I am now, I'm still just a Death Dog. That's what I do: I deal death."

I sat back in my seat. Quiet. Not sure how to counter his words. Words he'd said with so much despair and disdain it made me ache.

I stared far out the window as we drove along the old country road away from Frightmare Farms. I hoped to never see that place again. Daniel stopped the car when we came to a red light at the intersection for the main highway. He flipped on the blinker to go left. A sign at the T-shaped intersection pointed one way toward Rose Crest, and the other way to Apple Valley and then on to the city. I couldn't help thinking of my dad at City Hospital. I'd been so wrapped up in Daniel's return and learning about Pete's undeath, I hadn't been there to see him yet today. But the thought of watching him lying there in that hospital bed again was almost too much to bear. . . .

Until an idea hit me and I sprang forward in my seat.

"Death is not the only thing you have to give. I'll prove it to you." I pointed at the intersection. "Turn right."

"Why?"

"Because we're going to the hospital."

Daniel glanced at me with confusion, but he took the right turn anyway.

"I'm going to show you what you can really do. Who you really are."

It was time. I may have failed before, but I knew that, hand in hand with Daniel, we could do what needed to be done. What we were *meant* to do together.

Chapter Twenty-four

GIFTS OF THE HEART

I pulled the clothes we'd changed out of at April's house from the trunk of the Corolla. Daniel and I took turns changing in the backseat while the other stood outside the car. Getting past the nurses' desk at the ICU was going to be hard enough this time of night without our parading in there looking like a couple of emo-bandits. Plus, if my plan worked, I didn't want my outfit to put my dad into cardiac arrest. I'd had enough of this hospital for a lifetime.

Getting past the nurses' desk posed even more of a problem than I'd thought it would—even in my nice-girl ensemble. The ICU allowed visitors at night, but that didn't change the fact that I was minor and not allowed there after dark without a chaperone—as the nurse at the front desk reminded me.

"But he's over eighteen," I said about Daniel. "Can't

he be my chaperone? We're not staying overnight. Just give us twenty minutes. That's all I need." I made the saddest face I could possibly muster, wishing I had the talent to cry on demand. "I just need to see my dad. Pleeeease?"

The nurse didn't seem amused. "Your friend may be over eighteen, but only family is allowed."

"Maybe we should come back in the morning?" Daniel whispered, so soft only I could hear it.

I shook my head. I didn't know if I'd be able to work up this much courage again. If we were going to do this, it had to be tonight.

I grabbed Daniel's hand, lacing my fingers with his. "But he's my fiancé," I said. "I've read your visiting policies. That's allowed."

Daniel glanced at me, his eyes wide with surprise. Or perhaps shock. He looked away again, and I couldn't get a read on his expression.

My heart sank a bit. *So he really doesn't remember what happened?*

I squeezed his hand as if to say, *Just play along with me.* Daniel's hand clasped mine a little tighter in response.

"Just happened," Daniel said, rocking on his heels. "We came to tell her father the good news. Even if he's unconscious, we wanted him to be the first to hear it. Besides you now, of course." Daniel flashed her one of his most charming smiles, and even though the nurse had to be twenty years his senior, and clearly wasn't buying the story, I could tell that she wasn't going to be able to say no to him.

"Twenty minutes. That is all. You stay a minute longer, and I'll call security. You don't want to get barred from the ICU for the rest of your father's stay."

"Thank you," I said as she handed me a couple of visitor badges. She glanced at my hand as I reached for them, no doubt searching for an engagement ring on my finger. I pulled Daniel along the hall as fast as I could without running before the nurse could change her mind about letting us in.

When we got to Dad's room, I pulled the curtain partway closed over the sliding glass door the way Gabriel had. "We're here to help you, Daddy," I said, turning toward my still-unconscious father. Daniel stood quiet and still by his bedside, and I remembered that this was the first time he'd seen him in his injured state.

"I almost can't recognize him," he said with a catch in his voice. The swelling in Dad's face had gone down considerably, but the bruising was much more pronounced. Like his whole face had been blotted with blackish-purple dye. "I'm glad you brought me to see him. But I don't understand why we're here, or what this has to do with me. How could I possibly help him?"

"We're going to heal him."

Daniel looked even more shocked now than he had when I announced our engagement. "How?"

I explained what we were about to do, using Gabriel's almost exact wording so I wouldn't get it wrong. Daniel still had that shocked but solemn look on his face, but he nodded along like he understood.

"You need to clear your head," I said again after the explanation. "The first time I tried this with Gabriel, I wasn't able to push away my negative thoughts, and I ended up hurting my father more. I was afraid to ever try it again, but I had to use a similar method to turn you back into a human, and that worked. Now that I have you to help me, I believe it will work for my father, too."

"I'm not sure I'm the best person—"

"You're the only person." I looked deep into Daniel's eyes. "I need you to accept who you are. You're a Hound of Heaven, not a Dog of Death. Yes, part of your calling is to kill demons—only to protect the innocent—but *this* right here is what we were truly meant for. What the original Urbat were created for. Something only Urbat like you and I can do. Because we haven't lost our capacity to love. That's what we have to give the world."

I could see the struggle in Daniel's eyes. The fight to accept what I was telling him against what he'd come to believe about himself.

"You're not a monster. Not anymore. You came back something different. And deep down, I think you know what that is."

Like an angel.

I leaned in and kissed Daniel softly on the lips. When I pulled away, he closed his eyes for a moment so I could no longer see the battle in his head. Then he stood a little straighter and nodded. "I think you're right," he said, opening his eyes again. What I saw there was a solid look of determination.

"Are you ready to do this with me?"

"Yes. Anything for you." He glanced at my father. "For him."

Daniel held his hands out to me. We stood side by side next to the hospital bed, and I placed Daniel's hands on my father's chest. "Concentrate on the positive. You need to channel all your good energy and love."

Daniel closed his eyes, and so did I. I found myself digging deep down into my memory, pulling up every positive recollection of my father, and focused those thoughts into my hands. Only a few seconds passed before I could feel the energy buzzing between my hands and Daniel's. It swelled and pulsed, growing in intensity. One of my memories of my father suddenly shifted to an image I didn't remember at all—one of Daniel sitting in a chair across from my father at his desk in his office. They were alone, and I realized this wasn't one of my memories at all. It was one of Daniel's. We were connected once again. The images were murky, but I watched as my father told Daniel that he was going to help him find the cure to the were-wolf curse, and I felt the gratitude Daniel experienced in that moment. The connection continued, and I saw little clips of Daniel's life. And then I saw myself in one of his memories. Saw who I was to him from his mind's eye, and I wondered how I could have ever doubted the way he felt about me.

My heart swelled with love, and a great burst of power ricocheted through every cell in my body, engulfing me until I didn't know if I could hold it in any longer. With a great surge, all of that energy rushed through me, into Daniel's hands, and then into my father. And then I felt myself let go of Daniel's hands, and then I was falling. Collapsing next to the bed—only to be caught in Daniel's arms.

"Are you okay?" he asked, cradling me against him. "That was intense."

"Yes," I tried to say, but my voice barely made a noise. I didn't even have the strength to open my eyes.

A shrill chorus of beeping noises filled my ears. At first I didn't know where they came from, but then with a shock of horror I realized it was the sound of every single one of my father's monitor alarms. Indicating something was terribly wrong.

"Holy shit," Daniel whispered.

I'd been so sure I could do this. So sure it would work this time like it had for Daniel. *What have I done?*

"*Holy shit,*" Daniel practically shouted. I felt the

shift of his body as he turned me toward my father. "Look, Grace."

I forced my eyes open, even though they wanted to stay clamped shut—afraid to see what damage I must have caused to send all those monitors into such a frenzy. But then I saw what it was, and I understood.

Dad was sitting there. *Sitting up* in his bed, and he'd pulled the oxygen mask from his face—both of which actions would have set off multiple alarms.

"Gracie?" he asked. "What happened? Where am I?"

I couldn't believe it. He was awake. He was speaking. All the dark purple bruises on his face and arms had faded away.

"We did it." Tears streamed from my eyes. "We actually did it."

Daniel tried to set me on my feet, but I was too weak to stand, so he lifted me onto the bed, and I threw my arms around Dad's neck. "You're alive," I said between happy sobs. "You're alive, and you're okay."

Dad hugged me back. "Of course I'm alive. But what happened? Why am I here?"

Before I could answer his question, I heard the *woosh* of the sliding-glass door and an army of nurses swarmed into the room. "What's going on here?" one of them shouted at me.

"Get away from him," another nurse shouted, but then she stopped suddenly, staring at my father sitting up in his bed, looking perfectly healthy and uninjured.

She whispered something in what sounded like Spanish and made the sign of the cross in front of her chest and forehead. She went on in the language I didn't quite understand, but I did catch something.

"A miracle," she said. "It's a miracle."

Chapter Twenty-five

WORLDS COLLIDED

You'd think a miracle would be cause for rejoicing in the ICU. Instead, it brought on a barrage of questions for me and several not-pleasant-looking tests and scans for my father. The successful power transfer had left me completely drained of all energy, and Daniel and I spent the next several hours curled up in one of the waiting room sofas, drifting in and out of sleep.

I guess the nurse at the front desk decided to let us stay longer than twenty minutes, considering the circumstances, because it was just after seven in the morning when my father announced that he wanted to go home.

"I'd prefer to keep you here for observation," the doctor, who had been pouring over lab results for the last hour, said to Dad. "Perhaps run a few more tests."

"No more tests." Dad groaned. "I feel like a pincushion."

The doctor looked at the chart one more time. "We can't find anything *wrong* with you, which means we can't keep you here if you want to go. But I don't advise it. . . ."

Dad pulled the heart-rate monitor from his finger. "You heard the woman, Grace. They can't keep me here."

Under normal circumstances, I would have protested Dad doing anything against his doctor's advice, but in this case I knew more about his condition than anyone else in the hospital would be able to determine.

Daniel steadied me in his arms as I stood—my body was still a bit unstable and weak from the power transfer—and I took my father's hand. "Let's go home," I said, feeling more joy at that moment than I'd thought possible a few days ago.

"There's one more thing I want you to do before we leave," Dad said as we approached the elevators. He reached out and pushed the Up button instead of the Down. I knew immediately what it was that he wanted.

"Dad?" I looked up at him. "I don't know if I can."

"You can do it, Gracie. You and Daniel healed me, so why can't you do the same for your mother?"

"I don't even know if my powers would work on someone like Mom." So far, I'd only known the power to work on physical injuries. I had no idea if it had any effect on mental illness. For some reason, that just felt *different.* "And, I mean, what if Mom is the way she is because that's God's will for her?"

"Then I imagine it won't work if God doesn't want it to." Whenever Dad led a prayer circle for someone ill at the parish, he'd always qualify his pleadings to God for that person's restoration of health with "if it be Thy will." Dad gave me a reassuring smile as the elevator doors *ding*ed open. "Why would God have granted you this power if he didn't want you to use it?"

Daniel took my hand, giving it a light squeeze. "It's worth a try, Grace."

I looked between Daniel and my father, taking in the hope that brightened their eyes. If we could do this, it suddenly opened up so many possibilities. The things we could do . . . The people we could help . . .

"Okay," I said. I stepped inside the elevator with them, knowing that from this moment on, my life might never be the same again.

THURSDAY EVENING, ABOUT TEN HOURS LATER

I awoke to a mixture of sounds and smells so familiar and pleasant, yet strange and out of place from my current life, that it made my head swim. Little stars danced in front of my eyes as I sat up. I recognized the coral color of my sheets as my eyes focused, and I sighed with relief, knowing I was in my own bed. At home. But I had no idea how I'd gotten here. Couldn't remember anything except a vague recollection of getting into an elevator with my father and Daniel.

But where were they now?

A chorus of laughter sounded from the main floor of the house, answering my question.

I drew in a deep breath and sifted out the smells that permeated the air of my bedroom. Bacon. Eggs. Pancakes. And the sweet smell of maple syrup being heated over the stove.

Someone was cooking.

No one had *cooked* in this house since Mom had gone away.

More laughter drifted up the stairs and down the hall into my bedroom. There were too many voices mixed in the chorus for it to just be Daniel and my father. I breathed in again, and caught another now-familiar, underlying scent in the air—that of a dog who's been lying out in the sun, mixed with the distinct scent of *boy*. There were werewolves in this house. And not just Daniel. Based on the smell, there were several just down the stairs.

Despite the effort it took just to keep my weak, aching body sitting upright, curiosity got the better of me. Not to mention the gnawing sensation in my stomach triggered by the smell of so much food. When was the last time I'd actually eaten? I dragged myself out of bed, slowly changed into fresh clothes, and tiptoed my way down the stairs—only to find the dining room bursting with people and food.

Daniel, my father, Charity, Baby James, Brent, Ryan, Zach, Slade, and even Talbot were gathered around, dishing up heaping portions from platters piled high with all varieties of breakfast foods that filled every square inch of the table.

"She's up!" Dad said when he saw me in the entryway.

The crowd at the table cheered.

"Come eat." Dad waved me into the room.

Both Daniel and Talbot stood when I entered, but it was Daniel who rushed over and threw his arms around my shoulders. He pecked a kiss on my cheek. "How are you feeling? You passed out at the hospital."

"Tired but starving." My stomach hadn't stopped growling since I'd laid eyes on all that food.

"Sit. Eat." Daniel indicated the empty seat between his spot and Charity. I watched as my sister passed a pitcher of orange juice to tattoo-covered Slade. Little Baby James squealed with delight as he pelted Talbot in the face with a handful of scrambled eggs. Talbot laughed, swatting egg off his baseball cap.

I pinched my arm. Hard. Isn't that what you're supposed to do if you think you're dreaming? My two worlds—the Urbat, and my human family—had finally collided. But instead of the resulting explosion I had expected if that were ever to happen, they were breaking bread together? "What on earth is going on?"

From behind me came the last voice I had expected to hear. "Breakfast for dinner."

I whirled around to find my mother standing there, holding a tray of steaming French toast. My mouth popped open. How was she here?

"Your favorite," she said. "I was hoping the smell would rouse you." I noticed now that her fingers were still quite thin, but other than that, she looked so different from the vacant shell I'd seen when I'd visited her on Monday.

"Mom? But . . . but . . ." Fleeting memories trickled into my brain. Daniel and me standing over my mother as she lay in her hospital bed in the psych ward. The feeling of power rushing through my hands. Then I recalled passing out with fatigue onto the hard linoleum floor. "How long have I been asleep?"

"About ten hours," Daniel said. "I've never seen anyone so drained. I don't think you're supposed heal two people in one day like that. So don't go getting ideas that you can go around healing whole wards of people at the hospital at once."

My cheeks flushed with heat. I *had* been thinking something like that.

"How are you so okay?" I asked Daniel. He'd been part of both healing sessions, too.

"I slept for a good four hours myself once we got back here. But Grace, you should realize that most of the power came from you. I was just helping. You're the one who healed your parents."

"We hear you're quite the little miracle worker," Talbot said, his mouth full of egg.

I turned back to my mom and threw my arms around her neck, almost sending the tray of French toast flying. I kissed her cheek.

"I heard what you said," she whispered into my ear. "When you came to see me a few days ago. You said you needed a mother. That you all did. I know I can't try to be perfect anymore, but I'm trying my best to be what you need." I noticed now that even though her hair was washed and cleaned, it hung straight and unstyled around her shoulders, and she wore wrinkled slacks and a blouse under Dad's KISS THE COOK apron. Several slices of the French toast on the tray were browner than my mother would have usually deemed "acceptable" in the past, and that made my heart feel lighter.

She wasn't perfect, but she was *Mom*.

"Now go eat," Mom said, shooing us to our seats with an awesomely motherly tone. "Build up your strength."

"So where's Aunt Carol?" I asked as I headed for my seat. I realized I'd been gone all day and all night without calling her. I was expecting to get quite the earful about it.

"She left already," Dad said. "Carol was a little . . . overwhelmed by our return. Miracles are harder for some people to process."

"I wouldn't be surprised if she started claiming you faked the accident just to get a couple days off," Mom said. I'd never heard her talk so jovially about her sister.

"That'll go over well with Grandma." I sat at the table, and the others passed platter after platter of food in my direction. I shoveled chocolate-chip pancakes, eggs, bacon, and slice after slice of French toast into my mouth—filling up the empty pit that had been in my stomach for days.

In fact, the only one—at a table populated with almost all teenage boys—who ate more than me was Slade; he inhaled his food with the fervor of a death-row inmate granted his last supper.

Charity giggled next to me, and I was afraid it was directed at my lack of eating manners, but then I realized she'd locked eyes with Ryan, who sat directly across from her. A wide, goofy grin spread across his face. I picked up a banana-nut muffin and chucked it at him. It bounced off his forehead and landed in an almost-empty plate of bacon. But it had been just the trick to wipe that puppy-dog look off his face. He blinked at me.

"Don't. Even. Think. About. It." I picked up a second muffin and held it like a baseball about to be thrown.

"I wasn't . . . I mean, I was . . . But, um . . . your sister is cute . . . ," Ryan sputtered, and wiped at the little particles of muffin that clung to his forehead like a bull's-eye.

Charity turned as red as the raspberry jam on her pancakes.

The others broke into laughter. I acted like I was about to send the second muffin flying, making Ryan flinch. Instead, I took a huge bite and leaned my head against Daniel's shoulder. He wrapped his arm around my back. We laughed with the others for a moment, but my sight lingered on the half-eaten chocolate-chip pancake on his plate. French toast might be my favorite, but Mom's special pancakes were pretty much one of my older brother's most favorite things in the world.

Daniel grew quiet next to me. He bent his head closer to mine. "He should be here, shouldn't he?" Daniel asked quietly, as if he were tuned in to exactly what I was feeling. Which he probably was.

I nodded against his arm.

"Then I think that means you're ready," he whispered. "It's time to make things right with Jude."

Chapter Twenty-six

MOMENT OF TRUTH

STILL THURSDAY EVENING,
AROUND SEVEN THIRTY P.M.

Daniel and I drove slowly to the parish. A very yellow, and almost full, moon rose between the hills of Rose Crest, sending its ghostly light reflecting off the clouds in the night's sky. It was an oil painting waiting to happen, and I wondered just how long it would be until I'd ever have the time to pick up a paintbrush again.

Daniel parked the Corolla in the empty front parking lot. I realized now that, if everyone was at the house, Jude had probably been left alone all day.

I sighed, hesitant to reach for the car handle.

"You ready for this?" Daniel asked.

"Yes," I said. "No. Maybe. I don't know."

"All of the above?"

"Things didn't go so great the last time I came to see Jude. I kind of accused him of murdering that nurse at the hospital. You know, the one Pete actually killed?"

Daniel nodded. "Yeah, I can see how that wouldn't go over all that well."

"I don't know what to even say to him anymore. I haven't even been able to look him in the eyes."

"Then that's what I'd lead off with. How do you expect him to ever get better if his own sister won't even look into his eyes?"

A pang of guilt tugged at my heart. "I know. I think I've just been afraid of what I'll see there."

"Whatever it is, he can change. Everyone can. I believe that now."

"Everyone?" I looked into his dark eyes. "Even Caleb?"

Daniel hesitated, then cleared his throat. "Yes . . . I would have never said that a while ago. There was a time when I thought even *I* wasn't capable of changing, but you showed me the way." He smiled a little. "You were my saving *Grace*. More than once."

"But someone like Caleb, he's pure evil. How can you change that?"

"Gelals and Akhs are pure evil. They're nothing but demons. They have no soul. But Caleb, he's Urbat. He still has a human heart—which I think also means he still has a human soul. No matter how black it is. I have to believe there is still some light inside of him somewhere. Some spark of humanity. If he decided that he wanted to change—somehow try to make amends for all the horrible wrong he's done—maybe that means he could still be redeemed."

"As if he'd want to change," I said.

"I didn't say it was likely, but it's still possible." Daniel looked out at the parish. "I don't know, maybe it sounds stupid, but I guess I believe that everyone is *capable* of changing. It doesn't mean they *will*. Nobody can be saved if they don't want to be."

"So what about Jude? Do you think he *wants* to change?"

"There's only one way to find out."

I took a deep breath, knowing I couldn't put it off any longer. "I just hope he'll even let me speak to him, let alone listen."

"He'll listen, Grace. That's what's so special about you. Not only can you make people better—like the way you healed your parents—but you make people *want to be* better. Just remember that what he's going through is a lot different for him than it is for you."

"What do you mean?"

"The wolf—the voice you hear, trying to manipulate you—is a hundred times stronger after you've already given in to it. It's always there. Fighting it is a constant decision. Coming home, trying to beat the wolf, trying to make things right with the people I hurt the most were the hardest things I've ever done. The wolf was screaming in my head that I could never be forgiven. I don't doubt Jude is getting a similar treatment."

Daniel's words sank into my heart. I don't think I had realized *just how much* of a battle he had gone through when trying to overcome the wolf's hold on him. The battle that Jude was going through now.

"You just need to remind him that he is loved. That he *can* be forgiven. You're pretty good at that."

I felt a lift in my confidence, remembering what I'd done for Daniel once. And what I'd done for Mom and Dad. The kind of power I'd wielded in my own two hands today. It made me feel like a different person now than the one who'd tried to talk to Jude the first time only two days ago.

"Let's go inside." Daniel got out of the car and came around to my side. He opened my door for me. "Clear your mind, and I bet the right thing to say will just come to you. Jude isn't completely lost."

INSIDE THE PARISH

Our footfalls echoed through the empty stairwell as we made our way down to the parish's basement. Jude no doubt heard our approach. He stood at the gate of the storage cage when we entered the room.

"What are you doing here?" he snarled at me. "I told you not to come back here. . . ." His eyes narrowed in on Daniel. He took a sudden step back from the gate. "What is *he* doing here? Why would you bring him?"

"Hello, Jude," Daniel said.

Jude bared his teeth. "So the prodigal son returns—again. Did they have a feast for you? Did someone kill a freaking fatted calf in your honor? Because all I got was this damn cage." Jude grabbed the bars of his cell and rattled the gate.

I glanced at his eyes. They were hard and fierce, like a wolf about to attack. I dropped my gaze.

You shouldn't have come, the demon in my head snarled. *You only make things worse.*

"You and I both know you could leave that cage any-time you want," Daniel said. "I think you stay here because you want to. Because it's easier to be in there than with the ones who love you."

Jude let go of the bars. "You know nothing about me."

"I know more than you're willing to admit. I've been where you are now. Felt what you feel now."

"Shut up! You don't know anything. You can go to hell!" Jude spat in Daniel's direction.

"Jude, please," I said, trying to calm him down.

"I have nothing to say to you, Grace. I told you I never wanted to see you again."

"Jude, I'm sorry I accused you of killing that nurse. I can't believe I did that. It was a horrible thing to do. But I realized that that was my first instinct because I was still so angry with you. I didn't know what to believe." I approached the gate, gripping the bars with my hands. I looked my brother right in his silver, glint-ing eyes. "But I'm telling you now, I forgive you."

Jude blinked. When his eyes flitted open, I saw what I needed to see. Just the slightest flash of violet as his eyes softened briefly . . . before they went hard, glinting, silver, and twisted again. Something human still lived and breathed inside my brother. *Jude* was still there, and he needed to hear what I'd said—even if the demon inside of him would try to refuse it now.

But I was prepared for the fight.

"You forgive me?!" Jude roared. *"You.* Forgive. Me?" The hinges of the cage squealed in protest as he pulled on the bars. The whole gate would come crashing down if he wanted it to. I was tempted to step back, but I held my ground.

"So do I," Daniel said, stepping forward next to me.

"How dare you?" Jude asked. "You're the ones who should be begging *me* for forgiveness. You're the ones who did this to me!"

"I've said it before," Daniel said, "and I'll repeat it a million times if needed: I'm truly sorry for infecting you. I lost control, just like you're about to now. I don't know if I'll be able to ever fully forgive myself. Not until you forgive me first."

"That will never happen," Jude said, but his grip on the bars loosened.

"You're right, Jude," I said softly. He looked at me, almost surprised I'd agree with anything he had to say.

"I should beg you for forgiveness. But before I can expect to be forgiven, I need to forgive. So I'm telling you now, again, so you'll know without a doubt." I stepped as close to the gate as I could get and leaned my forehead against the bars. "I forgive you."

"Don't say that! You have no right to say that! I'm not the one in the wrong. Everything I've done is your fault. You two are the ones who did this to me." He roared and lunged at me as I stood in front of the gate. He grabbed my throat with one of his sinewy hands. "You shouldn't have come back here."

"Jude, let go," Daniel said, caution in his tone. "Don't hurt her. Don't go further down this path."

"The path you started me on?" Jude's fingernails dug into my skin as he started to squeeze my throat, cutting off my air.

"I've forgiven you," I rasped out, with what little breath I had left. "Now . . . will you forgive me? Will you forgive yourself?"

I could feel the power pulsating in Jude's hand. He could have killed me in one second flat—so why was he hesitating now? I looked up at his face, and it was almost possible to see the battle raging inside his head. His eyes flashing silver and then softening into violet over and over again. Strain marred his face, and the veins in his neck protruded.

"Jude!" Daniel shouted. He moved like he was about to intervene physically. I held my hand up to stop him. This was the moment of truth.

Jude's grip on my neck loosened just enough for

me to cough and sputter for air. Just enough to rasp, "Please, Jude. I know you're still in there. I know you're my brother."

"We love you, Jude," Daniel said. "We want to help you. We want you to come home. To *be* home. All you have to do is ask and we're here to help."

Jude's grip weakened, but he didn't let go of my throat. "Go home?" he asked. "You make it sound easy. You don't even know what you're talking about—"

"Being in this cage," Daniel said. "It's like being an addict who's been forced into rehab. Staying in here is what's *easy*. Yes, going home is the hard part. I know. I've been through it. I know what it's like to try to go back to your normal life, to have to face all the people you hurt on your path to destruction. I know what it's like to walk around with that terrible voice in your head, constantly tempting you. How every single waking moment is a decision to either keep fighting it, or just give in."

Ragged breaths heaved in Jude's chest. His fingers trembled against my throat. "I don't know. . . ." His voice caught. "I don't know if I'm strong enough to keep fighting."

"You are, Jude," I said. "I know you are. And I'm here to help you. We're both here to help you. But we can't unless you let us."

Jude's fingers slipped from my throat. He backed away and collapsed onto his cot, his whole body quaking in gut-wrenching sobs. "Help me," he cried against the canvas cot. "I don't want to be like this anymore."

I massaged my throat as Daniel went for the key that hung from the wall at the entrance of the basement. He unlocked the gate and pulled it open. The two of us ran to Jude and cradled him in our arms.

Daniel took off his moonstone pendant and strung it around Jude's neck. "You need this more than I do."

My brother clutched at the stone like it was the most precious thing in the world.

I brushed my hands through his hair and held him tight, rocking him until he wrapped his arms around me. One of his hands rested on the scar on my arm where he'd bitten me, infecting me with the Urbat curse.

"I'm sorry," he whispered. "I'm so, so sorry."

"I forgive you," I said one last time because he needed to hear it. I clasped his head with both of my hands and tipped his face so I could look him in the eyes. They were violet and glistening with tears—but they were my brother's eyes that I remembered. Mirror images of my own. "It's going to be okay," I said. "I promise."

I prayed with all my might that this promise would be one that wouldn't get broken.

Chapter Twenty-seven

ARRIVALS

We pulled into the driveway behind April's red hatchback and Talbot's blue truck. Every light blazed in the house, and I was sure the whole group was still here. Probably lying around sleeping like happy, fat dogs after a feast.

"I don't know if I can do this," Jude said as we got out of the car. He squinted at the lit-up house like it was almost painful to look at.

"It's time to come home," I said, trying to nudge him forward.

"What if they don't want me anymore?"

But I didn't get a chance to answer his question, and I didn't need to, because the front door opened, and Mom came running down the porch steps.

"Jude!" she cried, throwing her arms around him. It looked like she might suffocate him with her hug.

Dad appeared in the doorway. His mouth fell open, and his eyes got shiny with tears, watching the reunion of mother and son. "Are you sure about this, Gracie?" he asked, approaching slowly.

"Yes," I said, and squeezed his arm.

"Good girl." Dad swallowed hard and went to Jude and my mom. The three of them embraced.

"Let's go inside," I said to Daniel. He took my hand, and we left the others so they could cry and talk and embrace some more.

I was right about the rest of the household—they were fat-dogging-it all over the house. Brent and Zach were sprawled across the front room furniture, passed out napping, with hands resting on their full bellies. April, Charity, and James snuggled together on the couch, watching one of James's Playhouse Disney DVDs—but I couldn't help noticing that Charity's attention seemed to be a bit preoccupied. She kept glancing out the window at Ryan, who appeared to be getting a lesson in the finer ways of staking from Talbot out on the back porch.

"Hey," I said, trying to get the girls' attention.

Both April and Charity sat up when they saw me.

"You're back," Charity said.

"How did it go with Jude?" April asked.

"He's here," I said. "Outside with my parents."

April jumped up. "Do you think it's okay if I join them?"

"Me, too?" Charity asked.

"Yeah. The happier we can make his homecoming, the better."

I watched as April and Charity bounded out of the family room, leaving Baby James to suck on the edge of his blankey with blissful oblivion. At least I never had to worry about his running off with a pack of paranormal thugs.

"I'm going out back," Daniel said, hitching his thumb at Talbot and Ryan in the backyard. "I need to ask Talbot a few questions about the Shadow Kings."

"Okay," I said, and let go of his hand. I also wanted to hear everything Talbot had to say about the Shadow Kings, but at the moment, Jude's homecoming had to be my priority. I headed to the dining room and piled up a plate of food for Jude from what remained of the breakfast-for-dinner extravaganza.

I picked up the plate and was about to head for the kitchen to warm it up when I found Slade standing in the dining room doorway, blocking my exit. The dish almost dropped from my hands.

"I need to talk to you," he said, coming closer to me than he ever had before.

"About what?" I stepped back, but the table blocked me from going any farther.

"Why did you do it?" He grabbed my arm tight, almost tipping all the food off the plate and onto the ground. The tattoos on his skin looked garishly colorful compared to my pale arms. "I need to know why. I can't handle it anymore."

"Okay. What the heck are you talking about?" I pulled my arm from his grasp.

"Why did you save me from that Akh at the trance party? Why didn't you let it kill me?"

I put the plate on the table. "Why *would* I let it kill you? I don't want you to die." I didn't want to lose any more of the lost boys like I had Marcos.

Slade swallowed hard. "But I deserved it. I deserved to die." A look of genuine confusion passed over his eyes. "I disobeyed a direct order from you. I couldn't help you save your father. I couldn't go into that fire. You should have punished me for refusing to go. That's what Caleb would have done. But instead, you saved my life. Why? What do you have in store for me? What punishment could be worse than death by Akh? I can't handle not knowing when the ax is finally going to drop. Just do it now and get it over with. Kill me. . . ."

I put my hand on his chest, stopping him. "Whoa, whoa, whoa. No one is going to kill you. You're not even going to be punished. If you haven't noticed, I'm nothing like Caleb. Neither is Daniel. I understand why you couldn't go into that fire. You were afraid. I get that now. Werewolves fear fire because it's one of the few things that can kill them."

Slade nodded. "It can disintegrate an Urbat completely. Not even leave any bones behind. But the others were able to get over their fears and come to your aid. I couldn't. I was petrified. But I swear, I wasn't always such a coward." He licked his lips. "You know, I'd just been accepted to train as a smoke jumper—those guys who jump out of airplanes in order to put out forest fires?"

I shook my head.

"It's what I've always wanted to be—ever since I was a little boy. But the Shadow Kings took that away from me when they turned me into an Urbat. They took my whole life away." Slade ran his fingers over the colorful flames on his forearm, tracing the lines. "I ink my arms with tattoos of flames, burn myself with a lighter, like I thought I could fool myself into believing I'd overcome my fears. But when faced with it, I caved. I failed you."

"I understand. I really do." The wolf in my own head had almost prevented me from being able to save my father. For someone who'd wanted to be a firefighter all his life, I could understand the shame and agony Slade must feel. "No harm is going to come to you for that."

Slade grabbed my hand in a lightning-quick movement. "Thank you," he said, squeezing my fingers. "Thank you."

"Um. You're welcome." What else are you supposed to say when someone thanks you for not killing him? It's not exactly a situation that comes up often—at least for normal people.

Tears welled in Slade's eyes, shining brighter than

the steel bar in his eyebrow. Slade crying was the last thing I'd ever expected to see. Caleb had really done a number on these boys.

"What I don't get is that it sounds like you had a pretty good life—training to become a firefighter and all. How did Caleb even get his claws into you?"

Slade let go of my hand, almost as if he felt ashamed to touch me. "There was this girl. Lyla. Prettiest thing I'd ever seen." A slight smile pulled on his lips like he was remembering her face, but then his chin began to tremble. "But she was in trouble. Needed money. I'd been street racing since high school, best driver around, but the winnings still weren't enough. After a race one night, this guy approached me. Said his crew needed a driver for a job . . ." He glanced at the floor.

"You mean like for a heist?"

He nodded. "Normally, I'd say no. But the money he was offering was killer. Enough to pay Lyla's debts and bring her out to Montana with me for training. Enough to start a new life. Only thing is, when the job was over, the guy says I can't leave. That the job was my audition, and now I belonged to him. When I refused . . . Well, next thing I knew, I woke up in the warehouse with this. . . ." He pushed up his T-shirt sleeve and showed me the ragged crescent-shaped scar on his tricep.

I knew what it was, I had one myself. "Werewolf bite."

"And they had Lyla. Turns out the guy she owed money to was the same guy who'd recruited me. They'd used her. And then they used her again to turn me—to get me to give in to the curse they'd infected me with."

I imagined the scene unfolding in the warehouse. Slade waking up disoriented and confused, his arm throbbing with the burning venom of a werewolf bite. Caleb threatening Lyla, forcing Slade to give in to the raging wolf in his head in order to try to stop them from hurting her.

By the dark look in Slade's eyes, I could tell the scene was playing out in his mind, also.

"What happened to Lyla?" My voice was barely more than a whisper.

Slade's eyelids slid shut as he lowered his head. "She was the first person I killed after I turned into the wolf. I don't remember much of what exactly happened—I was in such a frenzy. I thought I was going after the guy who held a knife to her throat, but she ended being the one I killed. I don't know why I did it."

"The wolf wants you to kill the person you love the most. She didn't stand much of a chance once Caleb forced you to give in to the wolf."

"It wasn't Caleb."

"What?"

"He was there. Caleb was always lurking up above in the warehouse. But the guy who recruited me, the guy who forced me to do what I did to Lyla—that was Talbot."

I felt the air catch in my lungs. I shouldn't have been shocked by this revelation. I should have seen it coming from the very beginning, since I'd already known that Talbot had been in charge of "recruitment" for Caleb's gang of Shadow Kings. Talbot was the one who had supposedly had a *talent* for getting infected individuals to give in to the werewolf curse. He'd been given the task to recruit and change me—only he hadn't.

Supposedly, Talbot was a whole new man now.

"Why did you stay with them? After what they did to you?"

"Because after you kill someone like that—especially someone you love—you feel like the biggest piece of shit on the planet. You know that you can't just go back to your life again. But you've got this raging, screaming, selfish thing inside your head that doesn't want to be alone. And that's when Talbot and Caleb swoop in on you, telling you that you'll never belong anywhere else. But if you'll do what they want, then *they* can give you a home, and score after score, and a purpose. But really, I see it now, they just wanted me to be another foot soldier in Caleb's terrible army."

Deep down, I already suspected that each one of these lost boys we'd brought from Caleb's pack—even Brent and young Ryan—had probably been through a similar experience as the one Slade had recounted. Which meant that at some point, each of the lost boys had either killed someone—or at least wanted to—or else they wouldn't be full-blown werewolves.

But they'd each chosen to follow Daniel and me away from that warehouse, and to stay with us. Which meant they were each looking for a second chance.

And we could give it to them, just like the second chance we'd offered Jude.

I put my hand on Slade's shoulder. "Caleb may have treated you boys like his foot soldiers, but I want our pack to be a family. I know you've been hesitant to truly accept Daniel as your alpha. But you're welcome to be a part of this family, if that's what you want. No harm will ever come to you by us."

"Yes," he said. "I want to be part of this family."

"I truly believe we can learn to use our powers for good. Maybe you're still destined to become the best damn firefighter anyone has ever seen. Imagine the good you could do with your speed and strength?"

"But I'd still be afraid of fire."

"Talbot and the others were able to overcome their fear to help me. I think, deep down, you've got it in you to make a difference in this world—firefighter or not. And I want to help you. If you'll let me."

Slade was quiet for a moment. "Perhaps," he said. "But before you do anything else for me . . . there's one more thing I must tell you."

"You can tell me anything."

"I was stupid. I made a mistake. I shouldn't have let that Akh look me in the eyes. He read my mind. He knows where the other boys and I are staying. And I am afraid he may know where you live also. He got away, which means now Caleb knows. I would have told you sooner, but I thought . . ."

"Thought I might kill you?"

His nod looked more like a flinch. My stomach felt ill.

"Thank you for telling me. We'll find another place for you boys to stay—and Daniel, too. And don't worry about Caleb knowing where I live. He's always known that. He used to live in the house next door."

Slade's eyes went wide. "But that makes no sense. Caleb doesn't let anyone just *leave* the Shadow Kings. You should see the things he and Talbot made us do to guys who tried to run away. . . ."

I could believe, actually. The first demon I'd ever killed was a Gelal who'd left the Shadow Kings, and I'd been used as a pawn by Talbot to punish him.

"If Caleb knows exactly where to find us, then why hasn't he attacked yet?" Slade asked. "What is he waiting for?"

"That's a really good question," I said.

And now I was the one waiting for the ax to fall.

FIVE MINUTES LATER

I didn't have to wait long.

Only, the ax that fell wasn't the one I'd been worried about.

I was headed to the front door with Jude's warmed-up dinner, when a bright light filled the front window, making me shield my eyes with my hand. I heard Dad shout from the front yard. It almost sounded like he was saying my name, and then something like, "Run!"

"What the . . . ?"

The front door burst open. Strange light flooded the entryway as Mom, Jude, April, and Charity came into the house. Dad followed, shouting mine and Daniel's names. When he saw me, he grabbed me so hard it knocked the plate of food from my hands. "They're here! They've come for you. Get out of here. Run!"

Daniel rushed into the hall by way of the kitchen. Talbot and Ryan were right on his tail. The other boys who had been sleeping sprang to attention when they saw Daniel. No doubt Dad's screams had awoken them.

"The Shadow Kings?" I asked.

"No." Dad clenched my arm. "Sirhan and his pack. His entire pack is here, from the looks of it."

"What?" Daniel bolted for the door to get a look outside. Dad tried to stop him.

"Don't go out there. Take Grace and get as far away as you can."

"And then what?" Daniel asked. "If they want to find us, they'll find us."

Daniel went through the front door. The boys followed after him like his sentinels and fanned out on the porch. My father tightened his near-death-grip hold on my arm, trying to prevent me from following.

"You can't stop me, Daddy."

His nostrils flared. "I'm just trying to protect you."

"You can't. Not anymore. Not in this world."

Dad stared at me, the fear in his eyes moving from panic to sadness as he bowed his head. "I know. I've known for a long time the day would come when I couldn't anymore."

"Then let me go."

Dad released my arm. I followed the boys out onto the porch and stood side by side with Daniel. My father followed and stood in the doorway behind us. Jude stood next to him.

In the piercing light, I made out the outline of what looked like at least ten black cars—probably SUVs, from the size of most of them—facing the front of the house, their brights shining in our faces.

I kept my hand level with my eyes, wishing my superhuman vision wasn't quite so sensitive.

"They're trying to put us at a disadvantage," Ryan said, shielding his eyes.

"It's working rather well," Brent said.

Ryan punched him in the arm.

"I was just making a comment." Brent punched him back.

"Cool it!" I snapped. Brent and Ryan stood at attention now, except for their hands guarding their eyes.

Daniel was the only one who stood with his arms at his sides—as if he weren't hindered by the light.

"How do you know it's Sirhan?" I asked Dad. "That could be anyone. It could be the SKs."

"Because I recognized the insignia on the cars. You can't see it now, but I saw it when they first pulled up. There's a medallion of a wolf's head on their front grille. I was shoved into one of those cars by Sirhan's guards when they found me trespassing on their land. And that car"—Dad pointed at the outline of a smaller vehicle in the middle of the line—"belongs to Sirhan himself. He personally escorted Gabriel and me from the compound property after he decided to let me go . . . Which is apparently when he decided he wanted you—"

Dad's sentence was interrupted when all of the cars' headlights cut off at the exact same moment.

"Ahhh!" I winced. My eyes throbbed, and the sudden change in light left me blinded momentarily—left us all blind.

I heard a rush of movement, and seconds later the headlights of the middle car switched on—illuminating the silhouettes of at least forty individuals standing in my yard now.

I couldn't make out any of their faces; they were just tall, stark shadows in the headlights. They all seemed to be holding something long and pointed in their hands. One of them stepped forward, and the light from the car glinted off the tip of the object he held. It was a spear, the blade made of some sort of shiny metal—silver, no doubt. He seemed to be wearing some sort of cloak or robe; I couldn't help but think about the Grim Reaper from the haunted farm.

"Give us what we came for," the man said in a deep, rumbling voice.

Daniel reached out and took my hand in his, threading his fingers with mine. Without saying a word, the lost boys stepped closer to us—as if closing our ranks. I could see the muscles tensing in their arms and backs, looking like they'd jump the porch railing and attack at the first command from Daniel or me. Tension radiated off their bodies. I feared what might happen if they went wolf right in my front yard.

Daniel held his hand up, telling his boys to wait. "I'm afraid you're going to have to be more specific," he said to the spearman, sounding too calm for the situation.

The crowd stood steady. The same spearman spoke again, "Give us what we came for."

Was that the only thing he'd been ordered to say?

"Again, specifics would be nice." Daniel squared his shoulders. "You wanted Gabriel, but he's already returned to you. Wasn't that the deal, if Gabriel returned, you'd stay away?"

"But where is Gabriel?" I whispered to Daniel. "Maybe something happened to him. Maybe he didn't make it back."

The spearman put his hand to his ear. He seemed

to listen for a moment. Was someone talking to him through an earpiece?

He said something to the man next to him. Two other spearmen marched to one of the SUVs and yanked open the door. Something fell out of the doorway and landed in a heap on the pavement between two of the cars. I couldn't tell what it was until I heard him groan.

"Gabriel," I breathed out. "No."

The heap shifted as Gabriel raised his head from the pavement. "I am sorry," he said. "I did not leave soon enough. Daniel, I . . ."

"Sirhan Etlu speaks," the chattiest of the spearmen said. "Sirhan Etlu of the Etlu Clan speaks, and all listen. . . ."

The lights of the smaller car turned off. I blinked several times to help my eyes adjust once more to the change in light. When I could see clearer, I noticed that the crowd—which was indeed forty people strong— wore long velvet robes draped over otherwise normal street clothes, the hoods of their cloaks obscuring most of their faces. Almost all of their robes were a deep sapphire blue color, except for the ten closest spear bearers, who stood in the very front of the crowd facing us. Their robes were emerald green. The only person in the mob who was noticeably female was a young woman who stood among the green-robed ten. Her hood was lowered, so I could see the more delicate features of her face and the teardrop-shaped earrings dangling from her ears. I couldn't help staring at her. I'd never known another female Urbat.

Something else entirely had caught Slade's attention. He pointed at the smaller car in the middle of the SUVs. "That's an Aston Martin Rapide limousine." Slade whistled in appreciation.

All ten of the closest spear bearers pointed their weapons at him. "Sirhan Etlu speaks, and you will listen," the spokesperson said, with a fierceness in his rumbling voice.

A hand extended from the back window of the limousine. I wouldn't have noticed it if it weren't for the light of the almost full moon glinting off the large ring on one of the fingers. Something about the shape of the hand didn't look quite . . . human.

"Gabriel failed me," came a voice from the car. It was raspy yet loud at the same time. Commanding. A power radiated through it that made my knees feel like they weren't completely solid. Almost like I needed to bow down to the owner of the voice.

The sensation must have been shared by the robed crowd, because they turned on their heels and fell to one knee, heads bowed in the direction of the limo with one fist shoved against the ground.

"If he had been truly loyal," the commanding voice continued, "he would have returned the moment my guards informed him of my ultimatum."

Gabriel moaned. His head bowed low.

"Only he tarried, showing where his true loyalties lie. I had to see for myself who could steal the devotion of my very own beta. Bring this 'Divine One' to me."

Daniel let go of my hand and stepped forward.

"Don't," I whispered to him.

"Perhaps your own beta would be more loyal to you if you didn't treat him in such a barbaric way." Daniel stood tall. Taller than I'd ever seen him. How much had he grown in the last week?

Again, I felt that sensation in my knees, trying to fold me into a bow. But this time it was directed toward Daniel. The lost boys on the porch fell into one-kneed bows, in supplication to Daniel. I glanced back quickly and saw that even Jude had fallen in a bow to Daniel. But I was even more shocked and amazed as two robed men from the crowd turned toward Daniel also.

"Your time as alpha is growing to a close, Sirhan," Talbot, stuck in a half-bowing position toward Daniel, said with a laugh. "Can't you see that?"

Which was apparently the worst thing anyone could have possibly said at the moment.

"Take him!" the voice—I assumed belonged to Sirhan—roared. "Take the Kalbi boy before he corrupts any more!"

A group of spear bearers rushed at Daniel, who stood at the edge of the porch steps. The lost boys growled and crouched back, ready to lunge at Daniel's would-be captors. My insides shrieked, knowing a bloody battle was about to erupt in front of us. What would happen to my family? My neighborhood?

"Don't!" Daniel shouted.

Both the lost boys and the spearmen stopped mid-motion.

Daniel held out his arms out to Sirhan's men. "I'll go with them willingly."

Daniel, no! I thought as two spearmen grabbed Daniel's arms.

A sharp scream came from my right, and I watched in horror as Ryan jutted over the porch railing and flew at the guards. He swung his stake at the closest spear bearer—the young woman I'd noticed before—hitting her ear with his weapon. She screamed. Blood spurted from her head as she clutched at the side of her face—her ear barely hanging from a flap of skin.

Another guard swung his spear at Ryan's face, smacking him with the flat side of the silver blade. Ryan's whimper made me shudder as he fell to the ground. A blistering red burn in the shape of the spearhead welted up on his cheek.

"Stop!" Daniel shouted as the guard went in for a second blow against Ryan. "He's just a boy."

The spearmen glared at Ryan, but he dropped his spear at his side—obeying Daniel's command.

"Don't anyone else make a move," Daniel said. "I am Sirhan's prisoner, and I won't allow anyone else to get hurt on my part. Not tonight."

"No." I jogged down the porch steps. I strode right up to the guards holding Daniel. "No," I said again. "I'm the one you really want. I'm what you came for." I tried to bypass two of the spearmen to go straight for the window of the limo, but the guards crossed their spears in front of me, blocking the way. "Take me and let Daniel go," I shouted at the window of the limousine.

"Let me pass." I shoved the crossed spears out of my way. One of the guards grabbed my arm so hard it felt like my wrist might break.

"Why would I want a child when I could have the false alpha?" came Sirhan's voice from the limo window.

"Because I'm the Divine One," I said. "*I'm* the one you came here for."

"Lies. The Divine One is not an infant."

"I am older than I look," I said, but I realized that, to someone as old as Sirhan, I probably *did* look like an infant. "Tell them who I am, Gabriel."

Gabriel slowly pushed himself up to a standing position against the side of one of the SUVs. "She speaks the truth. I told you the Divine One was a teenage girl."

The guard holding my wrist gasped and let go.

"Lies and tricks," Sirhan said. "The Divine One is great and powerful. This tiny imposter should be killed."

"I am not an imposter." I didn't exactly know what being the "Divine One" meant to Sirhan and his pack, but based on what Sirhan said, it seemed as though the very *idea* of me had grown to mythical proportions.

They expected me to be powerful, and I had to do something to prove to them that I wasn't lying.

I turned toward the young woman in the green robe. She knelt in the grass, trying to hold her bloody, nearly severed ear in place. She looked like she was only a few years older than I was, but with the Urbat, you really never could tell for sure. I went and knelt next to her. "Are you okay?" I asked.

"Hurts like, you know, someone cut off my ear," she said, wincing. "Don't think I can heal this one. But hey, at least I'll save money on earrings." She smiled weakly, despite the pain that flashed in her eyes.

I almost laughed, not expecting her to be so . . . nice. "I can help you," I said, and cupped my hand over hers and pressed it against her head. Her fingers were warm and slick with blood. I knew I was supposed to draw on my love for someone in order to call on my healing powers, but I'd never met this woman before. We were strangers. Yet at the same time she fascinated me. The only other female Urbat I'd ever met. That made us connected, and I drew on that as I closed my eyes and concentrated my powers into the hand that was clasped over hers. I could feel the heat pulsing and swelling, growing as hot as a flatiron.

She winced and then let out a small cry.

"What is she doing?" one of the spearmen asked—presumably about me. "Get her away!"

One of the guards moved toward us.

"Stop," Daniel said. "She's healing your pack mate."

"Impossible," Sirhan called from inside the limo. "She can't possibly be strong enough. Only the most powerful of Urbats can heal others. And nobody can do it alone."

In my haste, I'd forgotten that it supposedly took two people to channel the healing power into someone else. Yet at the same time, I *knew* I could do it.

I *was* doing it.

The heat finally dissipated, and I stood, pulling the young woman up with me. I let go of her hand, and she dropped her own away from her head.

Gasps rippled through the crowd around us.

"Doesn't even hurt," the young woman said, prodding her newly healed ear. "I can't even feel a scar."

"You see," Gabriel called toward the limo. "No mere *child* could do that. Grace is the Divine One."

A deep, aching fatigue filled my body—the side effect of using my powers to heal someone else. But I tried not to let it show as I walked toward the limo. The spearmen didn't even try to stop me.

"You know who I am," I called to Sirhan. "And I know what you want, old man. But I'm not going to give it to you unless you guarantee that Daniel goes free— and that the rest of my pack, my family, go unharmed."

"Come closer," Sirhan's voice beckoned from inside the limo.

I walked slowly but deliberately toward the open window. The first thing I noticed was that the hand

I'd seen earlier indeed didn't look human. It was dark gray and leathery, mottled with short grayish-black hairs. No, it was fur. The fingers were unhumanly long, and looked even longer tipped with sharp, wolflike black claws. The hand was a freakish mix of beast and human.

"Look at me, child," Sirhan said.

My vision snapped from the beastly hand to the face that glared at me through the open window. I stifled a gasp, but let my eyes grow wide—dilating enough in the dark to really see what was in front of me: a face that was also a grotesque mixture of animal and human. He had yellow eyes and a snout instead of a normal nose and jaw. His ears, on the sides of his head, came to mutant-looking points at the top.

"Are you afraid of me, child?" he asked. His blackened gums held pointed teeth—like I was staring into the mouth of a wolf.

"No," I said.

"Then tell me, what is it that you think I want. What could you give me to ensure the safety of the ones you love?"

I looked him over—not only was he a mixture of man and beast, his body also looked decrepit and fragile. A thin plastic tube with two little nodules hung around his neck. I recognized what it was from the hospital—an oxygen feed. He must have pulled it from his animal-like nostrils just to speak to me.

"You're dying," I said. "And you want to be cured so your soul will be free from the wolf before you pass. Healing people isn't the only thing I can do, as I'm sure you've heard or you wouldn't be here. If you meet my demands, I will provide the cure for you."

Chapter Twenty-eight

WOLVES AT THE GATE

The smell of decay and wolf assaulted my senses with every breath I took as I rode in the back of Sirhan's limousine with the ancient Urbat. Sirhan's car wasn't a limo in the traditional prom-night sense of the word. It could hold only four people: the driver, a spear-man who sat up front, Sirhan, and me. The leather of my seat was so soft I finally understood why some people compared the feel of fine leather to butter. I'd never been in any vehicle nearly as nice as this one, but I couldn't find comfort inside of it. Not only was the smell of Sirhan almost too much to handle, but the dark-tinted windows made it impossible to see if Daniel and the others were truly following us like they were supposed to.

My nails dug into my skin as I held my arms crossed in front of my chest. It didn't help my nerves that

Sirhan's labored breaths as he sucked in air from his oxygen tank reminded me of Darth Vader. He didn't speak to me again, just kept looking occasionally in my direction and laughing until his mirth turned into fits of hacking coughs.

At Dad's insistence, Sirhan had agreed to move our negotiations to a new location—away from our curious neighbors, who kept peering out their windows at the spectacle in our front yard. My parents were going to have a devil of a time explaining what exactly had been going on. No doubt Dad would tell them we'd been rehearsing for a Christmas pageant or something. The only problem with that was then Dad would actually insist on our *putting on* a Christmas pageant this year just so he wouldn't be caught in a lie.

Great, I thought. *Just the thing to look forward to.*

An aching gripped my heart, and suddenly I *was* looking forward to something like that. Anything, really. Because looking forward, making plans, feeling like there would be anything beyond this night, was what I needed to keep my nerves at bay.

I didn't know if Sirhan or anyone else would go for my plan—or if he could be trusted actually to meet my demands in the end. Only time would tell.

We didn't go far. The only place that Dad could think of to hold such a large group was the social hall of the parish. One of the guards prodded me out of the limo into the empty parking lot with the point of his spear.

For a moment, I worried I'd been kidnapped, but I sighed with relief as the rest of the caravan of black Cadillac Escalades pulled in behind us. Daniel and my father got out of one of the vehicles; Talbot, Jude, and the lost boys soon arrived in other cars.

The spearmen shuffled us into the building, followed by a long procession of Sirhan's robe-clad people—or Urbats, to be exact. We stood around in the social hall, feeling like cattle herded into a corral.

Or perhaps a slaughterhouse.

Daniel gripped my hand hard. Almost like he feared he'd never get a chance to again.

"They're all looking at me," I said, and nodded toward the members of Sirhan's pack, who were staring at me.

"It's to be expected after what you did for Jordan. You're the Divine One, remember?" Daniel said. "You're the stuff of legends to them, and you proved them true."

"Oh. Yeah. That." Earlier in the week, I'd felt so completely alone. Now I felt claustrophobic, surrounded by so many people and their searching eyes. "Wait, *Jordan*?" Daniel knew that young woman's name?

But Daniel had already turned to one of the spearmen. "What now?" Daniel asked him.

"We wait for Sirhan."

"What's taking so long?"

The spearman furrowed his brow and rocked a little back and forth, looking like he was contemplating just how much to say. "Sirhan has his own medical staff. He won't exit the car until they've fully examined him and deemed it safe for him to be moved." His brow crinkled deeper. "He shouldn't have left the estate to begin with, if you ask me."

Daniel nodded. I don't know about him, but I was surprised by the spearman's honesty.

Minutes ticked by, and the silence started to wane. Sirhan's people started to talk amongst themselves, many pointing in my direction. The spearman Daniel had questioned left our side and joined the nine other green-robed spear bearers, who were huddled in the far corner, looking like they were engaged in some sort of debate. Some of the men who'd been wearing blue robes had taken them off, revealing regular old T-shirts and jeans underneath.

"What's the deal with the robes?" Jude asked from behind me. "They look like a bunch of wizards."

"My hypothesis," Brent said. "They're either for ceremony or post-transformation convenience."

"Post what?" Slade said.

"You know, the whole naked factor. Normal clothes never survive the transformation from human to wolf, which means you're always naked when you go back to being human. The robes are quite clever. Easily discarded before transformation, and there for the convenience of covering up your . . . stuff, when you change back."

Slade laughed. "I like the way they think. Waking up somewhere with a bunch of naked guys has always been my least-favorite part of this werewolf gig."

"Brent's right on both accounts," Daniel said. "During my time with Sirhan's pack, they always wore the robes when they thought a fight might break out. And they wore their brightly colored ceremonial robes to impress us."

"I'm always right," Brent said, flexing his muscles; I'm not sure how that had anything to do with being smart. "Which is why," he pointed at Ryan, "you should totally pick those blisters, like I said."

Ryan lifted his fingers toward the blistered spearhead-shaped wound on his face. "Are you sure?"

I swatted Ryan's hand away from his face. "Don't touch it. You don't want it to scar. Brent's just being . . . well, *Brent*."

"Can't you work your healing magic on it?" Ryan asked me, and then shot a glare at Brent. "It burns like a mother—"

"Watch your language," I snapped. "We're in a church." Bleh. I sounded way too much like my mom. I was glad she, April, and my siblings—the humans other than Dad, who had insisted on coming along—had been allowed to stay at the house. "It's caused by silver, which means I can't do much to heal it."

"I told you," Zach said to Ryan. "That's why nothing happened when you tried to heal it yourself."

"Pick at it," Brent said, a little too much glee mixed in with his sarcasm. "You know what a cool scar that would be?"

I rolled my eyes.

"Hey, freak!" someone shouted in our direction. I looked up just in time to see the young, green-robed woman come bounding up to Daniel and me. She stopped just before colliding with Daniel's chest—and punched him in the arm.

Daniel winced. She'd smacked him just below his still-healing bullet wound. But the wince quickly turned into a smile. "Jordan!" he exclaimed.

She laughed and jumped at him. Daniel caught her in a hug, gave her a quick squeeze, and then set her on her feet.

Both of my eyebrows went up in arches. So Daniel *did* know her?

Daniel looked at me and indicated the young woman. "Grace, this is Lisa Jordan. We met during my brief stay with the pack last year."

"The Divine One!" she practically squealed. She grabbed my hand and shook it with gusto. "I have to admit, I thought you'd be *bigger* or something." She shrugged. "But whatever. Thanks for saving my ear! Sweet, I think my superhearing is even a little better." As she pointed at her ear, I noticed that her dangling black teardrop earrings were actually made of moonstones.

"No problem," I said.

Lisa squeezed my hands and let go, then wrapped her hands around Daniel's wrists, bouncing his arms up and down with excitement. "I've missed you, freak. But I can see why you wanted to come back here. She's almost as pretty as I am."

I couldn't help staring at this Lisa Jordan. Not only was she still the only other female Urbat I'd ever met, but she was also gorgeous, with hair the color of candied walnuts and eyes a clear lake green. Her arms were toned, and her body was tall and slender like a runner's. She looked like she was in her early twenties, and I couldn't help wondering—if only for a fleeting moment—just how *well* she and Daniel had gotten to know each other before.

Lisa gave me a playful smile, as if she could read my thoughts. "Don't worry," she said, leaning toward me and still hanging on to Daniel's wrists. "Daniel is *way* too young for me."

I blinked.

"I turned twenty-one in 1985," she said, even though she still looked that age. "I don't go for teenagers. That'd be creepy."

"Oh." I laughed.

All the newcomers in the room looked like they were in their twenties, but some of them had more age behind their eyes.

Lisa leaned in closer to Daniel and took in a deep breath, as if drinking in his scent. "Yowza, but I do have to say, he's even more appealing now that he's got his true alpha on. Nothing quite like the smell of power to get my blood boiling." She smiled at Daniel. "I knew you had it in you. And you wear it well."

Daniel blushed. A full-on, red-in-the-face blush.

"Tell you what." She lowered her voice so it was barely a whisper—kind of pointless in a room full of people with superhearing, but whatever. "That was so darn cool how you got two of Sirhan's men to bow to you. Geez, I'm surprised Sirhan didn't take off your head right there and then for it. Even despite all this 'cure' stuff."

"What's up with Sirhan, anyway?" I asked. "Why does he look the way he does? All man-wolfy?"

Lisa shrugged and swept her long bangs out of her eyes. "That's what happens when the Urbat hit their nine-hundred-and-ninetieth year. Not only do they suddenly age rapidly—their body changes in other ways, too. It's like the wolf manifests outwardly even when they're in human form. One of the other Elders said he thinks that's why some human myths portray werewolves as anamorphic wolf men. Someone must have once found the body of a newly deceased ancient one." Lisa made a pouty face. "It's too bad, too. Sirhan used to be such a hotty. Looked almost just like his grandson, here." She squeezed Daniel's arm.

Daniel looked down at her with a little shake of his head, confusion marring his perfect face. "What did you just say?"

"I think she just called you Sirhan's grandson," I said, her comment just now clicking in my brain.

"Ah crap." Lisa put her hand over her lips. "I forgot that you're not supposed to know that," she said through her fingers. She looked across the room at the group of green-robed men. Two of them glared at her. They'd apparently been listening, and I wondered just how much trouble she'd be in for spilling this secret. But then she turned back to us. "But since that cat's out of the bag"—she winked at Daniel—"I might as well tell you that your last name isn't really Kalbi. It's Etlu. Like Sirhan Etlu of the Etlu Clan."

"It is?" Daniel's voice was barely audible. He'd always despised his last name. Kalbi meant *dog*. Kalbi connected him to Caleb. Reminded him of everything he didn't want to be.

"Etlu means *warrior*," Lisa said. "Caleb must have changed his last name when he was banished by Sirhan—by his own father."

Daniel looked more than shocked.

"So you're saying that Sirhan is Daniel's grandfather?" I asked, unable to hide the incredulity in my voice. "You mean, Sirhan turned away his own grandson when Daniel came to him seeking a home last year? That just . . . Grrr . . ."

"Think about it, Grace," Daniel said slowly, like he was processing his thoughts as he spoke them. "If I'm Sirhan's grandson, then that means Caleb is his son.

Or *was*, before he was disowned. Before Caleb caused the death of Rachel . . . his *own* mother. Imagine the betrayal Sirhan felt? His disdain for me makes all the more sense now."

"But you're nothing like Caleb."

"Sirhan doesn't see me that way."

"Then we have to make—"

The din of the conversations going on around us faded, and I realized I was the only one speaking. All the robed Urbat had turned their attention toward the doorway as three blue-robed men entered the room. One of them carried Sirhan in his arms, the second followed closely with an oxygen tank, while a third man dragged a chair from the parish's foyer behind him.

He placed the chair in the center of the room, and the two other men placed Sirhan in it. They stood behind him with one hand on each of his shoulders. All the other people in robes fell to one knee, bowing their heads toward Sirhan, with one fist shoved against the floor. At first glance, Sirhan, clad in a burgundy velvet robe, looked as regal as a king holding court. But looking closer, I realized that the two men who stood behind him with their hands on his shoulders weren't doing it just as a sign of respect—they were holding Sirhan upright in his chair.

At the same time, I didn't see this as a sign of weakness. No, Sirhan may not be *physically* powerful, but the respect and devotion he garnered from the rest of his able-bodied pack still made him the most dangerous person in this building. A single nod of his head could turn them all against us.

One more blue-robed man entered the room with Gabriel in his custody. The two fell to one knee like the others—Gabriel doing so without any prodding from his guard. Part of me was surprised Gabriel still respected his alpha, despite the way he'd been treated. Then again, Gabriel and Sirhan's history ran much deeper than these last few days. They had been as close as brothers for hundreds of years. Gabriel had told me once that it was the rapid aging process—and the proximity of death—that had changed Sirhan's behavior as of late.

"Very well," Sirhan said. He waved his withered hand, telling his bowing subjects to rise. "I do not have much energy left."

Sirhan's spokesperson knocked the hilt of his spear against the hardwood floor three times. "The Elders of both packs will convene in the center of the room for negotiations. Step forward."

The men in green robes moved quickly to form a half circle behind Sirhan's chair.

"That's me," Lisa said as she stood. "I better go."

"You're an Elder now?" Daniel asked.

"Duh," she said, swishing the fabric of her green robes. "Methuselah passed away from old age a few months ago. Sirhan wanted some young blood on the council—so I got the nod. Marrock"—she pointed at a large man in a blue robe with blond dreadlocks and a beard—"was super pissed off, as you can imagine."

Daniel nodded.

Lisa hurried off to join the half circle of Elders. One of them, a man with skin as rich and dark as espresso handed her the spear he must have been holding for her.

Daniel looked at me. "Um, does our pack have Elders?"

I shrugged.

Daniel motioned to my dad, Jude, and Talbot to follow us. I would have vetoed his last choice, but I figured he had his reasons. We made our own semicircle facing Sirhan.

"Let us get to the heart of the matter." Sirhan pointed one of his long, clawed fingers at me and beckoned me closer. "The Child Divine claims she can cure me. But what exactly does she want in return?"

I took a few steps in his direction. "Sanctuary. For Gabriel, Daniel, my family, and the rest of my pack. For this town, too. No one in Rose Crest is to be hurt by you or your people. Is that clear?"

"Lofty demands from one so young and small."

"I pack a pretty big punch." I waved my hand around the room. "Tell me, do you know anyone else who's ever cured an Urbat before? Do you know any other Divine Ones? I cured Daniel, and now I can provide the same for you. But only if you grant us sanctuary."

Sirhan narrowed his eyes. "Bring the Kalbi boy here," Sirhan demanded. "If he's been cured as you and Gabriel claim, then why does he still possess the true alpha nature?"

Two spearmen took Daniel by the arms, even though he didn't protest being brought only inches from Sirhan's monstrous face. Sirhan pulled the oxygen tube from his nostrils and scrunched up his snoutlike nose. After several wheezing breaths, taking in Daniel's scent, he curled his lips in a growl. "You are not Urbat," he said to Daniel. "What are you?"

"I wish I knew," Daniel said.

"But you do," I said. "You're a Hound of Heaven. A true one. With all the powers of the Urbat, but without the curse that's been passed from one generation to the next. From one infection to another. He's what God intended all of you to be."

It made so much sense when I said it, I couldn't believe I hadn't thought to explain it in those exact terms before now. Gabriel nodded at my words like he agreed with my conclusion—and for half a second, I thought I caught a look of recognition in Daniel's eyes when he glanced back at me. Like he finally understood—and accepted—it, too.

The Elders murmured among themselves. One of them leaned over and whispered something in Sirhan's pointed ear. The alpha nodded.

"All the power without the curse?" he asked. Something

gleamed in his yellow eyes. He waved at the guards, and they took Daniel to the side of the room next to Gabriel.

"So tell me Child Divine," Sirhan said. "How does this wondrous cure work?"

"It's simple really." I took another step closer to him. "You die."

ONE SECOND FLAT

Every razor-sharp spear in the room pointed in my direction.

"Whoa." I raised my hands. "What I mean is, the cure is death. Gabriel himself can tell you. It was his theory that I put to the test when I cured Daniel."

"Yes," Gabriel said. "The cure to the Urbat curse is to be killed by the one who loves you most—in an act of true love. Grace has proved that it works. Alas, there is no guarantee that you would survive the cure as Daniel did, but it would free your soul before you died. So you are not doomed to be a demon for all eternity."

That look in Sirhan's eyes faded, as if the hope that he could become perfect like Daniel faded along with it, but it was the freeing of his soul that he'd come here for in the first place. "Then how can *you* cure me, child? You don't even know me."

"I never said I could actually cure you."

Sirhan snarled. "You dared to lie to me, child!"

Five blue-robed men closed in on me, their spears

only centimeters from my face. "No!" I shouted. "I didn't lie. I said I would provide the cure for you, but *I* can't do it. You're right, I don't know you. I pity you. I have compassion for you. But only someone who loves you most can cure you."

Sirhan's lips dropped back over his pointed teeth. He pursed them tight for a moment. "Then it is hopeless. My Rachel is gone."

"Here's a whole room of people who love you—" I started to say.

"They are loyal; that is not the same as love," Sirhan said. "My true alpha essence keeps them devoted to me. But I have been far too cruel over the last year. No one in this room could possibly love me now. Love is against the nature of most Urbats, anyway. We are sad creatures, really. We hate to be alone. Our greatest drive is to be a part of a pack. Yet it is also part of who we are to never truly be close to anyone. We're too selfish for love."

"But there are exceptions to that. You and your Rachel? Daniel and I before he was cured?"

"True," Sirhan said.

"And I believe there is someone in this room who still loves you greatly. Despite the way you've treated him. He's loved you as his brother for nearly eight hundred years. That has to mean something, doesn't it?"

"Does she mean you, Gabriel?"

Gabriel nodded. "I am still your faithful brother,

Sirhan. No matter what betrayal you think I have committed. I came to this town, and I stayed here, because I wanted to learn more about the cure—for you. For me. For all of us. I am your beta, and I will be until the end."

"But can you kill me?" Sirhan asked Gabriel. "You, who hasn't raised his hand against another man for centuries?"

"What life I have I owe to you, my brother. I would have gone mad hundreds of years ago if you had not convinced your pack to let me in." Gabriel swallowed hard. "For you, I would do anything." He wrung his hands. I noticed they were trembling.

Sirhan sighed, looking even more weak and frail than before. Like he'd somehow aged another couple of decades in only a few seconds. He reached one of his beastly hands toward Gabriel. "Then do it now, brother. End my suffering. . . . Before it's too late and I pass from this world on my own."

"Not here. Not now. Alas, Sirhan, I will need time to prepare. Meditate. I want to ensure I am in the right state of mind for it to work. What I do for you must be an act of pure love." He paused for a moment. "There is also the issue of the Challenging Ceremony that should be considered."

"Yes. Tomorrow is the first day of the full moon, is it not?"

"It is."

Sirhan coughed. It sounded like a mixture of a growl and an asthma attack. "I do not know if I can hold on that long." He rolled forward awkwardly in his chair, as if trying to reach for Gabriel, but instead he slumped over his knees, his outstretched hand now pointing at the floor.

Gabriel knelt at his alpha's side and helped push him up. The guards held him steady. "You must. Two days is not enough to prepare for the ceremony. We need more time."

"What's this about two days?" I asked. "And what does the full moon have to do with anything?"

"Pack laws are stringent when it comes to the Challenging Ceremony," Gabriel said. "Not only in location, but also in timing. The ceremony would have to take place within a hundred paces of the location where the death of the alpha occurred. Pack laws also dictate that the Challenging Ceremony must happen at midnight on the second night of the full moon directly after the death of the alpha. If Sirhan were to pass either today or tomorrow—the ceremony must be held this Saturday evening. When the moon is at its fullest."

"It would be glorious, though, wouldn't it?" Sirhan mumbled, more to himself than anyone else. "A Challenging Ceremony on the night of the bloodred moon. So poetic. And all that p-p-p-power . . ."

I wondered for a second if Sirhan was rambling incoherently with some sort of rapid-aging-induced dementia, but then I knew what he was referring to. "The night of the bloodred moon? Does he mean a lunar eclipse?" I looked at Daniel. "There's a total lunar eclipse this Saturday. We're supposed to observe it for our astronomy class. Dr. Richards said that the moon would turn bright red during it." I looked back at Gabriel and Sirhan. "Does a lunar eclipse do something to the Urbat?"

"So much power," Sirhan said. "It would be so glorious."

"No, Sirhan. It would be far too dangerous." Gabriel looked back at us. "The way the sun, moon, and Earth align during a total lunar eclipse, something about it increases the power of the wolf tenfold. The draw of the wolf," he glanced at me, "would be overwhelming. And if an Urbat can channel the power of the bloodred moon, it would make him immensely powerful. A Challenging Ceremony held during the eclipse would be far too dangerous." He held Sirhan's hand, not seeming to notice the grotesqueness of it. "Alas, you must hold on longer, my brother. Two days is not enough for time for us to prepare."

"Very well. I've been alive for nine hundred and ninety-nine years. What is two more days?" He let out a low, raspy laugh. The he straightened up in his chair. With a labored swing of one of his leathery, withered arms he pointed at Daniel. "In the meantime, kill the Kalbi boy."

"What!" I screamed.

The five spears that had been pointed at my face were now positioned by their holders at Daniel, who stood tall and unflinching.

"This wasn't part of the deal, Sirhan!" I said. "Daniel is to get sanctuary."

Lisa stepped forward from the pack Elders and rushed to Sirhan's side. "Be reasonable," she begged.

"Keep your end of the bargain," Gabriel said.

Sirhan grabbed both Lisa's and Gabriel's hands with a fierceness I didn't think him capable of. Lisa's face twisted with pain. Sirhan's face resembled that of a rabid, deranged beast. "No!" he roared. "A true alpha who possesses all the power but without the curse. No son of Caleb Kalbi should be allowed to have that. No son of Caleb should be allowed to *live*."

"That's the wolf speaking, Sirhan," Gabriel said. "Come to your senses. The boy has done nothing to you."

"He has the blood of Caleb Kalbi, the most selfish and treacherous Urbat I have ever known. That is offense enough."

"Daniel and I are a matched set," I said. "If you kill him, then you'll have to take me, too. Then you'll have no more Divine One."

"That's no longer an issue." Sirhan clapped his mangy hands, and one of the spearmen turned toward me, the sharp blade ready to stab into my neck. "You already told us what we needed to know about the cure."

Crap, he did have a point.

"Sirhan," Gabriel said, "the girl still has so much more to give. And the boy may be our only hope—"

"Silence," Sirhan barked.

"Wait," I said. "Yes, Daniel has the blood of Caleb inside of him, but he also has yours. He's your grandson, for heaven's sake. But he's so much more than that. He's proved it time and time again. And he did once more when he freely gave himself over to you. Would Caleb have ever done that?"

"Tricks," Sirhan hissed between his wolf teeth. "How do I know it was not part of his plan to win my favor?"

"Daniel helped heal me," my father said from behind us. "He helped heal my wife, too. He's saved my daughter's life and my youngest son, also. Where Caleb is selfish, Daniel is selfless."

"Caleb is coming to the Challenging Ceremony," Jude suddenly spoke up from our semicircle of Elders. I'd all but forgotten that he and Talbot were here.

"It's true. He's amassing an army," Talbot added. "I used to be one of his generals, until my loyalties changed. The others have seen how dangerous his forces are with their very own eyes."

"I can also confirm this," Gabriel said.

Daniel, Jude, and I nodded in agreement.

"He's planning on tearing the ceremony apart and claiming the position of alpha of *your* pack, no matter the cost. Is that what you want?"

Rage burned in Sirhan's eyes. "Never."

"You kill Daniel now, and that's exactly what you'll be asking for," Talbot said. I felt a sudden pang of appreciation toward him.

"He is right, Sirhan," Gabriel said. "Daniel, as a true alpha, is our best shot at stopping Caleb from winning."

"No. You are to be my chosen successor, Gabriel, not the Kalbi boy. You are my beta . . ."

"I am your beta, yes. I am the caretaker of the pack. Alas, I am not the leader you are. I am not a fighter. I don't stand a chance against Caleb and his demon hoards. But Daniel has been chosen by a higher power. He is a true Hound of Heaven and a true alpha. It is his calling to take your place. Only he can lead us out of this dark time and defeat Caleb. I believe he and his alpha mate, the Divine One, have been chosen to take the Urbat to a new level. Imagine it. This pack led by a true alpha and the Divine One. A warrior and a healer. The Etlu and the A-zu. Together—"

"No! No! No!" Sirhan roared. "No son of Caleb will rule this pack."

"Sirhan," Daniel said. Every head in the room snapped in his direction. The true alpha essence radiated off his body like waves of pure power. The spearmen pulled their weapons back, ever so slightly. "The difference between Caleb and me is that I don't want to be alpha. I've never wanted to be a ruler, or a leader, or even powerful. All I've ever wanted to be is an artist. I embraced my true alpha nature only to save the ones I love. And now, if that means my calling is to do it again at the Challenging Ceremony in order to defeat Caleb— then I will do it. If there was any other option, I'd let this responsibility pass to someone else. But once you die, I will be the only true alpha left. Let me be your successor instead of Gabriel. Give me your blessing, *Grandfather*." Daniel's voice wrapped around that word like he'd never addressed anyone with that title before. "I will make you proud."

Sirhan slumped in his chair, clutching his clawed hands to his head. Again, he looked as if he'd aged another ten years in a blink of an eye. "I cannot think," he said. "The boy has confounded my mind. His words ring true, but the wolf inside of me screams something else."

"You're brain is addled by the aging, Sirhan. The wolf has too much control. Let the council decide, if you are not able. Who will be your successor?"

"What say the Elders?" Sirhan asked. "Advise me. Whom do you choose? The son of Caleb, or Gabriel?"

All the Elders huddled together—speaking in whispers so low I couldn't even make out their words with my sensitive hearing—except for Lisa Jordan, who came to stand in front of Sirhan.

"Your choice sounds more like, 'Son of Caleb, or Caleb himself' to me," Lisa said. "I don't need to deliberate. I cast my vote for Daniel now." She turned to him and bowed on one knee. One fist pressed into the ground. "And I will follow him into battle to defeat Caleb if need be."

"Here, here!" Gabriel knelt, fist to the ground toward Daniel. "I cast my vote also."

The other Elders took in the sight of Lisa and Gabriel, and for a second it looked like they'd made up their mind to follow their lead.

"This is bullshit," shouted a voice from the crowd.

I looked in the direction of the voice and found that the man with the blond dreadlocks had stepped forward. I thought hard, trying to remember the name Lisa had called him by . . . Marrock.

"I will not give my allegiance to this boy, true alpha of not," Marrock said. "He's, what, eighteen? Most of us have been alive since the French Revolution. What does he know of being a leader that I do not?"

Three men who stood behind Marrock nodded in agreement.

"If Gabriel is too weak to be your successor, then name me instead of this boy." Marrock looked like he wanted to spit in Daniel's direction.

"Sirhan didn't even trust you enough to name you to his council of Elders," Lisa said. "What makes you think he'd name you his successor?"

Sirhan was aging fast in his chair. "The council will decide," he wheezed out. "Marrock, Gabriel, or the boy?"

The council went back to deliberation, and I worried Marrock had thrown a major kink in Daniel's odds of surviving this day. But then the council turned toward Daniel. "Here, here, to the boy!" they shouted, and one by one they fell to their knees, shoving their fists into the carpet. They bowed their heads toward Daniel.

"So it will be," Sirhan said.

Many of the robed men dropped their weapons and copied the gesture of the Elders.

Marrock and five others in the crowd remained standing. "If that is what the council decrees, then I am no longer a member of this pack."

His robe swished behind him as he stormed from the room, the five other men followed him.

"Should we go after them," someone asked.

Sirhan lowered his head. "It's their choice to leave."

"I am afraid we will probably see them again at the Challenging Ceremony," Gabriel said. "For now, let us welcome Daniel Kalbi—"

Lisa pulled on Gabriel's robes and gave him a pointed look.

"Ah, yes," Gabriel said. "Let us welcome Daniel Etlu, grandson of Sirhan Etlu, and his pack into our ranks. Here, here!" he shouted.

"Here, here. Here, here," the kneeling men shouted over and over again, their chorus growing loud enough to rattle my eardrums.

"Here, here!" I called, clapping my hands. Dad and

even Jude joined my applause. Only Talbot stood still without cheering, but a smile played on his lips.

Daniel stood tall, as if soaking it all in. He'd never really had a family before, and now he had one almost more than forty people strong. After a moment he cleared his throat and raised his hands to quiet the crowd. "Um, you all can stand up now if you want."

Lisa laughed and clapped her hands as she stood. I ran to Daniel and threw my arms around his neck. But our joy lasted only a moment before Sirhan gave a great moan and crumpled in his chair. He looked even more withered and decrepit than before—if that's possible— like the last few minutes had added another hundred years to his body. His sunken eyes rolled back, closing halfway. I would have thought he was dead if it weren't for the deep-pitched wheeze of his breathing. Two of his men, his medical staff, I assumed, leaned over him, checking his vitals.

I let go of Daniel and sidled up to Gabriel. "What are we going to do? We can't let him die here in Rose Crest."

"We'll need to move him. Somewhere secluded but comfortable. Do you have any ideas?"

"My grandpa Kramer's cabin. It hasn't been used in a couple of years, but it's about a four-hour drive from here."

Sirhan's attendant shook his head. "He has had a long journey already today. I don't think it wise to move him tonight."

"Tomorrow then," Gabriel said. "We will find a place for him to stay tonight, and then set out in the morning."

"There's always my house," Daniel said. "He could take the master bedroom on the upper level."

"No, that location has been compromised," I said, remembering what Slade had told me about the Akh reading his mind. "No one should stay there."

Gabriel nodded. "He can take my room behind the parish. I would like to spend the night meditating in the forest before our journey anyway. I must prepare my mind before I can cure Sirhan." Gabriel took my hand. "I would like you to come with us to the cabin, Grace. Show me exactly how you cured Daniel, to ensure I do it right. You'll have to miss another day of school, I'm afraid."

When did my life get to the point that the idea of going to school felt like the abnormal part of what he had just said? "Of course," I said, even though I wasn't sure I could really *show* someone how to do it. But at least I could lend my moral support to the "kill the ones you love in order to save them" club.

"I would like you there, also, Daniel. As his successor, you should be there when he dies."

"Yes," Daniel said.

Gabriel let go of my hand and clapped his on Daniel's shoulder. "We must help Sirhan survive the next few days, then you will have an entire month to prepare for the ceremony."

"If he's in hiding when he dies," I asked, "could we keep it a secret? Just for a few days? Let the lunar eclipse pass, and then tell everybody. That way we could have another month to prepare even if he dies sooner."

"It would be against pack law," one of the Elders said.

"Yeah, but could we bend this law, just a little?"

Gabriel shook his head. "You could try, but once the Death Howl starts, everyone will know that Sirhan has passed. Secrets would do no good."

"What's the Death Howl?"

"When a true alpha dies, his pack will sense it. They will howl in his honor no matter where they are. It's some sort of supernatural phenomenon that can't be stopped. Other Urbats, even just plain wolves and domestic dogs, will pick up the call. After the Death Howl, word will spread quickly of Sirhan's death, and every Urbat who wishes to challenge for the position of alpha will know it is time."

"Oh," I said. Really, what else could I say?

One of the guards lifted Sirhan's frail body. Another took up his oxygen tank.

"I will show you the way to my quarters before I go on my sojourn in the woods," Gabriel said, beckoning them to follow him.

"Be careful in the forest," I said. "The sheriff has called for a full-on free-for-all on wolves. In fact, *no one*," I sent a pointed glance around the crowd, "should be going wolf around here unless you want to be a trophy on a hunter-with-silver-bullet's wall."

The crowd gave one another grave looks, but I hoped that would be extra incentive to keep their innerwolves in check.

"Thank you for the warning," Gabriel said, and left with Sirhan and his attendants.

"I hope Sirhan can hold on," I said to Daniel.

"Me, too," he said. His voice sounded like the weight of the whole world suddenly rested on his shoulders.

Chapter Twenty-nine

ANTICIPATION

The next couple of hours were spent making sleeping arrangements for our thirty-five or so unexpected guests. Rose Crest doesn't have any hotels, and most of the pack Elders weren't too keen on staying too far away from Sirhan, so Mom and I rummaged through the storage closets at the house. We pulled out blankets, old decorative pillows, and bolts of cloth—anything that could make a few bedrolls.

It was strange, really, that only a couple hours before I had been worried these Urbats were going to kill us—and now one of my biggest concerns was for their comfort as they slept on the cold hardwood floor of the parish social hall.

But now that they'd accepted Daniel as Sirhan's successor, and me as Daniel's alpha mate, they treated us with the utmost respect.

"I could only find stuff for about twenty people," I said when I showed up at the parish with a few boxes of old baby quilts, sheets, and sleeping bags.

"I guess it will have to do," Jude said, and took one of the boxes out of my arms. I smiled at him, remembering the time we'd spent together as siblings, sorting through boxes for the annual Thanksgiving charity drive each year. Working with him now almost felt like old times.

April grabbed a couple of sleeping bags.

Lisa Jordan picked up a set of threadbare *Star Wars*–themed sheets out of one of the boxes—the same set Jude, Daniel, and I used to make tents out of in the family room for movie night when we were little. "I don't think I've roughed it since 1991," she said. "Not since Sirhan took me in."

For some reason, I'd always imagined that a werewolf pack that lived in the mountains would be roughing it all the time. Living in campers or caves or something. However, based on the fleet of practically brand-new Cadillac Escalades—not to mention the Aston Martin Rapide—and the quality of the pack members' velvet robes, I'd started picturing Sirhan's compound looking more like a fine European manor with at least a dozen garages attached.

I guess if you've been around for almost a thousand years, you probably learn a thing or two about long-term investing. It was obvious Sirhan and his pack were swimming in money. No wonder someone like Caleb coveted control of this pack—I imagine it came not only with power, but also with Sirhan's estate.

"I guess some of them can stay at my house," April said. "My mom is on a business trip, and we've got two extra bedrooms."

I looked at her. April was offering her home to a bunch of werewolves to spend the night? For some reason, I wasn't shocked.

Lisa dropped the sheets and popped up on her toes. "Do you have HBO?" she asked. "Sirhan doesn't allow TV in the compound. I haven't seen a movie in years."

"Yeah," April said.

"And licorice. Do you have popcorn and licorice? We could have a girls' night!" Lisa looked happier than a puppy with a brand-new chew toy.

April smiled. "And I just got a new pedicure set."

Lisa squealed, clapping her hands on April's arms. "I haven't painted someone else's nails since the 1980s. You know how hard it is living with a bunch of grumpy old werewolves? Not another girl in sight for miles."

"You want to join us, Grace?" April asked with a hopeful smile. "Girls' night!"

"No, thanks," I said. "But have fun." I had way too much on my mind to think about movies and make-overs. I didn't foresee a "girls' night" anytime in my near future.

April looked at Jude. "It doesn't just have to be a

girls' night. You can stay at my house, too. I promise not to paint your nails."

"No." Jude shook his head adamantly.

"Ooh, is that your boyfriend?" I heard Lisa ask April when the two made their way to April's car. A small group of Urbat men followed after them, rolling their eyes. If they wanted comfortable beds to sleep on tonight, they were going to have to put up with the giggly girl squad.

I glanced at Jude, whose eyes followed April with a longing sort of look. "If you want to go with her, I'll cover with Mom. Just this once."

Jude shook his head. "I want to stay here tonight. Back in the cage in the basement."

"Are you sure?"

"I'm not taking the easy way out," he said. "I do want to be home. It's just that the full moon starts tomorrow. I can already feel its pull." He squeezed the moonstone pendant we'd given him in his fist. "I just don't feel comfortable sleeping in the house with the family yet. I think it's best if I spend the next few nights locked up. Just as an extra precaution."

"Okay," I said hesitantly. It had been such a big step to get him to want to leave his cage, I worried that locking him up again would be a step backward in his progress. But then again, his wanting to be locked up for the safety of the family seemed like a reasonable request. I just hoped he wouldn't stop fighting the good fight.

I walked with him down to the basement. I pulled the gate closed behind him and turned the lock.

"Take the key," he said.

I tucked it into my pocket for safekeeping.

"See you in the morning," I said before heading up the stairs.

Jude didn't answer.

ALMOST MIDNIGHT

Daniel and I decided that it wouldn't be safe for the lost boys to go back to the Duke house, so when I got back home, I wasn't surprised to find just about every soft surface in the house occupied by a teenage werewolf. Brent was already asleep on the living room couch; Ryan had made a bed for himself under the dining room table with stacks of pink accent pillows—that must have been donated by Charity because they came from the window seat in her room. Zach snored from Dad's easy chair, and Slade was staked out on the family room sofa, flipping through channels on the TV. Talbot sat on the floor in front him, sharpening a stake with one of my mother's kitchen knives.

I was glad they were here—not that the house was any safer, as far as Caleb's knowledge of it was concerned, but I guess I just felt comfort knowing where they were if something bad happened.

"Grace," Mom called as she came up from the

basement. "I just found a few more blankets with the camping gear. You mind running these back over to the church?"

"Sure." I sighed heavily, picking up my keys again.

"I'll do it," Talbot said. "I should be getting home anyway."

"Are you sure?" I asked, realizing that I had no idea where *home* was for Talbot. "You can stay here. Strength in numbers, and all that."

"I'll be fine," he said, lifting his newly sharpened stake.

Mom handed him the bundle of blankets. "You really are welcome to stay, though," she said.

"Thank you, but it's getting a bit crowded around here." Talbot's gaze locked on something beyond my mother's head. I followed his line of sight and saw that Daniel had just come through the front door. I'd wondered if I'd get to see him again tonight. Jarem, the tall, dark-skinned pack Elder—had insisted on introducing Daniel personally, and individually, to each member of the Etlu Clan.

I locked eyes with Daniel, and he smiled at me. My heartbeat kicked up a notch, and I barely even noticed Talbot say his good-byes and duck out the front door past Daniel.

"That Talbot is a nice boy," Mom said. She must have liked his farm-boy charm.

"Huh," I said. I couldn't take my eyes off of Daniel.

Something about him had changed. In the way he stood, the way he smiled, even the look in his eyes. He'd finally, fully accepted himself as a true alpha—and Lisa had been right: he wore it well.

Daniel's smile grew wider as he came down the hall toward to me. My legs ached with each inch he got closer.

"Well, I guess Daniel can take Jude's room in the basement since your brother isn't coming back home tonight," Mom said. "The bed is small but comfortable. Much better than the couch."

"Yeah, a comfortable bed would be good," I said. My face grew very hot, very quickly, realizing I'd said that out loud.

"Thank you, Mrs. Divine," Daniel said, not taking his gaze off of me. "That's very kind of you."

Yes, it was very kind. And slightly odd, considering Mom's usually not-so-warm feelings concerning Daniel. I started to wonder if her thoughtful gesture was a sign that her mental health still wasn't 100 percent, but then she grabbed me by the shoulders and propelled me right past Daniel before I could properly greet him, and ordered me upstairs to bed. That's when I understood her true intentions for offering Daniel superior sleeping quarters over the other boys.

Jude's basement bedroom was the farthest point in the house from mine.

But it didn't matter, because even two floors away, even with all the snores and noises of so many sleeping people in the house, I could still *feel* Daniel's presence. I found it impossible to sleep knowing he was lying on a bed in the dark somewhere in the same house as I was. There were still so many unfinished things—and unsaid words—between us. We'd barely had a chance even to talk about just *us* since he turned back into human.

How do you spend an entire night holding each other, and then let two floors separate you on another night?

I longed to see him, if just for a moment. Have a few seconds alone in the chaos of our lives.

I could just sneak down there for a few minutes . . .

Yet the idea of it felt downright *dangerous* as I contemplated it.

By three in the morning I couldn't stand it any longer. My body buzzed with so much anticipation and longing, I knew I wouldn't be able to sleep at all unless I could see him.

Just for a minute. Just a quick, "Hello, I love you, don't forget that," and a kiss and then I can go back to my room and sleep . . .

I tiptoed down the stairs, past the sleeping boys in the front room. Slade was still awake, watching infomercials in the family room. I almost turned back when he looked up at me.

"Um, just have to take care of something real quick," I whispered. "Don't mind me."

"Sure," he said, and nodded, a little too much *knowing* in his smile.

My cheeks grew extremely hot, and for a second I contemplated running back upstairs, but I realized I'd feel even dumber turning back with Slade watching me.

I held my head high, simply pretending I desperately needed a sweater from the laundry room, and opened the door that led down to the basement. I closed it tight behind me.

My feet moved on their own accord after that, propelling me quickly but quietly down the basement stairs. Right up to the door of Daniel's bedroom. My hand rose to knock, just to see if he was awake, but I stopped.

He was probably asleep. He was probably exhausted from everything he'd been through today. He probably would think I was nuts for waking him in the middle of the night just to say a quick hello. . . .

I dropped my hand to my side. It was dumb for me to have come in the first place. I turned, ready to tiptoe back up the stairs so he'd never know I'd been there, when the door opened behind me.

"Grace?" Daniel asked.

I looked back at him standing there in a wrinkled pair of flannel pajama pants, no shirt covering his perfect abs and stomach, hair all rumpled like he'd been tossing and turning. Like he hadn't been able to sleep, either.

"I hoped you come," he whispered. "I didn't think you would. But I'd hoped."

"You did?"

Daniel's large hands wrapped around my waist, pulling me against his bare, warm chest. Our mouths melted together, kissing in an urgent, almost-frantic way. He pulled me into his room, closing the door behind us.

"I only came for a quick hello," I said against his skin.

"That's all I was hoping for." He kissed me hard. "Hello," he said, and kissed me again.

"Hello," I said, and giggled until he cut off my laugh with his searching lips. His hands felt like fire, clasped against my hips.

"I should go," I said between kisses, not actually wanting to tear myself away.

"Yes, you really should." Daniel trailed his lips down my throat.

"I'm going to leave now." My fingers traced the muscles in his back as I shuddered against his chest.

Daniel's mouth left my collarbone, and he kissed my lips one more time, pushing me away from him in the same moment. "Go," he said. "Before I can't resist anymore."

I stole one more kiss and then backed away to the door. My hand was on the knob, my mind swimming, trying to recall what else I'd wanted to come down here for. . . . I'd wanted to talk to Daniel about . . . something.

"Wait, Gracie," Daniel said, but he stayed on his side of the room, as if trying to resist temptation.

"Yes?"

"There was something else I wanted to say. Another reason I was hoping to see you." He took one tiny step closer, the muscles in his body tensing. "Something happened at the hospital. You called me your . . . fiancé, remember?"

I nodded. "I was just . . . the nurse wouldn't let you in because you weren't family. . . ." *Should I lie?* "I just made that up. . . ." *What was the point of lying now?*

"But when we were doing the healing session for your dad," Daniel said. "When we were connected, I remembered something. No, not remembered really. But I felt something. . . . Like what you had told that nurse about us . . . Like it was just . . ." He ran his hand through his rumpled hair and bit his lip. He looked like he was searching for just the correct words to say.

"Daniel, I—"

"It just felt . . . *right*," he said.

My heart almost stopped—in a good way.

"We're engaged, for real, aren't we?" Daniel asked, taking two large strides closer to me. "It must have happened at the warehouse, right? That night we spent in Caleb's dungeon?"

I took a few steps closer to him, feeling my heart drumming, propelling me forward. "Yes," I said. "Yes, Daniel . . ." but my voice was almost completely drowned out by the ring of the telephone on Jude's nightstand.

I looked at it, perplexed. *Did that really just happen,*

now, *or had I imagined it?* Daniel stared at the phone, too. *Who the heck would call here at three in the morning?*

That couldn't mean anything good. . . .

The phone started to ring for a second time. My hand shot out, and I answered it before it could even finish its nerve-rattling sound.

"Hello?" I asked—half pissed off by the interruption, half frightened by what might be on other end of the line.

Nothing. Absolutely nothing but silence.

I looked at the caller ID—this whole situation feeling eerily all too familiar. "It was from the parish," I said. "But nobody is there."

"Maybe someone knocked the phone off the wall by accident and it was just a flyaway?"

"Do landlines make flyaway calls?"

I put the phone up to my ear again. "Hello?" I strained my superhearing to try to make something, anything, out on the other line.

What I heard, somewhere in the distance beyond the phone, made my blood run cold: the screeching cry of an Akh, before the line went totally dead.

"Akhs!" I said. "There're Akhs at the parish."

In a lightning-quick movement, Daniel grabbed the shirt he'd worn earlier off the dresser. He yanked it over his head and pulled it down over his abs. He grabbed the phone from my hand.

"What are you doing?"

"Calling my cell," he said. "I gave it to Gabriel before he headed off into the woods." He put the phone to his ear and waited a second. "Trouble at the parish," he said into the phone. "We're on our way. Meet us there." He slammed the phone down on its base and grabbed my hand.

We flew up the basement stairs, through the door, and out into the kitchen.

"Where're you lovebirds headed?" Slade asked from the couch.

"There're Akhs at the parish," I said. "Have to get there as fast as we can."

"Then let me drive." Slade was up and had grabbed the keys to the Corolla from the key hook before he was even done speaking.

I shouted to the other lost boys to wake up and follow us.

"I'm coming, too," Dad shouted as he came down the stairs in his pajamas.

"No! Stay here!" I said. I had no idea what we were headed into, and I wasn't going to risk putting anyone in my family in harm's way.

Chapter Thirty

FORCED HAND

OUT THE FRONT DOOR

We followed Slade to the car, and I was glad for his maniacal driving skills as we flew down the empty streets of Rose Crest and into the parish's front parking lot. The building seemed quiet and peaceful. No lights shone through the windows, and I started to wonder if I'd imagined hearing an Akh. I started to hope we were acting on a false alarm—but then I noticed that the front door of the building stood wide open, making any thoughts of reassurance fleeting as we dashed into the building.

I detected the smell of Akh and Gelal, not to mention Urbat, as soon as we entered the foyer. But there was another unexpected smell, like rotten eggs, that filled my nostrils. I wrinkled my nose, coughing. "What is that?"

"I know," Brent said, and he took off in the direction of the social hall. Slade and the other boys followed.

Daniel started to go after them. "No. Let them handle it. Come with me. I need to check on Jude. If someone called, it was probably him."

We darted down the stairwell leading to the basement. The air was clearer, and the rotten-egg smell faded the farther down we went. I reached for the light switch in the pitch-black basement, but nothing happened when I tried to flip it. "Power is out."

"It's okay," Daniel said. "I can see."

I concentrated my powers into my eyes until my night vision sharpened.

We rounded the corner and went straight for the gate of Jude's cage. Only it wasn't there—the gate, I mean. It had been ripped from its hinges and cast aside like the lid of a tin can. Jude's cot was overturned, his blanket splayed across the ground, with the TV set tipped over on top of it.

Jude was gone.

"What happened here? A struggle? Has Jude been kidnapped?" I asked.

"Or is someone trying to make it look like that's what happened?" Daniel crouched, inspecting the mangled hinges of the gate.

"What are you saying?"

"I don't know . . . But this gate was torn off from the *inside* of the cage."

"You guys!" Slade shouted down the stairs. "You need to get up here!"

Daniel let go of the gate frame and picked something up. He handed it to me. The moonstone pendant, tied to a broken string.

"You guys!"

I shoved the stone in my pocket without saying a word, and we bounded back up the stairs.

Slade stood at the top, holding what looked a like burned-up soda can in his hand.

"What is that?" I asked.

"Homemade flash bomb. We found gas bombs, too. They're all unconscious—everyone in the social hall."

"Are they okay? Are you sure they're not . . . ?"

"It's just knockout gas. They'll be fine but pretty nauseated in a couple of minutes. But Grace," he held up the soda-can bomb. "This is one of Brent's designs."

"What? I don't get what you mean. Brent's been with us this whole time."

"I mean, this wasn't just any old Akh attack. This was the doing of the Shadow Kings. They were here. They knocked everybody out."

I looked at Daniel. "But why would they just knock out all of Sirhan's men . . . ?"

"Sirhan!" Daniel shouted. He was out the door and around the building in matter of seconds, with Slade and me on his heels. We went down the alley between the parish and the school and almost ran right into Gabriel.

"I came as fast as I could," he said.

"No time to talk," Daniel said. "Follow me."

We ran toward the caretaker's apartment. I could see the door standing open as we approached. Something large and furry lay in front of it. Daniel and Gabriel didn't stop to see what it was and leaped over it in order to get through the door. But something caught my eye—the shredded fabric of a blue robe and the shaft of a broken spear, lying in a pool of blood under the furry thing. It was a wolf—one of Sirhan's guards, I realized. A dead guard.

I went through the doorway and almost tripped over another dead wolf.

"No," Gabriel cried. "No!"

My head snapped in the direction of the bed that took up most of the room. A withered, leathery, gray body lay on the bed. A silver spear protruded from his sunken chest. Blood darkened the fur all around the blade.

"They killed Sirhan?" Slade asked from behind me.

"No," Daniel said, leaning over the body, his fingers pressed to Sirhan's shriveled neck. "He still has a pulse. At least one of his hearts is still beating. He's not dead yet."

"What?" Gabriel felt his friend's wrist. "Yes, he's still with us. But not for long."

"Quick!" I said. "We have to move him. We have to get him out of here." I couldn't imagine holding the Challenging Ceremony in the parish. The Shadow

Kings had desecrated it enough with their attack. "He can't die here!"

"Keys," Slade said. "I left the keys to your car in the parish."

"Take these!" Daniel picked up a set of keys on the small desk and threw them to Slade.

"You want me to drive the Aston Martin?" he asked, wide-eyed. I could tell he was trying not to sound too excited, considering the circumstances.

"Yes. Get us as far away from here as you can," I said.

Daniel carefully but quickly broke the shaft of the spear so it only protruded about six inches out of Sirhan's chest. Then he wrapped Sirhan in the bedspread. He and Gabriel hoisted up Sirhan's beastlike body, spear and all, and we went running for the limo parked in the back lot of the parish. Slade unlocked the doors, and I held one open as Daniel and Gabriel carefully but quickly hefted Sirhan inside.

"Hold on, brother," Gabriel said, holding Sirhan's wrist.

I ran around the car and jumped into the front passenger seat.

"Go!" Daniel shouted, slamming the door once we were all inside the limo. "Drive as far out of town as you can!" He pointed in the direction of the main road.

Slade revved the engine and slammed on the gas.

We flew, faster than fast, out of the parking lot onto the road, and kept on careening toward Rose Crest's town limits. I was glad it was so late; we wouldn't encounter any other cars, as Slade wasn't exactly worried about staying in our lane. Instead, he drove right down the middle, straddling the double yellow lines.

We'd just flown past the LEAVING ROSE CREST, COME BACK AGAIN SOON sign when Gabriel shouted, "There's no time left! We're losing him."

"You want me to stop?" Slade shouted.

"No!" I shouted. Sirhan couldn't die here. Not out on the open road. We'd never be able to host a Challenging Ceremony here. We needed someplace secluded. Abandoned. Where no one in town would go.

I looked out the windshield at the upcoming intersection. "Hang a right!"

Slade turned the wheel, and we went sailing onto the old country road Daniel and I had driven down only the night before. "Seriously!" Slade shouted with glee. "Did you feel how the Aston handled that! I would kill to race this thing."

I gave him a sideways glance, hoping he wasn't being literal about the killing part.

"You're racing against time, now!" Daniel shouted.

I could see the apex of the Frightmare Farms barn just beyond the trees. "We're almost there. Take this left!"

Slade took the turn, clipping the back bumper on a post of a large FOR SALE sign at the corner.

"That's a bloody shame," Slade said.

"We're about to do worse. Keep going straight!"

"But there's a fence." He pointed at the closed entrance gate, guarded by a couple of scarecrows.

"Do it! Just keep going straight!" I ordered. "Hold on!" I shouted to the others.

Gabriel and Daniel clung tight to Sirhan. Slade cringed, slammed on the gas, and the front of the limo hit a metal gate. I braced against the impact as the gate burst open and one of the garish scarecrows went flying up in the air. It landed with a *thunk* on top of the car. It's eyeless face looked down on us through the moon-roof before it went flying off the car.

"Hay!" Slade shouted, and we plowed through a pyramid of hay bales. Hay exploded all around us, but we kept on sailing until we came to the center of the barnyard and I shouted for Slade to stop.

The limo swerved, sending mud and hay flying as we spun to a stop.

"You're insane!" Slade yelled.

"You're brilliant," Daniel said, pushing open his door.

"Sirhan's dying!" Gabriel screamed.

He and Daniel pulled Sirhan's shriveled body from the back of the car. If I'd thought the ancient alpha looked old before, it was nothing compared to how he looked now. Like leathered skin pulled tight over a skeleton.

Gabriel cradled Sirhan's head in his lap as he lay in the hay in the middle of the barnyard. "Sirhan," he said. Tears streamed from his eyes into his red beard. "Sirhan, I am here. I will keep my promise. I'll cure you before you die."

"Doesn't he have to be in wolf form?" I asked, looking at Sirhan's half-beast, half-human body.

"This is it," Gabriel said. "There is no separation between his two forms anymore."

"It's now or never," Daniel said, holding Sirhan's limp wrist.

"Deal the final blow," I said. "Let him die by the hand of the one who loves him most."

With a great scream, Gabriel slammed his hand down on the hilt of the silver spear that protruded from Sirhan's chest. It sank deep into his hollow rib cage, sending a gush of blood rolling into his already saturated fur. The body convulsed, but then with a final gasping wheeze, Sirhan's head lulled back in Gabriel's lap—dead.

We all knelt quietly in the mud, while Gabriel held Sirhan's body and cried, until right in front of our very eyes Sirhan's dead body began to transform. His short fur melted away, and his gray, withered wolf skin shifted into an olive human tone. The snout of his face shortened into a normal human nose, mouth, and dimpled chin. I couldn't help thinking, as I looked at the purely human version of Sirhan in the light of the moon, that I now knew what Daniel would look like if he ever lived to be a very old man.

"It worked, my brother," Gabriel whispered. "You are cured."

"Um, how do you *know* if the cure worked?" Slade asked.

"The transformation," Gabriel said. "Normally, when an Urbat dies, his body transforms into that of wolf. I always assumed it was a symbol that the man would remain a demon forever. But Sirhan's body has reverted to his human form. I have to believe that means his soul is free of the wolf."

"I think you're right," I said softly. "When I cured Daniel, his body turned human."

Without a word, Daniel leaned over his grandfather's body and crossed the old man's arms over his chest like a mummy I once saw of an ancient king.

Gabriel rocked back and forth until he flung his head back, looking up at the moon, and a great howl ripped out of his throat. The sound of it made my whole body shudder.

Daniel stood, his head arched back as well, and picked up the cry. Slade followed suit. And soon more and more voices—dogs or wolves somewhere in the distance—joined in, creating an unearthly chorus, filling the early-morning sky with sorrow.

The Death Howl had begun.

It would spread, like a wave in a stadium, until every Urbat knew it was time.

Forty-four hours.

In about forty-four hours, the Challenging Ceremony would start in this exact spot.

Chapter Thirty-one

GET THE MESSAGE

Slade drove us back to the parish, slower this time, though I could feel him itching to take the car at top speed again. When Gabriel got there, Sirhan's pack, looking groggy and ill from coming to from the knock-out gas, were waiting for us in the parking lot.

"The Death Howl," Jarem said to Gabriel. He had an accent that made it sound as if he'd grown up somewhere in Africa. "We heard the howling and carried the cry. What became of Sirhan?"

"It is finished," Gabriel said. "He was cured."

The others bowed their heads in reverence.

"His body is in the car. We should take him and the two dead guards into the woods and give them the send-off fitting of warriors."

Gabriel had explained to me on the way back that meant building a pyre and burning their remains.

They'd disintegrate completely in the flames.

A few of the Elders gathered together and left with Gabriel to take care of the dead. They had just pulled away when two cars came into the parking lot. April's red hatchback and Talbot's blue truck.

Lisa and April got out of the red truck. Talbot followed a few seconds later.

"We heard the howling," Lisa said as they met us on the parish lawn where we stood.

"So did I," Talbot said. "What happened?"

Daniel told them about the attack on the parish and what happened to Sirhan. Lisa wiped tears from her face. Talbot's green eyes grew stormy with what I presumed was anger as he listened to the details.

"Where's Jude?" April asked, her eyes flitting to the faces of Sirhan's men, who milled about in the parking lot, still groggy from the gas. "Did he go with the Elders or something?"

I hesitated, not sure what to say. "No," I finally said. "He asked to sleep at the parish, but we haven't seen him since the attack. I don't know if he ran away, or if the Shadow Kings took him prisoner." *It may even be possible he's the one who brought them here.*

April covered her mouth; she started to sink to the ground, but Talbot caught her up in his arms. She rocked a bit, clutching her hands close to her chest. "Tuesday is his birthday," she said. "I thought . . . finally—" Her voice broke off with a high-pitched yelp.

"We'll figure out what happened," I said.

"We need to be open to the possibility that Jude was the one who orchestrated this attack," Daniel said.

"Do you really think that's true?" I looked down at my hands. I know I'd thought the same thing just now, but I just couldn't accept it.

"Think about it, Grace. The door of his cage was ripped open from the inside. I could tell by the way the hinges were bent. The Shadow Kings knew exactly where everyone in the building would be. They had a plan of attack before they even got here. How would they know unless they had an inside man?"

"You're saying that Jude broke out of his cage and then let the SKs in?" April asked. "I just can't believe it."

"He asked to stay here last night, didn't he, Grace?" Daniel asked. "When he could have stayed in a comfortable bed at home?"

I nodded.

"And we don't know where he was every minute tonight before you locked him up again, do we?"

I shook my head.

Talbot nodded. "He could have sent the SKs a message to meet him here at a designated time," he said. "Told them where to find Sirhan and the others. Told them about our plan to try to postpone the ceremony past the eclipse."

"No, I don't believe it," I said. "He wanted to change. He wanted to be better." My encounter with Jude—our reconciliation—had seemed so genuine, I couldn't let myself believe that he'd betrayed us. "Maybe that Marrock guy is the one who—"

"I believed Jude, too," Daniel said. "I really did."

"Wait, isn't *that* your brother?" Lisa asked, pointing at someone who came stumbling into the parking lot only a few yards away.

"Jude!" April and I shouted at the same time.

He looked up at the sound of our voices. His stumbling walk shifted into an awkward, jerking kind of run as he came toward us. He passed right by April, who looked like she wanted to tackle him with a hug, and kept coming toward me. He raised his arm, and something metallic flashed in his hand.

"Jude—?" I started to say.

His eyes looked completely dead as his arm came swinging down, a knife in his hand, aimed right at my heart. I spun away just in time. April screamed. Jude fell forward, and his knife lodged into the grass.

Had my own brother seriously just tried to kill me? Had I been so wrong about him?

Jude let go of the knife, looking stunned. He stood and started walking in a circle.

"What the hell?" Daniel shouted. He and Talbot made a move to grab Jude, but he suddenly scrambled away from them with jerking movements.

He turned those dead eyes on me and stepped toward me, again with odd jerky movements, like part of him wanted to move in my direction, but his feet were fighting it. I recognized those odd movements. It reminded me of those dancing girls at the trance party. It was almost like . . .

Talbot swung around, a large rock in his hand, ready to bash my brother in the head with it.

"No!" I shouted. "Don't. He's in a trance."

Jude grabbed the knife out of the grass. His arm jerked back and forth as he swung it at me again.

Talbot grabbed him from behind and held him by his arms. The knife dropped from his hand.

"A trance?" Daniel asked.

Jude's head jerked back like he was trying to head butt Talbot.

"Yes," I said. "We have to snap him out of it."

"On it," Daniel said. "Sorry, friend," he said to an unresponsive Jude, and swung his fist right into Jude's jaw.

Jude's head turned sideways in response to the blow, and then it lulled forward. He looked like he was unconscious for a moment, but then his body began to convulse, like he was having a seizure, while Talbot held him upright.

"Is he okay?" I started to ask.

Suddenly, Jude's head snapped up. He looked right at me with his glazed-over eyes. His mouth opened and began to speak, but the words he said were not his own. "Sirhan is dead. The Death Howl is over. The ceremony will go forward tomorrow. You will come. You will fight. The Shadow Kings will lap the blood from your throat." Jude clamped his mouth shut, his face twisted as if he were trying to stop someone else from speaking with his voice. He shook his head, but two more sentences came out. "There, we will bring the child. You will fight, or he will die."

Daniel sent another punch across Jude's face. He slumped out of Talbot's arms and fell to the ground, in a faint.

"Well, those Shadow Kings could make a fortune writing creepy greeting cards," Lisa said. "That was some message."

Daniel scanned nearby rooftops. "Jude was being controlled, which means there was probably an Akh nearby, pulling the strings."

"I'm on it," Lisa said. "I'll search the grounds."

"I'll go with you," Talbot said. He stepped over Jude's body, and he and Lisa took off on their search.

"Is he going to be okay?" April asked. She knelt in the grass next to Jude. He moaned when she felt for his pulse.

A cold dread had filled me since the moment Jude had stopped speaking. "What did he mean about the child?" I asked. "That they'd 'bring the child' with them?"

"I don't know," Daniel said.

Jude rolled his head back and forth with a great

groan. He blinked up at me, looking dizzy. "Gracie," he said, and I was sure it was actually *him* that was speaking. "I tried to stop them. I tried. . . . They said they were going for him. . . . I tried to stop them, but it's too late."

"I know," I said, sitting next to him in the grass. I picked up his hand and patted it. "They got to Sirhan."

"No." He rocked his head back and forth. "Not Sirhan. They wanted him, I heard them say it. . . ." He blinked, blinked, as if trying to clear his thoughts. He squeezed my hand weakly. "Gracie, the Shadow Kings were headed for our house. . . ."

Chapter Thirty-two

EVIL DEEDS

Baby James was gone.

The Shadow Kings had taken him.

When we got to the house, we found the front room window shattered and another one of Brent's makeshift gas bombs under the coffee table. Mom and Dad, who must have been waiting up for us to return from the parish, were knocked out cold on the couch. Daniel stopped to check their pulses, but I ran straight up the stairs. Charity was unconscious in her bed, probably unaware that anything had even happened. But James was just gone.

Taken from his toddler bed, blankey and all.

We gathered a rescue party immediately. Every last member of the Etlu Clan volunteered to help us search for any trace of the Shadow Kings, but still we found nothing.

Nothing.

Nothing.

Every scent we followed seemed to evaporate into thin air. Every trail dead-ended. By eight thirty a.m., four hours later, we'd reconvened at the house to talk over new strategies.

"I don't understand," I said, pacing the front room. "How can there be no trace of the SKs? When they kidnapped me, Gabriel was able to follow their trail easily to find me at the warehouse."

Jude cleared his throat. He sat on the sofa next to April. "Gabriel only found the Shadow Kings because they *wanted* to be found. It was a trap, remember?"

I nodded, recalling that now.

"If they don't want to be found, they won't be found," Jude said. "That's how they got their name, the Shadow Kings are masters of hiding in the dark."

I scrubbed my hands down my face, pacing some more around the coffee table. The first time James had been taken from this house—stolen by Jude while he was under the influence of the wolf—before we found him, I'd thought that not knowing what had happened to him was the worst part. But this time, knowing who had him . . . Knowing what they were capable of doing to him . . .

Knowing was worse.

"I promised James I'd keep him safe," I said.

This is your fault, snarled the wolf. I'd gone almost a

full day without hearing its voice, and it almost startled me now. *You brought this upon them with your promises. Promises you can never keep.*

It's your fault.

It's your fault.

It's your fault.

I grabbed the closest thing to me—Dad's Bible from the coffee table—and chucked it through what was left of the front room window. Shards of glass shattered out onto the porch.

"This is my fault!" I cried. "I promised James I'd protect him. I promised him, and now he's gone. They took him from me."

Someone should to die for this.

I picked up another book and was about to throw it out the window, but Daniel grabbed my hand. He wrapped me in his arms, and I broke down, crying. "It's my fault."

"Shhh, Gracie," Daniel said, running his fingers through my hair. "Get ahold of yourself. They want you to lose control, but you can't. Don't let them win by giving in to these thoughts. Caleb is a sociopath. There's no way you could have predicted his behavior, or caused it to happen by making a promise. This isn't your fault."

I nodded against his chest, trying to let his words reassure me.

"If it's anyone's fault, it's mine," Jude said. He

picked up the knife that sat on the side table—the same knife he'd tried to kill me with when he was entranced.

"What do you mean?" I asked.

"The SKs came to the parish because of me. Because of a message *I* sent them."

"That *you* sent them?" came Talbot's voice from the foyer. He'd been standing there with the Etlu Elders.

Jude looked at the knife, twisting it in his hand, inspecting the silver blade. "That night you let me out of my cage to go visit my father in the hospital . . . " He glanced at April. "I didn't go straight to the hospital and back like I said. I stopped at an Internet café in the city and sent an e-mail to an account Caleb uses for fencing merchandise online. I sent him a message telling him that I was being held at the parish. I begged him to send the SKs to come get me. Begged him to let me rejoin his pack . . ."

Jude looked up at me. "But please remember, this was before I talked to you yesterday. Before I decided I wanted to truly come home. I was confused, and I didn't know what I wanted. I just thought, if they wanted me back, and they came for me, then that would make up my mind for me. . . ." He placed the flat side of the silver blade against his arm, rolling it up and down. He winced, and I could smell his skin burning against the silver.

"But when they showed up last night, it made me ill. They'd finally come, and I didn't want to go with them.

But the thing is, they weren't really there for me at all. They just wanted to get rid of Sirhan. But maybe they wouldn't have come at all if I hadn't told them about the parish. Maybe they wouldn't have taken Baby James. This is my fault." Jude closed his hand over the knife's blade, letting it burn the insides of his fingers.

"Jude, don't," I said.

The wolf in my head wanted me to rage at my brother. Blame him for even bringing the Shadow Kings into our lives in the first place. But I couldn't. Daniel was right, giving in to the wolf in any way was not an option now. I'd been strong enough to keep it almost completely at bay since Wednesday—since I'd found my ability to push away my anger and start forgiving—and it had felt so freeing not to have the wolf in my head. I wasn't going to willingly let it in again. I refused to feed the beast any longer.

I left Daniel's embrace and went to my brother. "You had no way of knowing that they'd do what they did. At least you know now that you didn't want to go with them."

"More important," Daniel said. "You know Caleb's e-mail address. We can use that to contact him. Maybe we can arrange some sort of ransom for James. . . ."

Jude shook his head. To my relief, he put the knife down and reached into his jacket pocket with his uninjured hand. "I stole your cell phone earlier," he said to April, giving her an apologetic glance.

She didn't meet his gaze, and I wondered if she was thinking about how he'd admitted twice now in one conversation to breaking her trust.

"I e-mailed Caleb's address already. This is all I got back." Jude handed the phone to Daniel.

He read the message out loud. It was the same one the SKs had delivered through Jude: "Sirhan is dead. The Death Howl is over. The ceremony will go forward tomorrow. You will come. You will fight. The Shadow Kings will lap the blood from your throat. There, we will bring the child. You will fight, or he will die."

I heard a high-pitched gasp from up the stairs, and I realized my mom must have been listening to our conversation from the landing. The knockout gas had left her extremely nauseous, and she'd supposedly been lying down since we got back from searching. This was the first time she'd heard the actual message.

"I tried e-mailing again," Jude said, "but the account has been closed."

"But what's the effing point of that message?" Slade asked from where he sat on the bottom stair. "Isn't it kind of a given that Daniel will be fighting in the ceremony? Why kidnap the baby in order to force Daniel into the fight? He'll already be there. There's got to be more to it."

"It's his backup plan," Brent said. "Caleb always has a backup. He's paranoid and always has to have something to fall back on."

"Yeah, but why demand that we fight when we're already going to? What's the meaning?"

"It means I'm going to be fighting in the ceremony," I said, standing tall. "Jude wasn't meant to succeed when he tried to stab me. He was trying to get my attention. The message was for me. Caleb wants me in the fight, and that's what he's going to get."

"No way," Talbot said. "You can't do what Caleb wants."

"But why would he want you?" April asked.

"Caleb has a *thing* for Grace," Talbot said with disgust.

I snapped a glance at him. "And you don't?"

He glared at me. "If Caleb wants you in the fight, then you should be as far from it as possible. Caleb—"

"No!" I shouted. "He said *I* fight, or James dies. Which means I'm fighting. When Daniel enters the ceremony, I'll be entering at his side. I probably would have regardless of what Caleb wants. I'm fighting, and you can't stop me. I'm not going to let anyone Wendy me."

"Wendy you? What the hell does that mean?" Talbot asked.

"Wendy, from *Peter Pan!*" I shouted at him. I'm sure I sounded completely unhinged. But I couldn't help it. "Peter and the lost boys get to go off fighting pirates while Wendy has to stay back and clean their stupid tree house because they want her to be their mother.

Well, I'm not doing it. I'm not going to be sidelined. I'm fighting for my baby brother, and that's final."

"She's being unreasonable," Talbot said to Daniel. "Tell her to sit this one out."

Daniel stood at my side. "If Grace wants to fight, she'll fight."

Talbot scowled. His behavior made no sense. He was the one who'd taught me how to fight in the first place, encouraged me always to use my powers. Why would he ever try to make me stay away from the Challenging Ceremony?

"If Caleb wants her in the fight," Talbot said, "then he either wants to kill her with his own bare hands, or he wants to make her angry enough that she'll try to kill him, forcing her to fall to the Urbat curse."

"That's not going to be a problem." Daniel placed his hand on the small of my back. "Because *I'm* going to kill Caleb Kalbi."

"Daniel?" I looked up at him.

"If I'm this thing, this true Hound of Heaven, and if God made me to destroy pure evil, then that's what I'm going to do. Starting with Caleb."

"But I thought you said only Gelals and Akhs were pure evil? Caleb is still human. You said he could still choose to change his ways. . . ."

Daniel shook his head. "This is the proof I needed, Grace. Doing this, taking Baby James to use him against us, it proves that whatever spark of humanity

I'd hoped still existed inside of Caleb is gone. He *is* pure evil—human heart or not. And I'm not bound by the Urbat curse. I can kill him without losing myself."

"Daniel . . ." I looked up into his deep dark eyes, which told me he was determined to do what needed to be done. He'd embraced his calling as a true Hound of Heaven.

"Excuse me?" came Jarem's accented voice from the group of Etlu Elders. "Have you considered that one of Caleb's intentions with this kidnapping is to prevent us from being properly prepared for the ceremony? Throw us off our game, as the saying goes. We have already lost several precious hours that should have been spent planning and making preparations."

The other Elders, including Lisa, nodded in agreement with Jarem.

"The message says that they'll bring your little brother to the ceremony," she said. "We have to assume he'll still be alive when they do. If there's no other way to find James, then we must accept that the best way to get him back is to be as prepared for the ceremony as possible."

Daniel looked at me, and I nodded. "So be it," he said.

Thirty-nine hours remained until the ceremony, and we were going to be ready for whatever Caleb and the Shadow Kings could throw at us.

Chapter Thirty-three

PREPARATIONS

The first thing the council decided we needed to do was get a proper lay of the land at Frightmare Farms. Get to know our battlefield. So most of the council of Etlu Elders, plus the other Elders Daniel and I had also selected—my father, Talbot, and Jude—headed out for the farm, with the lost boys in tow. It seemed the closer we got to the ceremony, the closer the boys wanted to stick to Daniel and me. I found their protective nature reassuring, if not a little annoying.

"What do we do if the owners show up?" I asked Gabriel on the way over to Frightmare Farms. It may have been abandoned as a Halloween attraction, but somebody still owned the place. It would be just our luck if the owners decided to take a midnight stroll on their property during the Challenging Ceremony.

"Not a problem," Gabriel said, checking the ancient-looking pocket watch he pulled from his jacket. "In about an hour's time, we'll be the owners of the land."

"What?"

"I noticed the 'for sale' sign when we were here with Sirhan. I called the Realtor and made a cash offer the owners could not refuse, on contingency of taking immediate possession of the property. One of the Elders is handling the paperwork and wire transfer as we speak."

"That 'for sale' sign was for a sixty-acre parcel of land around the farm. That must have cost a fortune."

"Until Sirhan's successor is named at the Challenging Ceremony, the council controls Sirhan's estate. Trust me, money is not a problem."

The caravan of Escalades pulled into the parking field near the farmhouse, and Gabriel led us all to the barnyard. The Elders, dressed in regular clothing, congregated around the spot where Sirhan had died, their heads bowing in silent reverence.

"How do they know that's the spot?" my dad asked as we watched them. Daniel and I had covered up the blood-soaked ground with dirt and straw before we left.

"They can feel it. I can feel it," Daniel said. "It must be some sort of pheromone footprint left behind when he died."

"Is that how the challengers will know where the ceremony will be?"

"Many will be able to sense it. And word will travel

fast for those coming great distances," Jarem said. "This is the epicenter," he continued, addressing the other Elders and holding out his hands at his sides. "Let the battlefield be determined from here."

I watched as eight of the Elders stood back-to-back right over the spot where Sirhan had died, and then they started walking with careful measured steps, radiating out like the spokes of a wagon's wheel.

Gabriel must have noticed my confused look as I watched them. "Pack laws dictate that the battlefield is to be measured out in paces. One hundred of them, creating a circle roughly 150 yards wide around the epicenter of where Sirhan died. This will be the challenging ring. Anyone who enters this ring after the ceremony has started will have to fight. Any fighter who leaves the ring will forfeit his challenge."

The Elders kept measuring out their paces until they'd created a giant circle, encompassing the farmhouse, barnyard, and the large dilapidated barn. Then Daniel, Jude, Talbot, the lost boys, and I gathered rocks and marked the boundaries of the challenging ring.

We gathered again in the middle, and Daniel mapped out the battlefield on a piece of notebook paper, showing the buildings and the barnyard and a thick black circle for the boundary line. I was more than happy that the circumference of the circle had barely skimmed the edge of the corn maze. I wouldn't want to have to take on fighters inside the maze again.

"Will you explain the rules?" Gabriel asked Jarem.

Jarem nodded solemnly, as if being asked was a great honor. "The beginning of the ceremony is quite . . . well, ceremonial, so to speak. Since Daniel will be fighting in lieu of Gabriel, the beta, Gabriel must present Daniel in the center of the ring as the prime challenger—the incumbent, if you want to think of it that way. There will be certain words said, and Daniel's face will be painted with specific markings that will signify his rank as the challenger to be beaten. Once Gabriel has retired, Daniel will then be required to invite any other challengers to step into the ring."

"How many challengers can we expect?" I asked.

"At a normal Challenging Ceremony, perhaps one or two. However, this ceremony will be different because of . . ." Jarem glanced up at Gabriel.

"Because of me," Gabriel finished for him. "The Etlu Clan is large and influential, not to mention wealthy. I am known well for my pacifist ways, and many of the other larger packs have been anticipating Sirhan's demise for quite some time, hoping they can easily take possession of this pack from my hands. The short timeline until the ceremony may prevent some from coming, but I would think it safe to anticipate *at least* five challengers—other than Caleb."

"So they'll come expecting Gabriel, but what they'll get is Daniel," I said. "A true alpha instead of a pacifist beta. That'll be a nice shock."

"Secret weapon," Ryan said, punching Daniel on the arm. "I bet a bunch of them will totally rethink challenging."

"Not necessarily," Jarem said. "We can use the surprise to our advantage; however, it cannot be our only strategy. Most Urbat would not challenge a true alpha—however, it has been centuries since a Challenging Ceremony involving a true alpha has occurred. Not since Sirhan was made leader after his father died. I am afraid, to many younger Urbat from packs other than ours, the very idea of a true alpha is merely a fairy tale."

Gabriel shook his head. "Even after we present Daniel as the prime challenger, I am afraid many of the other challengers may feel they have come too long of a way not to make a challenge for the position of alpha, regardless of the presence of a true alpha or not."

Daniel nodded. "So no matter what, I can't expect that Caleb will be the only challenger?"

"Certainly not."

"And what happens when there's more than one challenger?" my father asked.

"They must all fight it out. The last man standing wins."

"But Daniel can try working his true alpha mojo on them. Get them to submit to his authority?" I asked.

"Mojo?" one of the older-looking Elders asked. "What is mojo?"

"Essence, power, whatever." I waved my hand up

and down in front of Daniel. "He can do that thing that makes other people want to bow to him."

"Ahh," the Elder said. "Yes, that is Daniel's greatest advantage. That is the danger of trying to challenge a true alpha—you may end up one of his subjects instead."

I didn't like that word—*subjects*. Caleb ran his pack like a cruel dictator or general. Sirhan ran his pack like a somewhat benevolent king. To me, a pack seemed more like it should be one big, not-so-normal family. At least, that's how I'd run it.

"Not everyone will submit to the will of a true alpha," Gabriel said. "It only worked on a few of Caleb's boys in the warehouse, remember?"

I nodded.

"Your 'mojo,' so to speak," Jarem said to Daniel, "will only work on some. And certainly not Caleb. He did not even recognize the authority of his own father. Those who will not submit by choice will have to brought to the point of submission by force—or finished off altogether. You must be the last man standing in order to win."

Daniel grew quiet and still, I imagine absorbing all the information. He looked up at Jarem. "What do you mean 'finish them off'? What does it take to be the last one standing?"

"*Whatever* it takes. There are four possibilities once you, or any challenger, enters the ring. You can leave the boundaries of the ring voluntarily and forfeit your challenge; you can submit to another challenger and become his subject; you can be killed by another challenger; or you can be the last man standing and therefore the winner. You must understand, the Challenging Ceremony is a fight to either submission, or death."

I willed away the dread in my heart that pushed against the inside of my rib cage. I didn't like the idea of Daniel, or me, entering a fight to the death. My plan was to stay and fight until Caleb was taken care of, and Baby James secured, and then I would exit the ring, allowing Daniel to win. But that was making the very large assumption that Daniel and I would still be standing at the end of it all.

Daniel took in a deep breath and sent it out slowly through his teeth. "I won't kill the other challengers. Caleb, yes; any Gelals and Akhs who enter the ring with him, certainly. They're pure evil, and it's my responsibility to destroy them. But these other possible challengers? They don't deserve to die just because they've challenged my authority. I won't kill them."

"Once you enter that ring, you either submit or force the others to submit," Jarem said. "You kill or be killed."

"He's just as bad as Gabriel," a black-bearded elder named Bellamy said. Lisa had told me that he claimed to have once been an actual pirate of the Caribbean. "We lose the pack to Caleb no matter which coward we choose."

"He's not a coward," I said. "He's just not a five-hundred-year-old barbarian who thinks indiscriminate killing is the right thing to do."

"I'll fight," Daniel said. "I'll use my mojo, or whatever it is. But I won't kill any challenger other than Caleb."

Lisa looked at Daniel with pride in her eyes. "Your strategy will have to be to wound other challengers to the point that they'll beg to submit."

Daniel swallowed hard. I knew he didn't like the idea of wounding anyone like that, but he didn't protest Lisa's suggestion. It was better than killing random strangers.

"Then you'll lose," Bellamy said, shoving his face right up into Daniel's. "Maybe Marrock had the right idea walking out. You're too much of a child to understand what it takes to be a leader."

Daniel stood his ground against Bellamy, glaring into his eyes. "You're welcome to challenge me yourself in the ring," Daniel said, squaring his jaw. I could feel the power radiating off of Daniel's shoulders until the giant bearded man took a large step backward, away from Daniel.

"No," Bellamy said. "But don't say I didn't warn you. If you won't kill, you'll be killed." He pointed at me. "And your girlfriend, too."

Daniel glanced away when he mentioned me.

"Not necessarily." Talbot, who had been otherwise

silent, said. He adjusted his baseball cap on his head. "What if another challenger in the ring took out anyone who refused to submit for you?"

"There's no guarantee that would happen," Jarem said. "The other challengers will fight among themselves, certainly, but we can't just hope they pick each other off for us."

"But what it there was a guarantee?" Talbot asked. "What if *I* entered the ring as a challenger?"

Daniel narrowed his eyes at him. His brows furrowed. "You want to challenge me?"

"No. I'd be a ringer. I'd fight side by side with you and Grace, but I have no qualms about killing anyone who tries to harm her. I can be your backup executioner—if that's what the circumstances called for."

My father threw his hands up. "I cannot condone this idea. I can't listen to you all plan to kill people. . . ."

"Then maybe you should go home," Bellamy snapped at him.

"Even if it is the only means to get your son back?" Jarem asked him.

Dad closed his mouth and dropped his hands to his sides.

Daniel still had his eyes narrowed at Talbot. "And then what?" he asked him. "What do you do at the end of the ceremony?"

"Then I'd submit to you," Talbot said. "Ensure you're the last man standing."

"And what would you be getting out of it?" Daniel asked.

"Your trust. A place in your pack. Except for my brief time with the Shadow Kings, I've been on my own since I was thirteen. I want a place to belong." He smiled at Daniel—one of his warm smiles that made you feel like you'd been friends for ages.

"I like this plan," Jarem said.

Daniel gave a great sigh and looked at me. "You should have a say in this, too, Grace. Do we bring Talbot into the ring with us? You and I can fight, but we let him do the dirty work?"

I looked from Daniel, to Talbot, and then to my father. He turned away so I couldn't see his face. I imagine it would be hard listening to your little girl deliberating over whether or not people should be allowed to die.

"Okay," I said. "But only if circumstances absolutely call for it. I think every challenger, no matter how ruthless, should be given the opportunity to submit first."

"I agree," Daniel said.

"If that's what you wish," Talbot said.

Daniel extended his hand toward Talbot, and the two of them shook on it, sealing the deal. Something stirred in the pit of my stomach as I watched them. Most likely anxiety, knowing that in a little more than thirty-six hours' time, we'd all be fighting for our lives, side by side.

Other than the few rules Jarem had already told us about—the boundaries of the ring, and the last-man-standing-wins part—it started to become clear to me that the rest of the ceremony was pretty much a no-holds-barred free-for-all.

Weapons of any variety were allowed—except for vehicles. Challengers could choose to fight in either wolf or human form—the most advantageous choice being wolf, as most Urbat were stronger in that state. And any pack was allowed to send in as many challengers as they wished.

"Then how come the other packs don't send in tons of challengers? We're sending in more than one fighter? Don't they stand a better chance with more?" I asked.

"Usually only one champion is sent into the ring by their pack because they risk losing each person who enters," Lisa said. "Most packs are small. The Etlu clan is forty strong—or was before Marrock and his lackeys left and you all joined us. The Oberot Clan has twenty-seven members. But most of the other packs are less than a dozen members each. If you only have ten people in your pack, you're not going to risk five of your men. Even two would be considered too great a risk, you see?"

I nodded.

"It's the lone wolves you really have to worry about.

Challengers who have no pack of their own to be accountable to. They always fight the dirtiest."

"Who we need to be the most worried about is Caleb," Talbot said. "We're getting off track, worrying about anyone else. Any other challenger is merely a distraction. Caleb's coming here with an army of Gelals and Akhs and Urbats. Don't forget that. And he doesn't give a damn about casualties. He's planning on bringing as many Shadow Kings into that ring as he can."

"And he must have *a lot* of Gelals and Akhs," Daniel said. "Based on how many he was willing to send to that trance party."

"Is that allowed?" Lisa looked at Jarem.

"It's never been done before. Gelals and Akhs do not normally ever interact with the Urbat. But it is not against the rules."

I scrubbed my hand down the side of my face. A few minutes ago I was fretting over the prospect of our going up against a handful of challengers. Now it was sounding like a few dozen, or even more.

"What about the eclipse?" I asked. "Won't that make Caleb even more of a threat?"

"The ceremony starts at midnight," Lisa said. "The eclipse isn't supposed to begin until about twelve twenty-five. We'll just need to make sure Caleb is taken care of before it begins. They can last several hours, so the sooner we can finish this, the better."

"I imagine it would be best if we could concentrate

most of the fighting here." Daniel pointed at the open area he'd marked as the "barnyard" on his map. "Try to keep the fighting out in the open."

"But if the house and the barn are within the challenging ring, then people can take the fight in there, right?" I asked.

Jarem nodded.

"The barn doesn't worry me so much," Daniel said. "It's still pretty open inside. However, I've been inside the house. The rooms are small and cramped, and there are far too many places to hide. Chasing someone in there might end up being an ambush."

Brent suddenly jumped like he'd been shocked with a jolt of electricity "What if we got rid of the house?" he asked, an expression of maniacal glee on his face. "Made it go boom."

"What?" Daniel and I asked at same time.

"Are you suggesting we blow up the farmhouse?" Daniel asked.

"Why not?" Brent pressed his finger to the bridge of his nose like he was pushing up an imaginary pair of glasses. "Seeing that thing go up would definitely freak out the Shadow Kings. Ahks and Gelals hate fire almost as much as Slade."

Slade shot Brent a look like he wanted to pound him.

"What? I'm just saying. . . ." Brent shrugged dramatically.

"I like the way you're thinking," I said. "But what if

we could somehow lure as many of those Ahks and Gelals into the house before you blew it up? Get rid of the house, and get rid of as many of them at the same time?"

"Now you're talking!" I swear it was almost possible to watch Brent planning out a design for the explosives. "I'll need a remote trigger. . . ."

"Can this kid really build a bomb big enough to burn down the house?" Bellamy crossed his large arms in front of his chest.

"Believe me," Dad said. "He knows how to blow things up."

Brent gave my dad a sheepish smile. "Uh, yeah. Sorry about that."

Dad gave him a nod.

I looked at the other lost boys. "Do you think the rest of you could come up with some sort of plan to get as many demons into the house as possible? Some sort of lure?"

"Sure thing," Zach said, and Ryan agreed.

"If that house is going up in flames, I'm not going anywhere near it," Slade said. "I'd rather be fighting hand to hand in the barnyard with you guys."

"That can be arranged," I said, grateful for another fighter.

"Me, too," Lisa said. "I want to fight with you guys. I said I'd follow Daniel into battle, and I meant it."

Jarem looked at her like he wanted to protest. I wondered if it wasn't customary for Elders to join the fight, or if he had some sort of personal interest in wanting her out of harm's way.

Jude cleared his throat, drawing my attention. He'd been so quiet for so long, I'd almost forgotten he was there. He raised his hand as if he were a child in school. "What do you want me to do?"

I looked at Daniel. I have to admit, I didn't want Jude in the ring with us. I just didn't know if he was stable enough yet for such a fight. . . .

Daniel spoke up before I could. "I don't imagine Caleb will limit his attack to just those inside the challenging ring. I think we need to be prepared for the possibility that the rest of the pack may have to do some fighting on the sidelines. Would you be willing to help organize them?"

"Yes," Jude said. I could tell he was relieved that we hadn't asked him to enter the ring as a challenger.

"Our guards are trained in combat, but many of our other men are not fighters," Jarem said. "We've followed Gabriel's pacifist ways since the 1700s. We're out of practice."

"I can help Jude give them a crash course in fighting," Talbot said. "They're going to need all the help they can get."

FRIDAY, MIDAFTERNOON, THIRTY-THREE HOURS UNTIL THE CEREMONY

Gabriel made the call for the rest of the Etlu Clan to join

us, and we divvied up tasks and went to work. Daniel and a few of the Elders continued to debate strategy, while I sent Zach and Slade to the sporting-goods store on Main, to buy up as many crossbows and hunting knives as they could. Unfortunately, since the Death Howl last night, the mayor had upped the bounty on *any* wolf's head to ten thousand dollars—which meant there weren't very many weapons left in the store to begin with. I just hoped since our new farm was on a sixty-acre parcel of private land, we wouldn't get any unexpected hunting visitors tomorrow night.

Bellamy supervised a stake-carving committee on the front porch. Talbot and Jude set up a boot camp out in the barnyard for anyone who wanted to brush up on demon fighting. April took it upon herself to buy up all the tiki torches at her favorite costume shop in Apple Valley, and she and Lisa staked them in the ground at regular ten-foot intervals around the boundary of the challenging ring.

Brent drew up his plans for his explosives, and then we sent runners to three separate hardware stores in the county—so as not to raise any red flags—to get supplies. He set to work on constructing the bomb in the barn, with Ryan as his only *slightly* disgruntled assistant.

I tried to keep myself as busy as possible, rotating among the groups and assisting where I could, in order to stave off my growing anxiety about the ceremony, and my deep worry for James's well-being. Every time I felt the wolf's voice creeping into my head, I stopped for deep-breathing exercises while I held the moonstone we'd found discarded in Jude's cage.

Mom and Charity provided a lunch big enough to feed an army—Mom had thoroughly sanitized the haunted farmhouse's kitchen and whipped herself into a cooking frenzy in order to "keep up the morale of the people who were going to save her baby." I stuffed myself with food, mostly in order to keep my hands busy, and then rotated out to the barnyard to check up on Talbot's and Jude's progress in training a small group of the Sirhan's youngest pack members.

But from the looks of it, it wasn't going as smoothly as I'd hoped. . . .

"No, not like that!" Talbot barked at one of his students—a young Urbat with a closely shaved head. "Never try to stab someone while holding a knife with the blade pointing downward."

Jude and the others looked over at them. I leaned with my elbows on the rickety railing of the back porch as I watched.

"If you hold the knife like that, it's too easy for someone to take it out of your hand." Talbot's hand shot out, and, in almost a blink of an eye, he'd captured the knife from his pupil. Talbot turned the knife so the blade angled up and thrust it at his student. The young Urbat jumped back with a yelp.

Talbot sent another sparring thrust in his direction. "See! You can't grab this out of my hand, can you?"

The student shook his head. Talbot looked up then and saw me standing on the porch. He handed the knife over to the young Urbat and positioned it correctly in his hand. "Give it a try."

Talbot backed away as the guy started thrusting the knife awkwardly into the air.

He grabbed something off the top of a hay bale and jogged up the porch steps to join me. He leaned his backside against the porch railing so he was facing me and flashed one of his warmest smiles, like he was about to present some sort of peace offering.

"For you," he said, and extended his hands out, presenting me with a sword incased in a wooden scabbard. "I told you I'd get you a sword. If you still insist on joining the fight, then I want you to have the best one I've got."

I took it without saying anything and pulled the blade from the scabbard, inspecting it. I recognized it from one of our training sessions back when he was *my* mentor. It was a kung fu short broadsword, with a slightly curved steel blade and a wood-inlaid steel hilt. A tuft of bright red fabric was tied to the end of it.

"You remember how to use it?"

I nodded and sheathed the sword. As much as I liked it, I wasn't sure I wanted to accept any type of gift from him. I may have agreed to let him join us in the Challenging Ceremony, but he still made me feel a bit uneasy.

"How's it going out here?" I nodded toward the men training to stab each other.

Talbot hitched his thumbs behind his belt. "You know, for a pack that goes by the name Etlu, most of them fight like crap. The oldest ones at least have some skills from back in the day, but they sure haven't done themselves any favors by spending the last few hundred years meditating on the mountainside." He shook his head with disapproval. "What a waste."

"What, you think it's better they use their powers to go running around the city, knocking off jewelry stores and pawn shops?" I raised my eyebrows at him.

Talbot's expression clouded over. "You're still mad at me for earlier?"

I shrugged. I was still mad at him for so many reasons, let alone his insisting that I shouldn't be allowed to fight.

"I'm sorry, Grace. It's just that, you have this great healing power, and if someone you love gets hurt, like your dad, you can heal him. Maybe that makes you see life as not quite so fragile anymore. But what if *you're* the one who gets hurt? Who's going to heal you?" He looked at me with concern in his bright green eyes.

My shoulders dropped. "You and Gabriel tried to heal me once. After what happened at the warehouse."

"*Tried* is the operative word there. It didn't work

nearly as well as the way you can do it." He tapped the back of his shoe against the rungs of the porch railing. "Maybe you can teach me to do what you do. . . . Then maybe I won't be so worried about you going into the fight."

"I'm sure Gabriel already explained it to you when—"

"Honestly, Grace. I don't remember much of what he said. I was just so desperate to save you I couldn't really focus. . . ."

"Then that's probably one of the reasons it didn't really work all that well. You've got to be totally focused. Clear your mind and think about nothing but your love, or compassion, for the person you're healing. Try to picture him becoming whole again." I bit my lip, remembering what had happened the first time I'd tried to heal my father. "Otherwise, it can be dangerous. Like if you accidentally channel your fear, or anger, or hate."

Talbot gave a grave nod. "Is that what happened to your dad that first time? You said you ended up hurting him more."

"Gabriel said it's like letting your inner wolf attack the other person from the inside. The healing power backfired, and instead of repairing his injuries, it reopened them. I even hurt Gabriel. Reopened an already-healed gash on his face. But you've seen what it can do when used correctly. I've never experienced anything like it before."

Talbot held up his hands, almost as if he were examining them for healing potential. "That's some power to wield." He bit his lip.

"Healing people is exhausting, though. After I healed my parents, I fell unconscious for ten hours straight. That can't be a good thing to happen on a regular basis. It's not like I can go around healing an entire hospital of people at once, or anything. That would probably kill me."

"What about during a lunar eclipse?" Talbot asked. "Aren't our powers supposed to increase tenfold? Maybe if you could channel enough of the moon's power during an eclipse, you could do a lot of good for a lot of people."

"Or a lot of damage, if I wasn't careful." I looked down at my hands, thinking about how they could be weapons even more dangerous than the broadsword.

Talbot reached out and grabbed my free hand by my fingers. He drew it close to him and placed it over his heart, pressing it against his chest with his own. "Maybe you could heal the aching I feel inside my heart when I look at you."

"Talbot. Don't." I pulled my hand out from under his and started to turn away.

"I'm sorry," he said. "I shouldn't have done that. I get it. You're Daniel's, and he's yours. You're the perfect match. But I still want to be a part of your life, Grace. Any way I can."

"I don't know how that could work," I said, and stepped away.

"Hey, Talbot?" the young Urbat with the shaved head called from the lawn. "Is this right?" He swung the knife with an upward jab.

While Talbot's attention was turned away, I took the sword and went into the farmhouse to join Daniel and the Elders at as they huddled over a drawing of the battlefield.

And I didn't look back.

FRIDAY EVENING, TWENTY-NINE HOURS TO GO

We kept working until the sun started to set, and Gabriel announced that he and his pack were going to retire into a meditative state—as was their custom on nights when the moon was full. He told me it would be best if I took my family home, and we could resume preparations in the morning.

Mom, Dad, and Charity piled into one of the Escalades driven by Daniel, but Jude told me he wanted to be locked up for the night again.

"There's an empty silo in one of the adjacent fields," he said. "I can sleep there tonight during the full moon, and you can let me out in the morning."

The idea of his not going home again with the family made my heart feel heavy, but I didn't fight him on it. We walked silently together out to the silo. Before Jude could close the door between us, I pressed the moon-stone pendant into his hand.

He folded his fingers over it and closed his eyes with a sigh so heavy I suddenly felt guilty for keeping the stone to myself all day.

"Today was a hard day, Gracie," Jude whispered.

"I know. It's a lot of work, but we're getting closer to being ready for the ceremony. And we'll get James back."

"The preparations weren't the hard part for me. I almost welcome the ceremony because it's something I can focus on. It's thinking beyond it that's so hard. How can I ever hold James again and not burst from guilt, knowing that what happened to him was because I brought the Shadow Kings into our lives in the first place? And I have no idea how I'm going to go back to school, or walk into the parish during one of Dad's sermons, and pretend to be normal again. The idea of it is just *so hard*. . . ."

I nodded. I'd felt the same things to some lesser degree, but I knew that didn't really compare to how difficult it must be for him. "You can do it, though. I know you can."

He gave the slightest nod and pulled the heavy silo door closed. I hoped my words hadn't echoed empty in his mind.

Chapter Thirty-four

Where Soul Meets Body

When I pulled into the driveway of our house, I saw Daniel balancing up in the highest branches of the walnut tree. It almost looked like he was trying to reach out and touch the bright yellow moon above him. His head was tipped back, allowing moonlight to bathe his beautiful face. He opened his mouth, and I was almost afraid he was about to send a great howl into the night— but instead, he simply said my name as I approached.

"Are you okay?" I called up to him.

"I can feel it," he said, "the pull of the moon. It calls to me. I remember that from when I was stuck as the white wolf—feeling that undeniable pull, keeping me trapped. The white wolf wants me to heed it again. Wants me to set it free."

"I don't like the sound of that," I said.

Daniel dropped his gaze from the moon. "Neither do

I." He pushed off from a branch and jumped from the top of the tree. He landed with barely a sound in the grass in front of me. "I want you to know that when I say I feel the pull of the moon, or the pull of the wolf, I don't mean it the way you or Jude feel the wolf. It isn't some terrible voice anymore, trying to drive me to embrace any terrible thoughts. I'm not a danger to you."

"I understand that. The wolf that's inside of you isn't a demon. It's a pure Hound of Heaven."

"But at the same time, I still have to fight it constantly. It wants me to shed my human form and embrace my natural state."

"Are you saying that *being* the white wolf is your natural state?" I placed my hands on his arms. Heat radiated off his skin, and it reminded me too much of the night he'd spent fighting to stay human. I wrapped my fingers around his elbows, feeling like I needed to hold on to him. Keep him from going away again. "Not this? Not you? Not *Daniel*?"

"The white wolf seems to think so." Daniel returned my gesture, wrapping his own hands around my arms. He tapped his ring finger against my skin. "This is helping," he said about the moonstone ring on his finger. It was same ring Sirhan had worn, and Gabriel had presented it to Daniel after Sirhan's death—as a token of the grandfather he'd never really known. "And you're helping, too. Just being near you gives me the drive to stay in my human form. So I can be with you."

"Then you'd better stay as close as you can." I pulled him against me, embracing him as tightly as I could, even though he radiated enough heat to make me sweat.

"I'm not going to go wolf at the Challenging Ceremony," he said. "I'm afraid the draw of the white wolf will be so powerful under the eclipse that I might not be able to fight my way back again."

I nodded against his chest, knowing that not going wolf when the other challengers did might put him at a disadvantage. "My money is still on you," I said. "Even human you."

He let out a short laugh. "All my life I wanted to be normal. Now I'll just settle for having only two legs, two arms, and a human face."

"I like your face," I said, trying to lighten my heart.

"I like yours, too." He shifted his head close to mine and kissed me with lips that felt like fire. Our lips melted together until his body convulsed with a great shudder, and I knew he was still fighting the wolf. "Will you stay with me again tonight?"

"Yes," I answered, holding him tight.

"The white wolf is wrong," he said, and kissed my shoulder. "This right here—you and me together, under this old walnut tree—*this* is my true natural state."

"We always do seem to end up back here," I said. "It's comforting."

"It's home," he said.

I sighed into his arms, realizing that in a day's time, I

had no idea what *home* was going to look like anymore. If we failed at the Challenging Ceremony, this family that I'd been fighting so hard and so long to restore—to make whole again—could possibly be torn apart completely. I could lose everyone I loved.

But if we succeeded . . . If we got James back . . . If Daniel and I were to become the alphas of a whole new pack, I still had no idea what *home* would look like then. Would we be forced to leave Rose Crest to lead the Etlus? Leave my finally reunited family behind?

SATURDAY MORNING, FIFTEEN AND A HALF
HOURS UNTIL THE CEREMONY

I awoke to rays of sunlight streaming through the seams of the boarded-up front room window. Daniel and I had moved inside when it had gotten too cold for me out under the tree. We'd sat on the front room sofa, tangled in each other's arms. Daniel asked me to give him a word-for-word retelling of our engagement. "I want to be able to at least pretend I remember it," he said, but I knew he was looking for something to distract him from his inner battle against the white wolf's pull.

I told him stories until the heat of his body cooled, and he fell asleep with his head tucked against my shoulder.

He stirred next to me now, looking like an angel the way rays of sunlight danced off his golden hair.

I could hear my family in the kitchen, and the sounds of car doors opening and closing outside. The lost boys' voices drifted in through the broken window. It sounded like they were loading something large onto the back of Talbot's truck.

Daniel yawned and stretched next to me. "What's going on?" he asked, sounding slightly disoriented by sleep.

It was Saturday morning. The start of what would probably be the longest day of our lives.

"It's beginning," I said.

SATURDAY AFTERNOON, EIGHT HOURS TO GO

Daniel and Jude both chose to forgo Talbot's battle-training lessons, instead spending the day meditating with Gabriel in the grassy fields on the back acres of the farm. As much as I wanted them ready to fight, I knew it was a smart choice. With every hour that got closer to the sunset, even I could feel the pull of the full moon.

Lisa must have noticed, as she removed her teardrop moonstone earrings and offered them to me.

"Are you sure?" I asked.

"I owe you. I mean, I'm totally hot enough to pull off the one-eared look. But still, I'm grateful I don't have to." She gave me a devious smile. "I'll just have to make sure I don't go wolf tonight, though. Wouldn't want to accidentally kill you instead of a Shadow King."

"Thanks," I said. I closed my fingers over the two small stones and kept them locked in my fist all afternoon.

ONLY TWO HOURS LEFT

Mom served up a late dinner for everyone, and we spread out in the front yard of the farmhouse, filling our stomachs with as much as we could force ourselves to eat—for energy stores and all that. The way we all sat in small clusters, sharing plates of fried chicken and mashed potatoes, any passerby might assume we were at a family reunion. Only we were preparing for battle, not three-legged races or a water-balloon toss.

I sat on the front porch with Daniel, my parents, Jude, April, and Charity.

"Have any interesting plans for tonight?" April asked the group.

Daniel gave a slight laugh.

Charity picked up the fried chicken leg from her plate. "James loves these," she said. "He thinks they're little microphones. Remember how he'd pick a drumstick and hold it like this and sing 'Twinkle, Twinkle, Little Star'?" Her voice caught, and she put the drumstick back on her plate. She wiped tears from the corners of her eyes.

I put my hand on her back. "Except he always gets the words wrong," I said. "And he sings 'Tinkle, Tinkle, Little Star' instead."

Charity gave a sad smile, but then she started crying harder. "What if they don't bring him tonight? What if he's already . . . ?"

"We can't think like that," Mom said. "He's coming back to us. I know it. Grace and Jude will bring him home."

Jude lowered his head, and I watched as he clutched his moonstone pendant against his chest.

A few minutes of silence passed. I picked at the chicken on my plate.

The front door opened, making us all jump at the noise.

Gabriel stepped out onto the porch.

I looked up at him.

"It's time," he said. "The others will be here soon. Let us finish preparing."

Daniel and I stood and followed him into the farmhouse. The rest of my family followed us, while the Etlu Clan scattered to their various prearranged positions for the ceremony. April picked up two black garment bags from the musty old sofa in the living room. "I thought you two should have robes for the ceremony. Like everyone else," she said. "I made them myself."

"Thank you." I took the bags and handed the one marked with Daniel's name to him. I hung my bag over my shoulder and turned to my parents. I pulled the keys to the Aston Martin from my pocket and pressed them into Mom's hand. "I want you guys to take Charity and

April and start driving. Just keep going as far and as fast as you can. Go to Carol's or Grandma's. Just someplace far from here. In case something goes wrong."

Mom looked at the key and then back at me. "No," she said. "They're bringing James here. I can't take off to some other state. I need to be here for him."

"Mom, it's too dangerous. You can't be here. . . ."

"Meredith," Dad said, placing his hand on the small of my mother's back, "how about we drive a few miles down the road, out of harm's way. Grace can call us as soon as they've secured James, and we'll come for him."

Mom thought about it for a moment and agreed. "You won't come with us?" she asked me. "Even if I beg?"

"My place is here."

She nodded.

Dad stepped forward and hugged me. He traced a cross on my forehead. "God be with you."

Mom and April took turns hugging Jude and me tight, and then they left wth Charity and my dad.

Brent, Ryan, and Zach came into the entryway. Ryan and Zach held two hunting rifles at their sides— the same ones I'd stolen from those hunters who had tried to kill Daniel.

Brent held something out to me in a little black pouch.

"This isn't another trick, is it?"

The boys were enjoying staying at a haunted house

all too much, and they'd taken to trying to scare people at every turn with whatever leftover Halloween decorations they could find. I'd about lost my soul when Brent lured me up into the hayloft after lunch to show me "something vitally important." It had turned out to be a giant faux battle-ax, the size of a mountain bike that came swinging out of the ceiling at the press of a button. The stupid thing almost hit me in the shoulder, but the boys had thought the look on my face had been oh-so-funny.

"It's an earpiece," Brent said. "I got it from Sirhan's spokesperson guy. I've got the other one in my ear." He pointed at it. "That way we can communicate while you're on the battlefield."

"Good," I said. "You guys know exactly what you're supposed to do, right?"

The boys nodded.

"No mistakes," I said. "Wait for my signal before you do anything."

They agreed and then ran off to take their places upstairs. Their plan for tonight was our secret weapon against the Shadow Kings—but it was also an extremely dangerous plan, and I worried something might go wrong.

Gabriel put his hand on Daniel's shoulder. He looked at me. "I'll give you two a few minutes."

Gabriel bowed his head slightly and then went into the kitchen with Jude, leaving Daniel and me alone.

The second they were out of sight, Daniel pulled me into his arms. He held me for a full two minutes, neither of us saying anything. For a fleeting moment, I wondered if this would be the last time Daniel would ever hold me. Wondered if both of us would survive this night. Wondered if we should say a few last words . . .

No, I thought. *This isn't a time for farewells. I refuse to say good-bye.*

A horn honked outside. I glanced out the window. A long procession of cars rolled into the parking field beyond the house.

Daniel caressed his hands against my face, cupping my cheeks and brushing away with his thumbs the tears I didn't even know I was crying.

"This isn't good-bye," I said.

"Never, ever good-bye." He leaned in and kissed me in a way that reminded me of dark chocolate—both bittersweet and delicious, leaving me wanting more.

"They are here," Gabriel called from the top of the stairs. "The first of the challengers have arrived. Daniel, come with me, please."

I squeezed Daniel's hand as he broke away from me, and then I nodded to Gabriel—thankful for the few moments alone with Daniel. I wouldn't get another chance for that tonight. Not in that challenging ring, surrounded by spectators, come to watch as our futures were determined under the light of the bloodred moon.

Chapter Thirty-five

CHALLENGE

MIDNIGHT

I walked out onto the back porch of the farmhouse and stood at the edge of the steps in front of the battle-grounds. I tucked the earpiece behind my ear and straightened my moonstone earrings. A cold wind kicked up, tossing my robes around me as I unsheathed my broadsword.

I'd feared April would have gone with something sparkly with sequins for my ceremony garb, but when I'd zipped open the garment she'd given me, I found a beautiful hand-stitched ceremonial robe the color of a coral reef. Pinkish-orange fabric with a satin sheen—that reminded me all too much of my bedsheets at home.

I looked out at the boundary of the challenging ring, lit up by torches and the cascading light of the larger-than-life-looking full moon that presided over the battlefield. Only twenty-five minutes remained until the beginning of the eclipse. I prayed we'd be able to stop Caleb and his army before that happened. Otherwise, the moon would turn red, and all hell would break loose. The Etlu clan stood in a circle within the torches, the ceremonial "guardians of the ring," as Jarem had called them. They held their spears perfectly straight, despite the strong wind that whipped at their jewel-toned robes.

Beyond the guardians, I saw the silhouettes of figures waiting in the fields outside the ring. I caught the reflection of moonlight glinting in several of their eyes.

Urbats. Crowds of Urbats.

At least a hundred total from what I could make out.

"Are they all here to challenge?" I asked Lisa as I took my place next to her between two torches, unable to hide the worry in my voice. "There're so many."

"Spectators mostly." She steadied her spear in her hand. "I hope."

"Where did they come from?"

"Everywhere," she said. "A Challenging Ceremony is one of the few things that will bring Urbat out en masse." She scanned the crowd. "I count representatives from at least fifteen different packs in attendance. The Oberots sent their alpha and his son all the way from Russia. They wouldn't have come if at least one of them weren't planning on making a challenge. They've been keen on merging our two packs for quite some time."

"Any sign of Caleb?" I scanned the crowd once more, but I didn't see anyone I recognized. No Akhs or Gelals. No Shadow Kings.

Lisa shook her head. "It's starting."

She held her spear and stood at attention, looking toward the barn. Gabriel, in his burgundy robes, exited the barn. A second person followed, dressed in a robe that glistened like it had been spun from actual gold. The hood of the robe hid his face, but I could tell by the way he carried himself that it was Daniel.

Jarem, next to Lisa, began to hammer the shaft of his spear against the ground. It made little noise itself, but then Lisa and the other spear bearers joined in. Banging, banging, banging their spears against the hardened dirt floor until it sounded like the beat of tribal drums, heralding Daniel and Gabriel into the ring. The two walked in rhythm with the beat until they came to the epicenter of the challenging ring. Gabriel stood on the wooden platform Bellamy had built over the spot where Sirhan died. It was the place where the ceremony was to begin—and end. The winner would be declared from that spot.

I heard a low murmur from the crowd above the drumming, commenting and speculating as to why Gabriel hadn't entered the ring alone.

Gabriel raised his arms. The pounding stopped, and the crowd quieted.

"I know many of you came this evening believing I, as

Sirhan's beta, would be the prime challenger," Gabriel said. He spoke loudly, projecting his voice, even though there wasn't much need in a crowd with superhuman hearing. "However, two nights ago, Sirhan named a new successor. His grandson, Daniel Etlu of the Etlu Clan."

At Gabriel's signal, Daniel lowered his hood. His hair glistened in the torchlight, looking almost as golden as his robes. Three black lines had been painted under each of his eyes, and another black line ran from the top of his forehead to the tip of his nose—the ceremonial markings of the prime challenger, signifying that Daniel was the person to beat in order to be declared the new alpha. They made him look fierce and primal, like a tribal warrior.

A louder murmur came up from the crowd of spectators. Some wondering why they didn't know Sirhan had a grandson, others remarking as to how much Daniel looked like Sirhan in his younger years.

Gabriel raised his voice louder to be heard over the din. "Daniel is more like his grandfather than just in appearance. He is a true alpha."

Daniel stepped up onto the platform and looked out over the people who crowded around the outside of the arena now. I wondered if he was searching their faces, looking for his father. I could feel the power radiating off his body in waves.

"A true alpha," someone said with spite. I wondered

if the owner of the voice was reconsidering whether or not to make a challenge.

Daniel held up his arms like Gabriel had, and the crowd became completely still. "I, Daniel Etlu," he said, repeating the ceremonial words Jarem had taught him, "chosen successor of Sirhan Etlu and prime challenger, now call for all who wish to challenge my right to lead the Etlu Clan. Step into the ring to make your claim. All others should withdraw for their own safety."

Gabriel gave a slight bow to Daniel and quickly left the ring. He took his place as one of the guardians next to Jude on the side of the ring opposite of the barn.

"We're up," I said, taking in a deep supposed-to-be-calming breath.

Lisa, Talbot, Slade, and I stepped into the challenging field. We walked side by side until we came to stand behind the platform where Daniel waited. The crowd grew loud again with discussion as people realized that we were there for the sole purpose of backing Daniel up.

No other challengers entered the ring yet, and there was still no sign of the Shadow Kings. I searched the crowd for Caleb, while watching and waiting for the first real challenger to step forward. Based on the gestures and heated looks being exchanged between an older-looking Urbat and a man who looked like his son, they were debating over which one of them should enter the ring.

After a moment, the older man gave a nod to his son,

and the younger man passed between two guardians and stepped onto the field.

The crowd silenced, acknowledging the first challenger.

"That's Anton Oberot, son of Serge. He's the beta of the Oberot Clan."

The quiet continued as a second challenger stepped into the ring. He was large man dressed in army fatigue pants and a tight black shirt that showed off muscles upon muscles on his arms. He held something bundled in each of his hands.

"Who's that?" I asked.

"I don't know," Lisa said. "Most likely a lone wolf. Or possible a mercenary paid to fight for someone else."

"These first two are mine," Daniel said.

Three more challengers entered the ring together. I recognized the tallest of them right away. I assumed the other two would be fighting as his lieutenants.

"Marrock. I knew he'd show up." Lisa wrinkled her nose and tightened her grip on her spear. "He's mine."

"I'll take the other two," Talbot said. I wondered if he was trying to match Daniel in number.

Another challenger entered the ring—a woman swathed in layers of sky blue fabric, with golden bangles and henna tattoos decorating her arms.

"That's Mahira, alpha of the Varkolaks. She's

vicious," Lisa said. "She became alpha of her pack by ripping off the head of the beta at the last Challenging Ceremony I went to—he was her own brother."

I shivered in the cold wind, but then to my surprise, Mahira pulled the blue fabric from her shoulders and let the layers fall to the ground. She stood there completely naked in front of us, unabashed.

Slade just about fell over.

"Okay," I said. "Little Miss Naked is my responsibility. None of you boys will be able to focus while fighting her."

One last man entered the ring. He had hair almost as white as snow, even though everything else about him looked as if he were a young man. Everything else but his narrowed eyes.

Lisa gasped. "That's Christopher Varul. He's a pure blood. Varuls don't intermix with anyone who isn't pure. They don't allow Urbats like me—created by infection, not birth—into their pack. If he were to become alpha, he would no doubt get rid of everyone who isn't purebred."

"Now, we can't have that," Slade said, lifting his knife in the Varul's direction.

Another minute passed as we waited for anyone else to step forward and make a challenge, but the crowd stayed quiet and still with anticipation. Where were the Shadow Kings? Where was Caleb? Where was my little brother?

"Why the hell hasn't Caleb presented himself yet?" I asked.

"I don't know," Daniel said. He drew his long steel sword from the sheath under his robe. "What is he waiting for?"

The guardians began to hammer their spears against the ground. My heart beat with the rhythm, anxiety curling in my muscles. It was only fifteen minutes until the eclipse. How were we supposed to stop Caleb before it if he didn't show up?

And then I realized that maybe the eclipse was exactly what Caleb was waiting for.

The drumming of the spears reached an almost deafening thunder around us, then broke off into silence all at once. "Begin!" the guardians shouted.

We all looked at one another for half a second, and then with a great scream the lone wolf in the military pants went charging at Daniel. The other challengers followed only a second behind. Daniel would be the prime target of the challengers, and it was the task of the rest of us to pick them off.

The lone wolf broke away from the other challengers in a flat-out run. He let go of the bundles in his hands, revealing two long whips made out of chains. Silver ones, I was sure of it. He spun them in front of him like propellers.

"Damn, chain whips," Talbot said. "I should have thought of that."

The man with the whips lashed one out at Daniel, who twisted out of the way.

The rest of the challengers closed in on them. Our little pack of backup broke apart, and we each went after the targets we'd chosen.

I went running after Mahira, who loped toward the platform. She jumped with a great lunge and shifted into a large brown wolf in midair, only feet from where Mr. Chain Whips and Daniel fought.

"Hey," I shouted at her. I scooped a baseball-sized rock up and flung it with all my might at the back of the brown wolf's head.

She turned on me, growling.

"Come and get me!" I cried.

I waited half a second to make sure she'd taken the bait, and then I went running toward the barn, following the strategy we'd laid out beforehand—to draw the other challengers as far away from Daniel as possible.

I made it inside the structure just as the wolf nipped at my heels. I spun around and smashed the side of my broadsword against the side of her head. She growled and flew at me with her great, clawed paws. I used my sword to bat them away, but suffered a nasty tear in my swinging arm in the process. As a wolf, she was stronger than I was, especially since I had to be careful as ever not even to *want* to kill her.

She came at me again, jaws protruding from her lips. I changed sword hands, and with a measured blow, slashed into one of her front legs, spilling blood onto her fur.

She howled with pain and anger. I scrambled away and climbed the ladder up to the hayloft, thinking it would give me a moment's reprieve to heal the pulsating gash in my arm.

The brown wolf passed under the ladder. I wondered if she were contemplating changing back into human form in order to climb up after me. But I should have known better.

The wolf took ten paces back and then jumped up into the hayloft, landing only a few feet from where I sat. I clambered to my feet and ran, heading for the far end of the hayloft. The rotten floorboards creaked and cracked under my pounding feet, and I remembered that this was the area where that kid had fallen through the floor last month, forcing Frightmare Farms to be shut down. I jumped over a hole in the floor and ran for the window that overlooked the barnyard. Maybe I could make the jump?

The wolf growled. I glanced over my shoulder and saw her rearing back to leap at me again, claws extended. In a moment of either panic or brilliance, I threw my sword at the small metal box that protruded from the haunted barn's wall. It swung blade over hilt and slammed into the large red button on the box. The same button Brent had shown me earlier as a trick. The wolf lunged into the air, and I ducked as a thick, bicycle-sized faux battle-ax came swinging out from a metal contraption in the ceiling. I knew the ax wasn't sharp, but it caught the brown wolf midair and sent her flying backward. She hit the rotten floorboards with such force, they crumpled under her and she went crashing through the floor of the hayloft. I heard her whine as she fell, and then a sickening sound that made me flinch. I moved quickly and carefully over the cracking boards and gazed down through the hole she left behind.

What I saw made a shudder of nausea rip through me: the body of the brown wolf, skewered through her belly by a broken pole below.

The wolf whimpered and writhed and then fell silent and limp, hanging like a piece of bloody meat on the end of a kabob. I knew she wasn't dead. The pole was iron not silver, and it hadn't decapitated her, but she was most likely in terrible pain. The blood loss would keep her out of commission for quite some time.

A horrible shiver overtook my body as I looked down on her.

Close, child. Close, whispered my inner wolf. I could feel its glee over my near kill. Its anticipation of the next. *I am so close to being freed.*

Finish her off.

I cupped my hands against my ears to feel the calming warmth of the moonstone earrings, shaking my head. *No,* I told the wolf. *I have no intention of killing her. I don't want her dead.*

I backed away to the window in the hayloft and sucked in gulps of fresh air, trying to clear the wolf out of my head. However, the scene outside the window was anything but calming. I could see Daniel below, locked in battle both with Mr. Chain Whips and Anton Oberot. Daniel's adeptness with his sword kept Anton at arm's length, and his agility to spin and flip out of the way of the swinging chain whips seemed to frustrate his other opponent to no end. But Daniel was definitely on the defensive, trying to fend off both attackers at the same time.

Then in a move I didn't expect, and neither did Daniel, Mr. Chain Whips sent a lashing strike of one whip at Anton. It caught the Russian Urbat around the neck, and Mr. Chain Whips jerked his arm back, flipping Anton into the air and then slamming back down again. Anton clutched at the chain that was wrapped around his neck. I'm sure the silver was burning into his flesh. Even from the barn I heard Mr. Chain Whips laugh as he pulled his other whip back, ready to send it lashing into Anton's face. But as the whip went flying, so did Daniel. He reached out in front of Anton, catching the brunt of the whip's blow with his arm. The chain wrapped around his wrist, and before anyone could react, Daniel yanked the whip with all his might and sent Mr. Chain Whips flying over his head. He hit the ground several feet away and rolled over onto his back.

Daniel reached out and helped Anton to his feet.

To my surprise, the Russian made a small bow toward Daniel and then jogged out of the challenging ring. I assumed he'd withdrawn his challenge out of respect for what Daniel had done for him.

I was just thinking that not all of these challengers were bad people when Mr. Chain Whips scrambled to his feet and went flying after Daniel again.

I didn't see what happened next, as a commotion below me caught my attention. Lisa Jordan, going spear to spear, had driven Marrock into the barn. Talbot and one of Marrock's lieutenants entered behind them, fighting sword versus spear. It was only a matter of seconds before Talbot sent a slashing cut into the lieutenant's throat with the blade of his steel sword. Not a killing blow for an Urbat, but the man clutched at his spurting artery and dropped his silver-tipped spear.

Lisa and Marrock went at each other with their spears—spinning, jumping, and ducking out of the range of each other's thrusts in a way that reminded me of a kung fu movie. But Lisa shouted as Marrock sent a kick into her belly. She flew backward into a tower of hay bales.

"Watch out!" I shouted as Marrock raised his spear to stab her.

Talbot heard my call and snatched the fallen lieutenant's spear and sent it sailing into Marrock's back. Lisa rolled out of the way as Marrock fell forward into the hay, the spear still protruding from underneath his right shoulder blade. Talbot rushed at him and grabbed the end of the spear—I thought at first for the purpose of pulling it out, but instead Talbot twisted it with hard, cranking motions. Marrock screamed and screamed, and I knew the silver-tipped spear was not only slicing his insides, but also burning them at the same.

"Mercy!" Marrock begged between his shrieks of pain. "Mercy! I submit!"

Talbot twisted the spear again, his foot pinning Marrock down for better leverage. Marrock shrieked.

"Stop!" Lisa shouted at Talbot. "He's submitted."

Talbot only twisted harder.

"Stop!" I shouted at him from the hayloft, but he didn't seem to hear me, either. I took a running leap and jumped from the loft. I landed in a trough of hay and ran to Talbot, shouting his name. A look of complete and utter rage filled Talbot's eyes as he twisted the spear in Marrock's back. I was sure the eclipse hadn't started yet, but was it already having some sort of terrible effect on Talbot?

"Stop!" I sent my open hand sailing and slapped Talbot across his face.

He let go of the spear and stared down at me—that rage burning in his eyes. Then he blinked and clutched his palm over the red hand-shaped mark I'd left on his face. "What was that for!"

"He submitted. Let. Him. Go."

"Fine." Talbot grabbed the spear, yanked it from

Marrock's back, and cast it aside. "You're welcome," he snapped at Lisa, who gaped at him openmouthed.

"Grace! Grace!" I heard a voice shout. I couldn't tell where it came from at first, and I thought the wolf was shouting in my head again. Only it sounded an awful lot like Brent.

"Grace! Come in, Grace!"

I realized the voice was coming from inside my ear. I'd completely forgotten I was wearing the earpiece.

I put my hand to my ear. "What is it, Brent?"

"Still no Shadow Kings. What do you want us to do?"

"Stand your ground," I said. "They'll show."

Brent swore so loudly it made my eardrum rattle. "Looks like Slade needs some help!"

I dropped my hand from my ear and went sprinting back out into the barnyard. Daniel and Mr. Chain Whips were still fighting, but I didn't have time to ascertain the situation because Slade was running straight at us, down the middle of the field, with two giant wolves on his heels. "A little help here!" he called in our direction.

"I thought you were supposed to be handling one of those guys," I said to Talbot.

"I was a little busy," he said.

"You want us to stop them?" Brent shouted in my ear.

"No! Do not give up your position!"

Slade went barreling past us. Talbot flew at the larger

of the two wolves. Lisa, weaponless now, jumped onto the back of the smaller of the two wolves, pummeling her fists against the sides of its head. I sent my sword into its hindquarters, slicing a chunk in its left hip. It stumbled to the ground. I raised my sword, ready to swing at it again, but the beast lowered its head and tucked its tail between its legs. It whined in submission.

The larger wolf stopped short before sending Talbot flying off its back. Slade punched the beast in the face, but instead of retaliating against him, it spun around and faced Lisa and me. Its yellow eyes narrowed in on me. It scratched at the ground like a bull and then charged in my direction, with great galloping leaps.

I gulped and raised my sword, ready to defend myself against the attacking wolf. But before it could make its final bound, Talbot came flying down on top of it. With a brutal swing of his sword, he sliced into the wolf's neck. Then a second swing decapitated it completely.

"What the—?"

I stared at Talbot, amazed that he was able to pull off such an attack on the wolf, and revolted at the same time by what he'd done. "You . . . you weren't supposed to kill him unless it was a final resort. That was the deal."

He stared back at me with blood on his hands.

"I told you I'd kill anyone who tried to harm you," he said.

"Grace," Brent said in my ear, "the eclipse."

I looked up in the sky and watched as a red stain crept along the edge of the moon, like blood slowly soaking into a white sponge. The eclipse was just starting, but I could already feel a surge of energy raking down my spine. My powers were magnifying.

"Any sign of Caleb?" I asked Brent. I knew he had a better vantage point than I did from his hiding place.

"No."

I spun in a circle, searching every face I could see in the crowd. I was so sure Caleb would make his entrance the moment the eclipse started. It would be just like him to want to capture the drama of it all.

A ferocious roar ripped through the air, and I thought the Shadow Kings had finally arrived. But it came from Daniel's opponent, the Urbat who had lost both of his chain whips. He reached his hands up in the sky, seething and shaking, and I watched as his hands transformed into clawed paws. He fell to all fours, and his body rocked and convulsed. His army fatigues shredded as his body burst into the form of a giant, hulking red wolf at least twice the size of any werewolf I had ever seen.

"Whoa," Brent said. "Give me whatever steroids that guy's taking."

"It's the eclipse," I said.

The giant red wolf crouched in the straw ten yards away from Daniel.

"Do you want us to—?"

"No. Not yet."

Daniel squared his shoulders, standing tall and mighty. He opened his arms, his sword ready in one hand. With the other, he beckoned the wolf to attack with the inward wave of his fingers.

The red wolf reared back and leaped at Daniel. Daniel countered out of the way and sent a hard crack across the wolf's head with the hilt of his sword. The wolf shook off the blow and ran a few yards in the opposite direction away from Daniel.

I ran toward them, ready to back up Daniel if needed, but before I was even halfway across the field, the wolf leaped high into the air, straight at Daniel's right side. Daniel tossed his sword into his right hand and stabbed it up into the wolf's rib cage, then used brute force to swing the wolf through the air and slam it to the ground on its back. Daniel pinned it to the ground with the sword as the red wolf thrashed his clawed paws.

Daniel towered over the red wolf, and I could see the fierceness in his eyes. Not rage like I'd seen in Talbot, but the fierceness and determination of a warrior.

"Submit!" Daniel commanded the red wolf. I could feel the tidal wave of power crashing off his body. "Submit and I will spare you!"

The red wolf crumpled in submission. Daniel pulled the sword from his chest. The red wolf rolled over and crawled from the ring on its belly. That's when I noticed that many of the guardians around the ring were bowing to Daniel now. As if they'd heeded Daniel's call for submission also. I looked behind me and saw Lisa and Slade bent on one knee.

Only Talbot still stood. The bloody remains of his kill at his feet.

Daniel dropped his sword in the straw and clutched at his shoulder. He must have injured it again in the fight. He looked at me, his eyes softer now, and I ran toward him.

What now? I thought. With all the challengers gone, and Shadow Kings a no-show, did that mean it was over?

I was only feet from Daniel when Brent shouted in my ear: "Grace! Stop! The barn!"

I spun around and looked at the barn.

Nothing.

"Look up!"

My gaze flitted up to the roof, and I saw them, perched there like gargoyles. Rows and rows of Shadow Kings.

Caleb stood on the very apex of the barn's roof, a tin rooster-shaped weathervane spinning at his feet. "Sorry to miss the preshow entertainment," he called, "but I've made it just in time for the main event."

A horrible chorus of screeches, snarls, and howls echoed into the night as the waves of Shadow Kings charged down the roof of the barn and vaulted onto the battlefield.

Chapter Thirty-six

THE REAL BATTLE BEGINS

There were so many of them. So many Shadow Kings. More than I'd ever imagined. They just kept on coming, hurdling over the roof of the barn, filling the challenging ring. Caleb must have spent every moment of the last week creating and recruiting new Akhs and Gelals. I wondered how many of these Akhs had been regular teens at the trance party from earlier this week. I imagined empty homeless shelters and halfway houses. I tried to remember that they were already dead when I took my first swing at an Akh, slicing through its neck with my broadsword.

I could barely see Daniel, who was only a few yards away, just flashes of his gold hair or his sword as he took out demon and after demon that just kept on coming. Lisa, Talbot, and Slade, who had been on the other end of the 150-yard-wide battlefield, were totally lost from my vision. But the spray of Gelal acid and bursts of dust that went up in the air in that part of the arena told me that at least two of them were still fighting.

I took out three more Ahks and a Gelal with my sword, wondering why I had ever settled for a stake in the past.

However, not all the SKs were pure demon, and I had to pull back on one of my swings before I nearly took off the head of an Urbat teen. He growled and almost instantaneously transformed into a great hulking tan wolf right in front of me. He was almost as big as the red wolf Daniel had fought.

More growls rumbled out from Caleb's forces, and fourteen more boys burst into giant wolves—the speed of their transformation aided by the lunar eclipse.

I couldn't believe how huge the wolves were, and I knew Daniel would be even bigger if he transformed into the great white wolf. But I also knew he wasn't going let the white wolf free under the eclipse.

Caleb stood in the middle of it all, laughing like the madman he was.

"Now?" Brent shouted into my ear.

I'd almost forgotten about him in my struggle to keep up with the SKs and wondered how long he'd been shouting at me.

"Now!" I responded as the enormous tan wolf came volleying at my head.

I swung at it with my sword, but at the same moment

a great crack resonated through the air. A bullet whizzed past my ear, and the tan wolf yelped. He fell to the ground, his shoulder bloody where the silver bullet had hit.

"Tell Ryan to watch it," I shouted at Brent. "He almost hit me."

"These bullets don't fly right," I heard Ryan shout in the background in my earpiece.

"Cheat to the left," I said, remembering what the hunters I'd stolen the guns from had said. "You have to aim to the left of what you want to hit!"

Another gunshot fired, and a Gelal's head exploded as he came charging at me. His body kept moving for a full five steps until he burst into green ooze. I grabbed the closest Akh and used him as shield. He screeched as the acid hit his skin. I threw the demon at a black wolf; he ripped the Akh to pieces with no regard to the fact that they were on the same side.

I looked back at the farmhouse and saw Ryan, Zach, and Brent in the windows of the master bedroom. Ryan and Zach aimed the hunting rifles out of the broken panes.

"Again!" I shouted.

More gunshots rang out, sending Shadow Kings scattering. I caught sight of Lisa as she grappled with a tawny wolf. An arrow went sailing into the wolf's hindquarters from the direction of the farmhouse.

I looked up to see one of the Etlu Urbats standing

on the roof of the house with a crossbow. Two more archers joined him, just as we had planned. They took out several Akhs with their wooden arrows from their vantage point.

Several more gunshots rocked the field.

"Don't go hog wild on those bullets," I reminded them. I'd been able to get only two boxes of silver bullets from Mr. Day because he'd run out of them—having passed them out to all the hunters who'd come into town for the wolf hunt.

"Can you see Caleb?" I asked Brent. He'd disappeared somewhere in the chaos of the field.

"No," Brent said.

I swore. I heard a scream from somewhere in the crowd beyond the challenging ring, and I watched with great concern as several of the SKs started going after the guardians on the sidelines, not caring that they weren't supposed to be part of the fight. We'd planned on this contingency, and Jude and Gabriel jumped into action, leading the spearmen in a fight to protect the people outside the ring.

"I see him," Brent said. "Caleb's on the far north side of the ring, close to where it edges on the corn maze."

I looked out, but I couldn't see him from where I stood.

"Concentrate your fire on Caleb."

Two more shots rang out.

"We can't get at him. He's got too many SKs around him."

I nodded. Of course Caleb would be using his own men as a shield. "Just keep firing in his direction. Get him mad enough that he sends the SKs into the house after you. That's what we want."

I jumped and rolled head over heels to avoid the attack of an oncoming werewolf. I was locked in battle with it, when a barrage of gunfire and arrows pelted the north side of the field. Ahks screeched and Gelals snarled, and I heard Caleb shout his command. The demon hordes turned their attention on the farmhouse, their ghastly eyes locked on the boys who stood in the windows—my boys. Even the demons that had gone after the guardians outside the ring turned their attention to the house, clacking their claws and grinding their teeth.

One of the Akhs let out a great shriek, and fifty or so demons ran straight for the house.

Brent swore as he saw them coming.

"Hold your ground," I said. "Not yet."

I could hear Ryan cursing up a storm.

"Almost," I said.

The demon army jumped onto the back porch of the farmhouse. They crashed through the door and the windows and flooded the house.

"Not yet," I said.

"They're coming up the stairs!" Brent shrieked. He,

Ryan, and Brent stood in the frames of the windows, ready to jump.

When almost all of the demons had crashed into the house, I shouted, "Now!"

The boys sprang from the windows, clearing the porch below, just as I saw the first wave of demons enter the master bedroom. The boys hit the ground and started running faster than I'd ever seen them move—fueled by adrenaline and the eclipse. Zach had lost his gun in the jump, but Ryan clutched onto his with dear life.

The archers escaped the roof off the other side that led to the front yard of the farmhouse.

"Blow it!" I shouted as my boys neared the center of the ring.

Brent held out his hand and slammed his thumb down on the detonator he clenched in his fist. The boys braced for the impact of the explosion.

Nothing happened.

Brent looked down at the detonator. He mashed it again. Still nothing.

Demons started to claw their way through the second-story window, still intent on their prey.

"It's been disconnected!" Brent shouted. "I have to set if off manually."

"Brent! No!"

But Brent had already turned and rocketed back toward the house. He threw open a metal box that was attached to the outside railing of the porch. I knew from the design he'd showed me that there was a lead from that box to the explosives we'd planted under the house. "Don't worry, I'll have time!" His fingers moved quickly inside the box.

Ahks and Gelals dropped from the window onto the porch.

Ryan and Zach had made it to me on the field. "Hurry!" We all shouted at him.

"Got it!" He closed the metal box and turned to run from the impending explosion, pumping his fists up in the air like Rocky Balboa. But before he could finish the gesture, a Gelal grabbed him from behind, yanking him up over the porch railing by the neck.

"No!" I shouted.

I ran for Brent, but before I could get halfway there, the farmhouse exploded right in front of me.

It happened so fast, in the blink of an eye. Brent and the house and the demons were there when my eyes closed against the brightness of the blast. When my eyelids fluttered open, it was all gone.

Brent was gone.

Nothing left of him but the flames he'd created.

Chapter Thirty-seven

THE WARRIOR AND THE HEALER

THIRTY SECONDS LATER

I couldn't hear anything but a terrible, nauseating ringing in my ears from the explosion. I couldn't stand, either, the dizziness making my knees slam into the ground.

"No!" Ryan screamed as he ran past me, but I couldn't actually hear his shout over the ringing. I just saw his mouth shape the word. Felt the pain he radiated as he scrambled toward the flaming remains of the house. I reached out and tried to stop him from getting too close, but I couldn't. He slaughtered two Ahks who had escaped the blast with his rifle, and then he fell to all fours in front of the fire.

I rocked backward and lay on the ground, my head in the straw. I clawed the earpiece out and then clamped my hands over my ears. I concentrated my healing powers on my eardrums, willing the throbbing, pulsating pain to stop. The ringing eased slightly, and the pain lessened to a stinging ache, and I could hear well enough to make out someone shouting my name.

More than one someone, actually, I realized as I arched my head back, trying to get a look at the battlefield from where I lay. The action reminded me of when I'd been taken down by the wolves in Caleb's warehouse, and that made my head swim more. The challenging ring seemed eerily empty. Most of the Ahks and Gelals had been destroyed in Brent's explosion. A small bunch of them, shielding Caleb at the far north side of the ring, remained, and a few others scattered about the field. I could make out only five remaining werewolves in the smoke that rolled into the ring from the burning house. I wondered how many of the wolves had been defeated in combat, and how many had run for the hills after the explosion.

Daniel was one of the people who shouted my name. I could see his mouth moving as he fought two giant wolves that seemed to be trying their best to stop him from making it to my side. Their battle was bloody as they clashed in the air, and Daniel swung his sword at their flailing limbs. It all seemed to happen in surreal slow motion.

It probably didn't help that I was seeing the whole thing upside down from the way my head was positioned on the ground.

Talbot also shouted my name, and I rocked my head

so I could see him. He and Lisa were taking on two more of the terrible wolves. And even Slade and Zach, who were fighting off a few of the remaining demons, shouted at me. They all seemed to be waving their arms at me, as if trying to signal something. I was so disoriented from the blast that my brain took too long to process this information.

I rolled over onto my stomach so I'd be able to see normally, and looked up just in time to notice someone running at me, a spear raised in one hand, while the other hand waved me away. It was Jude. *Why had he entered the ring?*

His words finally made purchase in my brain. "Grace, run!"

I scrambled up onto my knees just as Jude sent his spear sailing over my shoulder. It hit something just behind me, and I heard the growl of a wolf. I turned my head just enough to see the open jaws clamp down on the collar of my robe. The wolf yanked me off the ground, and with four great bounding leaps crossed the entire challenging ring, with me as its prisoner. It didn't even seem to be fazed by the spear that protruded from one of its front legs.

ONE LONG PIERCING SCREAM LATER

The brown wolf flung me to the ground, my hip slamming against the hardened dirt. I looked up and found myself staring into the yellow, murderous eyes of Caleb Kalbi.

His wicked smile cracked across his face, reminding me of a garish jack-o'-lantern when combined with his glowing eyes. We were at the north end of the ring, just in front of the boundary line of torches. They sent garish shadows dancing around him.

"I am glad you listened to my message," he said.

I scrambled to my feet, ready to charge at Caleb. Two Gelals grabbed me by the right arm, and two Ahks grabbed my left.

"Where is he?" I seethed at Caleb. "Where is James? I came; I've fought. Just like you wanted. You said you'd bring him! Now where is he?"

Caleb leaned in close. "You'll find out soon enough."

I screamed and tried to smash my head into Caleb's face, but the demons holding my arms yanked me back. They pulled so hard it felt like they were attempting to rip me in half.

Caleb snorted. "You think you're strong enough to take me on?"

I grunted with pain. "That's what you wanted, isn't it? That's why you wanted me in the ring, so you could fight me yourself?"

"I wanted you in the ring so I could *destroy* you myself. One way or the other." He licked his lips. "You came into *my* house. You stole some of *my* boys. You made me have to leave *my* place. And now you will pay. I'll kill you myself, and then Daniel, in front of everyone. And all will know that Caleb Kalbi is the strongest Urbat."

Caleb's own words confirmed what I'd suspected all along. We'd humiliated him in his house, in front of his pack, and now he wanted the ultimate payback, in the most public form possible. To save face in front of the Urbat world.

That's why he didn't kill us when he attacked in the night. He'd *allowed* us—at least in his eyes—to live until this moment. I was shocked his message hadn't demanded that Talbot also be in the ring—since his former beta was one of his biggest betrayers. But maybe Talbot's fighting had already been a given in Caleb's mind. Like Daniel being in the ring was.

My thoughts flitted to my friends. I had no idea what was happening to them outside the circle of demons that surrounded Caleb and me.

Caleb snapped his fingers. The Akhs and Gelals yanked on my arms in opposite directions again. I screamed.

Caleb frowned at me with disappointment. "You're too weak," he said, circling me. "You're taking the enjoyment out of this for me. You're too human. Not enough fight. Not enough power. You should let your wolf come out and play." He smiled wide and evil. "Then we could really have some fun."

The mention of my inner wolf made it go crazy inside

my head. It wanted nothing more than to take Caleb on. *Let me out!* it shrieked. *Embrace me.*

My body convulsed, and I looked up at the moon. Half of its surface was stained a bright bloodred now, its power increasing. I felt like it was crashing in on me. I tried to concentrate on the moonstones in my ears. But their pulse felt so faint compared to the screams of the wolf in my head, compared to the power of the eclipse.

Let me free!

I thought about what Talbot had said about channeling the power of the eclipse. I arched my head back toward the moon, soaking in its rays.

"Stop fighting it," Caleb said. "I can see it in your eyes. You want to. Embrace the power."

"I'll show you power," I said, concentrating energy into my arms. I bent them in and then flung them out. Sending the Ahks and Gelals who'd been holding me soaring into the air. They crashed outside of the ring, and two of the guardsmen went after them with their spears. Caleb barked an order, and the rest of his demons came at me. I lunged for one of the tiki torches, yanked it from the ground, and staked it through three of the demons at once. The two Gelals and the black wolf that remained shrieked and ran from the battlefield, disappearing into the corn maze beyond the challenging ring.

Caleb stood alone, no longer surrounded by his

demon followers. He roared and threw himself to the ground, almost as if in a tantrum, but instead of kicking and screaming, he shifted into a colossal tan-and-gray wolf. He clawed at the ground with his massive paws as he pushed himself up with his front legs. He stood on all fours, his body seething with power, as he glowered down at me. His jaws opened, and he growled, revealing teeth as long as my thumbs.

I took a step back.

Oh. Freaking. Crap.

Caleb sent a clawed paw swiping at me. I spun out of the way, grabbed another tiki torch, and jumped on top of the hulking wolf's back before he could turn his body around. I hit him over the head with the torch, but all it did was shatter into thin strips of bamboo. The wolf reared and bucked, trying to throw me off, as he spun around. I caught flashes of my friends as the beast turned, still grappling in their own battles with giant wolves.

The wolf finally flipped me off, and I went sailing over his head and slammed into the wood platform at the epicenter of the ring. I felt my right leg crack in at least three different places as it smacked against the edge.

I heard a shout and saw Jude go running at Caleb. He'd found my broadsword and swung it at Caleb, only to be swatted away by one of Caleb's clawed paws. Jude flew several yards and landed on his side.

The tan-and-gray wolf charged at the platform. I heard running footsteps behind me. I glanced back and saw Daniel rushing at the back of the platform. The wolf lunged into the air, just as Daniel jumped at the edge of the platform and used it to launch himself right at the wolf. The two collided several feet above me, and Daniel sent several kicks and punches into the wolf, propelling him forward in the air. The wolf wrapped his paws around Daniel, and the two went crashing to the ground. The wolf let go on impact, and Daniel rolled away. He stood, his body in a stance to take another attack from the tan-and-gray wolf.

I heard a scream of rage and saw Talbot run his sword into a large black wolf near the barn. He pulled the bloody blade from its body and came sailing in our direction, swinging his sword above him with a battle cry.

The tan-and-gray wolf lunged at Daniel again. Daniel did an aerial side flip—like a cartwheel in midair—and as he twisted around, he caught the wolf's neck between his feet. He flipped the wolf around in the air by his head. Daniel let go and miraculously landed on his feet as the wolf was sent spinning away. It slammed into the ground right in Talbot's path.

Talbot thrust his sword down at the wolf's chest.

"No!" Daniel shouted at Talbot. "Caleb is mine!"

The tan-and-gray wolf rolled away and Talbot's sword drove deep into the ground. "Caleb killed my parents!" Talbot shouted, wiping sweat from his forehead. "I've been waiting for this moment all my life." He let go the sword and flung himself at the wolf, pummeling at it with his bare fists.

I tried to push myself up to standing on the platform, but my leg wouldn't have it. Suddenly, Slade and Lisa were at my sides, holding me up. I didn't see where they had come from.

The tan-and-gray wolf caught Talbot's arm in his teeth and flung him away. The beast stood, ready to go after Talbot. Daniel sailed at the wolf with a great superpowered lunge. He caught the wolf by the shoulders, holding the wolf's snapping snout from his face. The wolf's claws shredded Daniel's robes as he flailed.

With a great burst of power, Daniel threw the wolf away from him. It sailed several feet and then slammed, back first, onto the ground. Talbot rushed up and grabbed the wolf around the neck before he could regain his footing. The beast yelped and wailed, flailing his clawed paws, unable to break Talbot's mighty hold.

"You die now, Caleb," Talbot snarled into the beast's face. He tightened his grasp on the wolf's neck. I'd seen him snap a creature's neck with his bare hands before.

"No!" Daniel shouted. He grabbed the sword Talbot had discarded.

"What do you mean *no*?" Talbot asked through clenched teeth.

Daniel slammed his foot down on the wolf's chest and thrust the knife at his face until the tip of the razor-sharp blade was only inches from the furry patch between the wolf's eyes. "Change back," he demanded, power ripping the air around his voice. "Where's James? Change back so you can tell me!" He pulled the sword back slowly as if preparing to thrust it into the wolf's head. "Change, now!"

The wolf's body shook as it shifted back into human. Daniel now stood with one foot pinning Caleb's human body to the ground. Talbot still had his arms wrapped around Caleb's neck.

"Tell me where the boy is!" Daniel said. His voice had lowered, and I had to strain my superhearing to catch his words. The crowd—which had scattered out into the fields after the explosion—edged closer to the ring now, anticipating the end of the fight. Ryan had finally left his grieving place by the fire and come to stand on the platform with the others and me. Jude made his way toward us, holding his bloody side.

Caleb laughed, the noise sounded choked and desperate instead of maniacally gleeful like earlier. "A few of my boys have the child. Their orders are to kill him if I die."

Talbot tightened his grip on Caleb's neck. "Liar! That wasn't part of the plan."

"The plan?" I asked.

"I always have a fail-safe," Caleb choked out. "You . . .

kill me . . . and the last thing you will know . . . of the child . . . will be his screams."

"His screams," I said, trying to step forward on my broken leg. It buckled under me. Slade caught me up in his arms. "If we could hear James's screams," I whispered to him, "that means he's here. He's somewhere on the property!"

Slade sat me down on the platform. "We'll find him for you." He signaled to the others to follow him.

Ryan handed me the rifle. "Just in case," he said. "But there're only two shots left."

Lisa sprinted toward the barn; Ryan took off around the still-burning wreckage of the farmhouse; Slade headed into the corn maze. Jude jogged slowly, still holding his side, toward the field of spectators.

I snapped my attention back toward Daniel, Talbot, and Caleb.

"You've got it backward," Daniel said fiercely, with the sword still pointed at Caleb's head. "If any harm comes to the boy, you'll be begging me to end *your* screams. Now tell me where he is!"

Caleb gave him a wicked smile. "Then I guess we're at a stalemate, my son."

I concentrated hard on the idea of trying to send a telepathic message to Daniel that we were on James's trail. I couldn't just shout to him, for fear of tipping Caleb off—I didn't want to give him any reason to try to fight back again, or worse, to send the signal for

James's death before we found him. *We just need to keep Caleb at bay for a few more minutes*, I thought, directing it toward Daniel. Hoping he'd sense what I needed him to know.

"I don't do stalemates," Talbot said, and wrenched his arms with so much force, he snapped Caleb's neck, practically tearing his head from his body. Caleb convulsed, and his body shifted back into that of a giant tan-and-gray wolf. Talbot let go and backed away, letting the dead wolf's head loll onto the ground at an unnatural angle.

My hands clapped over my mouth, holding in a scream. But I heard one anyway: the pitiful shrieking cry of a child echoed out from somewhere inside the corn maze beyond the challenging ring. At the same time, the walls of corn burst into flames.

Jude, from the sidelines, turned in the direction of the cry. "James!"

Daniel's head snapped up, and he roared at Talbot: "What did you do? The boy—they've killed James because of you!"

Talbot was kneeling in the straw still, next to Caleb's body. "He was never going to tell us. The boy was as good as dead already."

My body shook with horrible cries. Daniel glanced back at me like he could feel my pain, then he reeled on Talbot, pointing his sword at him.

I could feel Daniel's pain now on top of mine as he

grappled with the decision of whether or not the thrust the sword into Talbot's chest. *Submit or die*, he seemed to be thinking.

Both of our heads snapped up as we heard another shout from somewhere in the corn maze. "I found him!" came Slade's voice. "I found James!"

"Thank you, God." I threw my hand over my mouth. I wanted to feel relief, but a maze of flaming cornstalks still stood between me and my toddler brother—and *Slade* was the one who had him.

Jude took off running toward the entrance to the maze. I wished I could follow him.

"You better hope that boy survives!" Daniel shouted at Talbot. "Now submit!" He bore down on him with all the radiating power of a true alpha.

Talbot glared back at him, hard breaths ripping through his body. He shifted, so he knelt on one knee, and shoved one fist into the ground. Just as it looked like Talbot was about to bow his head toward Daniel, Slade burst out of the flaming corn maze, clutching little James to his chest. His charred and tattered robes flapping behind him as he ran as far from the fire as he could.

"James is safe!" I shouted.

Daniel turned toward them.

Talbot rocked forward on his knee. "I'll never submit to you!" he shouted, and flew at Daniel. Before Daniel could react, Talbot swung his arm out and knocked the sword from his hand. Daniel grabbed him, and the two began to grapple.

"Did you really think I'd *ever* submit to you?" Talbot asked as they fought. "Think I'd be your lapdog? Even when I was with Caleb, I pulled all the strings. And I still did after I left him. Do you really think he was smart enough to pull off that attack on the parish? Stage this here tonight? That was all me."

"I wouldn't sound so proud," Daniel said, striking a blow against Talbot's shoulder. "Caleb failed."

"Because I wanted him to. I always knew I'd kill him in this ring, and then kill the prime challenger. Only I originally thought it would be Gabriel, not you. But I like this plan better."

What? Talbot had been against *both* Caleb and us at the same time? Playing us for fools against each other? Until it led to this very moment?

It took me a minute to process, but I still wasn't shocked. I'd always wondered why Talbot had worked for Caleb, despite knowing the man had been responsible for his parents' death. And ever since it was revealed that he once had been a part of the Shadow Kings, I was never really able to trust him fully. But the part that didn't ring true—the part that still confused me was the thought that Talbot had been against us *the whole time*. I guess, deep down, I'd believed that he *thought* he was in love with me. And even though I didn't return his feelings in any way, I just couldn't accept that the things he'd told me about the way he felt were lies.

I'd believed his professing that he'd do anything to be a part of my life—even if it meant helping Daniel become his alpha.

Talbot shifted fighting methods, and started using wing chun punches and blocks against Daniel—a style of fighting that kept your opponent at a very close range. Daniel returned the pummeling, block against hit, hit against block. Daniel was stronger and bigger than Talbot, but wing chun was designed especially for the small-sized fighter, and Talbot eventually landed an open palm blow against Daniel's chest. But instead of hitting him backward, Talbot clutched at Daniel's chest and screamed a great bloodcurdling roar of anger. His face angled up at the bloodred moon, and I watched as power visibly rippled through his body, into his arm, and through his hand into Daniel's chest.

Daniel's mouth fell open like a scream of pain should have followed, but no sound came out. His arms looked rigid at his sides—like they'd been petrified. I could see fear and confusion in his eyes, and I could tell he was paralyzed. Talbot's face bore the look of complete concentration as he squinted up at the moon and shoved his hand against Daniel's chest with all his might.

What was Talbot doing?

I thought I heard Daniel cry out. But then I realized

I'd felt his pain rather than heard it. A red stain suddenly erupted on his shoulder, soaking through the gold fabric of his robe. I realized it was blood, and it looked like it was bleeding from where he'd been shot by that hunter with a silver bullet. I felt another one of Daniel's screams and watched as the newly healed ragged scars on his wrist—where he'd taken the blow of the chain whip in order to save Anton—burst open.

I looked at Talbot's face, twisted with rage. The way he extended it toward the red moon reminded me of how I'd channeled the power of the eclipse in order to break away from Caleb's demons. I looked at his other hand, pressed firmly against Daniel's chest. The way Daniel's body quaked and shook like something was trying to rip him apart from inside.

"He can't be . . ." My breath caught in my chest so hard it hurt. I pushed myself up to standing, almost screaming at the sheer pain of my shattered leg. There was no time even to contemplate trying to heal it. I could feel Daniel calling for my help. I had to stop Talbot now.

"Stop," I screamed at him. "I know what you're doing, Talbot! Stop it now!

I lifted the hunting rifle Ryan had left for me.

Talbot's jaw clenched. He didn't let go. My body shook as I felt Daniel's screams of terrible agony. Talbot was channeling the power of the eclipsed full moon and using it to fuel the healing power—no, the *opposite* of the healing power—against Daniel. He was forcing his anger and rage into Daniel, attacking him with his inner wolf from the inside. Just like we'd discussed yesterday when Talbot convinced me to teach him about the power. When he'd *claimed* that he wanted to know only so he could save me if necessary. Using the claim of his feelings for me as a trick.

A bloody gash gushed from Daniel's face, another on his hand. Wounds he must have suffered and healed over during the fight. Blood soaked through the side of his shredded robe, where Caleb had clawed at him.

"You still want me to submit to you now?" Talbot asked Daniel. "Or do I need to dig a little deeper? What other past wounds does your body hold? Weren't you stabbed in the heart once—with a silver dagger? That's what all the stories I keep hearing about you say."

"Don't, Talbot!" I screamed. "Don't you dare! Don't do this!"

"What's the matter, Grace? You don't want me to rip a hole through your Daniel's heart? The same hole you caused?"

I lifted the rifle. The flickering red beam of the laser scope danced against Talbot's black shirt. It bounced up and down, betraying just how badly my hands trembled. I'd never pointed a gun at a person before. "This is loaded with silver bullets." *Two, anyway.* "And I know how to shoot it."

Talbot laughed. It was an airy noise, and I knew he was trying not to break too much of his concentration.

"Maybe that's the point, Grace. Maybe I want you to shoot me. Or at least I want you to *want* to shoot me."

"What does that mean?"

"I'm good at getting Urbats to give in to their inner wolves. Didn't Caleb tell you that once? I've got more style than him. I go after the heart of the matter." He pressed his hand harder into Daniel's chest, making his otherwise paralyzed body convulse.

"Don't! Stop, please. What do you want?"

"For years, I thought all I wanted was Caleb dead, and revenge on Sirhan's pack for not preventing the death of my parents. That's all I used to want since I was child—but Caleb's dead now, and I'm about to win alpha of Sirhan's pack, like I always planned. The only problem is, *you* made me want more than that." His face twisted, and I thought it almost looked like an expression of remorse. "With Daniel gone, I might actually get the thing I want most."

"So you've been pretending all this time? Ever since the warehouse, you've just been pretending to be on our side? What about all that crap you said about loving me, and how I made you want to be better?"

"No," he said. "You really did have an effect on me. You made me want to change for you." He glanced at me, slightly. "All I wanted when we left that warehouse was you, Grace. We could have been perfect together. Fighting demons. Saving the night. You're everything I want now, and I tried to be a better man for you. But you wouldn't let me change. You wouldn't forgive me . . ."

My throat constricted and I knew Talbot was right. In all of this, I'd never quite forgiven him. Never really given him a second chance like Jude and the lost boys. *I'd brought this upon us all.*

"What if I forgive you now?" I asked through gritted teeth. "You let Daniel go and I'll give you another chance—"

"It's too late!" Talbot shook his head. "You already told me you'd *always* choose Daniel," he said. "You *made me* want you, and then made it so I couldn't have you."

"And that's when you turned against us?" I asked. "You told the Shadow Kings we'd be at that party so you could rush in and save the day, didn't you? So you could gain our trust back. Then later you tipped off the SKs about our plan to prolong Sirhan's life. They attacked the parish because of you, not Jude."

"It was easy," he said. "Caleb didn't even realize I was playing him, too. All I had to do was find one of Caleb's Akhs and let him read my mind. Or at least the parts of it I wanted him to see. I fed him the plan to attack the parish, to take out Sirhan. I couldn't pass up the opportunity to harness the power of the eclipse, so I tricked the SKs into forcing the ceremony with Sirhan's death. Caleb had no idea I planned on killing him when he came here tonight."

"And James? Was that part of your plan, too?" I steadied my hold on the gun so the red laser dot settled on his chest.

"No, that one's on Caleb. He took the baby on his own."

"But he wouldn't have come that night if it hadn't been for you."

James almost died because of Talbot. I'd been able to keep my inner wolf at bay since my encounter with Caleb, but now its voice ricocheted through me like a scream in an empty corridor. *And now he's going to kill Daniel if you don't stop him.*

"The way I see it," Talbot said, "you either lower that gun and let me kill Daniel. Or you can decide to kill me and turn into a werewolf like the rest of us. No more of this Divine One shit."

"What would that accomplish? Do you think if Daniel's gone, I'll suddenly love you instead? Or do you think if I turn into the wolf, I'll suddenly like you better? Because then I'll be evil, and I'll want someone evil like you? You really think that would work?"

"It's worth a shot," Talbot said. "I don't exactly have anything to lose. I predict you'll go wolf before you can even pull that trigger. I know how this works. Caleb always tried to rush it, but I get to know my victims. Know exactly how to make them give in." Talbot slammed his hand against Daniel's chest, sending another jolt of negative power into him. I experienced

Daniel's whimpers of pain and frustration as he was paralyzed by the power, unable to stop Talbot himself. Blood stained his shirt under Talbot's hand.

The gun faltered in my grip as I tried to shake off the cries of the wolf, driving me to embrace it. Driving me to let it sink its teeth into Talbot. Rip out his throat for everything he'd done. *For what he's doing to Daniel* . . .

Talbot was right. He knew me too well. He knew exactly what was in my heart. He knew exactly what would push me over the edge. Force me to give in to the cries of the wolf in my head. I'd told him so myself. It would *always* be Daniel. . . .

"However will you choose?" Talbot asked. "You let me go, and I *will* kill him."

I lifted the gun and aimed the beam of the laser scope so it sat still and steady right over Talbot's heart. "I've made my decision."

Talbot didn't even blink. "You know that all you have to do is *want* to kill me, and you'll lose yourself."

"I know," I said.

I squeezed back on the trigger. A silver bullet exploded from the chamber.

I have no regrets. . . . I thought as the bullet hit Talbot squarely in the shoulder. He screamed, let go of Daniel, and stumbled backward. He clutched at the searing bullet wound and looked at me with shock and rage twisting in his glowing eyes.

"The difference is," I said to Talbot, "I didn't want to kill you. Just stop you. These bullets hit whatever is left of the target." I pulled the trigger a second time, taking out one of his kneecaps. He collapsed onto the hard dirt ground, shrieking and writhing in pain.

I dropped the gun and scrambled toward Daniel, on my hands and knees, unable to walk on my fractured leg. But then Jude was there, pulling me against his side, and he carried me to where Daniel lay in the straw.

Jude set me down, and together we lifted Daniel so he was sitting up. Blood seeped from the gash in his cheek. But what worried me more was the blood soaking through his shirt. I pushed it up over his chest, but to my surprise the blood that was there had streamed down from the reopened bullet hole in his shoulder. Not a single mark marred his chest.

"It's okay," Daniel said, gritting his teeth. "He couldn't get to my heart."

"Why?" Jude asked.

"Because *this* heart doesn't have an old wound to rip open."

I nodded, understanding.

"What do you mean?" Jude asked. "Did I miss something?"

"When I stabbed Daniel last year, he was an Urbat with two hearts layered one on top of the other. But I killed that creature, and Daniel was essentially reborn.

Perfected. This heart, this single heart, has never been broken. There was no hole to rip open."

Shifting so I was sitting at Daniel's side, I started to help him remove his robe so I could get a better look at his shoulder.

"Water," Daniel said. "My throat is so dry."

"I'm on it." Jude stood, ready to go fetch something for Daniel to drink.

"Thank you, brother," Daniel said, and clasped Jude's hand before he could go.

"You're welcome . . . brother." Jude squeezed Daniel's fingers and let go, turning to leave.

"His heart still deserves to be broken," came Talbot's voice. My vision snapped to where I'd left him writhing in the dust. He'd moved two paces to the right. His arm pulled back, and a silver-tipped spear flew at Daniel's chest like a javelin.

My hands were tangled in Daniel's robes. I couldn't react fast enough. Jude shouted and threw himself in front of Daniel. His cry turned sharp as the spear pierced through his chest and out his back. He landed on his side, one arm extended out, the other lying limply on the shaft of the spear.

I struggled to free my arm and let go of Daniel, scrambling to Jude. I looked up as Talbot ran, hobbling and stumbling on his injured leg toward the burning field of cornstalks. The guardians let him pass— abiding the rules of the ceremony that was still technically going on—but before I looked away, I thought I saw someone in a green robe go after him.

"Jude!" I said, turning my full attention on him.

His pleading eyes looked up at me. He grabbed weakly at the spear shaft. The amount of blood that pumped out of his chest confirmed my worst fear—he'd been stabbed through at least one of his hearts.

With a silver-tipped spear.

One of the few blows that could kill an Urbat.

"Jude, no!"

He'd reacted before I could. He'd thrown himself in front of the spear. He'd saved Daniel's life.

"Gracie," he said. "Please." He tried to place his hand on mine. His following words made no sound, but he mouthed them to me with that pleading look overtaking his eyes.

I shook my head and grabbed him up in my arms. His head lolled in my grasp. His eyes rolled back under their lids. I checked the pulse in his neck. He was unconscious, but not dead. Not yet. The pulse was almost too weak to detect. "No. Hold on, Jude. You're going to be okay. You're going to be okay." I turned toward Daniel, who struggled to his knees. "I promised him that. I promised him everything was going to be okay. We have to do something. We have to heal him."

I broke the shaft of the spear and yanked the spearhead out through his back. I pushed down and pressed my hands over the wound in his chest. Blood pooled under my fingers as I tried to concentrate whatever positive energy I could find into him.

"Help me," I said to Daniel. "Help me. I can't do this one alone."

"Gracie, you can't," Daniel said, pulling at my arms. "You can't heal silver."

"But we can at least try," I shouted at him, not letting him pull my blood-soaked hands from Jude's chest. "Help me, damn it! We promised to help him."

Daniel let go of my arms. He placed his hands over mine.

Tears flooded down my face, but I forced my mind to clear. I thought of every positive wonderful moment I'd ever shared with my brother. Building Ewok forts in the family room, climbing trees, sitting on a rock beside Grandpa Kramer's pond with our fishing poles. Power poured from my fingertips, but it wasn't enough. My mind centered on another memory. The one of Daniel and me holding Jude in his cell at the parish. How it felt when Jude said he wanted our help. How it felt to know my brother was finally coming home.

Power surged through my fingers into his chest. Exploding under my hands so forcefully it made me fall backward. I sat up and looked at Jude. He still lay there with a gaping, bloody wound in his chest.

"It's not enough," Daniel said. "You can't heal silver. You can't save him."

Jude's eyes flitted open. He extended a couple of fingers toward me, but he couldn't lift his hand.

I caressed my fingers down Jude's face. "Can you hear me? Can you try to transform into a wolf?"

Jude tried to speak, but no words came out. His head nodded ever so slightly.

"Then it is enough," I said to Daniel.

Jude's body began to twitch and convulse, trying to make the transformation. I placed my hands on his chest. "It's going to be okay," I said, and channeled my energy into him again, giving him enough strength to make the change.

Jude let out a gasp, and the transformation completed. His gray wolf form lay under my arms now. The gaping wound spilling blood into his fur.

"Close your eyes," I told him.

The wolf's violet eyes slid shut.

I picked up the broken spear, wrapping my fingers around the shaft. So much energy had drained out of me from trying to heal Jude, I could barely even lift my arm. Daniel clasped his hand over mine so we were both holding the spear.

"Together," he said.

Hand in hand, we lifted the spearhead and plunged it deep into the bloody hole in the wolf's chest. Its body convulsed and then lay still.

"I love you," I whispered to Jude, and pulled the spear out.

I wrapped my arms around the wolf and counted my heartbeats. Thirty of them. Until the wolf melted away and it was my brother's body that lay in my arms again.

In the end, this was my terrible gift—my savage grace. In order to cure Jude, I had to kill him. Some people I could heal; some people I could restore to life, but for others—like Jude—the only gift I had to give was death.

And in giving it, I'd freed his soul.

Everything was going to be okay.

I held Jude until I was sure he wasn't coming back. I brushed his hair off his forehead and kissed the scar that was just above his left eyebrow. I laid his head on the ground. Daniel held his hand out to me as if he knew what I needed. He helped me stand, and we leaned our weight into each other for strength. Both injured, but still whole. Together, we stared out at the crowd that had gathered at the edge of the boundary line. Our friends stared back at us: the lost boys—all but Brent. Lisa with Baby James in her arms and Jarem at her side. Gabriel and the other Elders. The Etlu guardians of the ring.

Beyond our friends crowded the spectators—more witnesses who'd watched the hardest moments of my life played out in front of them.

Someone pounded his spear against the ground with three loud smacks, then every member of the Etlu Clan fell to one knee, one fist shoved to the ground and their heads bowed toward us. Some of the other spectators followed suit.

I looked up at Daniel. He squeezed my hand and answered the question I hadn't asked out loud. "Yes," he said. "It is finished."

And we were the last ones standing.

Chapter Thirty-eight

WAKE

I sat on the porch swing, staring out at the orange sky that painted a perfect backdrop to the walnut tree where Jude, Daniel, and I had spent so much of our childhood playing up in its branches. I took in deep gulps of early evening air. It was cold and icy in my lungs, but the sharp pain with each breath felt somewhat invigorating.

Like I was actually waking up for the first time in three days.

What had happened in the many hours that followed the end of the ceremony had pretty much been a blur. I'd been exhausted, mentally fighting off the fatigue that tried to overtake my body after having poured so much of my power into Jude in order cure him. But there'd been no time for rest. So many things needed to be done, so many decisions needed to be made, and so many people now looked toward Daniel and me as the ones to make them.

The Elders had wanted to give Jude a warrior's send-off—burn his body like they did with the five Etlu guardians we'd lost to the Shadow Kings during the ceremony. But I refused, knowing Mom would want Jude to have a proper human funeral. Which had left us to deal with the legal ramifications of his death—to explain what had happened to him in a way the sheriff and the rest of the town could accept. It was Daniel who'd come up with the solution. Jude's body had still held a terrible gash in his side, where he'd taken a blow from Caleb's claws.

"Jude died in a wolf attack," Daniel had said. "We went wolf hunting, looking to win the ten-thousand-dollar bounty. But the wolf attacked us, and Jude, in the process of saving my life, grappled with the wolf, killing it, but was fatally injured by his own weapon. We'll bring Jude's body, along with one of the smallest of the wolf carcasses, to the sheriff as proof. Everyone will know that he died to save my life. Everyone *should* know that."

The sheriff had bought the story. The mayor declared Jude a town hero for saving us all from the terrible wolf and awarded our family the prize money. Dad donated it to the homeless shelter in Jude's name. And because of Jude's sacrifice, the whole town had turned out for tonight's memorial. I'd been obliged to retell the lie of how Jude had died over and over again in front of the crowd of mingling neighbors, parishioners, and the occasional superhuman werewolf, all here to pay their respects to Jude.

Today we should have been hosting Jude's nineteenth birthday party; instead, we were hosting his wake.

I'd come outside to escape for a few minutes. I'd retold the lie so many times I had almost started to believe that false story myself. But I didn't want to forget the truth. I wanted the pain of it, mixed with the icy stabbing of the night's air, to keep me feeling alive and awake.

Two things I knew Jude wasn't anymore.

Part of me had hoped that he'd rise again, like Daniel had when I'd cured him last year. But really, deep down, I'd known he wouldn't. Killing Jude hadn't been an ultimate sacrifice the way it had been for Daniel, because I'd *known* when I plunged that spear into Jude's heart that I wasn't sacrificing my soul to save him. What I'd done for Jude had freed his soul, but it wasn't enough to restore his life.

And I wondered if it was better this way.

Or at least if it was what Jude had wanted.

The words he'd mouthed to me just before I tried to heal him—the words he'd been too weak actually to say out loud, still echoed in my head, even though they'd made no sound. "Let me go," he'd tried to say, with desperate pleading in his eyes. "Let me go. It's easier. . . ."

Jude hadn't been able to imagine a future for himself.

And perhaps dying a martyr—sacrificing himself for Daniel and me—had been the easiest way out he could see. . . .

I shook my head. Jude had died a hero as far as everyone was concerned. His last words I'd keep to myself. No one else ever needed to know.

I heard the creak of wooden porch steps and realized I wasn't alone. I looked up and saw someone standing there wearing a black sheath dress and bright coral-pink tights. She held a small, brightly wrapped package in her hands. I blinked several times, wondering if I really was awake after all.

"Hey," Katie Summers said.

"Hey," I said back.

"I know I didn't know your brother, but I wanted to stop by and tell you that I'm sorry for your loss."

I nodded. "Thanks." I wiped at the tears pooling in the corners of my eyes.

"I heard what he did for Daniel . . . ," she started to say.

"Yeah. Wolf attack." I sighed, knowing she'd probably want to hear the false account from an "eyewitness" just like everyone else.

Katie shook her head. "No. I know what really happened. So don't worry, you don't need to lie to me."

I raised my eyebrows.

"Slade told me. And I know what you all did for me at that awful party. I'm afraid Slade and Brent didn't do the best job convincing me that I'd drunk some funky Kool-Aid." She smiled a little. "So thanks, you know, for helping to save my life. You're pretty cool, you know that?"

I gave a little laugh.

She tapped the present she held with her coral-pink-painted fingernails. I could tell the design on the wrapping paper was hand drawn, and it reminded me of the get-well present she'd wanted me to give Daniel last week. The one that was still tucked in my backpack upstairs. Had she really brought another present for my boyfriend to my brother's funeral?

"Um, this is for Slade," she said about the package. I realized then that the brightly colored drawings on the paper were the same design as the flamed tattoos that inked Slade's arms. "It's a stopwatch."

"A stopwatch. For Slade?"

She blushed a bit. "Did he tell you he's thinking about trying out for the fire department again?"

I shook my head. He hadn't said anything to me, but I wasn't surprised. Slade had seemed like a completely different person ever since he brought Baby James out of the fire. Like a man who'd found a reason to live again.

"I thought I could help him train," she said. "The stopwatch is so we can make sure he doesn't do the drills *too* fast, if you know what I mean."

I smiled and nodded.

"So do you know where I might find him?" Her cheeks

went almost as bright as her pink tights. Obviously, Slade had made quite the impression on her when he saved her from that Akh at the party.

"My guess is in the garage. He's been working on the Aston Martin."

"The Rapide?" Her eyes grew wide. "You know, I've got a thing for automotive design? I have got to sit in that car."

"Be my guest," I said, and gestured her inside the house to join the rest of the town. My heart felt a little lighter, knowing that Slade had met his match. Even on a sad day, people should still be allowed to find some happiness. I wondered if Slade would come with us when Daniel and I left with the Etlu Clan, or if this meant he was planning on staying here.

About a minute later, I heard the front door open, and Daniel came to sit with me on the porch swing.

"I brought you something to eat." He placed a paper plate piled high with honey-glazed ham and a concoction of cheesy shredded potatoes with cornflakes on the top, which my mom had always called funeral potatoes. The name felt a little too poignant at the moment.

"Thanks," I said, and Daniel wrapped an arm around my shoulders.

We sat in comfortable silence. I picked at my food while Daniel used his feet to rock the swing back and forth. Beyond the squeaks of the metal chains as we swayed in the swing, I listened to the noises of the gathering inside the house. As much as I'd needed a few minutes away from the crowd, I didn't know how I was going to handle leaving any of them behind in a few short days.

Since Sunday we'd been locked in debate with both my parents and the Elders as to when and how to facilitate Daniel and me moving to the mountains of Pennsylvania in order to lead our new pack. Many of the Elders wanted to whisk us away immediately, but Dad wanted to keep us until Christmas at least. Mom made an unwavering argument that the pack should allow us at least to finish high school before taking us away.

I could tell she was desperate not to lose another child so soon. I didn't want to go, either. Didn't want to leave my family, or my town, or the things I wanted out of my future behind. How could I live with the pack in seclusion in the mountains and still use my powers to help the rest of the world? But what else could we do?

Daniel and I had won the responsibility for the pack, and it's not like I could expect them, more than thirty strong, to keep sleeping on the floor of the parish's social hall indefinitely.

I heard a guffaw of laughter from inside the house. It sounded like a mixture of Bellamy, Gabriel, Jack Headrick, and Mr. Day's voices. Last I'd seen them, they'd been exchanging travel stories over the refreshment table. I thought about Katie and Slade probably in the garage together. And I'd seen Ryan and Zach discussing hockey with a couple of guys from my school. I watched now as Jarem and Lisa came around the house from the backyard. They walked close together, their hands not quite touching, but almost.

And that's when the idea came to me, forming in my mind the way I could see a painting coming together in my head before I'd even touched my brush to canvas.

I pushed myself up from the swing, careful not to put too much pressure on my still-healing leg, and called to Lisa and Jarem, who stood near the driveway: "How do you think the pack would feel about relocating permanently?"

Lisa, Jarem, and Daniel all looked at me.

"How so?" Lisa asked, approaching the porch with Jarem.

"We—the pack anyway—own a sixty-acre plot of land outside town now. Do you think the pack would be willing to move? Start over there with us? We could build whatever kind of estate we want on the grounds. It's far enough outside town for privacy, but close enough that we could still have a relatively . . ."

"Normal life?" Daniel asked, with a wry smile.

"As normal as a couple of teenage alphas of a werewolf pack can get." I smiled back at him. "But I think it'd be good for the pack, too. They've lived cloistered away for so long, they've forgotten about the good they can do for the rest of the world with their powers. I think it would be good for them to start *living* a little more." I nodded to Jarem, who had a slightly skeptical look in his eyes. "We'd put the decision to a vote, of course. I mean, it's their lives, too, we're talking about."

Lisa popped up on to the porch and hugged me. "Well, I, for one, welcome a change in scenery. Oh, and cable TV." She looked at Jarem. "And a movie theater. I haven't been on a date since 1986, you know?"

"Date?" Jarem spoke the word like it was completely foreign to him.

"You'll see," she said. "And you'll like it."

"Moving the pack to the farm?" Gabriel asked. He stood in the open doorway, looking out at us. "It is a good idea. I have grown a bit fond of Rose Crest myself. I think I would like to stay on as your father's junior pastor, if he will let me. And I have a feeling the rest of the pack will follow the two of you anywhere."

Daniel squeezed my hand with approval. We discussed logistics for a while, and then I excused myself and went back into the house to find April. She sat alone in the dining room next to the display of pictures of Jude that Mom had put out on the table. I could tell that not getting a chance to say good-bye to Jude had hit her hard, and I hoped *not* having to say good-bye to me soon might help lift her spirits.

"When you're up for it, I'd like to see more of your costume designs," I said as I sat next to her, holding her hand. "I think we're going to be sticking around, and I'm going to need my Alfred."

She nodded. After a minute she whispered, "Do you think we'll find Talbot? Stop him from hurting anyone else like he did Jude?" She wiped at her eyes. "Do you think we'll ever even hear from him again?"

"Yes," I said. If there was one thing I was sure of in this world, other than the love Daniel and I shared, it was that Nathan Talbot would try to find a way to be a part of my life. . . .

A conclusion that was confirmed later that night when I crawled into my bed and heard my phone buzz with a text. I knew it was from Talbot, even though the number was blocked, because it read: *You want to be a superhero still, Grace? Well, every hero has a nemesis. And I'm yours.*

Chapter Thirty-nine

RENEWAL

I hadn't heard anything again from Talbot since the text, but I knew it was only a matter of time before he'd try to do something else to get our attention. In the meantime, I had enough on my plate to keep me busy—making arrangements to rebuild on the farm property, move the entire the pack and their belongings across several states, and, of course, there was *school*. Both Daniel and I had a lot of missing assignments to make up for if we wanted to graduate on time.

I had quite a bit on my mind, but I still couldn't believe that I'd completely forgotten about my trip to the Print & Ship two weeks ago. That is, until I passed Mr. Barlow at the Day's Market on Saturday afternoon. He came up to me as I waited for Stacey to ring up my groceries—enough sandwich fixings and potato chips to feed a pack of thirty men and my lost boys, with the appetites of wolves, who'd been framing out a house all afternoon. Barlow raised his eyebrows at my shopping cart's contents, but he didn't ask about it. Instead, he pulled a folded-up piece of paper from his knapsack. "It's nothing *official,* of course," he said—and winked at me. "But I thought he'd like to know right away."

THIRTY MINUTES LATER

It was still hard to walk past the place where Jude had died, but I knew I'd eventually get used to it. The framing of the new house—the first of the buildings Daniel had planned for our new property—was going up quickly. We were trying to beat out the first snow of the season that the weatherman was predicting would hit Rose Crest by Thanksgiving. I dropped off the lunch fixings with Zach—who'd figured out he had quite the talent for cooking under my mom's tutelage—and made my way to the barn, where I knew I'd find Daniel poring over his design plans for the house. He'd taken to it so quickly, it made me wonder if Trenton had an architectural emphasis in their industrial design program.

Daniel dropped his pencil when he saw me, his whole face lighting up. I smiled back, hoping the day would never come when he'd stop looking at me like that. I asked him to come with me, and we walked hand in hand until we came to the old tree we'd discovered in one of the back acres of the property—a walnut tree, even older and larger than the one in my family's front yard. I'd already started thinking of it as "our tree."

"I have something for you," I said, and handed him the letter from Barlow.

Daniel took the paper and read it out loud.

"Dear Jack—

"Just wanted to let you know that we on the admissions board are very impressed with the two applicants from your school—Daniel Kalbi, especially. Although his essays were a bit rough, I must say that his portfolio blew us all away. We haven't seen this level of talent, and an obvious passion for industrial design, in a freshman applicant before. While we won't be sending official acceptances until after the new year, I'd think it is safe to say the Amelia Trenton Art Institute will be happy to welcome Mr. Kalbi into our program. . . ."

Daniel's voice trailed off, and he looked at me. Shock and confusion filled his eyes. "I don't understand," he said. "I never turned in my application. With everything that happened . . . I hadn't even had time to think about it. I haven't even mentioned it because I thought it was pointless now. . . ."

"I turned it in for you. Back when you were still stuck as a wolf. I wanted to make sure you had a decent future to come back to . . . and then I completely forgot that I'd done it."

"You did this for me?" He pulled me into a bear hug. "But what about you?" he asked. "I'm sure you're the other applicant the letter was talking about. I bet you'll get in, too. . . ."

"No." I shook my head. "I only had time to do one application, so I chose yours. I guess I thought maybe I might find time for mine later . . . but you know, with everything . . ." I shrugged.

"You sacrificed Trenton so I could have it?" He looked down at the letter. "But that's not right. Maybe we can write to this admissions guy, get him to take a late application."

I shook my head again. "It's okay. Really. I know now that Trenton isn't for me. I think I only wanted it because you wanted it so bad. I could never bring myself to even start filling out the application once I read that one essay question. The one that asked how I was going to use my talents to make the world a better place? That made me realize that I have a different calling in life."

"What do you mean?"

"I love art, I really do, and it's obviously going to be a part of my life forever. But I don't live and breathe design the way you do. I don't see myself being able to use it to make the world a better place like you can. But I can't stop thinking about all the hurt and sick people out there. Wondering how I can help them. I think that's what I want to do with my life, after school. Use my healing talents to help people. Maybe I'll have to become a social worker or a nurse. . . ." I almost laughed, thinking about how my mother had always wanted me to consider becoming a nurse like her and how I'd *hated* that idea. "That way I can choose people to help on a case-by-case basis. Get to know them personally so I can heal them."

"And not become a crime-fighting superhero?" Daniel flashed me one of his almost devious-looking smiles. "You have a talent for that, too, you know."

I smirked. "Who says I can't do both? Heal people by day, fight demons by night?"

"*And* help run an entire pack of reformed were-wolves. Sounds like you'll be busy."

"We'll both be busy. You with Trenton and all."

Daniel tapped the letter against his hand. "Is this dumb?" he asked. "With everything that's happened? With all the responsibilities we have now, should I really even still be *thinking* about Trenton?"

I felt both his hope and his pain at the same time.

"Trenton is only a few hours away. We'll find a way to make it work. You can still be an alpha and have the normal life you always wanted, too—well, as normal as any of this is *ever* going to get. But we have each other for help. You can be a leader and an artist, just like I can be a demon fighter and a healer."

Daniel nodded. He slowly folded up the letter and slipped it into his jacket pocket. When he pulled his hand out again, he held something else in his closed fist. "I have something for you, too. I was going to wait, but

I don't think I can anymore," he said. "But first you need to do something for me."

"What's that?"

"I want you to close your eyes." He nodded at me to do so.

I dropped my eyelids. "Okay, now what?"

"I want you to try as hard as you can to forget when I proposed to you in Caleb's dungeon."

"What? Why on earth would I do that?"

I opened my eyes, ready to protest his request face-to-face, but I found Daniel kneeling on one knee under the branches of the walnut tree.

"What are you doing?"

"I want you to forget when I proposed to you before. I want you to stop thinking I did it only because I thought we were going to die—and wondering if I think you said yes only to make me happy in that moment." He tapped the side of his forehead. "I've felt those worries inside of you."

"Daniel, I . . ."

He held out his hand, with something small clasped in his fingers that glinted in the afternoon sun. A ring. White gold with a large round diamond in the center and a smaller purple stone on either side that reminded me of the color of my eyes.

"I want you to forget all that, because I want this to be the moment you remember. The moment we *both* can remember." He cleared his throat. "Grace Divine, *now that* all this crap is over, and when we're out of school, and you take some time off from kicking bad-guy butt, *and* healing hapless strangers," he said, embellishing the words I'd told him he'd used the first time he proposed, "will you marry me?"

I clasped my hand to my face, as if trying hold back the tears that suddenly sprang up in my eyes. "Isn't that just kind of a given?"

"I'd still like to hear it, so I can burn it into my amnesia-riddled brain."

"Yes," I said. "I'll marry you." I put my hand on my hip. "*After* Trenton."

Daniel laughed. The next thing I knew, he'd engulfed me in his arms—his lips melting against mine, my fingers curling in his hair, and my body aching with so much anticipation. For us. For our future.

For the unknown.

Acknowledgments

I am told space is limited for acknowledgments because I wrote such a freaking long book, so while I'd love to gush on and on about all the people I owe my extreme gratitude and adoration to for helping this book even exist, I will attempt to be brief with my appreciativeness. (Though, obviously, brevity is not one of my strong points. Heh. Heh.)

First and foremost, the two people who deserve the most thanks for their extreme patience, long plotting sessions, dishing out plenty of encouragement, and knowing just the right moment to tell me to stop freaking out and get back to work—are my husband, Brick Despain, and my editor, Greg Ferguson.

Ack! Look at that, I'm already losing briefness . . .

Okay. Take a deep breath, Bree. Focus. Stop elaborating and just get to the point.

Ready?

Alright.

Additional love, gratitude, and (too quick) thank you, thank you, thank yous also go out to the following: Ted Malawer and Michael Stearns from Upstart Crow Literary. The other awesome people from Egmont USA: Doug Pocock, Elizabeth Law, Mary Albi, Regina Griffin, Nico Medina, Bonnie Cutler, Robert Guzman, Alison Weiss, and Katie Halata. Joel Tippie at JDrift Designs. Jose Torralba for your always-gorgeous cover photography. My parents, Nancy and Tai, my siblings, in-laws, nieces, nephews, and other extended family members, neighbors, and friends who continue to offer ongoing support and enthusiasm. The SIX: Brodi Ashton, Emily Wing Smith, Valynne Maetani Nagamatsu, Kimberly Webb Reid, and Sara Bolton. My two little boys who try to be patient when mommy is working. And a special shout-out to our dear friends Michelle and Brent Sallay—Brent, you finally made it into one of my books. I hope you're happy, man.

Whew.

I did it! I did it! I managed to thank everyone without running out of roo